The Illusion of Murder

FORGE BOOKS BY CAROL McCLEARY

The Alchemy of Murder

The Illusion of Murder

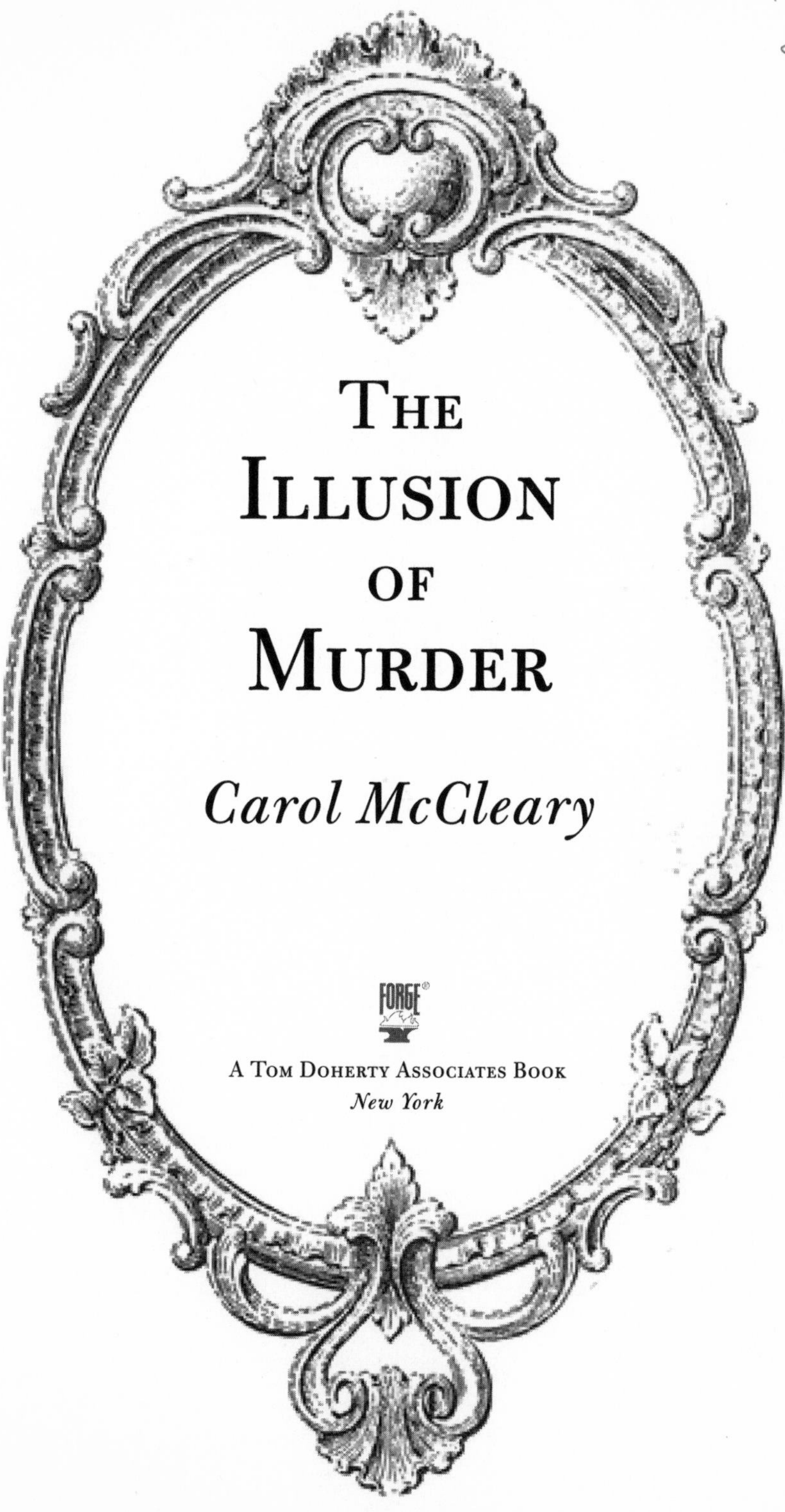

The Illusion of Murder

Carol McCleary

FORGE®

A Tom Doherty Associates Book
New York

THE ILLUSION OF MURDER

A Forge Book
Published by Tom Doherty Associates, LLC
175 Fifth Avenue
New York, NY 10010

www.tor-forge.com

Forge® is a registered trademark of Tom Doherty Associates, LLC.

ISBN 978-0-7653-2204-3

First Edition: April 2011

Printed in the United States of America

0 9 8 7 6 5 4 3 2 1

To Hildegard,
who doesn't know the beauty, kindness,
intelligence, and wisdom that she possesses.
But that is what makes her so
extraordinarily special.

ACKNOWLEDGMENTS

As Nellie Bly so adequately put at the end of her book *Around the World in 72 Days*:

> To so many people this wide world over am I indebted for their kindnesses that I cannot thank them all individually. They form a chain around the earth. To each and all of you, men, women and children, in my land and in the lands I visited, I am most truly grateful. Every kind act and thought, if but an unuttered wish, a cheer, a tiny flower, is imbedded in my memory as one of the pleasant things of my novel tour.

I could not have expressed it better, except I would like to add to Nellie's debt of thanks.

After I wrote *The Illusion of Murder*, I began my journey to reintroduce Nellie Bly to the public with my first novel, *The Alchemy of Murder*. To all the countless libraries and bookstores throughout the world who supported my novel, and to all the wonderful people who so graciously bought *The Alchemy of Murder*, thank you from the bottom of my heart.

There are a few people I want to thank for their kindness and special words of cheer. They are: Richard at Flowers by Richard in Manhattan; Heather Rees; Michael A. Giaquinto; Helena Cordeiro; Laurie and Ian at The Underground Bakery.

To Kareem Jr. and Amy Brogan, my first new Young Adults who sent me e-mails thanking me for introducing them to Nellie, "Thank you, I am thrilled and honored that you love Nellie. She truly is an inspiration to us all."

I would also like to thank the people "behind the scenes" who are invaluable to me and Nellie: Harvey Klinger, my Maxwell Perkins; Bob Gleason, my editor; Linda Quinton, a very special lady at Tor/Forge; Ashley Cardiff, extraordinary assistant to Bob Gleason, and to Whitney Ross, who so graciously stepped in and helped me—Merci-Merci; Cassandra Ammerman, my publicist, whom I'm very lucky to have; and Helen Chin, my copyeditor, who did an incredible job.

A few new special little critters were born this year . . . Ella Krische, Arshay Fischer, Dustin Gregory Anderson, and Gavin Si Ying Krische. I want to welcome you to our world and may you learn about Nellie Bly, because her courage and determination are something that I believe will be of great value to you in this crazy world of ours . . . Good Luck!

In memory of
Kathleen Ann Carr,
a beautiful gal with a heart of gold.
Like Nellie, she left us too soon.

The Illusion of Murder

PREFACE

I discovered that Egypt is a land of both mystery and magic, an exotic place where trees talk and men turn staffs into snakes, so it should not have come as such a surprise to me that death would also be mysterious in this ancient, haunted land of pyramids, mummies, and the eternal Nile . . .

Journal of Nellie Bly, 1889

Those words were recorded by Nellie Bly, the world's first female investigative reporter, during the race around the world she made in 1889 to beat the record of Jules Verne's fictional hero Phileas Fogg in the novel *Around the World in 80 Days.*

That journey of nearly 22,000 miles by steamship, carriage, and Iron Horse brought her not just into contact with exciting and exotic cultures during Victorian times, but into the intrigues of great nations at a time when ancient magic and a mysterious prophecy of the Sphinx threatened to stain the Nile red with the blood of foreigners.

While Nellie's adventurous journey was related for the public in her book *Around the World in 72 Days*, those of you who have read Nellie's previous accounts of her investigations are aware that she also maintained a secret journal of what actually happened during her investigations, beginning with the murder and mad science she encountered when she spent ten days in a madhouse in order to get a "man's" job as a reporter.

Many readers are already familiar with the fact that the discovery of Nellie's secret journals—found in the rubble when the old building that housed her employer, the New York *World*, was razed—has been the subject of both litigation and accusations that Nellie's actual accounts were liberally altered to include murder and intrigue.

This accusation is firmly rebutted.

While it was necessary to make modest editorial corrections to the journal, the reader may once again rest assured that they may compare our truth and veracity to that attributed to that lioness of literature, Lillian Hellman, by none other than author Mary McCarthy.

THE EDITORS

Nellie Bly

SETTING OUT ON HER RACE AROUND THE WORLD
WITH A SMALL VALISE

PROLOGUE

19th Dynasty Burial Chamber
Ancient Site of Tanis
Egypt, 1889

I discovered that Egypt is a land of both mystery and magic, an exotic place where trees talk and men turn staffs into snakes, so it should not have come as such a surprise that death would also be mysterious in this ancient, haunted land of pyramids, mummies, and the eternal Nile.

That I could suffer a bizarre death in this strange land had not occurred to me until now, as I stand cold to the bone, staring down at the long black snake I've stepped on.

I don't dare lift my foot, I can't even breathe; I just stand stiffly in place, the toe of my shoe pressing down on the serpent as it thrashes and tries to coil.

Darkness is closing in as a burning torch on the dirt a few feet from me fades. When the bundle of sticks burn out, there'll be just me and the snake—in the dark.

In the dark where? A burial chamber, for sure. A sarcophagus is off to my right and I can make out on a wall a scene from the *Egyptian Book of the Dead*—the aged painting of a boat that has the head of a lion, a tail and clawed feet at the stern; aboard are wailing women, some with hands outstretched, others covering their faces—mourners for the dead.

The stone coffin, pillars, and faded hieroglyphics are the only remnants of what was perhaps the magnificent tomb of some long-dead pharaoh. Once filled with unimaginable treasures, it now has dust and cobwebs; thieves have taken everything but the ghosts.

Shouting for help will do no good. No one knows I'm here except the person who imprisoned me; someone with murder in their heart I've yet to put a name or face to, but who knows I'm trying to flush them out.

The snake's tail whips against the side of my leg and I nearly jump out of my skin.

I have no idea of what kind of snake it is, but the country is famous for its asps—deadly horned vipers and cobras. Cleopatra tested their venom on condemned prisoners to find out which killed the fastest and most painlessly before she had one bite her.

How I came to be imprisoned in an ancient tomb with one foot on a snake and the other on my own grave has me wondering how I've so quickly managed to offend the gods of this ancient land. A mystifying artifact of Egyptian black magic is the source of my troubles and I had been forewarned—possession of it has already caused blood to soak into the primordial dust of the Nile valley.

It is not the first time I've stepped into a snake pit, so to speak, but never before so literally; it's at times like this that I wonder if there is something about me that attracts the strange and the dangerous.

My name is Nellie Bly and I'm a reporter for Mr. Joseph Pulitzer's New York *World.* With too much boldness for my own good, I bullied and bluffed my way into having the newspaper send me on a race around the world in which I must beat the "record" set by Phileas Fogg in Jules Verne's novel, *Around the World in 80 Days.*

That it was the thirteenth day of my journey when I made landfall in Egypt should have also told me that this was not an auspicious time to visit a place where priests once made people eternal with dark magic and the land blistered under ten plagues hurtled by the almighty Jehovah.

The snake twists and thrashes violently and I press harder—at least I think I do. My body is blue cold, I can't feel my toes and my knee is shaking wildly as if it has a life of its own.

Did something move at the sarcophagus?

I'm sure I saw something move.

Dear God, let it be a trick of the light.

The fading torchlight is casting eerie shadows. There couldn't be anything in the stone coffin, not something alive, unless it's true that Egyptian priests could embalm in a way that preserved life for aeons.

More snakes?

The thought of being in the dark with snakes, and scorpions, and spiders, and God knows whatever else lurks in ancient tombs causes the shaking in my knee to work its way up to my hip, and my whole body trembles. I want to cry but I can't spare the strength and instead press down harder on the snake—or maybe I just think I am pressing harder. My foot is so numb I can't feel anything under it.

The torch flickers and hisses as if it's burning through the last of the pitch. I have to get to it and somehow keep it going until I can find my way out of this nightmare. There has to be a door somewhere.

My knees and my courage are turning to mush and I keep imagining

I'm letting up the pressure on the struggling serpent. Or maybe I'm not imagining it.

I know I can't keep this awkward stance any longer. I have to do something now before the darkness completely embraces me.

The creature underfoot thrashes violently, whipping its whole body. It starts slipping out from under my shoe and I scream as I push down on it again, my heart pounding so hard that I'm breathless and sway dizzily, almost losing my footing.

Shutting my eyes tightly, I ask God for help. I don't think He will listen; unfortunately I'm one of those people who never talks to Him unless I'm up to my neck in alligators, but I try anyway though I don't think that the Good Lord would approve of my present association with the dark side of Egyptian magic.

I can't be left blind in the darkness with a deadly snake. I need to get both feet on the snake and jump up and down until I'm sure it can't harm me and get to the torch before it dies.

I start to bring up my other foot up as I look down.

It's gone.

The snake has slipped out from under my foot.

Mortified, I can't move, can't breathe. It could strike at any second.

Mother of God, how did I get myself into this mess? Ancient curses, magic amulets, esoteric mysteries from the *Egyptian Book of the Dead*, murder and fanaticism—it's all insanely bizarre for a young woman from Cochran's Mills, Pennsylvania, population exactly 534.

As the darkness closes in on me and my breathing takes on the hoarse rasp of a death rattle, I ask myself what I could have done differently when I decided to flush out a killer in a land blessed by the sun and damned by ancient curses.

PART I

Day 13

I shall now speak at greater length of Egypt, as it contains more wonders than any other land, and is preeminent above all countries in the world for works that can hardly be described.

—Herodotus (450 bc)

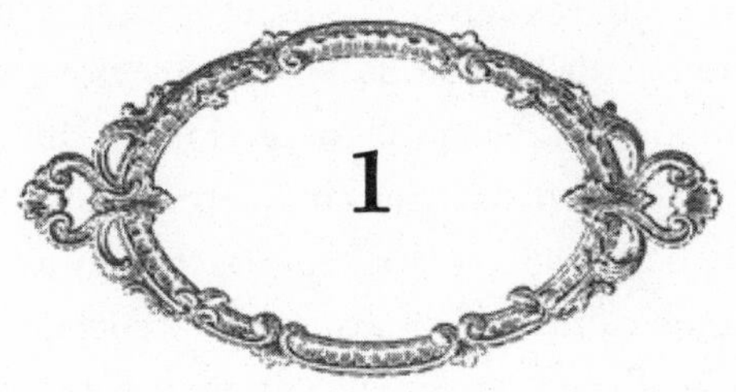

1

Port Said, Egypt • November 27, 1889

Thirteen days after I left New York, the *Victoria*, the ship that will see me all the way to Ceylon in the Indian Ocean, anchors in the bay at Port Said, the gateway to the Suez Canal. The bay is too shallow for large ships to reach the docks and they must lie out and be fed coal for the boiler by coolies on barges.

My effort to beat the eighty days around the world record of Jules Verne's Phileas Fogg has progressed nicely. By carriage, train, and ships—the *Victoria* being the third ship to convey me—I have put over five thousand miles under my feet.

Particularly gratifying is that my membership in the female gender has not in the least delayed or otherwise hindered my travels. Mr. Pulitzer had planned to send a newspaper*man* on the assignment because he believed the race too dangerous and strenuous for a mere woman.* But more about that later.

When I hear the anchor chain clanging, I dress to go out on deck and get my first sight of the ancient land by dawn's early light.

As I step out of my cabin, a man down the corridor is closing the door of his room behind him. He gives me a studied look as if to judge whether I have come out because of him, then turns away without a "good morning" and hurries to the companionway that leads to the outside deck.

He's dressed rather oddly for a passenger, more the work clothes of a

* Pulitzer's concern was well taken. The world of 1889 was infinitely more dangerous than today, not to mention the lack of modern conveniences—no airplanes, automobiles, credit cards, ATMs, not even cell phones! A time when "high-tech travel" was on trains called Iron Horses and steamships had auxiliary sails to use when the boiler failed. —The Editors

sailor, and he's carrying a small sea bag not unlike what I've seen sailors tote. Most unusual about his clothing is that the pants are a little too long, the shirt a bit too roomy, striking me as borrowed or bought on short notice.

An intense-looking gentleman perhaps close to thirty years old; I've offered a "good day" a couple of times in the passageway since I boarded at Brindisi, Italy, two days ago, but have gotten hardly a nod in return. He takes his meals in his cabin and appears very preoccupied with his own private affairs, so much that he forgets common courtesies. A man on a mission, the boys back in the newsroom would say. Caught up with his own importance, I'd say.

Had he asked, I would tell him that he'd have more success keeping his own affairs from public scrutiny if he acted less like a nervous squirrel hiding nuts.

Out on deck, the last lingering moments of night along with a fine mist hanging in the air make my first impression of Egypt not the golden land of the eternal sun, but the gloomy outline of a dark city with a line of buildings along the shore appearing as a great serpentine beast with humps that had lain down along the water's edge.

No gaslights glow in windows or on street lamps, and there is not the telltale bounce of carriage lamps that one expects in a city. When I crossed the Mediterranean, I left behind the world of modern conveniences, of steam-powered engines and Mr. Edison's newfangled electric lights, and stepped into a land that had changed little over the centuries.

A chant coming from a tall, slender tower silhouetted against the breaking dawn reminds me that I have arrived in the Islamic world. It is a call to prayer made by a muezzin from a balcony near the top of a minaret that rises next to the domed roof of a mosque. Neither spoken nor sang, the summons to face Mecca and pray is strange to my ear—a mournful wail as if a plea to Allah for mercy and bounty in a harsh, dangerous world.

I spot the peculiar passenger from my corridor and realize why he's dressed in work clothes—he's standing on a small wood platform being lowered to a rowboat below. He must be in hurry for him not to have waited for the accommodation ladder, a gangplank that will be placed on the side of the ship later to assist passengers in boarding shore boats. Urgent business, perhaps even a family emergency, speeding his exit from the ship? But why the sailor's garb?

A movement at the railing on the deck above catches my eye. Someone—a man I think, but I'm not sure because the individual is wrapped in a hooded overcoat—is at the rail, watching the passenger being rowed ashore.

My neighbor at least is entertainment on an otherwise dark and gloomy morn.

When the call to prayer ends, a violent gush of wind blows from shore, buffeting the ship and creating an eerie murmuring in the rigging.

"The poisoned wind, the A-rabs call it," a crewman says as he passes by. He pauses and catches my eye. "They say it comes out of the desert to blow us foreigners back to where we came from and there's plenty in Port Said who believe it. Don't go ashore without a good man's protection, miss."

A passenger slipping ashore under cover of darkness, a watcher in the night, a wind full of menace?

I return to my cabin to freshen up for an excursion ashore, wondering what other curious things await me in the uncanny land of the Nile.

2

The night before we anchored, Herr Von Reich, a gentleman from Vienna, invited me to join him on an excursion to the city's native bazaar our first day in Port Said, where, he assures me, I will find the mysterious and unimaginable, along with everything under the sun to buy, from rings to rugs and "even a camel if the captain will let you bring it aboard."

Accompanying us will be Lord and Lady Warton, a British couple who have business ties with Von Reich, an engineer and inventor who once worked in Egypt.

There are sounds of discord when I'm back on deck to meet my companions at the accommodation ladder. Arab boatmen below are shoving and shouting at each other in a mad haste to be the rowboat closest to the platform that passengers step off of at the bottom of the stairway.

Von Reich grins down at the chaos. "We need only one boat and there are six warring to serve us. Lord Warton and I will clear the way with our canes. You ladies should keep your umbrellas handy."

Both men carry Penang lawyers, thick walking sticks with bulbous, leaded heads.

As I follow the two men down the nearly vertical, narrow stairway on the side of the ship, Lady Warton, coming behind me, says, "You'll find that a sharp blow from a cudgel is the language these natives best understand."

I glance back at the cost of nearly losing my footing, and make a gasp instead of a retort. Having been formally introduced to the woman only last night, and in light of their generous acceptance of my presence, it would be ill-mannered for me to point out that a stick beats more ugliness into a person than it ever beats out.

The steep stairway sways and scrapes against the side of the ship and I hold on tight, wishing I was wearing trousers instead of a long dress that makes it likely I will take a neck-breaking tumble. For sure, it was an inconsiderate man who made up the rule that only men can wear pants.

At the bottom platform I bite my lip as the canes swing right and left to drive back all but one boat. Lady Warton lashes out at a grabbing hand with her umbrella, but I have no intention of using mine in such a rude manner against fellow human beings. It's obvious that rowing passengers ashore is the only way these boatmen have of earning their bread and it's a small loaf at that.

Having been a factory girl living hand-to-mouth until I was eighteen because I had been forced to leave high school due to a heart condition, my sympathies lie with the poor wretches.*

Von Reich and Lord Warton board a boat to assist us ladies and I step aside so Lady Warton can go on first. Swells lift the platform and I step back, reaching for the support of the railing when a boatman on the other side grabs my arm and I am literally dragged into his rocking boat. It happens so quickly I only get out a "Well!" after I'm seated.

Von Reich shouts, "We'll see you on shore, Nellie," and I give a brave little laugh and hold on to the sides of the boat for dear life, finding myself a prisoner of four Arab rowers who are naked except for loincloths.

This is an adventure, I tell myself, a mantra I repeat when it appears I am going to hell in a handbasket and have no control over the situation.

I smile at the man who had dragged me aboard. "Get me to shore dry and I shall be very grateful."

He unleashes a long statement in Arabic and I just smile and nod. I have no clue as to what he is saying, but I am sure he understands and is agreeable to my needs. I wish I could tell him how sorry I am that my companions found it necessary to administer the cane so freely and lavishly, and that I marvel at their stubborn persistence even while cringing under the blows.

I am reflecting upon the unkind attitude I heard expressed aboard the *Victoria* by Europeans and Americans about people of less fortunate

* Nellie lied about her age to maintain a "girl reporter" image. She was actually twenty-one when she left the factory for a reporter's job. She was twenty-five years old in 1889. Leaving school because of a "heart condition" was also a fib. She left school to work because her widowed mother could not afford to keep her in high school. —The Editors

nations when I realize the rowers have stopped rowing and we are rising and rocking in swells a hundred feet from shore.

The man I had spoken to gives me a nasty smirk, holds out his hand, and says in perfect English, "More money or you swim."

I stare at him—*gape at him*—thoughts and emotions convulsing in my head like the shifting patterns of a kaleidoscope. Manhandled, kidnapped, and now I'm threatened and blackmailed by people I sympathize with.

Rising in the unsteady boat, I raise my umbrella and tell the ungrateful devil, *"Get me to shore!"*

3

Safely ensconced in an open carriage with my companions as the sun's oppressive heat beats down on us, we make our way along a narrow, unpaved Port Said roadway alive with people and animals, the swirl of dust, and noise from every quarter—a street symphony punctuated with the bray of donkeys, the shouts of street vendors, and the glee of children.

Two- and three-story buildings, with large enclosed balconies that project out far enough to shade the crowded passages below, shoulder both sides of the street. The balcony windows, made of wood tarnished by time, are latticed with lovely Eastern motifs.

The uncommon sights, sounds, and smells wrinkle Lady Warton's nose but are a feast for the eyes of a young woman from Cochran's Mills, Pennsylvania, population exactly 534.

My companions busy themselves talking about the strategic importance of the Suez Canal while I smile in wonder as a cloud of pigeons on a terrace above take wing as a black-veiled woman walks among them like a magician releasing an entire flock.

We pass a train of camels carrying firewood, kicking up dust on an old man with hard years etched on his face sitting cross-legged on the curb, loaves of flat bread for sale lined up on newspapers beside him; a fat merchant wearing a red Turkish fez and straddling a small donkey clutches a metal box tightly to his chest as a fierce Saracen with a wicked-looking curved sword clears the way in front of him.

The streets are alive and the people have a strange flavor to me: servants—*slaves*, Von Reich says, despite the pretense of slavery being illegal—get up from sleeping on the ground outside of houses and go inside to work; men and women are clothed from head to foot in long, loose-fitting cloaklike garments. Girls without veils and women with their faces hidden go to a nearby well to draw water and carry it back in clay pots balanced on their heads; a little boy leads a cow with a rope from house to house, milking the cow into jars brought out by householders. The milk boy carries a stuffed toy calf to fool the cow into giving milk.

"Would a cow really believe a stuffed toy is her child?" I ask Von Reich, our expert on everything Egyptian. He had spent a year advising the government on an engineering matter.

"Perhaps not in America, but in Egypt, who knows? In this strange land, where it is said that the sphinx rises on moonless nights and runs across the desert like a jackal, and mummies dead thousands of years rise from their tombs, the unexplainable is not always unimaginable."

We rumble by a line of men balancing bulging goatskin bags on wood poles across their shoulders.

"Public water carriers," Von Reich says.

Their bodies are skeletal, as if the hot desert sun had melted away all their flesh except for a layer of skin as rough as papyrus. Though they're not in shackles, they remind me of a chain gang. "How do they survive such hard work in this brutal heat?"

"Necessity."

My companions for the day appear to be strange bedfellows not only to me, but to each other. The Viennese inventor is relaxed and amiable, even a bit of a *bonhomie*, while the British peer and his wife appear aloof, standoffish to the point of snobbishness, but I suppose they have a common ground in business. Von Reich has told me he is traveling with the Wartons to Hong Kong and on to Washington, D.C., on a business matter concerning an explosive he has patented.

The Austrian introduced himself to me while I was walking on the deck the first morning at sea after we left Italy.

A dapper gentleman with well-cut clothes and a starched mannerism, Von Reich is built broad with a closely shaven head and a gold monocle custom manufactured to fit comfortably and securely in his right eye; a flamboyant mustache with long curved ends that resemble the handlebars of a bicycle defies gravity with the help of a generous application of wax. His style of dress and mustache is very much in vogue with men of wealth and position and those who imitate such models of success.

It always amazes me to what great lengths men go in order to portray a certain look. And they say women are vain.

I was secretly amused when after several overtures on board toward me in his blunt, Central European manner—approaches that my mother would have deemed cheeky—I asked if *Frau* Von Reich will be joining him en route.

After assuring me rather stiffly, "Frau Von Reich is faithfully awaiting my return," he broke out laughing and told me that the only Frau in his family is his mother.

He certainly is a handsome figure of a man, but a shipboard flirtation is not in the stars for me. As I tell myself each morning, I have rivers to cross, mountains to climb, castle walls to storm, dragons to fight . . . and in this case, pulling a man along would slow me down.

After I refused an invitation for a walk on the deck and a libation afterward, his ardor cooled significantly.

However, when he told me that he was going with friends to the bazaar, I boldly hinted that I would be delighted to join him. Cheeky of me, indeed, but I am cabling my experiences back to New York and it will provide local color.

Kids swarm across the street, causing our carriage to stop. A bike rider wearing an Arabic robe with a closely drawn hood quickly swerves to avoid them. His front wheel catches in a deep pothole and both man and bike go down hard.

"I hope he's okay," I blurt out.

"What does it matter if one of these lazy natives is bruised?" Lady Warton asks.

Charming woman. Her husband refers to her as Eleanor, but she is Lady Warton to me, Eleanor being much too sweet for the woman's sour personality.

As the bike rider gets up, his hood parts to show the side of his brown face, but oddly enough a flash of pale white skin above the boot on his right leg is also exposed. Rather than the sandals that the Egyptians prefer for their hot climate, the bike rider's footwear appears to be the same type of brown boots I've seen on British soldiers.

Brown face, white legs, army boots. How odd is that?

I start to share the observation with my companions when a racket erupts that sounds like the hounds of hell have broken out of their cage.

"Good gracious!" Lady Warton snaps. "What is that horrid noise?"

"Hopefully it's not trouble with the Mahdi," Von Reich says.

"What's the Mahdi?" I ask.

"A fanatical group who have unleashed a jihad, a holy war, to drive the British and other Europeans from Egypt and to kill Egyptians who consort with them. The name actually refers to a Muslim messiah, a Christ-like figure who will return to Earth during the End Days to rid the world of evil."

I recall reading about the movement. "Are they the fanatics who defeated a British army several years ago?"

"Actually, it was a British general leading an Egyptian army that was overwhelmed by vastly superior forces. Cutting off the head of Chinese Gordon, the general, and mounting it on a pike fired the movement. Had the self-proclaimed Mahdi not died of typhus, he may well have continued down the Nile, driving Europeans and the Egyptians who tolerate them into the sea."

"Is there any danger to tourists?"

"There have been incidents of violence against foreigners but we will be safe." He pads his chest near his heart. "Lord Warton and I are armed."

Wonderful. After battling rowboat pirates who threaten to cast me into the sea, I have been dropped into a hornet's nest of murderous terrorists.

"The Egyptian government's rather ineffective, isn't it?" I ask. "Under British control?"

"Yes, the government went broke and couldn't pay its debts. However, the real interest of other nations isn't Egypt herself, but the Suez Canal. The country that controls it can put an economic stranglehold over other countries."

"Britannica rules the seas," Lord Warton says, "and that little ditch scratched into the sand is a strategic route to India and the Far East."

A mounted company of Egyptian cavalrymen with British officers trot by, heading in the direction of the noise.

"What do you think is going on?" I ask Von Reich.

"Noise can mean a celebration or trouble. This sounds like trouble."

"Our troops can handle any situation," Lord Warton says.

I didn't point out to him that the troops were Egyptian; only the officers were British.

The clamor grows louder and our carriage driver pulls off the road as a large crowd of men comes up the street shouting a repeated phrase. The Arabic words mean nothing to me, but it's the same violent tone I once heard from a mob that had gathered after strike breakers left union men dead that frightens me.

A squad of foot soldiers led by a British sergeant double-times smartly into place near us and our male companions leave us to speak to the non-com as the crowd gets closer.

Perhaps a hundred men are in the crowd, no women, though a number of children are prancing along. Most of the men are wearing the *djellabah*, a loose-fitting hooded robe that is the universal male attire unless one is working in the water or at the beach.

It doesn't strike me as an organized demonstration, at least not in the sense of people in a parade, but more of a crowd that was sparked into action spontaneously.

Egyptian horse soldiers with British officers, perhaps the ones we saw earlier, are in single file on both sides of the advancing crowd, acting rather like cowboys herding cattle.

Time to return to the ship, I think. Too inhibited to show a yellow streak, I keep it to myself as our gentlemen return with the British sergeant.

"Sergeant O'Malley says we will be safe this close to his troops," the British peer tells us.

The sergeant touches the rim of his pith helmet with the tip of his finger in greeting. "Don't worry, ladies, we won't let the rabble get out of hand."

"What are they shouting about?" I ask.

"The Father of Terror," Von Reich says.

"The Father of Terror?"

"That's correct, madam," the sergeant says. "That's what they call the Great Sphinx. Seems a tree told them that the sphinx was going to get up from where it's squatting at Giza next to the pyramids to drive us demon foreigners from Egypt."

It occurs to me that the bike rider I saw might be a British spy on the lookout for troublemakers.

Sergeant O'Malley busies himself lining up his men to assist in crowd control while our driver gets our carriage off to the side of the road.

"Trees talking!" scoffs Lady Warton, sounding personally offended, as if they were talking behind her back. "What will these ignorant people imagine next?"

She appears wedded to hats with netted veils and wears them even on the ship. I assume she has facial blemishes she doesn't wish to share with the world or wishes to protect her skin from sun damage.

Something about my expression causes the woman to direct her ire at me. "Young woman, I suppose *you* believe in talking trees."

I smile sweetly. "Well, I was thinking that not far from here God spoke to Moses from a burning bush and commanded him to lead his people from Egypt."

Von Reich doesn't say a word but it is easy to see that his jaws are clamped tight to keep a laugh from exploding.

4

Our carriage is pulling up to the arched stone entrance to the bazaar when a man on a bike passes us.

"Isn't that the same man who took the spill?" I ask.

Von Reich shakes his head. "I really can't say."

"Has the same boots," I mutter, more to myself.

"Shall we enter the Den of Thieves, ladies?" Von Reich asks as we step down from the carriage.

He had described the marketplace as a caravansary, a place where camel caravans stop to drop off and take on loads. I expected a sprawling dirt field with camels, tents, and a bit of dung underfoot.

Instead, passing through the gate we go back in time, not to the ancient Land of the Pharaohs, but to medieval Baghdad of the *Arabian Nights*, to Ali Baba who spoke the magical "Open sesame" to steal the treasure of the Forty Thieves, and to the mystifying Arab quarters called *casbahs*.

The bazaar is dark and twisted, mysterious, and puzzling, all at the same time; an exotic blend of people, merchandise, and animals that plays out as if it is planned by an artist for his canvas. Rather than a world of organized shops, it is a menagerie of tiny cubbyholes crammed with merchandise pouring out like horns of plenty, some selling spaces so small they are no more than cupboards.

The passageways, scarcely wide enough for two people walking abreast, are covered with canopies of Nile reeds, turning the walkways dark and shadowy even in daylight. The muted light, and hooded robes and turbans add to the mystique and the fathomless mysteries of this culture that has lived along the Nile for thousands of years.

People press up against walls to keep from being trampled as donkeys and camels laden with goods force their way through the walkways, yet no one seems to be bothered. The chaos is organized.

The atmosphere is spellbinding as a contortionist prances along with us, twisting his limbs in impossible positions, while a tumbler makes great leaps in the air, jumping, bouncing, and rolling like a rubber ball. As with the camels, people simply move out of their path.

I catch the pungent scent of spiced Turkish tobacco from an open-air café where men wearing the ubiquitous hooded robes drink muddy Turkish coffee and mint tea from tiny glass cups and share water pipes called hookahs.

Copper pots and carpets are for sale, as are clothes ready to buy, cloth ready to be sewn, and cloth still being woven on looms—cotton, lamb's wool, and goat hair. A man takes a live chicken from its cage and with one quick blow, chops its head off—blood splats on his robe, mixing with the blood of chickens now roasting over hot coals. "Genuine" papyrus paintings of pharaohs in chariots and dancing girls with their bosoms bare can be purchased for the cost of a pack of gum back home. There are flutes, drums, bells, cymbals, jewelry, and spices. . . .

Goods are everywhere; there are no bare spaces, not even the passageways themselves, some so narrow we are almost shoulder to shoulder with merchandise.

The exotic Eastern marketplace is everything I imagined and nothing I expected. I'm sure if I looked close enough, I would find frankincense and myrrh, and perhaps behind the public facades of shacks lining alleys, I could buy treasures looted from the tombs of pharaohs.

"I find the stench of a marketplace insufferable but his lordship enjoys contact with the natives," says Lady Warton, fanning herself with a very pretty pink silk fan that has the design of small flowers on it. "He served in Morocco for a year with the Foreign Office, advising the local officials about growing grains."

"He's a farmer?"

"Of course not! He has farmlands on his estate. Naturally the farming is overseen by his manager, not by his lordship."

"Of course," I murmur, keeping myself from wondering aloud why the Foreign Office didn't send the farm manager to Morocco instead.

Ragged beggars with bodies so dirty that their skin is hardly discernible from their fouled rags come up to us with outstretched hands and heartrending pleas. *"Baksheesh, baksheesh . . ."*

Lady Warton glares at them and swings her umbrella to shoo them away. "Go away, go away."

I give them coins, remembering my mother's admonition whenever she saw a person with a deformity: "But for the grace of God go any of us."

"Feeding lice only causes them to multiply," she says.

"Sorry."

Finding myself ill at ease with her insufferable attitude of superiority, I button my lips as any well-mannered guest should. The boys in the newsroom have an expression for her ladyship's type, one that I willingly embrace: *rich bitch.*

Lady Warton had obviously been born with a silver spoon—one filled with vinegar. She and her pompous husband no doubt believe that their position in the world is due to nothing less than the divine rights of kings, rather than an accident of birth.

Surrounded by strange sights and smells brings to mind a book I'd read, the adventures of Allan Quatermain, the hero of H. Rider Haggard's tale *King Solomon's Mines.*

"Isn't this place exotic?" I offer.

"Exotic? My dear, you are surrounded by half-naked, unwashed natives who eat and drink things that poison the stomachs of civilized people. The Côte d'Azur is exotic. This is a wasteland."

"I find it captivating. Egypt is a place to come in search of adventure. If I had been born in a different time and place, perhaps I could have been an adventurer searching for lost treasures."

Lady Warton stares at me as if I have something dribbling down my chin.

"Are you feeling ill, your ladyship?" I ask.

"Frankly, my dear, I am deeply disturbed and puzzled by the concept of a young woman tromping around wild animals and savage natives in search of treasure. That is certainly not a proper ambition for any *woman.*" She surveys me with a look of contempt that sweeps from head to toe. "One has to wonder how a young woman who possesses ideas that are the proper attributes only of men was raised."

I turn away and bite my lip. I've learned to rein my temper because being a reporter carries with it the necessary evil of having to deal with all kinds of people, but I draw the line at remarks about my upbringing. If she says another word about my mother, I will knock her on her noble fanny.

My reaction to her is aggravated by my resentment of people who have licked the cream off the top all of their lives. Not having to earn their bread, they don't understand that there is more to life for women than just being the helpmates and sex slaves of men.

I soon wonder if we aren't going in circles, for the alleys seem to be a confusing intricate network of passages that all seem to repeat themselves.

"Does your husband know where he's going?" I ask Lady Warton. "I'm lost in this maze."

"His precious sister in England specifically requested that he get her a trinket from a particular dealer she heard about here, so we must humor him."

We enter the jewelry section, where tiny merchant shacks offer jewelry boxes and trinkets of every kind, from copper bracelets to gold chains, anklets, and nose-rings of leaden-looking silver and brassy gold.

Lord Warton says, "We're getting close, I'm sure of it."

His wife leaves me to join him and Von Reich drops back to walk with me. He takes my arm as we stroll along, watching beggars and the purveyors of "ancient" artifacts competing to relieve people of their money.

"How do they talk?" I ask him.

"Who?"

"Trees. Do they speak to people passing by, that sort of thing?"

"Only with the written word. You see all around you the elaborate artful swirls and waves of the Arabic language, none of it decipherable to us of the West. Those flowing lines are sometimes repeated in nature, on tree leaves, carved in the sand by the wind—"

"So the pattern on a leaf is interpreted as words, and fanatics start shouting it's a message from God."

"Exactly."

I confess, "I'm afraid I'm not doing too well with Lady Warton. I don't want to be a bad guest, but anything I say seems to offend her."

"You're at a disadvantage, trying to hold a conversation with a woman who has never used her brain. As you pointed out with the Bible story, that trees talk here should not come as a surprise. Egypt is part of the Holy Land, a place of mystery and magic, where an angry God sent plagues of pestilence to punish a stubborn pharaoh, where staffs turn to snakes, and the sea itself parted for God's favorite." He squeezes my arm. "But you must appreciate that it is also a place of dark magic, of pharaohs with eternal lives, mummies that rise from their graves—"

"And a sphinx that gallops across the desert—and eats foreigners."

"*Ja!* In this ancient land there are few precise boundaries between what is . . . and what might be."

"I'm not a person who embraces the supernatural. Perhaps because so much of my life has been spent on keeping a roof over my head and putting food on the table, I leave the uncanny to those who have the time and energy. But ever since I walked out on deck this morning and saw Egypt through mist and darkness, I've felt *something*." I shake my head. "I can't explain it, and certainly won't share it with my editor in a cable for fear he'll believe I have brain fever, but I've had a sense of not being alone."

We come into a clearing where a crowd is gathering around a man standing on a small mound and holding a staff.

"You have to see this," Von Reich says, and steers me toward the man who wears a long black robe and white turban that rises to a peak and has a dark green band.

"Good Lord!" I exclaim. "That's a snake, not a hat band."

A cobra fanning its neck and showing its fangs is wrapped around the turban.

"That evil creature is looking at me," I tell Von Reich. There is no doubt about it, the thing is staring right at me.

"Nasty devil, isn't he?" he says with a laugh. "It's easy to see why the pharaohs used the cobra as a symbol of their power over life and death. The Egyptian cobra they call the asp is one of the most venomous snakes in the world."

"What happens if it gets off the hat?" I ask.

"Someone dies. But it's sewn on so it stays wrapped around the turban and can't move its head enough to bite."

It doesn't look sewn on to me. "The man's a snake charmer?"

"More than that; he's a *Psylli*, a magician who handles snakes," Von Reich says. "They're not just marketplace entertainers. *Psyllis* are descendants of an ancient tribe of desert people who work wonders with snakes, especially the *Naja haje*, the deadly Egyptian cobras. They're exposed to snake bites while still young and claim they have an immunity. They're said to be servants of Wadjet, the Green One, the Egyptian goddess with a snake's head.

"Stories about them go back thousands of years. A *Psylli* was sought out by Julius Caesar to draw out the poison from Cleopatra when she had an asp bite her, but she was already dead when the magician got there.

"An even older tale is from the Bible. The pharaoh's magician-priests who dueled with Moses and his brother Aaron were *Psyllis*."

"The ones who turned staffs into snakes?"

"Yes, their favorite trick, and it is a clever bit of conjuring. Today they earn more money drawing out snakes from people's houses than from entertaining people. It's not uncommon for snakes to get into houses and once inside they can be impossible to find—until a cobra reaches out from under your bed and bites you."

I shudder at that thought.

"*Psyllis* go into homes and sing a tune that the snakes find seductive enough to leave their hiding places."

The magician speaks to the crowd and Von Reich interprets the gist of what is being said.

"He's going to show us his power over snakes and then he will forever immunize people from snake bites—for a price, but not a bad investment considering how many people die of bites in the country."

I'm wondering how many people die from the "cure" when Von Reich grabs my arm.

"Watch this!"

The man raises his staff into the air and points it in our direction—then tosses it right at us. The wood rod hits the ground and instantly turns into a wiggling snake that coils and rises up, fanning its head.

Gasps erupt, including mine, and we move back. Von Reich keeps his own cane in front of the serpent to attract its attention as we backpedal.

The four of us regroup and walk away, the snake having been captured and placed in a sack by one of the magician's attendants.

"Please, tell me how it's done," I say to Von Reich as the Wartons stop to examine a rack of jewelry. Aboard ship he had told me that he was an amateur magician and showed me several clever card tricks.

"Obviously, the man calls upon the snake goddess to empower him."

A man with a big flamboyant mustache has to have an ego to match, so I play on his conceit to draw out the answer. "I'm sorry, I just thought you might know, being a magician yourself."

He pretends to look around to see if anyone is within hearing range.

A man coming toward us is selling scarabs and I keep an eye on him as we walk. The "beetles" were the most powerful amulets of the ancient Egyptians, used to ward off evil spirits, to slay enemies, and now to fleece tourists. I've already decided that I would pin one on my dress as a memento of Egypt.

"The *Naja haje* cobra has a unique characteristic," Von Reich says. "A spot on the back of its head when pressed causes the snake to extend itself full length and become rigid. It snaps out of its paralysis when it's tossed by the magician and hits the ground."

I raise my hand to signal the scarab seller to come over but he turns to a man who is suddenly by his side. The man's wearing a hooded robe, a *djellabah*, but a distinguishing feature of his clothing draws my attention: British Army boots.

It's the bike rider I'd seen earlier.

From the expression on the scarab seller's face, I sense tension between the two of them. The seller turns to move away and the hooded man grabs a scarab and abruptly spins around and starts to walk toward us.

The scarab seller yells in Arabic and the bike rider breaks into a run but he goes only a few paces before an Egyptian steps in front of him, his back to me, and I see the flash of a blade.

It all happens so quickly; I see it, but my mind won't accept it—the Egyptian has stuck a dagger into the gut of the bike rider.

Murder is being committed before my eyes.

The dagger man shouts, *"Allah Akbar! Allah Akbar! Allah Akbar!"*

God is great!

5

The two men face each other, so close that the bike rider grips the wrist of the assassin as if they are about to dance, his face a mask of surprise, his mouth open, almost as if the assault left him with an unfinished question, asking *why*. . . .

The assassin pulls the bloodied dagger out of his victim's stomach.

Staring down, the wounded man puts both hands over the spreading patch of blood on his abdomen.

The assassin strikes a second time, shoving the blade into the man's abdomen again. The bike rider's legs fold and he drops to his knees, then onto the dirt as his attacker holds the bloody dagger high in the air yelling again, *"Allah Akbar! Allah Akbar!"*

He turns toward us, dagger in hand, his robe splattered with the victim's blood.

"Shoot him!" Lady Warton shouts to her husband.

Lord Warton seems paralyzed, frozen in place, his jowls quivering as he stares at the dagger man.

My feet won't let me move. Like the British lord, I just stand and gawk at the man coming at us with a bloodied blade.

Von Reich pulls out a double-barreled derringer and fires. The bullet knocks the man back, his own face mimicking the surprise that his victim had shown only moments before as he falls backward onto the dirt.

Quick strides bring Von Reich hovering over the man. The assassin looks up and says something in Arabic as Von Reich takes careful, deliberate aim and fires, the bullet catching the man in the center of his forehead, snapping his head back against the ground, his legs twitching, and then he is perfectly still.

The second shot brings me out of my trance and I rush to the bike rider who has gotten back up on his knees. He clutches at me, grabbing at my clothes. Seeing him close up, I realize he's my neighbor passenger on the *Victoria* who made such an unorthodox departure from the ship earlier.

I try to hold him up but he slips back to the ground and I kneel beside him and cradle his head. *"Get a doctor, he's still alive!"*

He grabs me, pulling me closer.

"It's all right, we're getting a doctor."

He's trying to tell me something and I let him pull me inches from his lips as he whispers something I don't catch. "What?"

"Amelia . . . Amelia . . ."

That is all he says before he fades in my arms and I feel the life slipping away from him. He spoke with a British accent.

Lord Warton grabs my arm, and pulls me up and away from the man.

"We must get a doctor!" I yell.

"There's nothing you can do."

"No!" I struggle to get back to the man, hoping he might still be alive but knowing he isn't.

Lord Warton's holding me tightly as he pulls me away while Von Reich and others crowd around the body. He finally releases me when Von Reich takes my arm.

"He's dead," Von Reich says.

I jerk my arm away. "Leave me alone!" He's right, there's nothing I can do, but I need time to gather my wits and let it sink in.

"What did he say to you?"

"Amelia."

"What?"

"His wife's name, Amelia, that's all he said. We must get him a doctor, maybe there's something . . ."

Von Reich shakes his head as he reloads his pistol. "A doctor can't help him now."

"You poor dear," Lady Warton says, leading me away with another firm hold on my arm. "His lordship and Von Reich will take care of everything. You've been through enough."

Lord Warton looks up from kneeling beside the bike rider and yells to her. "Go back to the boat. Von Reich will see that you get there safely."

"But we can't just leave." I plant my feet firmly in the ground. "The police—"

"You're not in America!" Lady Warton snaps. "This is *not* a civilized country. If we are to sail with the *Victoria*, we must hurry to the carriage before we get involved in a deadly dispute between two natives."

"Natives? The man's a British passenger on our ship."

"Why do you say he's British?" Von Reich asks.

"I saw his face . . . heard his voice—"

They steer me back toward the bazaar entrance as we talk.

"I saw and heard what you did," Lady Warton says. "His face was brown, he's obviously a native."

"No, I'm sure he's British."

"That's not possible," Von Reich says. "He appeared Egyptian to me."

"You had a momentary glance at a hooded man," Lady Warton says.

"I saw his face."

"He's brown."

"Not his legs."

"His legs? What about his legs?" she demands.

"His robe pulled up when he fell off his bike on the road. I saw white skin."

Lady Warton gives Von Reich an exasperated look. He shakes his head and says, "Nellie, I saw only brown skin."

"I know what I saw. He spoke English."

"Many Egyptians speak the Queen's English. We run the country," Lady Warton says.

Holding back tears, I raise my chin and stand my ground. "The man is a passenger on our ship. I will not abandon him even in death."

"I'll take another look at the man," Von Reich says. "Keep going, we can't have the carriage leave without us when word spreads of trouble."

He hurries back in the direction we had come. Still gripping my arm firmly, her ladyship deftly marches me out of the maze and straight to the carriage as easily as if she'd left bread crumbs to guide us.

We're at the carriage when Von Reich comes back, breathing hard. "I've examined the man thoroughly."

"Arab?" Lady Warton asks.

"All over."

"I have to see for myself." I start back for the entrance to the bazaar.

"Get involved and you'll be detained for questioning," Von Reich says.

That reaches home and stops me in my tracks. "Detained for questioning" meant not finishing the race. I hesitate, shifting from one foot to the other, not knowing which way to turn.

Lady Warton turns to board the carriage. "I don't know about you, young woman, but I have no intention of staying for months in this God-forsaken hell while the slow wheels of bureaucracy grind down."

The mere thought of it chills me even in the dry, hot desert air.

I hate her words—they're hard and cruel—but I know she's right. "I suppose there's nothing that can be done for the poor man." It sounds like an excuse, even to me, but it's also the truth. "What about Lord Warton? Shouldn't we wait for him?"

His wife shakes her head. "He'll be fine. His lordship has had plenty of practice in dealing with natives."

Von Reich helps me board the carriage. My knees are shaky and I still fight back tears. "She's right, Fräulein. You cannot imagine what a nightmare the police of these backward countries are like. Things can get very ugly."

Things already start to look ugly as we board the carriage. A crowd has gathered and the driver looks worried. "We must hurry. Word spreads."

"What do you mean?" I ask.

"A Mahdi follower was martyred by an infidel. The Father of Terror is rising to drive the infidels from our land. That is what people are saying. We must hurry," he says again.

We've not gone a hundred feet before a mob pours out of the marketplace from different arteries chanting, *"Allah Akbar! Allah Akbar!"*

We duck and cover our heads with our hands as stones start flying at us.

The carriage takes us out of the reach of Stone Age weapons, but anger and fanaticism travel faster than the wind. All along our path, men on the street shout angry words and shake their fists at us.

I can't stop thinking about the man we left behind at the marketplace. A man who died in my arms and spoke his last words to me. He wanted me to do something for Amelia, whom I assume is his wife. How do I find her? What do I tell her? That her husband's life was spilled on the dirt of a Port Said marketplace? That if he's a foreigner, the local people would celebrate the death as a sign from God?

If he's a foreigner? The doubts of my companions have me wondering if the man really was the secretive passenger I'd seen disembark before dawn. I saw white skin on the bike rider, but it's possible that it wasn't the same man. I wouldn't recognize my own brothers if they were covered head to toe in Egyptian robes.

"You must stop agonizing over what occurred," Lady Warton says, reading my thoughts. "Life is cheap in these backward countries. They express themselves with violence because they have no books or newspapers. Unless you can breathe life into the dead, there is nothing you could have done."

"Except make sure his wife Amelia is notified of his death."

"Did he tell you his wife's name is Amelia?" asks Lady Warton.

"No, I just assumed—"

She gives me a dark look that says I will never learn. "You must have heard an Arabic word that sounded like the name."

I keep my peace rather than cause a confrontation. I'm certain he was speaking his wife's name in his last moment. I've not a clue how, but I shall see that the man's wife is properly notified. But at the moment I need to get my feet solidly back under me and keep focused on the demands of the race I have undertaken.

The tragic events in the marketplace were not imaginable when I took up the challenge and sailed from New York. Told that a man would be sent because a race around the world was too great a task for a woman, I told Mr. Pulitzer to go ahead and start his man—and I'd set out for another newspaper and beat him.

When the powerful publisher finally yielded, he gave me only three days' notice to prepare for the trip. But the path that brought me to Egypt had not just been Jules' remark in Paris that a woman was not capable of making the trip in the eighty days his fictional hero had managed, but had begun two years earlier when no New York newspaper would hire me as a reporter because I am a woman.

To prove that I was as capable as a man, I set out on my own to expose the shocking conditions at a woman's insane asylum by getting myself committed as a patient. It required that I convince a boardinghouse landlady, policemen, three psychiatrists, and a judge that I was a lunatic. The final diagnosis stated that I was a hopeless case, quite incurable, requiring a commitment to the notorious women's asylum on New York's Blackwell Island.

I spent ten days in the madhouse and wrote an exposé for Mr. Pulitzer's newspaper that revealed the brutal conditions mentally ill women were subjected to at the asylum.* That venture not only got me a job as an investigative reporter on Mr. Pulitzer's New York *World*, but ultimately took me to Paris, its magnificent world's fair, and a confrontation with preternatural evil.

Returning to New York, Jules' taunt that women are too fragile and require too much baggage for such a trip stayed with me. *Poppycock!* I felt—nothing more than sentiments stewed up by men who underestimate the power and determination of women just because society forbids them to wear pants. "Nellie's Folly" is what the other papers will call it if I fail. Worse, the effect that failure will have upon the ambitions of women to succeed in a man's world will be severely damaged.

This is why I accepted the challenge and why I must succeed.

* Nellie also wrote a book in 1887 called *Ten Days in a Madhouse* about the exposé that brought attention to the terrible conditions in the women's asylum. Her experiences in the madhouse ultimately led her to Paris and the events told in *The Alchemy of Murder*. —The Editors

I was certain I could do it. The available transportation—steamships, trains, and carriages—are all about the same as those used by Phileas Fogg sixteen years ago, but two great advances have reduced travel time: the Suez Canal, making it unnecessary for ships to sail all the way around Africa's Cape of Good Hope; and the completion of the transcontinental rail line from San Francisco to New York.

Knowing that I would have to sometimes scurry to make connections, I brought only one small handbag, a valise about sixteen inches long and seven inches wide. I never realized the capacity of an ordinary hand-satchel until dire necessity compelled me to exercise all my ingenuity to pack one with two traveling caps, three veils, a pair of slippers, toilet articles, an inkstand, pens, pencils, copy paper, pins, needles and thread, a dressing gown, a light jacket, a silk bodice, a small flask and a drinking cup, several complete changes of underwear, a liberal supply of handkerchiefs and fresh ruchings, and most bulky and uncompromising of all, a jar of cold cream to keep my face from chapping in the varied climates I should encounter.†

The travel dress I put on the day I boarded a ship in New York is the same one I wore today and will wear for the entire trip of nearly three months. I also have an ulster to keep me warm.

The evening before I started, I went to the office to say good-bye and to obtain two hundred pounds in English gold and Bank of England notes.‡ The gold I carry in my pocket, with a few pieces hidden in the heel of my left shoe. The Bank of England notes are in a chamois-skin bag tied around my neck. Besides this, I have some American gold and paper money to use at different ports as a test to see if American money is known outside the forty-two states and territories.

Even though it was quite possible to buy tickets in New York for the entire trip, because I might be compelled to change my route at almost any point, no itinerary was made; the only transportation I arranged on leaving New York was my ticket to London.§

† Veils were in fashion and also commonly used to hold ladies' hats in place. Ruchings were lace trim on collars and sleeves that could be taken off and washed. —The Editors

‡ Two hundred British pounds equaled U.S. $1,000, the equivalent of about U.S. $25,000 today. Not an excessive amount to take considering that she had to pay for all her accommodations and transportation for nearly three months en route and this was an age before credit cards and ATMs. —The Editors

§ Not buying tickets for the entire trip was a good decision because she missed the mail boat

A fellow reporter suggested that a revolver would be a good companion piece for my travels, but I had such a strong belief in the world's greeting me as I greeted it, that I refused to arm myself. I knew if my conduct was proper I should always find men of any nationality ready to protect me.

The life's blood of two men soaking the dirt of the marketplace had made the suggestion that I carry a revolver sage advice.

Raucous noise jolts me out of my thoughts and I tense up as a group of people turn onto the street. Women at the head of the procession are shrieking and wailing. "The Mahdi?"

"A funeral procession," Von Reich says. "The barefooted women in front howling the loudest and tearing their clothes are professional mourners."

"What nonsense is that?" Lady Warton demands. "Why in God's name would they hire people to make those awful noises and rip their clothes?"

"It's how they honor the dead—the more grief, the more the dead person will be missed. The black-robed women wait outside the house like a flock of crows until they're told the deceased has passed and then they begin their expressions of grief, all the way to the cemetery and until the last shovel of dirt is thrown."

I close my eyes tightly and turn my head to avoid looking at the group as they pass, but it does no good—the wails for the dead penetrate my bones, chilling my marrow.

Who will cry for the dead men in the marketplace?

We reach the beach where several boats are available to take us out to the ship.

"You ladies stay here and I'll find our boatman," Von Reich says.

He returns with a disgusted expression on his face. "It's arranged, but the boatman would not permit us even to board until I paid him. His price is double what he charged to bring us to land. These people are robbers."

"And murderers," Lady Warton snaps.

---

in London and instead crossed the English Channel to Boulogne, traveled across France and down the boot of Italy to Brindisi by rail and carriage, where she boarded the steamship *Victoria* for Port Said. —The Editors

7

The moment our feet are on the deck Lady Warton excuses herself, proclaiming a "horrid headache" and heads straight for her cabin and her headache powders.

Perhaps it is only my strained state of mind, but as she flees I'm left with the singular impression that in her estimation I am somehow responsible for her distress rather than the fact we had witnessed two violent deaths in the marketplace.

Instead of going directly to my cabin, I walk on deck, pacing swiftly from stern to bow, a habit I have of wearing off nervous energy and mulling over the day's events before I retire.

This time I need to walk off ragged nerves. My body aches because I've been so tense. I watched two men die today. Who will cry for them? And how will their deaths affect me? Touching the side of my neck, I can still feel the dying man's breath as he whispered his last word to me—"Amelia."

I know I've left the violence at the marketplace and the rage on the streets where a mob thirsted for blood—*my blood*—yet I sense that I've carried some of the malevolence back to the ship with me, just as I brought the dust of Port Said on my shoes.

They were still coaling the ship from a barge when we boarded, dust-covered men with sacks of coal rushing up the steep gangplank between the barges and the ship. The men are not working quietly. Judging from the noise, every one of them is yelling something that pleases their own fancy and humor.

The frantic bustle is soothing in an odd sort of way. It's an image long to be remembered, and just for the moment the aching memory of the horror in the marketplace fades.

I don't know the identity of the bike rider who died in the marketplace, but regardless of who he was, in the morning I'll ask Lord Warton what happened after we left and if anyone is planning to locate the dead man's wife. If not, I shall attempt it. The man's resemblance to a fellow passenger and the British accent still bewilder me, but I have to put aside my doubts and move on.

Returning to my cabin, I find the steward's luggage cart parked outside the door of the man I had thought was killed in the marketplace. The door is cracked open.

Passenger names appear on slips of paper tacked to cabin doors and this one bears the inscription: JOHN CLEVELAND.

I hesitate briefly, my good sense telling me to move on and to mind my own business, but my curiosity prods me to peek in. I nudge the door open a bit more. Raymond, a ship's steward who also serves as my attendant, is placing clothes on the bed. Behind him are two steamer trunks.

I push the door farther open.

"Madam? Can I help you?"

"Is Mr. Cleveland around?"

"No, he went ashore."

I glance at the clothing on the bed and the trunks. "Is Mr. Cleveland leaving us?"

"Yes, he's staying in Port Said. I've been instructed to send his luggage ashore."

"Really? Who told you he was staying?"

The steward avoids my eye. "Those are my instructions, madam."

"I'm just wondering if the instructions are correct. I saw Mr. Cleveland a short time ago and he never mentioned that he was leaving."

"The instructions came from Lord Warton."

"I see." But I don't—not at all. Lord Warton tells me that the dead man isn't my neighbor on the ship and then has instructions for the man's possessions to be left behind. That makes it all as clear as mud. Except for one thing. "Lord Warton isn't on board the ship."

"Her ladyship delivered the instruction for him."

"I see . . ." More muddy waters, though it is readily apparent that Lady Warton received instructions to which I had not been privy and neglected to share them with me.

"I'm only obeying instructions, madam."

He's getting defensive, probably thinks I suspect him of stealing. "Of course, go on with his lordship's instruction."

As he turns back to his task, I add, "Raymond, I have a dreadful headache. Would you please go to the infirmary and get me some powder?"

"I got headache powders for you yesterday—"

"Yes, I know, but I need more. Here—" I pull a three-pence coin out of my pocket and slip it into his hand. "I'll watch Mr. Cleveland's possessions until you get back."

Resisting the impulse to give him a push out the door, as soon as he is gone I start searching—for what, I don't know. I haven't a clue as to what to look for, but I obey my instincts, which are screaming that something is not right.

Why the devil makes me do these things has always been a mystery to me. As a fellow reporter once told me after I had narrowly escaped a brothel owner's wrath, someday I'd end up sticking my nose in the wrong place and getting it chopped off.

Quickly checking dresser drawers, I find them already emptied. Leafing through the items on the bed reveals an ordinary collection of shirts, collars, cuffs, shirt fronts, bow ties, and other accessories. Taking care not to ruffle the clothes too much, I press down on the clothing to feel if anything is hidden beneath . . . and find nothing.

The two streamer trunks are unlocked and empty.

In a box on the floor are books and a case of fine kitchen and dinner knives with the name of a cutlery manufacturer in Liverpool. Inscribed on the cutlery case is his name: JOHN J. CLEVELAND.

One of those gallows humor thoughts I am inclined to get at the most inappropriate times suddenly flies through my head: A cutlery salesman is stabbed to death by a knife.

His choice of books is odd only because there is nothing on cutlery. He has a book on hunting rifles, a thin volume called the *Handbook on Egypt*, and a hefty tome entitled *Compendium of Laws of the County of Yorkshire.*

A small piece of paper marks a page in the law book. Written on it in pencil are a series of numbers that have no apparent order, at least not to me. It makes no more sense to me than if I sat down and wrote numbers at random, but the numbers must have meant something to Mr. Cleveland.

Shamelessly rummaging through the man's possessions, I find no indication that he has a family—no pictures of a wife or children, no letters.

So who is Amelia?

Even if she is a lover rather than his wife, might he not have a picture of her? Some keepsake such as a lace handkerchief with her favorite scent or a farewell note?

I hear footsteps in the corridor and almost drop the book. *I'm going to be caught.* I shove the paper back in the book, the books back into the box, and race for the door, opening it and stumbling out as the heel of my shoe snags on the threshold.

Getting my balance, I stare at a man who has opened the door to a cabin on the other side of the corridor. The footsteps I had heard were his. He stares back.

"I . . . I—" No alibi comes to my normally liquid tongue and I give him a smile instead.

"Good evening," he says.

I choke on a reply as I hear two voices coming from the stairwell that leads into the corridor. *Lord Warton and the steward.*

I leap forward and rush at the man, causing him to step backward into his room and nearly fall over a piece of luggage. I step in and slam the door behind me.

For a moment, we just stare at each other, his mouth agape.

"You'll catch flies," pops out of my own mouth.

He starts to say something and I can see that words fail him.

He is older than me, perhaps in his late thirties. My first impression is that he needs a shave, a haircut, and a bath. Soap, hot water, and a good scrubbing by the ship's laundry would also make his clothes presentable. His appearance suggests he came aboard directly from an expedition of some sort rather than a hotel.

A tall, handsome man with sapphire blue eyes and an athletic build, he appears perplexed, perhaps even slightly amused that a short runt of a woman has forced herself into his room, although his jaw dropped at the sudden invasion.

"What I meant is, your mouth was open. You can catch flies that way if you aren't careful."

"Who told you that?"

"My mother, when I was a little girl."

My mouth is flapping nonsense but my ears are tuned to hear the sudden banging on his stateroom door I expect at any moment, along with a demand that I come out and face the music.

He nods in a knowing manner. "I can see that your mother, dear woman that she no doubt is, probably spared the rod too much with her daughter. May I ask why you have stormed into my room?"

"I . . . I—"

"Yes, I've heard that much."

He is British, something I had already assumed from his appearance and clothes.

"I'm trying to avoid a masher."

"A masher? On the ship? Come, we'll inform the captain . . . after I thrash the man."

I hold out a hand to keep him from getting around me to the door. "No, we can't."

"Why can't we?"

"I . . . I—"

"Perhaps the truth might come out easier?"

I sigh deeply and lean back against the door. I don't know why lies are getting stuck in my throat. A compulsion to tell the truth has rarely crimped my speech.

"I did something I shouldn't have done. A man was murdered—"

"You murdered a man?"

"No, of course not, a man was killed at the marketplace. Two men, in fact."

"Yes, I heard something about that. A dispute between locals."

"No, the man first attacked was British. I'm sure it was Mr. Cleveland, the cutlery salesman across the hall."

He starts to say something and opens his mouth wide enough again for flies and then closes it.

"You think I'm mad."

"Not at all," he says, calmly. "I think that something I ate or drank came from the Land of the Lotus Eaters and has caused me to imagine that a young woman has barged into my room and is telling me a wild story about the death of a cutlery salesman in a marketplace."

"Lord Warton says the dead man is Egyptian, but I say it was Mr. Cleveland."

"And what does Mr. Cleveland say?"

"You haven't been listening to me. Mr. Cleveland is dead."

"Miss—?"

"Bly, Nellie Bly. I'm an American. Mr.—?"

"Selous, Frederick Selous." He gave me a gentlemanly nod-bow. "I am British and it is obvious that you are an American. No proper British woman would barge into a strange man's room at night. However, the fact that you are American, madam, does not make Mr. Cleveland dead."

"The fact that you are British, sir, does not make Mr. Cleveland alive."

"Quite true, Miss Bly. But the fact that I spoke to Mr. Cleveland only a few minutes ago does mean he was not murdered earlier in the marketplace."

Oh Lord . . . a big hole has opened under my feet and I am falling into it.

8

I'm sure I left Mr. Selous's stateroom on two feet, but when I'm in the corridor and his door slams behind me, I feel I've crawled out on broken glass.

"Nellie girl, you did it this time," I moan out loud.

Mr. Cleveland alive? I can't believe I have been so bullheaded, stubborn, and stupid.

The corridor is empty—praise the Lord for that—and I walk slowly, in a mental fog, toward my cabin at the far end. How will I face Von Reich and the Wartons tomorrow? More importantly, how do I get myself into these things?

"Madam!" a voice behind me snaps.

I whip around. The steward has come out of Mr. Cleveland's room and I brace myself for the accusations that I am certain will start flying. Full of guilt, I'm ready to confess my sins.

"You forgot your headache powders."

I breathe a sigh of relief. "Thank you, Raymond."

My head is really ready to explode.

After taking the headache powders, I throw myself on the bed and cover my head with a pillow and groan into it. What a fool I have made of myself! It'll be all over the ship by morning.

My short time in Port Said has been nothing but dreadful. Witnessing a murder and what amounted to an "execution" in a medieval bazaar, then being chased by a mob of murderous fanatics confirms Mr. Pulitzer's opinion about the dangers of international travel.

Somewhere along the line I have made a complete fool out of myself with important people who have been kind to me and who I will be seeing every day for the next several weeks.

The last realization prompts me to pour another glass of water and add more headache powder.

I can only conclude in my defense that the dark side of Egyptian magic has reached out from a secret tomb buried in the desert sands and turned the day into a nightmare.

What grates me most is that Lord Warton will likely attribute my insistence that the dead Egyptian in the marketplace was John Cleveland to the combination of too much sun and the weakness of a "female disposition." And I have provided all the necessary ammunition. A hysterical female, for certain, is what I have managed to make myself.

I should never have challenged Lord Warton's assessment of the identity of the dead man. He is a lord, after all, even though I'm not quite sure what that means—is he an earl or a baron? Whatever his title, it's something very prestigious because everyone from the captain to the other passengers fawns over him. Compared to a nobleman, what do I know?

A thousand regrets swirl around me as I take off my dress to shake the dust out of it. As I'm giving it a good jerk, something drops out and hits the carpet.

A scarab, the magic amulet of the pharaohs.

"Where did you come from?" I ask as I examine it.

The stone beetle is a couple inches long and an inch wide, larger and heavier than the ones I've seen used for jewelry. Red with black eyes and a black spot on its back, the beetle has six brown legs and two short tentacles.

The only way it could have gotten into my pocket was from the dying man as I held him. Why would he put a symbol of Egyptian magic in my pocket? It was his last physical act, besides uttering the name Amelia.

What is so important about the scarab that a man is murdered over it—and caused him to pass it to me with his dying breath?

Nothing about its appearance makes it appealing. It lacks gems or fine workmanship that would give it value beyond a marketplace trinket. The flat bottom has two snakes on each side, their heads meeting at the top, but no other symbols or hieroglyphics. The scarab's back is smooth with no distinctive horizontal or vertical lines. It does have an unusual feature—it's meant to be opened. A crack along the side suggests that it's two pieces wedged together.

A piece goes flying as I pry it open with a nail file and bangs against the wall, breaking into pieces. In a cavity between the two sides is a key, one that has a familiar look to me.

My father had a similar key that he used to remove the big metal cover from a piece of machinery at the mill he operated in Cochran's Mills when I was a child. When he bought a new machine, he gave the key to me because I loved the bulky, odd shape of it. I still have it, safely tucked away in my jewelry box at home.

The mill was started by my father and named for him, Elizabeth Cochran being my true name. Those who have followed my career know that when I got a job as a reporter I was forced to take the pen name of Nellie Bly to hide my identity because news reporting is considered immodest employment for a woman.

A key that belongs perhaps in a factory, around machinery, is my feeling about the one in my hand. Nothing about it strikes me as Egyptian. It's definitely the product of an industrialized country.

My world has taken another flip. That was no dispute between locals in the marketplace, but something smacking of intrigue. But why had the key been slipped into my pocket?

The man on the bike that exposed white skin, the man whose dying words were spoken with a British accent, a man with a face I'm sure I'd passed in the corridor—it had to be Mr. Cleveland. Lord Warton taking charge of his luggage, sending it ashore . . . it can not be a coincidence.

A Brit named John Cleveland died in the marketplace in a dispute over a key hidden in a cheap scarab. I'd stake my life on it.

Staring at the key, I wonder if I have done exactly that.

I push the thought aside. I'm on a British ship. No one can harm me. I hope.

Still, I had no clue as to why he gave me the key. Or why the key was important to the dying man. What would it mean to Amelia? Assets he wanted his family to receive?

It all sounds very logical and reasonable except for some other unanswered questions: Why was Mr. Cleveland running around Port Said disguised as an Egyptian? Why was the key concealed in the scarab? Why was Lord Warton hiding the fact that the man was British?

Finally, of greatest significance at the moment: How could Frederick Selous believe he'd spoken to Mr. Cleveland if the man had died in my arms?

Is there an intrigue that involves the British and the religious radicals trying to drive them from Egypt? But Warton doesn't strike me as a spy. Not that I have met any, but I do have a reasonable notion that spies are clever and devious. Warton is stuffy and arrogant, rudely so, and my impression is that he is more force-fed educated than bright and scheming.

And his insufferable wife—that mean-spirited woman doesn't fit my romanticized notion of how a spy's wife would act.

It seems to me Lord Warton is much more likely to have stumbled accidentally into a murderous situation at the bazaar than being involved in some intrigue. If so, why hide that the murdered man is British?

Protecting the precarious British situation in Egypt would be the obvious motive. Having served in the diplomatic corps, Lord Warton would be sensitive to the fact that Egypt is a tinderbox really to explode. His first instinct might have been to hide the fact that Mr. Cleveland was British. It might serve as fuel for the radicals in their campaign to win converts.

I slip back on my dress because none of this makes any sense if Mr. Cleveland is still alive. And there's a man down the corridor who says he is.

FREDERICK SELOUS ANSWERS the door only after I have knocked several times. The door is jerked open to reveal that he is a bit disheveled and not in good temper. I suspect he had already dozed off.

"I need to talk to you."

"Miss Bly, it is—"

I make a frontal assault again, stepping in, with him making hasty steps backward. Being caught standing at a man's door at a late hour would be scandalous.

He backs up, staring at me as if I have entered with a snake in hand. "You are completely demented."

"I am a newspaper reporter for the New York *World*. I smell a story."

"For your information, I am also a newspaper reporter."

My turn to gape. "No!"

"Yes."

"What paper? The London—"

"The Cape Town *Lion*."

"The what?"

"A newspaper in South Africa."

"Never heard of it."

"Miss Bly, that statement exposes your ignorance of history, geography, and sociology. Africa was populated with humans when dinosaurs still roamed New York."

It is obvious that this is not a man I will win many arguments with. He is pliable to a frontal assault by a small woman, but once the conversation turned to more heady subjects, he becomes a giant.

"Mr. Selous, I need to ask you a very simple question. What did Mr. Cleveland look like?"

He takes a deep breath. It is easy to see that he is struggling with the temptation to remove me physically from his room. But I am confident that a proper Brit would hesitate to manhandle a woman just as an American would.

Hopefully.

"The man," he says, slowly, deliberately, "was perhaps in his thirties. Medium build. Average height. Hair . . . brown, I believe. Eyes . . . I'm not sure. My inclination is to say brown."

"Medium built, brown hair, brown eyes, would fit most of the men in the Western Hemisphere."

He gives me a tight grin. Like a dog ready to bite. "I am certain that is neither the fault of Mr. Cleveland nor me. Now, madam, would you mind leaving my room so I can get back to bed?"

"Where were you when you spoke to him?"

"I was standing beside my luggage on the beach, waiting for a boat to take me to the ship. He told me his name was Cleveland and asked me to tell the captain he would be staying ashore in Port Said. A business matter, he said."

"Ah . . ."

He controls himself. "What does 'ah' mean? You make it sound as if you have had a revelation from the gods on Olympus."

"You had luggage with you, obviously boarding the ship for the first time. The man knew that you wouldn't recognize him while passengers who had come across with him from Italy would."

"I was the only person on the beach."

"Very convenient."

"What does *that* mean?"

"Don't you see? You don't know that was John Cleveland; it was just a man who walked up to you and—"

"*Miss Bly.* I am not in the habit of being approached by *dead men* and asked to carry a message. Now, I suggest you take your hysterics out of my cabin before I am forced to have you removed by ship's officers."

I could see that a harmonious relationship with the man who has identified himself as a fellow reporter is impossible.

I open the door to leave but pause after stepping out to put a parting shot over his bow.

"I don't know how reporting is done in South Africa, but from your attitude I must assume your efforts are restricted to news of weddings, funerals, and dog bites."

After delivering that fine retort, I slam the stateroom door shut hard enough to wake the dead.

Whipping around, I'm doomed to meet the steward again coming out of Mr. Cleveland's stateroom.

Seeing me leave a man's room at night, the rogue gives me a knowing grin.

I give him a searing glare that wipes it off his face.

FREDERICK SELOUS IN THE HEART OF AFRICA

9

I return to my cabin but pace like a trapped animal, with more questions buzzing in my head. Wouldn't Cleveland have come back to the ship to secure his own luggage rather than leave matters to a stranger on the beach? And orders for his luggage to Lord Warton?

One conclusion I reach is that the key must be put in a safe place until I can figure out what to do with it. The best place I can think of is the secret compartments in my shoes.

The dear shoemaker who made my shoes for the trip suggested that I let him make the heels hollow, so I'd be able to put some gold coins in them. "That way if your purse is stolen, you shall still have some money."

The pieces to the scarab are evidence I can't hide so I do the next best thing. I toss them out my porthole.

With that resolved, I should be able to sleep, but it isn't possible. Thoughts are pecking at my head with the beat of a woodpecker. Instead, I throw on my ulster and head for my hearty stern-to-bow walk on the deck in the hopes of burning off nagging thoughts.

Raymond, the steward, is lowering luggage down the side of the ship in a net as I come out on deck. I'm sure the trunks are the ones I saw in Mr. Cleveland's stateroom.

A shadow falls over me as a man comes up to the railing and stands beside me.

"I couldn't sleep, either," Mr. Selous says.

He appears a bit hesitant at having approached me. Perhaps he hadn't realized it was me until it was too late to politely flee. Or is he implying that I'm the cause of his lack of sleep?

"Mr. Cleveland's luggage going ashore." I nod down at the meshed bundle being lowered.

"Quite," he says, using that uniquely British listening response.

"I suppose Mr. Cleveland is anxiously waiting on the beach for the boat to bring his luggage to shore." I facetiously stare at the distant beach that is too far and too dark to see anything on. "Can you see him?"

Mr. Selous makes a guttural sound that conveys he is sorry he attempted to be polite and now is *quite* done with my intrigues. He turns to leave as a shout comes from below.

A steamer trunk has slipped out from the meshed bundle, striking the side of the boat waiting for it. The trunk snaps open as it hits the boat and falls into the water, opening for a second before a boatman grabs it.

"It's empty," I whisper.

"What?" Selous turns back and peers over the side. "It's too dark to see—"

"I saw when it hit. It's empty."

From his expression I think he's trying to give me the benefit of the doubt but is uncertain as to whether I deserve it. He starts to say something, then appears to shrug it off and pushes away from the railing.

"Good night, Miss Bly. We should both get some sleep and rise early, for tomorrow we pass through the greatest man-made waterway in the world."

I stay at the railing for a moment, staring down where the luggage is being unloaded onto the boat. The trunk is empty; a fact that brings more woodpeckers pecking in my head.

When I turn to leave I make eye contact with the steward.

I give him a frown that lets him know that I am no fool, that I know there are shenanigans afoot, and get back an unexpected dark look.

Learn not to signal your punches, I tell myself on my way down dim stairwells and corridors to my cabin.

A dark figure appears ahead of me at the far end of a corridor before disappearing into a stateroom—the woman in black who I've glimpsed on deck during my walks. I've taken a fancy to the notion that the mysterious woman who wanders the decks at night is none other than Sarah Winchester, heir to the Winchester Repeating Arms Company fortune.

The name she boarded under was "Sarah Jones," and the widow Winchester is known to travel incognito in her own Pullman car with the shades down and to use a false name when staying in a hotel.

I haven't shared my theory about the woman with anyone else because

I hope there'll be a story behind it. It wouldn't be the first strange tale told about the woman.

Mrs. Winchester fell into deep depression after the untimely deaths of first her daughter and then her husband, and came to believe that she is haunted by the ghosts of the thousands of people killed by the famous Winchester repeating rifles that helped win the Civil War and massacred much of the nation's Indians.

That she has only worn black since the death of her loved ones is just one of the more mundane rumors about her strange behavior; another is that she is using her vast fortune to build a house with an endless number of rooms because a spiritualist advised her that as long as she kept adding rooms to the house, the ghosts of the Winchester dead would not attack her.*

I first saw the woman come up the gangplank after I boarded at Brindisi, Italy. It wasn't her widow's black garments and net veil that were memorable, but the coffin being carried by porters behind her.

Both woman and coffin disappeared into a first-class stateroom and neither has been seen since—except for the fleeting glimpses of her that I've had at night.

Her first name, widow's clothes, and reclusive habit all add up to the Winchester woman, but it's the coffin that clinches my conclusion that it is indeed the eccentric woman. While I've never heard of Mrs. Winchester bringing a coffin along during her travels, such an oddity would fit the public image of the woman—and provide me with a new slant on her eccentricities for a story.

Is it the body of her young daughter in the coffin? Or her husband?

The thought of sleeping with the dead in a stateroom gives me goose bumps . . . a goose walking over my grave, as my mother would say.

I make sure my door is securely locked before I put on my nightgown. I'm about to undress when there is a knock on my door.

Certain it is Lord Warton coming to accuse me of searching Cleveland's room, I open the door and find Von Reich instead.

"I thought I should check on you and make sure you're well."

I lean against the door frame and rub my forehead. "My head has split in two and I've lost one of the halves."

* Mrs. Winchester kept the house under continuous construction for the last thirty-eight years of her life, from 1884 to 1922. Once seven stories high, it was damaged in the great earthquake of 1906 and is now only four stories, with 160 rooms, 47 fireplaces, and 10,000 panes of glass. The number 13 appears in various motifs around the house. —The Editors

"After what you've been through, it's amazing you have any head left. Tomorrow the Wartons and I are taking another day excursion—"

I shake my head no and even that hurts. "I am going to stay aboard and rest."

"I'm sorry to hear that. We are going to feast with a sheikh in the desert that will be like nothing you have ever imagined, then we are visiting the ruins of ancient Tanis, the city that once was the capital of Egypt. But since you—"

"I'm coming!"

He grins. "We leave before the dawn. To avoid the sun. And trouble." He starts to leave and turns back to me. "It's rather like the Biblical Revelation, isn't it?"

"The feast?"

"No, no, the story of the Mahdi. The Muslim holy book says he'll return to Earth amidst a reign of war and destruction much like the Bible says the Four Horsemen of the Apocalypse will create."

He looks at me for a long moment. "I told you that you must expect the unexpected in Egypt. It's an ancient land, one still haunted by thousands of years of intrigues, wars, and hexes."

"What's the surprise for tomorrow?" I ask.

He raises his eyebrows. "A miracle, dear lady; you shall stand witness to a true miracle."

Von Reich leaves and I carry his words to bed with me.

Holy war, apocalyptic horsemen of war and death, the intrigues of modern nations and ruins of an ancient one—all mysterious and exotic, and nothing that I expected when I made the impulsive decision to race around the world.

Now I'm to witness a miracle.

I could use one at the moment. So could Mr. Cleveland.

I feel bad that I had mentally ridiculed him for acting so secretive. He had his reasons, though whatever intrigue he was involved in, he hadn't played it well, not at least good enough to keep from getting himself killed.

The invitation from Von Reich sounded to me as innocent as a pickpocket with his hand in my purse. With the Mahdi on the warpath, I have to wonder if the miracle won't be that we get back to the ship with our heads still on our shoulders.

I would have passed on the invitation, but it's just too convenient that we all ended up in the marketplace as murder was coming down. I have to find out if it was a coincidence or something else.

Exhausted from the day, I sit down to take off my shoes. Right after removing one shoe, I stop. A movement from the corner of my eye catches my attention and I look up.

Something—a shadow, a figure—is at my porthole.

Gripping my shoe, I slowly get up to see "what" if anything is there. Just inches away from my porthole a man's face abruptly appears. Someone might as well have thrown a spider in my face. I drop my shoe, and the face, draped by a gray striped hood, disappears as quickly as it came.

Without any thought, I run for my door, throwing off the other shoe I still had on and barrel out of the doorway, racing down the corridor to the companionway and out to the deck.

Breathless, heart in my mouth, I make myself slow down so as not to draw any attention and cautiously walk down the deck toward my porthole.

Several male passengers are mingling about, enjoying their evening cigars and brandy, none in Egyptian hoods. I look in every direction trying to figure out where the hooded man went.

My feet are wet from the deck's evening washing and even though it is not cold, my body shivers. Putting my chin and shoulders up, I'm determined to strengthen my resolve. I know there was a face at my porthole with the same hood as Mr. Cleveland's when he was killed in the marketplace. Whoever is trying to frighten me can go to hell.

I march back down the deck to the companionway, meeting Frederick Selous returning to his cabin.

Staring down at my bare feet and lack of a night coat, he asks, "Is something wrong, Miss Bly?"

"Does it look like something is wrong to you, Mr. Selous?"

I leave him with that until I am past him. He pauses at his cabin door and appears wishing he could say something.

"Don't worry, Mr. Selous, I don't frighten easy. In fact, when I get scared, I get mad."

I strut into my cabin six feet tall and filled with strength.

Once my door is shut behind me I collapse against it and try to get my breathing back into a normal rhythm. Then I lock it and shove the cabin chair under the handle.

What the devil? What insanity is this? Someone's idea of a bad joke?

No, not a joke, but something much more cruel—an attempt to frighten me, perhaps even send me running to the captain screaming that the ghost of John Cleveland has paid me a visit. If someone wanted to discredit me, that would certainly be grist for the mill.

I hadn't gotten a good look at the face in the porthole, all I saw was a dark face half hidden in the hood of a cloak, but I have no doubt that it meant to frighten me into believing it was him.

I draw the curtain over the porthole before slipping into bed, still angry and tense from the invasion of my privacy. The face in the window had served a powerful purpose—it brought home the fact that the murderous rage that spilled blood in the marketplace has followed me back to the ship.

The small cabin suddenly makes me feel confined, with an eerie sense of being cornered. I'm no longer certain I'm safe aboard. I feel exposed, even trapped, rather than safe and cozy because I don't know who I can trust and there's no place to run and hide.

The key had cost John Cleveland his life. Now it is a magnet bringing the danger and intrigues to me on a ship I should feel safe aboard.

And I lied to Frederick Selous.

I do get scared.

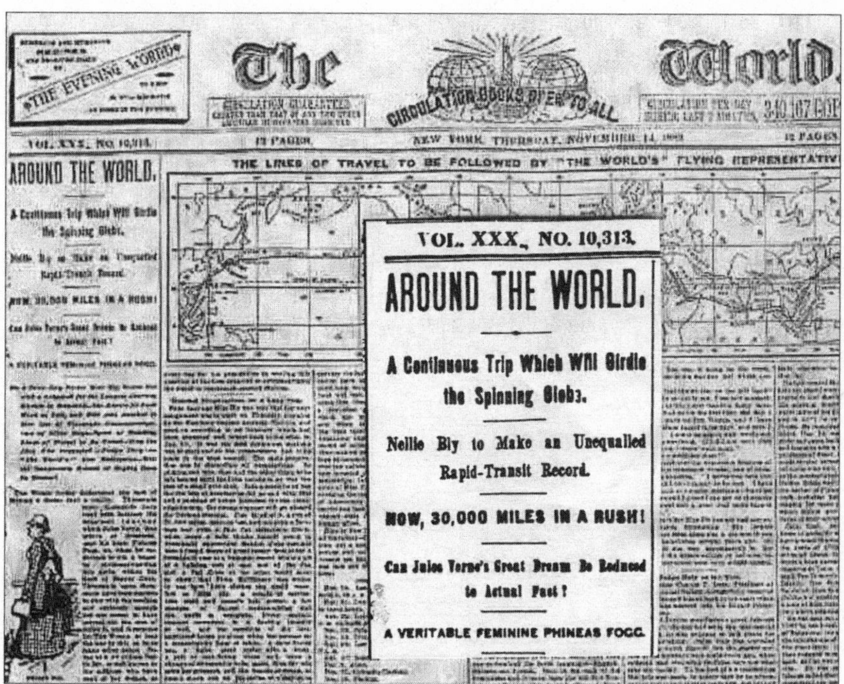

THE EVENING WORLD

The World

CIRCULATION BOOKS OPEN TO ALL

THE LINES OF TRAVEL TO BE FOLLOWED BY "THE WORLD'S" FLYING REPRESENTATIV

VOL. XXX., NO. 10,313.

AROUND THE WORLD.

A Continuous Trip Which Will Girdle the Spinning Globe.

Nellie Bly to Make an Unequalled Rapid-Transit Record.

NOW, 30,000 MILES IN A RUSH!

Can Jules Verne's Great Dream Be Reduced to Actual Fact?

A VERITABLE FEMININE PHINEAS FOGG.

NEW YORK *WORLD* NOVEMBER 14, 1889
THE DAY NELLIE LEFT ON HER TRIP

TRAVEL CLOTHES AND VEILS OF VICTORIAN WOMEN

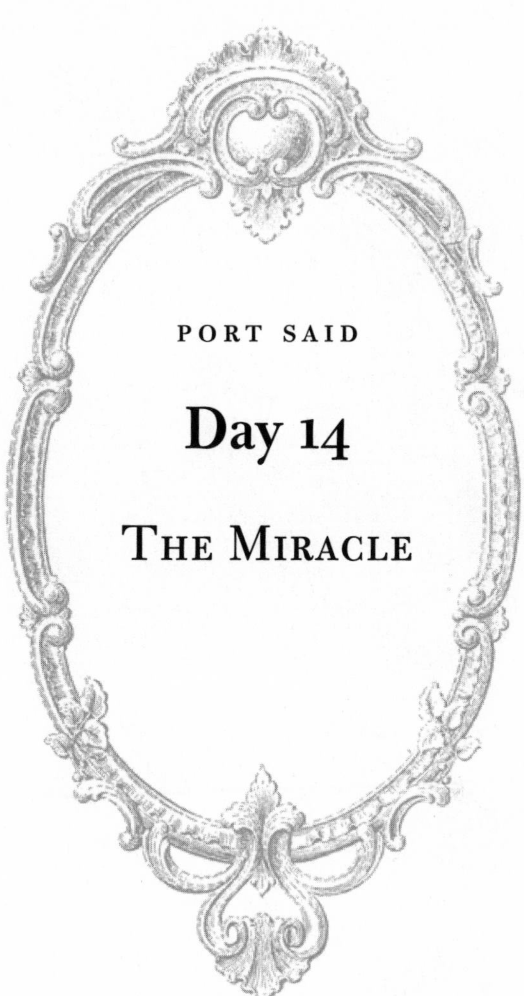

PORT SAID

Day 14

The Miracle

LIGHTHOUSE AND ENTRANCE TO SUEZ CANAL

10

Riding in a carriage through Port Said in an early dawn darkened by angry clouds, I no longer see the land of the eternal Nile as an enchanted place created with an artist's brush to satiate my senses with the strange and exotic. Instead, I feel as if I have been transported back to the malevolent Egypt of the Old Testament, where mighty pharaohs who called themselves living gods ruled with the whip and the God of the Israelites turned the Nile red with His wrath. Only this time, the blood that taints the waters might be my own.

I try to shake off the feeling of gloom and doom and anxiety about whether an angry mob might drag me from the carriage, but the murder of John Cleveland and the deadly rage of the Mahdi has cast a long shadow in my mind, feeding doubts, confusion, and fears that I can't share with my companions or anyone else on board because I don't know whom to trust.

I regret I accepted the invitation but struggle to grin and bear it—with clenched teeth—as I sit in a carriage fit for a king en route to a feast given by a Bedouin sheikh at the ruins of a great city of antiquity.

Von Reich is pleased with our transportation. "The sheikh sent his own carriage for me. It would not have embarrassed a pharaoh."

The gilt carriage has ornate carvings of snakes curling up around the poles, black tongues of the reptiles hissing toward the sky as if they are challenging the gods. Fish with vibrant colors of green, yellow, and turquoise that appear ready to leap off the poles are mingled between the snakes; sitting on top of each pole are white doves of peace each holding a bright lime-green leaf in its beak.

A silk canopy made of the most soothing sea-blue turquoise protects us from the sun. Aquamarine, azure, and violet overstuffed pillows with gold tassels are laid out on the seats for us to sit on.

Two fierce-looking Bedouins armed with rifles and swords on camels ride as our escort. So much for the white doves of peace . . .

From their conversation earlier on the beach road as we waited for the conveyance, it's obvious my companions are pretending that nothing happened yesterday in the marketplace. Rather than the shocking events and the possibility that we will be attacked by another mob, they chat about the lack of good service and food aboard the ship, the poverty of Egypt, the unusual scenery . . . anything except that the blood of men had been spilled on the dirt of the marketplace before our eyes.

The pretense leaves me tense and unsettled, with questions and no closure and a sense of distrust, especially of Lord Warton. I have no doubt he's the instigator of the game. He gives me solemn looks, communicating to others that I am an hysterical female who was so traumatized by the murder—and execution—that bringing up the subject would cause an imbalance in my delicate feminine constitution.

I've handled crooked politicians, convicted murderers, burly street toughs, and tough editors who would make mincemeat out of the pompous British lord. I have worked undercover as a madwoman in an asylum to expose the abuse of the mentally ill, walked mean streets as a prostitute to investigate how their male customers treat them, taken employment as a maid to show the abuse of servants, even danced in a chorus line and received shooting lessons from Annie Oakley . . . all without upsetting my female disposition.

I feel like asking the haughty gentleman exactly what he has done, besides trying to show Moroccans how to grow wheat, a task his employee would be far more qualified to perform. Or I could remind him that yesterday he had proved himself unable to handle the deadly encounter with the assassin when he froze in fear and confusion as a man with a dagger came at us.

Our carriage is rumbling over Port Said potholes when the British peer catches me by surprise by mentioning yesterday's incident.

"What did the man in the marketplace give you yesterday?"

"Excuse me?"

"Someone told the police he passed something to you."

"What is he supposed to have passed to me?"

"That is the question, young lady, what did he give you?"

"If someone believes they saw me being passed something, let them tell me to my face. I don't intend to answer to an anonymous accusation."

Lady Warton pats her husband's arm as his cheeks color from what he no doubt considers my impertinence. "Let's talk about more pleasant things, dear."

I had avoided an outright denial just in case someone actually did see the man slip the scarab in my pocket. I'd like nothing better than to take the key out of my heel and have a spirited discussion about it, but my instinct is that if I give it to Lord Warton the key will find its way to the bottomless pit of British bureaucracy.

Learning the truth about Mr. Cleveland's death and carrying his last word to his loved one are a responsibility I have accepted . . . not to mention Lord Warton made a mistake when he set out to make me look ridiculous.

What other malice he has toward me is still to be decided. At the very least, he has appointed himself protector of whatever involvement his country has in the marketplace incident, a task I sympathize with because I would do it myself if I felt Mr. Cleveland was American. But two thorns are under my claws—the truth needs to be exposed to ensure that there was no skulduggery involved by men or their governments. And, more than anything else, a man was murdered before my eyes, a man who selected me as the recipient of his last wish, to carry an object to his beloved.

Regardless of my feelings, I am an invited guest and it would be rude of me to say anything, especially since the Wartons have a business relationship with Von Reich, who is doing his best to make me feel welcome. But the matter has not dropped with me.

Von Reich points to the two-hundred-foot tall, brick-walled lighthouse near where the canal meets the Mediterranean.

"The Statue of Liberty, that colossal statue the French put up in New York Harbor three years ago, was originally meant to be placed here to commemorate the Suez Canal. The original design was that of a fellah, an Egyptian peasant, with beams of light from a headband and a torch he held."

"How did it end up in New York?" I ask.

"Money. The khedive of Egypt ran out of it and the *Light of Asia* peasant turned into the goddess Liberty and became *Liberty Enlightening the World* in New York Harbor."

I make a mental note of the Egyptian connection to the Statue of

Liberty to include it in a cable back to my editor. Everyone knows that the statue was a gift from the people of France and that Monsieur Eiffel had built the frame in much the same fashion he did his much-criticized tower in Paris, but the fact that the concept made its way from Egypt will be of interest.

As we leave the city, Lady Warton turns the conversation to me. The woman seems slightly bemused—or amused, I'm not sure which—by the fact that I am a working woman who is making a daring trip around the world.

"My dear," Lady Warton says, "you must tell me so I can advise the ladies I play bridge with . . . Why would any young woman work in a man's profession and race around the world to beat a man's record?"

I smile politely. "It's a challenge and I believe I am as capable as any man." Personally I would have liked to ask her if she ever goes outside without asking her husband about the weather.

Lord Warton's face again contorts with displeasure as if my very existence sours his stomach. "We can all hope that women will stay in their place and not attempt to imitate men."

"Now, now, dear." His wife pats his arm again. "We must not pick on our guest. She's still young, but will someday learn what really matters in life."

I return a very forced polite smile and resist the urge to be catty. How dare they judge me and the other women who have to work for a living! What keeps me from lashing out besides politeness is that I know these pompous snobs have had so much given to them—and have accomplished little themselves.

Unlike Lady Bluenose, I have had to work for my daily bread and it has never struck me as God's will that I should labor as hard as a man for less money or opportunity.

My impression of these two is that their noses are blue because they are stuck up so high. Their mannerisms strike me as that of two aristocrats who are mildly amused by the customs of the unwashed masses.

The first time I saw Lady Warton as we passed each other on deck, rather than meeting my eye and my smile, she observed my garments and shoes. Since my entire luggage consists of a single valise that's capable of holding only the barest necessities for a journey that will take close to three months, I don't have the luxury to change outfits several times a day like her ladyship and her snooty female friends who waddle down the deck like geese in a pecking order. Each one of these women came aboard followed by a long line of porters shouldering trunks.

Coming to the top of a ridge, the desert unfolds before us as a purple-gray carpet in the dull light. The road is a stony dirt track hard enough to support the carriage wheels. Far beyond, like a desert mirage, is a vast expanse of water.

"Lake Manzala," Von Reich says, "the eastern delta of the Nile. Tanis and our rendezvous with the sheikh are on the other side at a tributary of the Nile."

"It looks as big as a sea," I say.

"It's quite large. The Suez Canal actually runs through the east edge of it."

A caravan of camels moves across the sands, their long, slender necks flowing in unison with their rocking gait. They give an exotic air to the desert and I cheer up a bit, reminding myself I am away from murderous mobs and the face in the porthole.

Von Reich purchases dates from a cameleer whose animals are laden with them. It's my first taste of the oval-shaped desert fruit and I find them sweet and mushy.

A shadow passes over the sands as a falcon gracefully glides above us, blue-gray feathers glistening in the sunlight. He slants his body to the left and dives. Just before he appears certain to crash into the ground, his claws come out and grab something from the sand. When he soars back up into the sky a rodent is struggling in his grip. I'm in awe that the raptor has spotted such a small thing in this vast ocean of sand, yet at the same time I feel pity for the little critter.

The two Bedouins riding as our escort to the rear had also watched the falcon and smiled when it captured its prey. With their head cloths around their faces, leaving only a narrow slit for vision, the men appear unfazed by the cloud of dust kicked up by the carriage.

In their desert robes, mounted on camels that appear clumsy yet seem to move with the grace of the wind itself, these desert warriors are romantic figures to a young woman.

"My brothers and I against my cousins . . . my brothers, cousins, and I against the world," Von Reich says.

His comment catches me by surprise. "Excuse me?"

"The Bedouins have a view of the world that is narrowly restricted to their own families, which is the meaning of the phrase. It's often spoken by them as the code they live by. It's said that a Bedouin owns only three things—his clothes, his animals, and his women."

"What do the women own?" pops out before I can control my tongue.

"A lifetime of misery."

Lady Warton gives our escorts a frown. "Bathing water is definitely not on their list of possessions. They smell worse than their camels."

We board a small steam launch that huffs and chugs across the lake. I would prefer a sailboat, but Von Reich says the steam launch is faster and we don't have the time to spare.

With my practical traveling cap attached securely on my head, I have a hard time not laughing as Lady Warton struggles to keep her dainty canary feather hat attached to her head with a veil as winds skipping across the water pummel us. I'm envious of the pith helmets the men wear, smartly secured with a chin strap. The lightweight hats made of a corklike material provide shade and holes for heat to escape.

In their pith helmets and white linen suits, the two men look very much like white colonials coming to do their duty as masters. Lady Warton also wears white, an unfortunate color for all of them since the damp wood seats leave a brown patch on an unmentionable area.

When the sun comes up, they glow like snowballs.

Our boat passes a long narrow craft loaded with bales of cotton; men aboard chant as they row with long oars, a rhythmic song of labor carried by the breeze to us.

It takes little to imagine Cleopatra and her court attendants instead of cotton bales and a slave master cracking a whip over the heads of the rowers.

"What are you smiling about?" Von Reich asks.

I just shrug my shoulders because I can't explain. The gentleman from the city of Mozart and Strauss, the Vienna waltz, and the glittering court of the Hapsburg emperors, would not understand how different this strange land is to a young woman who once thought she would spend her entire life underpaid and worked to the bone in an industrial town factory.

11

Ruins of the ancient city of Tanis are visible as our steam launch brings us to a dock in the late afternoon. I am more eager to see the antiquity site than to sit down to a meal with a sheikh. The thought of having come nearly six thousand miles and not getting a glimpse of the remnants of the golden civilization along the Nile would have been a thorn in my claw.

A servant is waiting to escort us to the sheikh's tent. "A short walk," he says.

My eyes light up as I step back in time to the ancient city.

"Tanis was built a thousand years before the birth of Christ," Von Reich says, "around the time God sent plagues to punish the pharaoh who wouldn't let the Jews return to their homeland and parted a sea for Moses."

Always the showman, Von Reich adds, "We are walking in the footsteps of mighty pharaohs who were worshipped as living gods. The great civilizations of Greece and China had yet to arise when the monuments that you're about to see were made—temples and tombs and statues that have excited and puzzled people for thousands of years."

He leans closer and speaks in a confidential tone so as not to be heard by the others. "Do you know what I like most about you, Nellie? How little things excite you so much and make you smile so brightly."

Little things?

"You've missed your calling, Von Reich," Lord Warton says. "You should have been a tour guide. Tell us about Tanis."

"Tanis was capital of Egypt several thousand years ago. The city had access to the sea and was an important port until it was finally abandoned because of the rising waters of the lake. Its most important complexes are the Temple of Amun, the king of gods, who is usually represented as a man with a ram's head, and that of Horus, a god of the sky and war.

"The city has been ravaged by time and by tomb robbers, and much of the area has gone back to desert, but be aware—the spirits of gods and kings still walk among the stone vestiges of its magnificent past."

Scattered about like the stone garden of a giant are granite statues and monuments, some colossal in size, many lying prone, all radiating the exotic and mysterious with their strange shapes and sacred writings.

I'm already writing in my head the story that I will send with my cable back to New York.

"Some very fine artifacts were found here by an English Egyptologist who spent several years working the site," Von Reich says. "There are probably many more, but excavation is time-consuming and expensive, so it comes in spurts."*

"He must cry," I say.

Lady Warton asks, "Who's crying?"

"Him." I gesture at a fallen statue of what appears to be a pharaoh. Standing upright it would be several times my height.

"He has had to lie there and just watch over the ages as thieves carry away the treasures of his city."

She gives me a look that expresses at the same time both a question of sanity and contempt for my thinking process. I suppose in her world of tea parties and formal balls, stone kings don't have feelings. But as I stand here, humbled in his presence, and look at his finely chiseled features—large eyes; a bold, almost Roman-like nose; a full mouth, all a bit worn by time—I still sense his power and majesty and can't help but believe he's watching.

The beauty and timeless workmanship of all these fallen edifices are testimonials to the greatness of the people who built them.

"It appears to me," Lady Warton says, "that this place needs masonry work and a good coat of paint."

I'm choking back a retort that I know I'll regret when I hear Von Reich shout, "Come here!"

* In 1935, a French archaeologist unsealed a Tanis tomb overlooked by looters and discovered treasures that rival those of King Tut. On a lighter note, Tanis is the city where the Ark of the Covenant was found in the first Indiana Jones movie. —The Editors

We gather around an obelisk, a tall, narrow, freestanding pillar that has a pyramidal shape at the top. Hieroglyphs cover the granite surface.

"Obelisks were placed in pairs at the entrances to temples with the picture writing we call hieroglyphics on them. Do you know how it happened that we were finally able to read ancient Egyptian glyphs?"

Without waiting for a reply, he launches into an explanation of the Rosetta stone, which I already know a bit about, having seen it at the British Museum in London. The dark, pinkish-gray stone slab that is about four feet tall, two feet wide, and a foot thick, had commands of a pharaoh inscribed on it in both ancient Greek and Egyptian hieroglyphs two thousand years ago.

Officers of Napoléon's army of occupation discovered it at the town of Rosetta, not far from Tanis, about ninety years ago and somehow it found its way to London. I recall a comment from a curator at the museum that the stone was found about the same time Napoléon's cannoneers were shooting the nose off of the Great Sphinx of Giza during cannon practice.

"By translating Greek," Von Reich continues, "the lingua franca of the ancient world and a language well known to us, and comparing it to the hieroglyphics, the secret behind the Egyptian symbols was revealed."

I slip away leaving the others huddled together as the "expert" on ancient Egyptian writing rambles on. I much prefer to walk among the ruins. Maybe I'll stumble onto some artifact other explorers have overlooked.

Behind the crumbled ruins of pillars, I find a stately granite sphinx. Close by is a statue of another pharaoh and more stone structures.

Something I've read comes to mind. "The longer man lives upon the Earth, the more the ground grows ancient beneath his feet . . ."

Standing on ground where history has been made, I picture men toiling in the scorching heat as whips rain down on their naked backs because they are not working fast enough. Perhaps thousands of people died to build the city and centuries later many of the monuments are still here—a testimony more to the common people who built them, than to the pharaohs.

The huge statue of the long-dead pharaoh intimidates me. The way his penetrating eyes bear down puts the fear of the unknown in me and I'm not one drawn to the occult. Without a doubt, they made him this size so people would tremble before him.

The most menacing feature is the king cobra placed on the front of the crown—its neck fanned into that distinctive cobra hood, indicating that it is ready to strike a deadly blow whenever it desires.

"What do you think about your tombs being looted and monuments broken and scattered like stone weeds?" I ask the pharaoh.

"I am eternal."

I nearly jump out of my shoes.

A man wearing a long black robe that cloaks him from the top of his head down to his sandals is standing in the shadow of the colossal monarch. A narrow gap in the hood exposes little of his features.

"That is how he would answer your question."

I glance back to make sure my companions examining the hieroglyphics on the obelisk are still within shouting distance.

"He is eternal, like the Nile." He steps forward and I can see he is elderly, with wrinkled features and wisdom's white beard. "He and the river will be here when those who sacked his tombs and cities are dust scattered by the wind."

"Do you work here?" I ask.

"I am a caretaker for all this." He waves at the ruins around us. "A city of vanished glories, containing only what the thieves of history have left behind."

He appears educated; not a fellah farmer or laborer.

"Are you an Egyptologist?" I ask.

He gives me an appraising look. "Nothing so grand. When the Englishman Flinders Petrie was working the site, I had the privilege of overseeing the workers. What little knowledge I have comes not from books, but from working with others, mostly foreigners." He studies me for a moment. "You are not British."

"I'm American."

"An American . . ." He seems taken back by my nationality and ruminates for a moment before he finally says, "Egypt sees many foreigners, British, French, Germans, Italians, but few Americans. You are the first I have met, though I've heard it prophesized that someday your young country will be a great power like the ones in Europe that have colonial empires wrapping around the globe."

"We don't need colonial empires. We have strong arms and natural resources aplenty in our own country. America's very large and we've barely scratched our riches."

Yankee boasting, rather inane, but the hinges of my usually oiled tongue are rusted in the presence of this old man who seems to bear the wisdom of the ages on his shoulders.

"Who is this gentleman?" I gesture at the giant statue of the pharaoh.

"Ramses the Great. Unearthed by my crew while working with the English archaeologist."

"Ah, Ramses. The pharaoh of the Exodus who caused Egypt to suffer ten plagues when he refused to let Moses and the Jews leave. His army was swept away in the Red Sea when he tried to pursue the Jews after the waters had parted for them."

I didn't add that about everything I knew about Egyptian pharaohs was either learned in Sunday school . . . or came from Von Reich. I nod at the sphinx. "What a magnificent creature."

The sphinx is six feet high and about twice that long; its body is taut, its claws extended, giving the impression of being ready to leap.

Von Reich had explained that sphinxes with the heads of people, rams, or even birds of prey were often lined up as sentries to protect temples. This one has the head of a pharaoh, perhaps Ramses himself. I've never seen a picture of one of these enigmatic creatures without experiencing a sense of awe, and now I'm actually standing before one.

I walk around the sphinx as I speak to the man. "I think I saw his brother in the Louvre museum in Paris."

"Yes, one of the sphinxes from Tanis is held prisoner in the French museum."

Held prisoner? An interesting way to put it, but I suppose if a foreign country removed the Liberty Bell from Philadelphia I would view the act in much the same manner.

"He must also cringe at how the city has crumbled," I say. "I've heard the winds that swept off the desert can be brutal."

"It's the sea breezes that have blown invading armies to Egypt's shores that have ravaged the remnants of our past. The great powers of Europe have plundered the treasures of Egypt since Roman times," his hoarse whisper tells me. "There are more obelisks and sphinxes and treasures of the pharaohs in London, Paris, and Rome than in Cairo or Alexandria. Some of them got there because of the greed of my own people. Even our kings filled their coffers with monies they obtained selling our treasures to foreigners."

He swept his hand at the great stone edifices around us. "Left alone, these ancient monuments of a lustrous age would have defied even the scorching desert winds that can flay the flesh off a camel, but the hands of Man are too ruthlessly covetous to leave the treasures untouched."

"That's unfortunate, yet from what I've seen, Egypt is a beautiful land with a proud history, but too poor to protect the remnants of its splendid past. What would have happened if foreigners hadn't taken the treasures to museums?"

"They would be home," he says.

I change the subject to something not politically explosive. "There's a fable about the sphinx that appears in schoolbooks back home. We call it the Riddle of the Sphinx because a female sphinx stopped passersby and asked them this question: 'Which creature goes on four legs in the morning, on two during the day, and in the evening upon three?' She strangled anyone who failed to answer the question correctly."

The caretaker smiles and nods. "I know the puzzle from Flinders Petrie. People crawl on all four as babies, later they walk on two legs, and finally in old age they need a cane and that gives them a third leg." He gives me a narrow look. "But you must not think that the power of the sphinx is a tale for children. To us who know her well, the Great Sphinx at Giza is the Father of Terror."

"Yes, I heard that shouted in Port Said. People believe that the sphinx will drive foreigners from Egypt."

"It is said that the Nile will turn red from blood again, as it once did when Allah punished the pharaoh. Only this time it will be the blood of foreigners that colors the river."

I turn away from the chilling prophecy as I hear my name shouted. My companions are coming up the hill and I wave at them.

"Over here," I yell, when I realize the statues and stone wall are blocking their view of us.

As they reach me I say, "This gentleman—"

He's gone. I hurry around the sphinx and the pharaoh.

"What in heavens name are you doing?" Lord Warton demands.

"He was here a moment ago."

"Who was here?" Von Reich asks.

I throw up my hands in frustration. "We were talking about the Great Sphinx killing foreigners—"

"The sphinx was talking to you?" Lady Warton asks.

"No, of course not. I was talking to a man about it. He's disappeared."

Lady Warton offers me her umbrella. "You better keep your head shaded, dear. The heat is making you delirious."

12

I've been in circus tents smaller than the sheikh's pavilion.

The sprawling tent is held up by a forest of poles, with the sides rolled up to let air circulate. Off to the right of the colossal pavilion is an oasis with trees and date palms surrounding a pond.

A sea of sand and then in the middle of nowhere a small lake surrounded by grass and trees . . . one of God's miracles, my mother would say.

"Is the sheikh the head of a Bedouin tribe?" I ask.

That gets a chuckle from Von Reich and a snort from Lord Warton.

"He's actually a prince and a pasha," Von Reich says, "because he's the brother of Tewfik Pasha, the Egyptian king they call a khedive. He has palaces in Cairo and Alexandria but he puts up a tent in the desert once a year to impress people with his Bedouin roots."

"There is no Bedouin blood in the line," Lord Warton says with contempt. "The ruling family dates back to a Turkish officer of Albanian descent who won a bloody power struggle after Napoléon's army left. They have as much Bedouin ancestry as my bird dog."

Drinking at the oasis are Arabian stallions, horses of the desert noted for their intelligence, speed, and grace, and the wonderfully awkward and charmingly ugly camels. The horses and camels appear to be the animal world's version of beauty and the beast.

"Arabian horses and camels are considered among the finest gifts of Allah," Von Reich tells us, "the horse for its beauty and the camel for its strong back."

Over our heads as we enter the pavilion are hanging baskets of flowering plants, hundreds of them, adding a sweet scent along with moisture that is a relief from the parched desert air. The entire interior is carpeted with thick Persian and Turkish rugs. Golden candelabras as tall as a person are everywhere.

"What in God's name is this?" Lady Warton asks, staring at knee-high tables scattered throughout the tent. The short, round tables are surrounded by saddles and cushions.

"When a Bedouin comes to dinner, he sits on a rug and brings in his camel's saddle to rest against," Lord Warton says. "We used them in Morocco, too, though not the dinners you attended."

"We're expected to sit on the floor and eat? How uncivilized," she grumbles.

I stare around, fascinated by the sheer opulence of it all. I can't even imagine what this "Bedouin" tent must have cost. Or how many of the peasants they call fellahs have broken their backs in the cotton fields that produce the country's cash crop to provide it.

Von Reich seems to read my mind. "Eastern potentates are probably no richer than European royalty; they merely display their treasures more spectacularly. But it's what people demand, isn't it? We want to see our royals wearing something more valuable than paper crowns because it's a sign of posterity for the whole nation."

The porcelain plates lining the tables are exquisite. In the center of each marble white plate is a dark blue image of a warrior pharaoh in a golden chariot drawn by one horse. His arm is raised high, ready to hurtle a spear at a charging tiger.

"Bone china," Lady Warton says. "It's made with ash from calcified ox bone. That's what gives it that brilliant, but brittle look."

"Where are the utensils?" I ask.

"You eat with your fingers and *only with your right hand*," Von Reich says. "The left is for *personal* use and considered unclean."

"Obviously, they don't have enough civilized facilities for relieving one's self," Lady Warton sniffs.

"Dinner is served with gold and silver utensils in his palace, but using one's fingers is for his desert-warrior image." Von Reich leans closer and says in a low voice, "When you sit, don't have your feet pointing directly toward someone else. The Egyptians consider it bad luck."

"Thank you. Anything else I should know?"

"Let the men do the talking." He grins and gives me a wink. "Women are considered decoration."

With that said, the two "gentlemen" leave us to mingle, abandoning me to her ladyship who scowls around with the sourpuss expression that appears painted permanently on her face.

"I need to quench my thirst," Lady Warton says as she heads for a bare-chested man dressed only in big bellowing, yellow pantaloons, and a red turban. He's holding a large silver platter filled with glasses of pomegranate juice.

Von Reich told us earlier that the foreign men attending the banquet will be mostly European businessmen and some military officers. I see a few other European women present, no doubt the wives of the men attending since a single woman would not have been invited, nor would any Islamic women.

The women remind me of those at the high-society tea parties I used to cover for the *Pittsburgh Gazette*—overdressed and overpowered. Like Lady Warton, they wear flowery silk or lace dresses that are fastened in the back with tiny buttons smaller than the tip of my pinkie, which require assistance from maids.

Making no claims to being a great beauty, I dress for comfort, preferring clothing that is simple, with little lace, frills, or those prickly petticoats intended to make dresses full, or as one dressmaker told me, "ladylike."

Von Reich and Lord Warton had changed from their traveling clothes.

A few of the European men are in black or dark gray morning dress, the daytime version of white tie with its cutaway coats, striped pants, and silk top hats, but most wear the same type of white linen suits that Von Reich and the peer wear.

Military officers are all dressed pretty much the same, from pith helmets to boots with highly starched uniforms in between.

While a few Egyptians and Turks present wear Western suits and fez hats, the only men who seem to appear comfortable in the warmth of the afternoon are the ones in traditional Arab desert clothing that permits air to circulate—flowing white tunics with sleeveless cloaks made of cotton, linen, or silk, all of light colors, blue, green, yellow, that extend just below their shins, while loose tasseled belts of braided gold silk adorn their waist. Even their rope sandals look cooler than most footwear.

A weapon is one accessory all the males agree upon—the British with their Webley revolvers, the French with their officer's version of the Chamelot-Delvigne. The Arabs have hanging from their belts scimitars or daggers decorated with pearls, diamonds, all sorts of precious gems, weapons that lack the range of a pistol, but no doubt as effective if one has been raised cutting his teeth on such blades.

I would not have been surprised to find women carrying derringers in their satchels, especially French women who tend to be worldlier than most other women because their country is at the crossroads of everything international.

It's rather amusing to watch the British and French men sipping the rich, Turkish coffee out of those dainty little demitasse cups . . . the Westerners look so out of place, their pinkies sticking straight up in the air. I'm sure they'd rather be drinking a brandy but the Egyptians are teetotalers—at least in public.

A low rumble erupts that slowly vibrates into a loud, deep boom as a large gong is struck and bronze trumpets blare as a group of men arrives on camels.

It's obvious that the man in front is our host—he's riding the only pure white camel. His Bedouin robes are silk, not cotton or wool, and are trimmed with precious stones—glittering rubies, sapphires, and diamonds. But the real clincher is that a servant goes down on all fours beside the sheikh's kneeling camel so the sheikh can step on him as he gets off the animal. I wince as he steps onto this human footstool . . . the sheikh is not a small man; he must be close to two hundred pounds.

He walks on a red carpet that has been rolled out from a table heavily guarded by Saracens with long swords—and pistols tucked in their waistbands.

"I'm afraid you ladies must fend for yourselves for a while," Von Reich says. "His lordship and I have been invited to join the sheikh at his table." There's a little pride and male superiority in his tone.

As they head for his table I do a double take at someone who takes a seat next to the sheikh—Frederick Selous, the Dark Continent explorer who claims to have talked to a dead man on the beach.

Before I get over that surprise, another man emerges from a dark area behind the sheikh and joins them at the table—the marketplace magician, the one Von Reich called a *Psylli*.

I start to tell Lady Warton that I shall run screaming from the tent if John Cleveland materializes, but she has slipped away to get another drink. When she returns, I ask if Von Reich and her husband are friends of the sheikh.

"Von Reich met him in Cairo. My husband has never met the man, but they have a common interest—horse racing. My husband breeds racehorses, and the sheikh requested he join him to discuss their animals."

"I love horses. I had one of my own. I've been in quite a few shows and won ribbons at county fairs in the States."

"How nice." She makes it sound as if I have won a consolation prize at a penny arcade.

Keeping a polite smile plastered on my face, I groan inwardly, telling myself that I have to stop trying to hold a civil conversation with this disdainful woman and simply make listening responses to whatever she says.

The sheikh sits down at his table and claps his hands. We are now allowed to sit.

The soulful wailing of a woodwind instrument fills the tent as barefooted, veiled women enter. They're dressed in lush purple silk garbs that cling to their bodies, emphasizing their graceful contour. Yellow scarfs, fringed with coins, are tied around their hips.

Every feature of these women is exquisite—long, silky black hair, golden skin, ample breasts, and well-endowed hips—and all are perfectly proportioned. Swaying to the hypnotic music, they extend their arms outward, beckoning us to join them. The top part of their garb slips ever so slightly off their shoulders as their hips sway in a circular, hypnotic motion to the rhythm of the music.

Tiny cymbals held between their fingers make quick snapping clangs, as incredible feats of flexibility are performed with their belly muscles. Gradually they bend backward until their tresses sweep the carpet. Shouts from the men grow deafening as they perform this inverted feature. Like the men, I find myself captivated with the women's hips as they sway with such sexual precision, back and forth, till they are still. Then the yelling stops and I start breathing again.

What a gravity-defying, erotic movement to watch.

"Raqs Sharqi," Lady Warton whispers, "the dance of the Orient, claims to be the oldest dance in the world."

"Amazing," is all I can say.

The gong shatters the silence and brings us out of our trances as the women leave as exotically as they came.

Male servants enter carrying silver platters laden with vegetables grown on the Nile Delta—carrots, onions, tomatoes, radishes, and turnips—wooded bowls filled with couscous, and crystal bowls overflowing with shredded coconut, honey, dates, figs, olives, grapes, and pomegranates.

It's all so lavish, but also wasteful because it's impossible for us to eat all this food. I'm sure that in Port Said there are families that would survive a month on just a few platters of the food served here.

Two men carry in a platter that holds a lamb and place it in front of the sheikh who plucks the eyes out of the lamb and pops them in his mouth.

I force myself to keep a poker face. He *really* looks like he's enjoying them. But as my grandmother always said, "To each his own, said the old lady when she kissed the cow." I'm just glad I'm not eating the eyes.

He proceeds to cut off a leg and then takes a stuffing of dates and figs from inside the belly with his right hand. When he's done the lamb is passed to another table where a man cuts out the tongue.

I'm quickly losing my appetite, but my real focus is not on food as I keep a surreptitious eye on the men at our host's table.

No coincidence, is my reaction. I can't tell what they are talking about, but I wouldn't be surprised if it is about me, the key, and John Cleveland. And maybe the snake man is telling them he could put a cobra in my bed.

"Have you eaten something that disagrees with you?" Lady Warton asks. "You have the oddest look on your face."

"No, I'm fine. I was just thinking about what a small world it is."

She raises her eyebrows. "In what way?"

"Oh, all these people from so many places. Look—even the snake magician from the marketplace is here." Unable to resist the temptation, I add, "I wouldn't be surprised if Mr. Cleveland paid us a visit."

She gives me a crocodile smile. "Let's hope he does so you will be able to dismiss those silly notions about him being dead."

Touché! Wonderland's queen has chopped off my head again.

Dishes are cleared away and once again the gong booms. Dozens of men wearing the traditional long loose garments of cotton or rough wool, with full sleeves and hood, appear outside the tent.

The men lie down on the sand, arranging themselves in a row like sardines, side to side, each one pressed so close to the next there is not the slightest space between their bodies, as if they're forming a floor. A man casually walks down the line of bodies.

Lord Warton and Von Reich join us after the sheikh leaves his table where Mr. Selous and the magician remain huddled together in what appears to be a deep conversation.

"Why is that man walking over them?" I ask Von Reich.

"To make sure that this human plank will hold."

"Hold what?"

"They're preparing for a ceremony called *Doseh*, which means treading.

"Treading?" I ask.

"Yes, but it's best not to tell you what's going to happen. After it's over, if you like, I'll explain why it's done."

Trumpets blare and the sheikh appears astride a white Arabian stallion led by two grooms. Its thick mane flows down his side, his tail high in the air.

The sheikh makes a clicking noise with his tongue and the grooms let go of the stallion.

The horse advances with long, exaggerated steps, stepping up onto the human plank.

The big Arabian stallion with the sheikh aboard must weigh close to fourteen hundred pounds.

And it's walking on the men!

13

"The treading," Von Reich tells us, enjoying his role as scholar, "is a ritual done in memory of a miracle performed by a Muslim saint. The saint rode his horse into Cairo over earthenware jars without breaking them. It's believed that the sheikh who reenacts this ceremony cannot hurt the prostrate men, just as the saint didn't break the jars. If any of the men die, it's due to their sins."

Another couple had joined us to hear the man from Vienna's explanation.

"That's horrible." I see it as an act of arrogant oppression by the mighty against the helpless. I had gaped at the brutal spectacle, unable to move an inch, as the horse's powerful hooves had come down like sledgehammers, on one man and then the next. "Why doesn't the sheikh just use jars as the saint did?"

"And take the chance of cutting the hoofs of his prize stallion? His horses are much more valuable," Lord Warton says.

Everyone—except me—gets a good chuckle over the sheikh prizing his horses over his subjects, egging the peer on. "The noblest of men and desert nomads love, admire, and cherish their horses—"

"Sometimes more than their wives," Lady Warton interjects.

"I'm speaking of Arab men, my dear." Lord Warton grins at the other men. "Wouldn't you agree that if one has several wives, as many of these Arabs do," he pronounces it A-rabs, "sometimes they'll find sweeter dispositions in the stables than in the main house?"

The men enjoy another chuckle.

"There's a line from Sir Walter Scott's *The Talisman*," Lord Warton says, "which describes the impression of the Crusader knights of King

Richard the Lion-Hearted when they first encounter the magnificent Arabian horses in the Holy Land: 'They spurned the sand from behind them; they seemed to devour the desert before them; miles flew away with minutes—and yet their strength seemed unabated . . .'"

"The prophet Muhammad said every man shall love his horse," Von Reich adds. "Bedouins will go without food before they would let their horses starve."

"But what about the men who have to endure the sheikh's horse?" I ask in vain, knowing these people have no compassion for the underdog.

"The peasants consider it a privilege to be treaded upon," Lord Warton says.

"Really? I wonder how any of us would feel if we had to lay on the ground back home and let royalty walk their horses across our backs."

Von Reich gives me a small grin, but I get stony silence from the others. When they start comparing Arabian horses to quarter horses, I wander off, heading for the back of the tent in the direction I had seen Mr. Selous and the magician exit.

Strange bedfellows, the magician who was performing where a man was killed and the Brit who talked to the dead man. The two are huddled together, walking slowly, talking too low for me to hear. Very discourteous of them, not speaking loud enough for me to eavesdrop.

The two disappear into the ruins and rather than running to find them and making a perfect fool of myself by getting caught, I veer off to see the ruins by light of flaming torches that have been set up to permit guests to enjoy the antiquities.

It's a bit eerie seeing the ancient monuments under the ghostly glow of the full moon and the flickering torchlight, but a few other people are wandering about, too.

I come around a pillar and find myself abruptly face to the face with the magician. He is not blocking my way, but not moving, either; just standing still, staring at me with the blackest eyes I've ever seen. I give a quick look about, but his British companion is not in sight.

Forcing a smile and a "Good evening," I start to go around him when I spot a scarab hanging from a gold chain around his neck. Not a brother to the one slipped into my pocket, the magician's amulet is a blood ruby, almost heart shaped and encrusted with precious stones.

Worth a fortune, I think, as I raise my eyes to meet his. Not at all what one would expect a marketplace magician to be wearing. Neither were his clothes, which were not the simple cotton he'd worn yesterday, but were black silk trimmed with pearls.

"Do you know the magic of the Heart Scarab?" he asks in heavily accented English.

"No, but I would certainly like to hear it."

"A bearer of the Heart Scarab is assured of rebirth after death."

"I see . . . and how does it do that?"

"When people die, the gods weigh their hearts. Hearts that are full of sin are heavy and are eaten by the destroyer of hearts. But if the dead person's heart is replaced with a scarab before it is weighed, the sins are not discovered and the person is reborn."

"Is that how Mr. Cleveland managed to get from the marketplace to the beach where he spoke to Mr. Selous? And stare at me through a porthole? His heart was replaced with a scarab?"

He gives me a glare that would cow a two-ton Tanis sphinx.

"You are on sacred ground where gods still walk. Their wrath falls upon those who mock them."

His staff comes out from where it's concealed beneath his robe and I flinch back but the rod taps the ground with a solid sound as he sweeps by me, leaving me cold at the bone despite the hot night.

I shake off the willies and keep an eye out behind me for snakes as I head deeper into the site. What a creepy character. Put him on the front porch and I wouldn't have to worry about trick-or-treaters on Halloween.

That he wasn't surprised when I mentioned a dead man talking to Frederick Selous didn't astonish me; he probably got an earful of that subject at the sheikh's dinner table. But he could have at least raised a curious eyebrow about a porthole Peeping Tom.

More regrets about having come on the excursion start stacking up in my head and I shake those out, too, determined not to let an Egyptian bogeyman keep me from my chance to soak in some more of the land of pharaohs. I'm happy to visit the ruins without Von Reich's pedantic chatter and Lady Warton's caustic view of everything, including me.

Night is falling, the sky taking an ashen glow as an early full moon rises behind a thin blanket of dark clouds. Torches have been placed in a number of places to light significant monuments for guests who wander out for a look, but I see only a man and woman, and I take a path different from theirs to have some solitude.

Tanis is a ghost city, its greatest monuments shattered, the dusty souls of its ancient dead scattered by the desert wind, but the faint moonlight takes just enough edge off of the darkness for a little imagination to bring its past glories alive. It's not hard for me to imagine a pharaoh on a golden chariot, his soldiers using their spears to push back crowds staring with awe at the living god.

My feet take me far enough from the tent for the music and party sounds to fade, taking me past the Great Temple of Amun and beyond to where a short fence has been put up at an excavation site near the Temple of Horus.

A large cavity has been opened and fenced with stalks of river reeds, but the desert sand that coats everything makes it appear that the whole project had been abandoned years ago. The opening reveals a crudely excavated stone stairway, steep and broken with missing steps patched by wood supports. The broken stairwell disappears into a pool of darkness that the moonlight doesn't penetrate.

The crudeness of the opening makes me wonder if it wasn't done by thieves rather than professional archaeologists, and what priceless treasures the tomb held before tomb raiders vandalized it.

A smaller fence is about thirty paces away next to the end of a tall wall where a torch is mounted. I mosey over to see what it's guarding and find another cavity, a hole about six feet wide. As with the fence at the stairwell, the reed fence is flimsy, not meant to hold a person back but just to mark the opening.

I edge closer, bracing myself with my left hand against the granite wall, careful not to put any weight against the fencing which appears ready to blow away with a strong wind. The flickering light from the burning torch at the end of the wall is at my back and casts little light into the hole but there's enough moonlight for me to see a mound of rubble ten or twelve feet down. From the debris and irregular shape of the hole, I assume that I'm standing on the roof of a tomb or whatever the chamber below is, and that the opening was created by accident, perhaps from a cave-in when the area was excavated by workers inside the cavern who had entered through the stairway I'd seen.

The rest of the room is lost in a dark void but it doesn't take much for my mind's eye to envision markings on the walls, perhaps the tale of a war won by a pharaoh, a royal marriage, or the god-king getting sage advice from a god.

I'm leaning over the opening, trying to see more, when a shadow is created in the light of the torch behind me and I hear the crunch of a footstep.

"Is someone—?"

A black blur comes at me and impacts with the side of my head, the blow slamming me against the wall. My legs collapse and I go down to my knees, head spinning, putting my hands out in front to keep from going down on my face. Something drops next to me—a rock—and I see a swirl of a cloth being manipulated. My senses are half knocked out of me but I realize I'd been hit by a rock wrapped in cloth material. The cloth goes over my head and around my throat, a knee goes into the small of my back, and the cloth is jerked back to strangle me. I pull on it and try to twist out of it, my head spinning from the blow, with blind panic giving me some strength. Suddenly the pressure releases against my throat and I take in one gasp of air before something slams against my head again and I see stars.

I feel hands all over my body, exploring, searching, pressing, and grabbing, the strength of them telling me they are a man's hands. Fingers squeeze my breast and I get a flash of my drunken lout of a stepfather who touched me offensively, and I raise up, pushing back against the man pawing me, banging my head back against his chin.

The grip on me is relaxed again and hands go behind my shoulders and give me a shove, forcing me forward against the reed fence, and I scream as the fence parts like feathers against my weight and my whole body pours through as I plunge into the abyss.

I hit bottom, the wind exploding out of my lungs as a burst of light in my head leaves my mind dark.

14

I lie sprawled out, not moving and with a strange sense in my head that I'm still falling down a bottomless pit. As I reach out to break my fall I realize that my hands are already on solid ground, as is my whole body. I've landed on a layer of sand covering the rubble pile created by the cave-in. The fine grains of sand feel soft and cool when I grasp it through my fingers and push back with my feet in a weak attempt to move. I feel more sand with hard objects beneath.

Struggling to get up, I raise dust and such, clogging my windpipe, polluting my lungs, and I start choking, unable to keep the cloud of particles that's floating in the air from getting in my nose and mouth and eyes. I clamp my teeth together to try and filter the air between them, making it a little easier to breathe in the stifling atmosphere.

Looking up at the opening above lit by moonlight, I sway dizzily, and I have to balance myself to stay upright in order to keep from falling. The opening is much too far away to reach, even standing on the debris.

A torch that must have fallen with me is lying on the ground. It puts out little light, leaving the area around me lost mostly in dark shadows. I have to keep it going.

Taking a step I feel something move under my foot and I look down and freeze in place.

I've stepped on a snake.

It slips out from under my foot and I frantically put my foot back down on it, pressing down just behind its neck.

It thrashes, whipping its body back to hit the side of my leg. I feel it slipping out from under my foot again and I follow it with my foot, pressing harder, trying to keep the toe of my shoe close to its head so it can't bite me.

I don't know what to do. I can't move, can't reach the torch, can't even bend down to grab a rock. Fright chills my blood. I feel faint and sense a loss of feeling in the foot holding down the snake.

"She just wandered away from the table," Lady Warton tells Lord Warton, Von Reich, and Fouad, the sheikh's majordomo.

Frederick Selous joins the group in time to hear the statement. "What direction did Miss Bly go?" he asks.

Lady Warton waves vaguely toward the back of the pavilion. "I don't know, I wasn't paying attention."

"Has anyone checked to see if she's returned to the launch?" Selous asks.

All the guests but the group from the *Victoria* had left the pavilion, most of them returning to their steam launches.

"Yes," the majordomo says, "I sent a servant to check. She has not been there. No one remembers seeing her anywhere on the grounds. I'm told she spoke earlier to the site's caretaker. I have sent a man to his house to discover whether she told him anything that would provide a clue as to her whereabouts."

Lord Warton snorts. "Frankly, it wouldn't hurt my feelings if the young woman was left behind when the ship sailed."

"She's on a race—" Von Reich starts.

"The race be damned. She's been nothing but a nuisance, starting rumors about what happened in the marketplace."

Frederick Selous gives Lord Warton a restrained smile. "I think our first concern should be her safety."

"Of course," Lady Warton says, "that goes without saying, though I share your sentiments about her," she tells her husband. "It's just like the foolish young woman to wander off when our boat is ready to take us back to Port Said."

"What efforts are being made to find Miss Bly?" Selous asks the majordomo.

"I've sent servants to scour the area. The problem besides the darkness is that there are so many perils. Thieves have dug many holes in search of treasure, sometimes reaching burial chambers."

"Are the openings marked?" Selous asks.

"Only a few are fenced because one cannot keep up with the work of those who lust for the treasures of the pharaohs. There have been hundreds of pits dug over time. Thieves will often cover the opening to their holes so they're not obvious."

"The thieves work at night?" Von Reich asks.

"Yes."

"So Miss Bly could have run into these tomb raiders?"

"Anything is possible," the majordomo says. "She could have simply wandered away from camp and lost her way back. And there are more dangers in the night than ones who walk on two feet. There are packs of lions and jackals—"

"Human jackals, too, I imagine," Selous says. "How much Mahdi activity is there in the area?"

"The fanatics are found everywhere in Egypt where there is sand," the majordomo says.

Selous nods at a large group of guards who don't appear to have any tasks except to stand around and talk and smoke.

"You say servants have been sent out to look for the young woman. Can you have guards join the search?"

The majordomo smiles with false sympathy. "I regret that His Highness has more servants to spare than guards."

It's gone.

Dear God, the snake has slipped out from under my foot.

I don't move an inch, but I'm shaking so badly I'm sure the snake will interpret it as movement.

Looking in front, in back, all around, I don't see it. It's slipped away into the darkness. It could be coiled and ready to strike the moment I move, but I can't stand in place. The torch is fading, the shadows thicker. I have to get to the torch and use it to find a door or I'll be entombed with the snake and whatever else is lurking about.

I'm sure I saw something move at the sarcophagus a moment ago. I don't want to even think about what could be in the stone coffin or anywhere else in this chamber with morbid images from the *Egyptian Book of the Dead* on its walls and pillars.

Letting out a sob, I go for the torch, sure that I'll feel the snake's fangs biting into me before I reach it. I grab it off the ground and wave it to keep the flame going. It's just a bunch of sticks tied together and dipped in pitch. The light it casts is hardly more than a kitchen match, but it's all I have.

Raising it up, I can make out the opening above that I'd fallen through. Much too high for me to reach.

Most of the chamber is lost to me in shadows and darkness, with a slight edge taken off a pitch-black area in the direction of the stairwell I'd seen from the outside.

It makes sense that the chamber I'm standing in is accessed by the stairway and that what I see across from me is a small doorway. I don't rush for it because I can't see well enough to know if there's a big pit between me and the door—not to mention that whoever pushed me in might just be waiting there to finish me off. And finish his search, too. The man wasn't feeling my body out of lust—he was searching for the key, I'm sure of it.

I don't see or hear anything that tells me anyone is up there at the opening. I have no idea where my companions are or the caretaker, for that matter, and don't know if one of them might even have given me the shove, but I had to try and let someone know I'm in harm's way.

"Help! Help!" I yell up. *"I'm down here! I need help!"*

No one is coming, I know that, but I yell out of desperation anyway. The thought that I may never make it out scares me, but I can't let it control me. *Take a step,* I tell myself, *one step at a time, just keep moving, never give up, never stop fighting back.*

There must be a way out the door that I think leads to the stairway. I don't know what or who is on the other side of it, but if it's someone who is coming down to finish the job, I am already trapped, so I must drive myself forward and meet my enemy head on rather than have him jump on my back.

Moving toward the door takes me out of the light that comes from the opening above and I step slowly, cautiously, praying the snake has returned to its hole.

My foot hits something that feels like wood. Squatting down to get a closer look I make out the shape of a ladder covered by sand, at least it seems to be a ladder of branches tied together by twine. Not at all what an archaeologist would use, the rickety-looking thing doesn't feel very sturdy and most likely was made by locals who come down and hunt for artifacts.

I don't dare use it to go up the opening because whoever shoved me in might still be up there, so I keep moving in the darkness toward what I believe is a door and stairway. Until I hear the tumble of rocks breaking loose.

Is someone coming down the stairway to finish the job?

Backing away, I nearly fall when my foot hits the ladder again. Grabbing one end, I pull it up, completely out of the sand. It's surprisingly heavy and awkward but my adrenaline is pumping. I start raising it, trying to keep my footing as I push up, one rung at a time, getting it higher and higher until I lift it into position in the opening above. It reaches through the hole just far enough to keep the frame upright.

Starting up the crude steps, rocks and dirt rain down on me as the ladder breaks loose some of the debris at the top. The ladder is so rickety, I can't imagine it held the weight of a man; it seems more for children. A rung breaks as I take a step and I grab on, taking some of the weight off under my feet by holding tightly onto the two vertical posts.

Another step and it feels like the whole thing is just going to disintegrate and collapse in a heap. *Slowly,* I place my feet toward each side, hoping that there will be more support because that's where the rungs are tied to the vertical posts.

Another two steps and I reach up for the lip of the opening and feel the ladder shifting under me. I freeze in place, tightly holding on to both vertical posts to keep them stable, but the ladder starts to twist, one post moving away; I can't keep it straight and I hear the twine holding the rung under my foot snap as I reach with my hand for the rung above. I barely get a handhold when the steps under my foot let loose and I start to twist and fall and let go, hitting the floor on my feet and pitching forward.

Sheer panic gets me back on my feet as the sound of someone coming down the passageway becomes obvious.

I look around for a weapon. But what can I use? A piece of the ladder? The dry rotted wood would hardly batter a fly. Bending down to grab a rock I see what looks like a black whip. The whip moves and I nearly jump out of my skin.

A snake.

It starts to move away from me as a door opens and light flows into the room as a man enters. I only see a black figure.

Screaming, I grab the tail end of the snake and throw it at the man coming toward me. It hits him on the chest and falls to the ground. He quickly picks up the snake and steps toward me, coming into the light that's shining from above.

Gripping the writhing snake behind the head, he holds it up to me. "Good snake. Eats rats."

The caretaker smiles at me.

"I heard your cries for help."

15

Why me? Why am I so lucky to nearly get killed and end up subjected to the tender mercies of a dreadful woman who probably gives out pieces of coal to mudlarks at Christmastime?

Out of the chamber and reunited with my companions, Lady Warton helped brush me off, but it came with such unspoken disapproval that her attitude shouted at me.

No one else said a word, but the verdict expressed on each of their faces was the same: I clumsily "fell in." I had leaned too close and the fence gave way, I fell, hit my head, and imagined being assailed by a strange man. The other scenario, offered by Von Reich to assuage my anger, was that I had run into a tomb robber who wanted my purse and jewelry. I was too embarrassed to mention that his hands violated my body, searching for the key.

I pretended to accept Von Reich's assessment only because I couldn't counter with my belief that I had been attacked for the key—not without revealing I have it. I came close to revealing the motive when I told him that the man wasn't a local but one of the guests who followed me after I left the tent.

"Why would a guest do that?"

"Because they . . . they—I don't know," I stammered, tripping over my tongue as I swerved verbally to avoid mentioning the key.

"Who would do such a thing?"

"Anyone!" I snapped and walked off in a huff to kill the conversation.

"Who" could have been anyone in the pavilion, from the sheikh to his guests, who knew I had gotten the scarab in the marketplace. That included my companions, Frederick Selous, the snake-loving magician, and, I had to admit, just about anyone else in the tent who had a secret interest in the marketplace intrigue.

I know I was attacked and nearly killed for the key but even I find holes in my story because I can't reveal possession of the key to fill the gaps. There is nothing I can say, nothing I can do, to repair my reputation. All but the man who attacked me are convinced that I have a weak female constitution that drives me to hysterics.

I'm so angry I need to blow off steam, I need a good scream, but that would really seal their opinion of me. If they knew that in New York I once actually convinced a host of doctors that I was hopelessly insane . . .

We're approaching the dock to board the steam launch for the trip back across the delta when an eerie sound floats in the night air to us . . . not one from an animal, but a deep, steady rhythmical chant that pierces my soul like sharp daggers.

"What's that horrible noise?" Lady Warton asks Von Reich.

"Ababdehs," Von Reich says. "Nomads who wander through the desert, always on the move. They have been around forever, long enough to have witnessed the rise and decline of ancient Egypt. It's said the proof of their existence over the millennia is written on the sands. Every night the men sing and dance by their fires, chanting praises to Allah. If memory serves me correct, they dance in a great circle, moving incessantly from left to right, to the faithful moon of Shawwal. They believe the chant presages success for the sword of the Prophet."

"What about the sword of the Prophet?" Lord Warton asks.

"They're chanting about how much blood of infidels will be on it."

"Look . . . there they are." Lady Warton points off to our right.

In the distance a group of people are chanting and swaying under the light of the full moon. Dressed in flowing garments of white, they appear ghostly as they lift their arms at the moon.

"Are they pointing something at the moon?" she asks Van Reich.

"Yes, curved palm stalks, just part of their ritual."

It makes no difference that their eerie howls and ghost dancing send cold chills down my back and up my legs. It doesn't matter if they are putting a curse on me. I don't care if the sphinx gets up from where it's crouching and runs down the Nile, turning the waters red with the blood of foreigners.

All that matters to me at the moment is that someone had tried to kill me, another stain of blood on my great adventure around the world.

A morbid sense of dread follows me back to the ship because I know I have not left danger back at Tanis.

16

I am a messenger of the Father of Terror.

Ahmad Kamil bows his head to Allah one more time before slipping into the still dark water of Port Said Bay.

His time has come. Tonight he becomes a warrior for Allah.

I am a messenger of the Father of Terror. He repeats the phrase as a mantra while he slowly swims, cloaked by the dark of night and careful not to draw attention by splashing. His instructions are to board the steamship *Victoria* unnoticed and before the ship leaves the port.

His objective is the bow of the ship, which he has been told is the best place to avoid detection because the area is crowded with anchor hoisting and other machinery and equipment. He has been warned to stay away from all other areas even late at night since many passengers sleep on deck instead of in their cabins because of the oppressive heat.

I am a messenger of the Father of Terror, Ahmad sings silently to himself.

While rumors race like wild fire that the sphinx itself will rise against the foreigners who occupy the land, it is not the powers of ancient Egypt that Ahmad has sworn homage to, but one that has flowed down the Nile River valley from the Sudan and ignited the minds and hearts of the people: *Jihad,* the Struggle, a holy war to rid the land of infidels and Egyptians who have sworn false promise to Allah.

The war against the Europeans and unfaithful Egyptians had been proclaimed by the Mahdi, the "Guided One," whose appearance on Earth has ushered in the End Days and the Yaum al-Qiyamah, "Day of the Resurrection," when the world will be rid of error, injustice, and tyranny.

Ahmad joined the battle by the faithful that will make the land pure for the return of the Mahdi because those who toil in the Struggle are to be among the Chosen.

To join the Struggle one must be a warrior for Allah, a *mujahid*, with a willingness to be a martyr for the cause.

A poor fisherman, death to Ahmad would be freedom from a harsh life of relentless desperation just getting enough food each day to stay alive. He has no wife or children because he cannot feed them, but his parents and the people of his village will honor his name when they are told of his deed.

Giving his life will be an opportunity to honor the will of Allah and receive the rewards given martyrs.

Ahmad knows he will not return from the task assigned to him. He will take a life and give his in sacrifice and receive his reward on the Day of the Resurrection—paradise for an eternity.

When he was told a woman must die, he was at first shaken, even frightened. Like all the men of his village, he was raised to protect women. But if her death is the will of Allah, so be it.

Reaching the thick, bow anchor chain, Ahmad mounts it, using hands and feet to pull himself up until he is able to belly over the bow railing.

On deck he crouches down, looking around to make sure he's alone before he loosens the rope strapping down the canvas cover to a lifeboat and quickly slips underneath.

Peeking out from beneath the cover, he remembers as a boy standing on the river bank and watching crocodiles hiding in the murky waters, just their eyes and snouts above the water as they waited patiently for a victim.

Now, he will be that patient crocodile.

"The woman will come to you," his leader told him.

Nestled inside the lifeboat, his mind swirls with what he had been told after he was named the chosen one:

My mission for Allah is to deliver a message in blood.

I will be blessed and enjoy the fruits of paradise for an eternity.

I am a messenger of the Father of Terror.

Allah Akbar!

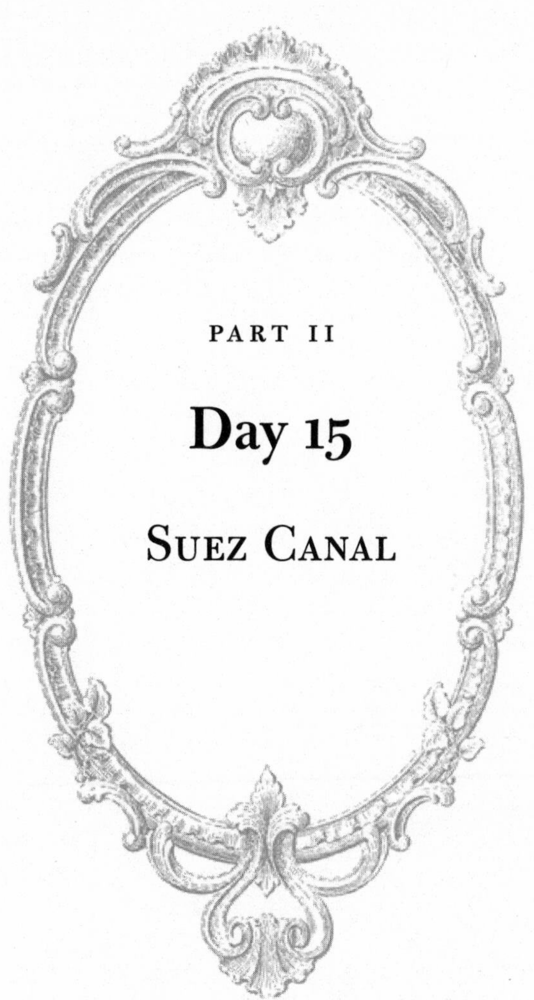

PART II

Day 15

Suez Canal

17

Getting a look at the Suez Canal dragged me early onto the deck when I would have preferred to stay in bed and bury myself under the blankets. Having no desire to be stared at or hear gossip about a young woman who imagines dark plots and cries "Murder!" I am at the rail when most of the ship is still asleep.

The famed canal is an enormous ditch with high sand banks that the ship moves through so slowly, no breeze is created over the deck. Even this early, the thick heat presses down, making it feel as if I'm standing on a hot plate.

The oppressive air puts me in a brown study. A normal reaction to seeing one of the greatest man-made monuments in the world would have put me into a high state of excitement, but my body is still sore and my anger still raw at being nearly killed.

"It's really quite amazing, isn't it?" The question gives me a start.

Frederick Selous edges next to me at the rail. This time he has obviously approached me when he could have avoided it.

Having such a gentlemanly air about him, I tell myself not to badger him further about what occurred between him and the ghost of Mr. Cleveland. It would be beating a dead horse.

"Yes, it is, though it's really just a big ditch."

"Quite, but it's one hundred and twenty miles long and connects two great bodies of water. There were doomsayers who predicted that it would cause the Mediterranean to pour into the Red Sea with such force the entire planet would be thrown off kilter."

He is fresh shaven and has had a haircut.

"Bath, too," he says, amused by my examination of his toiletry. "I roused the ship's barber early out of fear passengers who saw me would think I was a pirate who'd boarded the ship." He leans beside me on the railing. "I was away from civilization for a week taking a look at Mount Sinai. 'Fraid what little water we had couldn't be wasted on washing."

"Did you find the Ten Commandments?"

"Actually, my friends were convinced Noah's Ark was there, but we didn't find it, either. See that caravan." He points to my left at a camel caravan paralleling the canal. "They call camels ships of the desert, but that is no doubt what the caravanners are saying right now about this ship."

"Why would they call our ship that?"

"Because the ship is lower than the sand banks of the canal, and from a distance you can't see the water, making it appear that the ship is actually moving on sand. Truly a ship of the desert."

"That must be a marvelous sight. Have you seen it?"

"Yes." His eyes drift out to the desert and I feel like he's looking past me to places no one else sees.

He is a striking figure of a man: tall, broad chested, with well-carved features that are both aristocratic and sensuous. I find few men able to convey both personal warmth and a strong masculinity, and Frederick Selous manages both.

While he impresses me as strong and assertive, I also detect a reserved side to his nature, perhaps even intellectual, not at all like most newspapermen I've met, and certainly a far cry from the boys in the newsroom back home who like to roll up their sleeves, put up their dukes, and wade into a story—when they aren't spitting tobacco juice into a spittoon.

All those admirable qualities about him dim in comparison to the fact that I can't trust him. His discussion on the beach with a dead man can be excused because anyone who had not met John Cleveland would have taken the man's identity at his word. But Selous's presence at the sheikh's table, his suspiciously intense conversation with the marketplace magician, and his coziness with Lord Warton means I not only can't rely on him to be an ally, I sense he is deeper into the quagmire than he puts on.

Not one to live in silence for long, I fill it with words. "It must be the greatest man-made construction project in history."

"I suppose that's true, since we really can't count the Great Wall of China because it was built in segments over the centuries."

"You've seen the canal before?"

"Many times."

"On news assignments?"

He smiles. "I'm not actually a reporter, at least not a professional one and certainly not the caliber of one who is racing around the world on a story. I decided to take a sea journey and a Cape Town newspaper kindly asked me to send back observations of my trip. I'm a big-game hunter."

"Is that a profession? Or a sport?"

"In my case, a profession."

I had never met a big-game hunter, though I have read stories of men who explore trackless jungles on the Dark Continent in search of wild beasts and adventure.*

"You should read *King Solomon's Mines.* You'd probably enjoy it. It's about a safari hunter, like you."

Mr. Selous gives me a quirky smile, as if I said a joke and don't know it.

"Yes . . . I should. Egypt's quite a fascinating country, don't you agree?" he asks. "So much colorful history and astonishing monuments."

"I've seen little of it, but what I have seen has made a lasting impression upon me." That is an understatement.

He looks away and then back to me with sympathetic eyes. "What happened in the marketplace was a terrible thing for any woman to witness."

"For *anybody* to witness."

"Quite so. Having the poor devil speak his dying words to you must have given you an even more significant connection to the tragedy."

I nod. "Ah . . ."

"There is that *ah* again. What revelation have you received from the gods this time?"

"Lord Warton told you the man spoke to me. Or was it the magician who told you about Mr. Cleveland whispering to me?"

He appears at a loss for words for a moment. "You certainly don't beat around the bush, do you? It was his lordship who told me you had held the man in his last moments. As for the magician, I told him about the snakes that have tried to put me in an early grave more than once."

* Frederick Selous was more famous to Victorians than Nellie. The most notable African explorer and big-game hunter in an era in which such men were admired as the epitome of manhood, Selous was the inspiration for H. Rider Haggard's hero in *King Solomon's Mines*, which inspired more than a century of books and movies about adventures and the search for ancient treasures, including the Indiana Jones movies. —The Editors

"Did Lord Warton attribute my belief that the murdered man was British to female hysterics?"

"Lord Warton was concerned for your female constitution under such trying circumstances, as any gentleman would be."

"Mr. Selous, for your information, I have traveled without male protection across the American Wild West and untamed Mexico. Besides fighting my way up in a field dominated by men, I have gone into slums, prisons, and madhouses to cover stories, and have interviewed murderers, prostitutes, and thieves. Let me assure you that my female constitution is just fine. It is my sense of justice that is being trampled."

He raises his arms. "I surrender!"

"I don't take prisoners."

"Yes, I can see that. I've faced charging rhinos that are less aggressive than you."

I suppress my ire and turn back to the canal, in need of changing the subject before I make a fool out of myself or worse—put him so on guard he never slips up and exposes his true part in the intrigue.

"I left New York so suddenly, I didn't get a chance to research places I'd see. Is it true that the lives of one hundred thousand laborers were sacrificed in the building of the canal? A ship's officer told me that."

"I'm sure the authorities were not counting the bodies, but I have heard that estimate and from stories about how the canal was dug. I have no reason to doubt the figure."

I pat my face with my handkerchief. "This heat is quite oppressive. We could use a good sea breeze."

"Yes, but we won't see one until the ship can gather speed. Ships have to travel slowly, no more than five knots, or they create wakes that erode the sand walls." He hesitates, as if he's making a careful choice of words. "That incident in the marketplace, what convinces you that it was John Cleveland? Were you acquainted with Mr. Cleveland?"

"We weren't formally introduced, but passed each other in the corridor several times during the voyage from Brindisi to Port Said. As he lay dying in my arms, I'm certain I looked into the face of Mr. Cleveland."

"But you never spoke to the man? Or heard his voice?"

"True on both counts. But we can assume that he had a British accent."

I didn't mention that I knew he was British because I'd searched his room.

"Yes, that is a reasonable assumption. But just as you know, British accents are like American ones—they vary according to where one is raised. And there are many places in the world where the local peoples—"

"Yes, I am fully aware of the fact you Brits have scattered your accent around the world. But you haven't spread white legs, have you?"

That gives him a pause. "White legs?"

I describe the fall the "Egyptian" took on the road.

"And you are certain that the man on the bike is the same person you saw in the marketplace?"

"Yes."

"Frankly, I'm forced to question your powers of observation. If a hundred of these followers of Muhammad appeared before us right now, I would venture that we would remember robes and hoods but few personal features. Why am I to believe that your powers of observation are any better than that of the rest of mankind?"

That does it. "*Mr. Selous* . . . I see no evidence that entitles you to be a judge of me. You were not there. *I was.*"

He holds up his hands in surrender again. "You're correct, you were there. My concern is that you have been put through so much trauma in a short time. First the violence in the marketplace, then that accident at—"

"Accident? You mean the attempt to kill me?"

"Miss Bly—"

"If you'll excuse me, I have rivers to cross, mountains to climb, and castle walls to storm. Important matters. I'll leave you with your errands for Lord Warton."

I stalk off, my stomach and jaws tight. What insufferable insolence, but I'm irked at myself for being ruled by my emotions. Angry tantrums not only keep me from learning anything, but confirm Warton's opinion of me. It's hard, though, to maintain a reporter's detached, professional assessment of the situation when I'm the bloody damn victim.

18

Barely able to keep from boiling over, I go down the deck to another spot as far away as I can get from him and everyone else. And I keep an eye out for Frederick Selous. Something tells me I am not rid of the man. He doesn't appear to be a man who steps aside from a problem—even one acting like an angry bee. But at the moment I'm tired of dueling and wish I could have an ally rather than an opponent.

What have I gotten myself into? Why I'm staying in the mess as a target is another good question. An easy way out would be to hand over the key to the ship's captain and publicly admit that the man who whispered his last word to me was an Egyptian. But if I turn tail and run, I would do the same the next time I am confronted by a threat of violence. Shakespeare said something about meeting danger head-on so it doesn't get the advantage and that's what my instincts tell me I must do. It's not like I can jump overboard and swim to the next port.

A moment later Mr. Selous leans beside me again on the railing.

I don't give him the benefit of even a glance. "I'm going to ignore you in the hope you will go away. Rail leaning has become a bad habit on your part, at least when it's next to me."

"What about dragons? Do you also fight dragons during your storming of castle walls and other adventurous activities?"

I turn and lock eyes with him, hoping to see beyond his rich blue eyes and into his soul. "I have a strict policy of not harming dragons. There are so few left in the world outside of children's stories."

"Did I mention I considered a career in law before I took up hunting?"

"That doesn't surprise me. Your manner is that of a bullying lawyer."

"Yes, I deserve that. But may I ask you what I believe would be a lawyerlike question?"

"Why? To discredit my observations?"

"I can assure you that is not my intent."

"But is that Lord Warton's intent?"

He chews on that for a moment. "As an American, you may not be fully aware of all the ramifications of the presence of my country in Egypt. I have spent my entire adult life in Africa and I am acutely sensitive to the situations we face in our colonial empire—and the fact that the Mahdi movement along the Nile is the most violent opposition we face at the moment."

"If you're trying to tell me that Lord Warton has the best interests of his country in mind, that has occurred to me. But he hasn't come to me as a gentleman and expressed that. Instead, he treats me like I am a foolish woman with a wild imagination. And he acts as if he has some official authority concerning the matter, rather than just being a witness, as I am. Who exactly is Lord Warton, other than a man who inherited a title?"

Mr. Selous leans closer and speaks in a confidential tone. "I became acquainted with him yesterday for the first time, but I do know he has served in the Foreign Office. Briefly and without distinction. Rumor has it that the only thing that entitled him to a position was his title and old school chums."

"In other words," I whisper back, "his lordship is probably not a spymaster."

He clears his throat and hides a grin behind his hand. "I'm not aware of all his activities, but that is not a role I would pen for him if I were writing a story about the marketplace killings. More likely a chance bystander, but as a staunch British gentleman, ready to defend queen and country if he sees a threat."

He gives me an appraising look. "I suspect that Lord Warton's reaction to your slant on the situation may well be colored since he believes you're a reporter noted for, shall we say, sensationalism?"

I give him the smile that Mr. Pulitzer once described as the grin of a barracuda.

"I believe that I am noted for my objective reporting, sir, and that it is the wrongs of those I investigate that are sensational, not my reporting." I tap his lapel with my forefinger. "I am not a threat to queen or country. I just want the truth. If someone would reveal it to me, you may rely upon my discretion and the fact that I would act in a manner that neither you, Lord Warton, nor your Foreign Office would find fault. You can report that to him."

"You're right, you deserve the truth. The Good Book says that the truth will set us free. And I apologize for approaching you as an inquisitor, even if it was with the best of intentions. I trust that you are a person of great moral responsibility and would not do something that could result in furthering the already terrible toll of death and disorder the Egyptians are suffering. Now please, tell me exactly what you observed in the market-place."

I laugh and shake my head and get a frown in return.

"I'm not laughing at you," I say, "it's just that you are the same as me, always peeking under the rose to see what is hidden."

He grins and offers his arm for a stroll. "I confess that sometimes I also get pricked by the rose when I stick my nose under to snoop. Would you care to accompany me on a quest to find a cool drink, perhaps lemon-ade? And share with me the details of what you observed?"

WE SIT ON DECK CHAIRS shaded by an awning and sip lemonade as I relate what occurred from the time I first observed the victim on his bike and later at the marketplace.

I omit my search of Mr. Cleveland's room and the discovery of the scarab and key.

"So you believe that he spoke his wife's name," Mr. Selous says.

"That was my impression. I'm certain he said 'Amelia,' not an Arabic word. Whether Amelia is his wife is yet to be seen, but that she's a woman in his life is probable."

"Did you find anything of interest when you searched his room?"

I keep from giving a start. Fortunately, it's too hot to make any quick movements, giving me a chance to mull over the question. He saw me leave the room, but doesn't actually know I searched it. I have to tell him something, throw him a bone so he doesn't think I'm being evasive.

"Not really. He's a cutlery salesman from Liverpool."

"With a wife named Amelia?"

"I found nothing about a wife. But I had only made a quick search." I yawn and stretch. "I suppose Lord Warton told you that I had tricked the steward into leaving me alone in the room."

He gives me a grin. "Actually he hadn't, but I assumed as much since you escaped out of his room and into mine when you heard them coming. You also recognized the luggage being taken off last night."

Damn! . . . He bluffed me into a confession.

"Empty cases," I point out. He doesn't respond but I don't let the subject drop. "You didn't see the trunk open?" He said he didn't last night, but I wonder what his response will be now that we are on friendlier terms.

"No, I must confess, I didn't, but I don't doubt that's what you thought you saw."

"Thought I saw?"

He holds up his hands to block my attack. "Sorry, I didn't mean to put it that way. It's just that it was dark and happened so quickly. And I really can't imagine why anyone would conduct a charade about the luggage."

Neither could I.

"You saw nothing of interest in your search?"

"Not really. I found his lack of personal correspondence unusual but he may have only recently begun his journey away from home. He had a book about Egypt and one on the laws of Yorkshire."

"Doesn't seem unusual."

"I suppose not. There was a series of numbers on a piece of paper in the law book." I give Mr. Selous a mischievous grin. "Perhaps he's studying the law also."

He shrugs. "Perhaps. The incident at Tanis, is there any possibility that you were overcome by the desert heat—"

"And fainted because of my frail female disposition? Or perhaps from a lack of oxygen when I was strangling myself."

"Yes, I see we should avoid Tanis. May I ask you this: If a man's life depended upon your testimony, could you with complete confidence state before God and a jury that it was John Cleveland who was murdered in the marketplace?"

I give a big sigh and lean back, fanning myself. *The white of his leg. The British accent. Amelia. The key I can't tell him about. John Cleveland's sudden decision to stay in Port Said. The empty steamer trunk.*

It all adds up to a scheme to keep the dead man's identity a secret. But what if I had only seen his face and not the white flesh? I had not really taken much notice of Mr. Cleveland. So what was it that made me think it was him?

"I admit there was nothing distinguishing about the man's face that leads me to conclude that it was him. However, my impression is that it was."

"You didn't answer my question. It calls for merely a simple yes or no."

I fan my face more furiously. "Is this the way you badger your wife? A demand for simple yes-and-no answers?"

"I don't have a wife."

"I can well understand why!"

"Madam—"

"Sir . . . I suggest you direct any further *lawyerlike* questions to Lord Warton or anyone else but at my doorstep. Good day!"

"Miss Bly!" he yells as I hurry away.

I swing around—reluctantly.

"We'll stop at Ismailia shortly to pick up passengers. There will be time for a brief visit ashore to see the khedive's palace. Will you join me?"

I make a small bow. "I shall be honored to do so, kind sir."

It is a relief to go below and get away from the sweltering heat of both the air and the cross-examination, but I had discovered three things of importance:

I need more proof that the dead man is Mr. Cleveland.

Frederick Selous wants me to accompany him on a trip to shore.

And he is not married.

Von Reich steps out of the smoking lounge as I come by.

"Nellie, how are you feeling?"

"Hot and sore." I could have added that I am more angry about the damage to my reputation than the bruises to my body.

"I see that I have competition for your favors," he says. "That Englishman who wanders in jungles." He gives me a knowing look. "A friend of Lord Warton's."

"Hmmm." I suspect there is more to come. "You're also a friend of Warton."

"A business acquaintance. He needs money and can open doors for me." He glances around. "I happened to see Warton and the jungle man huddling together at a very early hour. Watch out for them."

What was that all about? I wonder as I head back to my cabin.

Certainly not jealousy on Von Reich's part. He distributes his attentions toward women aboard rather indiscriminately. So why did he give me a warning?

I like the man from Vienna, finding him amusing, though not the Romeo he obviously aspires to be. He might have confided in me as a friend, or more likely out of sympathy for the terrible situations he inadvertently put me in.

Now what am I to think about Mr. Frederick Selous and his interest in me after I find out that he plotted with Lord Warton before approaching me on the deck? He didn't approach me as a single woman he could casually pass time with aboard. For sure, he has joined with Warton to make sure that Nellie Bly, reporter, keeps silent about the murder in the marketplace.

Finding Mr. Selous both interesting and attractive despite his machinations, I shall be disappointed if his only interest in me is to sabotage my reputation.

I'm tempted to ask the steward what was done with the contents of the empty trunk I'd seen, but decide to leave well enough alone. But I'll be on guard, especially with the gentleman who has invited me for a shore excursion.

19

Mr. Selous and I board a small boat to go ashore after we anchor at Ismailia. The boatmen who swarm the ship to carry passengers gathered at the bottom of the ship's ladder suddenly become quiet and well mannered after Mr. Selous shouts down at them.

I don't know what he said—something in Arabic, I imagine—but I'm certain that his size and powerful voice are intimidating. No doubt the long-barreled six-shooter in the holster strapped to his hip also influences their decision to act in a civilized manner.

"Planning to bag big game?" I ask.

"Just a precaution. The pilot boat carried news that there have been more disturbances in the country, though none reported in Ismailia."

He starts to say something else but stops, and I don't leave well enough alone.

"You were about to confess that you brought the pistol because I might be a Jonah. I certainly hope I'm not a magnet for trouble."

"What I *was* about to say, is that I hope our little excursion ashore doesn't bring any more hell into your life."

"So do I."

Lord Warton stares down from the railing as our little boat pushes off and nods to Frederick. Catching my eye, he gives me a nod, too, and I throw back a small smile that only includes my lips. If he reads my eyes, he'll know exactly what I think of him.

As usual, his manner is haughty and condescending. And it isn't the fact that he's standing on a much higher vessel at the moment that leaves me the impression that he believes he's looking down at someone beneath him.

Ismailia Bay is hot and calm and flat. I feel as if I am on a wooden plate floating across a pot of hot water. Frederick—he insists I omit "Mr." and "sir" when addressing him—sensibly provided for a very large umbrella to protect me from the sun.

His own protection is a wide-brimmed safari hat that is rounder and appears softer than a cowboy hat. It reminds me a bit of the hats worn by the Argentine cowboys called gauchos. He's dressed very casual in a lightweight tan shirt and pants, and well-worn, knee-high brown boots.

"To protect against snakes in the jungle," he says, when I glance at the boots. "But I don't expect to be bitten in Ismailia."

Beggars, tumblers, and sellers of trinkets compete for our attention and for coins on the beach. A magician shows us a clever sleight-of-hand trick with a disappearing bead in a handkerchief and I reward him with a coin.

"Are you aware that a number of magicians from around the Mediterranean region boarded the ship at Port Said?" Frederick asks.

"No. Why are they on aboard?"

"A magic conference in New York, I'm told. One of those preternaturally wealthy American robber barons with an interest in the spiritual world has invited the finest magicians on Earth to demonstrate their powers. A rather large monetary prize awaits the conjurer whose trick can't be guessed by a committee of judges."

"Perhaps one of them can show us how Mr. Cleveland can manage to be both dead and alive at the same time."

He stops and searches my face with his eyes. "What must I do to convince you that I am not lying to you about having spoken to John Cleveland?"

"I believe you are as mistaken about having spoken to the man himself as much as you believe I am mistaken about him dying in my arms." Brushing a bit of lint off his coat, I look into his eyes with all sincerity. "The matter can be resolved by having one of those magicians who've come aboard conjure him up."

"Mind what you wish for. Stranger things have happened in the land of the pharaohs."

FREDERICK HIRES A CARRIAGE that takes us into the town. Ismailia is quieter and smaller than Port Said, a place the ship stops only because the government mail contract requires it. The streets are unpaved and even more rutted than at the Mediterranean port, but at least there are no mobs shouting for the blood of foreigners.

I spot an English language newspaper office, the *Ismailia Post*, housed with the cable office, a not uncommon arrangement since out of town news comes by wire.

"I try to pay my respects at news offices as often as I can," I tell Frederick, certain that as a thoughtful gentleman, he will urge me to make a brief stop.

He glances in the direction of the establishment. "Yes, quite." He suddenly points at a store selling musical instruments. "Those drums are fired clay with sheep's guts stretched over one end. They make a rather good sound."

I turn cold, then angry. *"Stop the carriage."*

I startle both Frederick and the driver, who reins in the horse and looks back at me.

"You can have this back." I shove the umbrella at Frederick and step down from the coach, slamming the door behind me.

Frederick stares gravely at me. "What are you doing?"

"I saw your look. You're trying to divert me from the cable office. You invited me along to make sure I don't send my editor the story about spies in the marketplace."

"Regardless of what you think, you must understand that you risk arrest if you send an inflammatory cablegram."

"I don't intend to send one. But when I do, you will not be able to stop me."

I wave down another carriage and tell the driver to take me back to the beach.

I am so mad, I'm ready to howl at the moon and foam at the mouth.

The scheme to keep me on a leash and my lips sealed smacks of Warton in his role as the self-appointed, self-righteous arbiter of my conduct.

I didn't plan to send a cablegram. I had considered it, but rejected the notion because I'm a foreigner in what amounts to a war zone and I know I could be arrested if I dashed off something sounding of spies and government cover-ups. Besides, I would be going off ill-prepared because I don't have all the facts. If the story was proved to be wrong, my reputation as a credible journalist would forever be tainted.

The newspaper world in New York is a battlefield, where a publisher's heart beats with the same rhythm as the paper's circulation figures. Mr. Pulitzer would drop me like yesterday's news if I made a mistake that allowed his competitors to hee-haw.

The same is true about the race I've undertaken. Sitting in a jail in Egypt, or even being detained for questioning for a few hours while my boat sails, would cost me the race . . . and my career, my very lifeblood. The *World* has made my trip a lead story, boasting that its reporter will succeed. If I don't beat the eighty-day mark, I will not only curl up and die from shame, but Mr. Pulitzer will make sure I am a pariah in news reporting.

By the time I reach the beach and hire a boat to take me out to the ship, my anger has evaporated, and the heat and dark thoughts have filled me with weariness and a sense of anxiety to which I can't put a name.

I feel so alone, so exposed, halfway around the world from friends and family, and not a soul I can turn to. Lord, what I would give to have the man who has trekked pathless jungles and faced charging beasts as a friend and ally. Instead, with every word and thought, my relationship with him goes deeper into a morass.

I realize that the source of the anxiety when I'm being rowed out to the ship is a question.

When is the next shoe going to drop?

Once upon a midnight dreary, while I pondered weak and weary . . . sings in my head as I take my late-night constitutional from bow to stern. Perhaps the poem slipped into my thoughts because it was a night in the "bleak December" that Poe's raven knocked on the door of the lover distraught over the death of the lovely Lenore.

December has come to me, too, and this first day of it is indeed a bleak one—the dark and angry clouds that hung over me have followed me aboard and put me in a melancholy gloom. The thick atmosphere from heat coming off the Arabian Desert presses down on me despite the stingy breeze provided by the forward motion of the ship.

It's a starless night with a moon that is a pale ghost doing nothing to relieve the darkness, bringing to mind my mother's belief that ghosts are spirits who have stayed behind because they have unfinished business and need help to cross over to the hereafter.

John Cleveland, of course, is the ghost haunting my mind's attic and I haven't been much help in getting his spirit to rest in peace. I don't want him to end up like Edgar Allan Poe's character whose soul is trapped beneath the raven's shadow, to be lifted—"Nevermore!"

Stop it! Groaning, I hit the side of my head with my palm to knock some sense into it. I don't know why my mind is always conjuring up these strange thoughts. I'm too superstitious, too willing to accept that there is phenomena beyond my five senses. I've even been wondering whether breaking the scarab and throwing it overboard brought an ancient Egyptian curse into my life.

I don't have to worry about threats from the spirit world—I have plenty to deal with in this one. I just have to keep my own feet grounded and remind myself that the man who instigated Mr. Cleveland's death puts on his pants one leg at time, the face in the porthole was a real person trying to frighten me, and that the only ghouls around are done on stage with mirrors.

When I reach the bow, I give a quick look behind me to make sure no one is watching because I don't want to get caught and really give the captain a reason to throw me overboard. Slipping under the rope, I ignore the NO ENTRY sign.

The bow is the least-visited area of the ship, roped off to keep passengers from strolling through because it's where the equipment for hauling up the anchor and raising sails is stored. There's also a danger of being swept overboard as the ship plows through the sea.

I enjoy my late-night visits to the bow because it gets both port and starboard breezes when the ship is underway, and unless the anchor is being raised or lowered, it's the quietest place onboard. When we're in rough seas, I sometimes sneak onto the bow to feel as if I'm riding a giant sea creature as the ship plows deep into waves and then rears back up, blowing back saltwater spray.

I know I'm not the only one violating the captain's order. The woman in black, also a nocturnal deck walker, uses the area, too. Knowing she desires privacy, I'm careful to avoid the bow when I see her there. I'm glad I don't see her tonight for I really need this time to be alone.

Away from the deck lights, it's midnight black as I carefully step over chains and steel cables, and weave around the big winches and lifeboats. I reach the forward end of the ship, my little haven of peace and quiet, and I suddenly realize how tired I am as I lean on the railing and let the warm wind ruffle my hair and clothes. Heat tends to drain my energy and we've had days of it in this hot, dry climate that is also afire with political passions.

I hear something behind me and turn as a man slips out from under the canvas cover of a lifeboat—an Egyptian, clad only in a loincloth.

With a large knife.

Letting out a yell, I make a dash amidships but my foot trips on a cable stretched between machinery and I go down, hitting the deck full and flat facedown. His feet find the same cable and he goes down to my left with a startled cry.

I get myself up in a panic and he rises as I do, with the knife in his hand.

I scream and turn to run again but my feet slip out from under me as I spin around and fall sideways, hitting my head against the metal housing of machinery and drop to my knees. The man with the dagger is suddenly upon me, knocking me against the metal housing again, sending me back to the deck.

A whirl of motion, grunts, and heavy footfalls erupt around me, and I realize someone else has joined the battle.

I raise my hands to protect my face and curl in a fetal position as feet stamp around me. The fight is suddenly no longer hovering over me and I hear a startled yelp and look up to see two dark forms at the rail, one of them going over. From the shape of the dark figures, it was my almost naked attacker who went overboard.

It's too dark to make out anything about the other person except he must be a man and he's gone, too, down the deck, leaving me there with my head spinning.

Someone hovers over me again and I let out a startled cry.

"Are you all right?" the woman asks in English.

The accent is not British, but continental, French, I think.

A whiff of perfume comes from a female figure wearing a veil. For a second I think it's Lady Warton, but the face beneath the veil is close enough for me to realize it isn't.

"I . . . I—" I'm not certain what my condition is. I am still on my back and my head is swimming.

"What's going on here?" The shout comes from a few feet away.

I recognize the voice as that of the first officer.

Without a word, the woman leaves.

As I am assisted to my feet by the ship's officer, I can still smell the woman's lingering perfume. I'm certain she is the woman in black who also walks the decks at night.

She left me with a sense of haunting familiarity about her features, one that I can't put a finger on. For certain, she is not the eccentric Mrs. Winchester, who is much older and dowdier than the woman in black.

Another certainty is that whoever tried to kill me at Tanis had come back to finish the job.

Questions bounce around like rubber balls in my sore head.

Who was my rescuer? Obviously, a man who did not want to stay around to receive my thanks because he wanted to keep his identity a secret. The woman in black did likewise.

Someone has tried to murder me again. Stowing away and lying in wait took planning. Have I gotten the entire Mahdi movement into a murderous rage against me because of the key in the scarab?

Maybe destroying that scarab wasn't such a good idea.

21

Miss Bly, because of your insistence to my first officer that you witnessed a man go overboard, we have done a roll call of all the crew and passengers and everyone is accounted for . . . *everyone*."

The captain has tight jaws and is not in good humor.

I was taken to the ship's infirmary to be checked by the doctor. When the captain came in, I quickly learned that an attack on a passenger aboard the ship is a scandal he eagerly wants to avoid.

"I told your officer I was attacked by an Egyptian wearing a loincloth."

"We have no Egyptians aboard—not even stowaways. And, young woman, the last time I looked, none of the passengers were wearing loincloths."

"Which means that whoever attacked me went overboard."

The ship's doctor, who has been puttering in his medicine cabinet to find a salve for my scrapes, says, "We have had incidents in the past where thieves have come up the anchor chain while we were—"

"We were underway, doctor," the captain snaps. "There are no thieves aboard the *Victoria*."

"Of course not, captain," the doctor says.

"What about the witnesses?" I ask. "The man who came to my aid, the woman who—"

"No one lays claim to having seen the alleged incident."

"Alleged? Are you implying that I made up the attack?"

"I am merely giving a commonsense interpretation to what you have reported. You sneaked into an area that is off-limits because of hazards, tripped, and banged your head. That much of your story is evident. Your report that a man came at you with a knife and that someone intervened is still under investigation. Your exact statement to my officer is that you blacked out after striking your head and that all you saw around you was a blur of dark figures. Is that an accurate rendition of what you have previously stated?"

"I did bang my head, but—"

"Doctor, exactly what injuries did this young woman incur during her *trespass* in the restricted bow area?"

"A few bruises and scrapes, a blow to the head—"

"A blow to the head. The fact that she became disoriented and even blacked out briefly shows it was a pretty severe blow, does it not?"

"Oh yes, yes, perhaps even a concussion."

I could see that I had lost the doctor, not to medicine but to the demands of keeping his job. "The head injury occurred because I was attacked."

"My dear," the ship's doctor says as he applies ointment to a scrape on my arm, "you took such a nasty fall, I'm afraid your memory is not solid. I won't be surprised if you have occasional blackouts for the next few days. You're a very lucky young woman."

"Will there be any permanent impairment to her?" the captain asks.

"No, though she could have a short-term effect. How severe, I can't say, but I believe with plenty of rest, she should be back to normal in a few days. In the meantime she might still have hallucinations."

"Hallucinations!"

The two men give a start and freeze in place. If Mr. Selous, the great hunter, had heard my retort he would have likened it to the howl of a wounded jungle cat.

I lock eyes with the captain. "It was a personal attack on me. A planned murder."

The captain turns shades of red and purple and appears to be suffering apoplexy. I hope he doesn't drop dead, if for no other reason than it might delay our passage.

He gains his composure and turns to the doctor with a meaningful look. "You do recall that we have been warned that this young woman suffers from an overabundance of imagination and paranoia. I suspect that the entire episode is a case of female hysteria generated by a blow to the head. There was no attacker, no gallant rescuer; it was all conjured by the imagination of an impressionable young woman who has read too many penny dreadfuls. Don't you agree, doctor?"

"Most definitely. Yes, most definitely."

The captain stiffly spins about-face as if he were in a military parade, jerks open the infirmary door, and steps out, pulling it closed in a slam behind him.

Before the door closes, a mirror on the wall reflects the image of two men standing in the corridor outside the infirmary.

Lord Warton and Frederick Selous.

I slip off the examination table to confront the two slanders but am stopped by the doctor who grabs my arm.

"Miss Bly, you're aboard a ship. Under the laws of the seas, the captain has exceptional authority over you, powers that can be exercised with little restraint." He gives me a fatherly smile. "If you cause trouble, he'll put you ashore at the next port and you will have to complete your race by swimming."

22

My anger turns from hot to cold fury as I head for the stateroom of the woman in black who had hovered over me at the bow. Hot anger is for bursts of temper. When I get an icy chill, my intent is to wreak vengeance and havoc. "Pink," my mother has said, using my family's pet name for me, "you are the meanest when you are silently angry."

Hysterical female, indeed. Those pompous, ignorant bastards. And I make no apology for my language.

I can understand the captain's eagerness to protect the reputation of his ship, though I draw the line when it is done at the expense of both the truth and my reputation.

I'll stop short of a confrontation with the captain because the ship's doctor is right—I could be put off the ship and forfeit the race. But I can't let an attempt on my life go unanswered or have my credibility trampled. Spotting Selous with Warton outside told me what side he had picked again. War has been declared, the lines drawn, no quarter is to be given.

I'll need allies in the battles to come and the woman who came to my aid on the bow is the most likely, and only, candidate at the moment since the man who threw my attacker overboard will not come forward.

Although I'm hesitant to call on the woman because she goes to extreme lengths to protect her privacy, I need to know what she saw on the bow.

Did she see the struggle? If she did, it would rebut the hysterical female accusation the captain has stained my reputation with.

Puzzlement over the features I'd seen under the veil still gives me pause, one of those thoughts that sits in a back corner of my brain and teases me. Sometimes they're revealed after a long, solitary walk during which I'm able to concentrate and other times I erupt from sleep in the middle of the night with an answer to the puzzle.

There's something about her that strikes a chord, yet I can't put my finger on it.

With so much on my mind, and my reputation at stake, I decide a frontal assault is necessary.

Pausing at the woman's door, I take a deep breath, and tell myself to relax. Barging in as I did with Selous could alienate her.

Tapping lightly on the door, I wait for a response. None comes.

Tapping a little harder, I wait.

Harder even, a good, strong pound because the woman is probably asleep.

"Perfectly obvious," I mutter to the door. The woman is not going to open it.

Has she been forewarned by the captain that I might pay her a visit? Or is she so intent upon maintaining her privacy, she will not open the door even if the ship is sinking?

I am tempted to yell that the ship is sinking but stop myself. Causing a panic aboard would only confirm the captain's opinion of my mental state and get me deposited ashore with my luggage at the next port.

"All right." The door is not going to be opened to my knock. That is a given.

Resisting the temptation to give it a good kick, I turn to leave, but driven by one of those impulses I'm helpless to stop, I turn back to the door and try the handle.

The knob turns and I push open the door.

Across the room a woman in a long black negligee is lounging on a plush velvet quilt on the closed hood of a coffin. Beside the casket is a tall golden candelabra, with little globs of wax sliding down the candles like tear drops.

Lazy smoke curls up from a cigarette held on an ivory holder as she looks up from a magazine and glares at me.

"How dare you?"

"I . . . I—"

She slips off the coffin lid and comes at me, no doubt to slam the door in my face.

I stare at her in paralyzed astonishment. It's not possible. It's unbelievable. It can't be.

"My God . . . you're . . . you're—"

She lets out a shriek and grabs me, almost jerking me off my feet as she pulls me into the room and slams the door behind us.

23

I am sorely tempted to leave her behind at Suez City," the captain says.

He invited the ship's doctor, the first officer, Lord Warton, and Frederick Selous to the sitting room of his quarters for brandy, cigars, and a discussion about the young newspaperwoman who had become a nuisance aboard.

"More's the pity, but I don't dare. Her employer, a man named Pulitzer, would lynch me with printer's ink in his newspapers if I caused her to lose this ridiculous race she's conducting."

"Yet she needs to be reined in," Lord Warton says.

"She's very centered on this incident in Port Said," the doctor says. "Not that she shouldn't be. It must have been a terrible trauma also to Lady Warton and yourself, of course."

"Quite so. Her ladyship was upset by the incident, but she has not turned it into a *cause célèbre* to embarrass our country."

"Ships sailing in this region do occasionally suffer thieves and stowaways," the first officer says. "It sounds like she may have had the bad luck to run into one that came aboard when we were anchored."

"You didn't actually see anyone attacking her, did you?" Lord Warton asks.

"No, but I got there after the man who supposedly came to her aid had fled. It's strange no one has come forward to take the credit for her."

"It certainly wasn't me," Lord Warton says. "I would have thrown *her* overboard."

The first officer nods at Frederick Selous. "And it wasn't you, Mr. Selous; you were playing cards with the captain and me. So who—"

"It doesn't matter if someone had assisted her," Lord Warton says, "we're dealing with a woman who has not only an imagination, but both an appetite and an outlet for sensationalism. Pulitzer's newspaper in New York thrives on providing vulgar thrills to its readership." He takes a long drag off his cigar and blows the smoke in the air. "It's our duty to ensure that she does not upset the delicate political balance in Egypt by having her take unrelated incidents and create a bloody mess for us."

"Hear! Hear!" the captain offers with his raised glass and the others follow suit.

Lord Warton sucks another drag and again stares up at the ceiling as he slowly blows smoke.

Selous, quietly observing the man, has concluded that the peer loves the limelight.

"It goes without saying," his lordship continues, "that my friends in the Colonial Office would hold the steamship company and its employees responsible if this young woman is permitted to damage our position in regard to the canal."

The threat was unnecessary, Selous reflects; the ship's officers are not only patriots but smart when it comes to protecting their employment. If the shipping line got barred from use of the canal, it would be forced out of business.

As the discussion rumbles on, Selous savors his brandy, swirling it, sniffing it, to avoid participating in the conversation. Something outside the room, at the bow of the ship precisely, required his attention and he wanted the session to get over with as quickly as possible.

Listening to Warton speak of his brief service in Morocco as if he had been at the right hand of the foreign secretary himself, Selous has a hard time to keep from smirking.

Having spent the last two decades mingling with Colonial and Foreign Office personnel, he had heard a bit about Warton and knew infinitely more about Warton's type—a man who got his job because of whom he knew rather than what he knew.

Selous, third generation of an immigrant French-Huguenot line Protestant that fled persecution in France, had a different view of the world than the peer. His name, Frederick Courtenay Selous, was not "British" sounding, a fact that got him into more than one fight at school with Warton types who counted their roots back to the Saxons.

Selous had heard that the first lord in the Warton line had been a wool merchant who bought his title by providing the king an eighty-gun ship of the line.

No other Warton had worked for a living since.

Although the situation with the American reporter has made them allies, Selous knows that Warton considers him his social inferior despite Selous's personal accomplishments, his adventurous spirit, and the fact his family has a long history of success in business and science.

He had heard that Lord Warton was a slow burn, not one to jump into anything new or radical. With financial problems due to bad management of his estates and being unlucky at cards, he'd gone into government service not for queen and country but because he needed the employment—and the contacts it gave him.

He had now left public service after a short, undistinguished career and had a reputation of being accessible to business interests that wanted to do business with the government. Some, like Von Reich, were foreigners.

"Egypt is a tinderbox," Lord Warton says, "ready to catch afire and fill the Nile with blood. When it does, thousands will die, our own people among them, not to mention that a loss of the Suez Canal would have political and economic ramifications around the world."

Lord Warton locks eyes with the captain. "I recommend that any cables Miss Bly gives to the purser to send at our ports of call be reviewed by me to ensure there are no politically explosive false allegations."

The captain looks to the others and back to Warton. "Rather unusual, don't you think, spying on a passenger's cables—and censoring them."

"Based upon my connection with the government, you can consider the request as an official one."

Selous stifles a yawn. The man's a complete ass.

"Most business passengers prefer to send their own cables when they reach ports," the captain says.

"Well, then, something will have to be done about that, won't it?"

"That tactic has already been met with a resounding defeat," Selous says.

After the captain's meeting ends, Selous wanders on deck, smoking a cigar, making his way toward the front of the ship. He waits in the darkness at the bow area, making sure no one is in sight, and then slips under the rope barrier to the area where Nellie was attacked.

With little light coming from the moon and a thousand nooks and crannies for a small object to hide, finding anything on the deck is not going to be easy, but being a great hunter he has an eye for fine detail—a broken limb in a forest of trees, a single crushed leaf among thousands, the smallest detail can reveal his prey.

He knows the ship's officers have inspected the area, but their examination would have amounted to walking to the bow and, short of tripping over a body, finding nothing of interest because they didn't know how to look.

Evidence of a struggle on deck is obvious to him: smudges made by the bare feet of one man, the scuff marks made by the shoes of another as two men struggled, their feet trying to gain purchase on the damp deck as they shoved at each other in a fight to the death.

Using the soles of his shoes, Selous wipes out the marks.

Reconstructing the fight from the evidence, he finds what he had come to look for; it slid into an opening at the base of a piece of machinery—the crude, wooden-handled dagger the assassin had wielded.

Giving a quick look around to make sure he is not observed, he tosses the weapon overboard, hearing a faint plop as it hits the water and begins its journey to the bottom of the sea.

Making his way back to his cabin he thinks about the newspaperwoman who has thrown a kink into the best-laid plans of men—and nations.

She has botched things up on many levels. It's easy to see that she will keep getting in the way—if she manages to stay alive.

25

They're trying to murder me, not you. They thought you were me, that's why you were attacked."

The statement from the woman barely penetrates my brain because I'm in a state of shock after finding out her identity.

I can't keep from staring impolitely at her.

That she just took credit for being the intended victim of the deck attack on me is unimportant. All that is completely irrelevant at the moment as my mind tries to deal with the incredible sight in front of me.

Had Cleopatra left her tomb and wandered around the boat in widow black, I would not have been more surprised.

"Sarah Bernhardt," I whisper.

"Yes, yes, I've already told you, in the flesh."

"The Divine Sarah."

Sarah Bernhardt is not a person, at least not in the sense that I am one, that the president of the United States and the occupants in the next stateroom are persons.

The Divine Sarah is a living goddess.

The most glamorous actress in the world, the most revered tragedian, most beloved, most sensuous, *the most everything*, with fame, scandal, and love affairs that provided juicy tidbits for gossip columns and afternoon teas all over the world.

The woman every woman desired to be; *the woman every man wants to love.*

From reading gossip columns I know that she was born in Paris, her mother was Jewish, her father probably Dutch, but no one knew for sure because his sole contribution appeared to have been slipping into her mother's bed just long enough to contribute his seed.

Sarah cloaked herself in glamorous scandal as other women hid themselves behind layers of clothes and respectability. Struggling to earn a living as an actress, she became a courtesan, her beauty and charm making her a favorite paramour of nobles and royalty.

Her love affair when she was nineteen with Belgium's Prince de Ligne produced her only child.

As she grew in years and fame—she had to be over forty as she paced in front of me, but looked a decade younger—she had become a living legend, the Divine Sarah, the greatest actress in the world, and an Aphrodite whose rich and famous lovers were rumored to include even the Prince of Wales, a playboy whose romantic romps to Paris were legendary.

She goes back on top of her coffin with her long cigarette holder and blows cigarette smoke at me. "Young woman, we must get beyond your amazement that I am on board."

"I thought you were that Winchester woman."

"Who?"

"It's too complicated to explain. What are you doing on board . . . incognito? Hiding in your cabin?"

Sarah slides off the coffin again and paces with the nervous energy of a caged animal in the small room, using her foot-long ivory cigarette holder as a music conductor's baton to highlight her words.

"I cannot reveal my mission. It is a matter of importance that is unequaled in human affairs."

I have no idea what she is talking about, but it sounds important. Exciting, in fact. "Unequaled in human affairs" brought to me images of the march of armies on darkling plains, war ministries called into secret sessions, dispatches carried through the night by spies on galloping horses.

She is the greatest actress in the world and I naturally assume that she is playing a role, but it didn't alter the fact that there had been a murder in the marketplace and attempts at Tanis and now aboard the ship.

It cannot be a coincidence.

The world's greatest actress, the consort of kings and millionaires, the toast of three continents, is telling me that she is involved in the same intrigues I have become entangled—but she won't tell me her role, though she has cast me as her understudy for the attack on the bow of the ship.

Just as important, she offers me no clue as to what game is being played that could mean war between nations.

As I watch her pacing, I realize that while I have solved the mystery of the woman in black, I have not made any headway as to why a man died in the marketplace or why an epidemic of violence seems to hover around me like a maelstrom ever since.

Had I not been such a dunderhead, I would have realized the real identity of "Sarah Jones" days ago.

Everyone knows the Divine Sarah sleeps in a coffin because it helps her understand roles involving suffering and tragedy.

Life has taught me that if one is to be somebody, it can only be after death.
—Sarah Bernhardt

26

Trying to get Sarah to sit still and discuss the situation is about as easy as stopping the ship by dragging my foot in the water. It is not so much that she is flighty, as bursting with energy. I suspect that she needs a release after being cooped up in a cabin for days.

When she finally sits quietly back down on her coffin, and has me sit in a chair, she gives me an assessing look.

"I've heard about you," she says. "My steward says you're an eccentric, rich American heiress, traveling about with a hairbrush and a bank book, with nothing to do, so you do strange things to get attention."

At first I'm furious and then I break into a giggle. "I am guilty of having a hairbrush."

"Who are you exactly?"

"Exactly, I am a newspaperwoman. I have done a number of exposés that have brought about social reform or exposed corruption."

As she asks pointed questions about my career, I give her details explaining how I got started as a reporter when I was working in a Pittsburgh factory, doing the same laborious job as a man but only being paid half a man's wage.

Angered by a *Pittsburgh Dispatch* article that essentially said a woman's only worth was as a helpmate to a man, I wrote a letter to the editor pointing out the injustice of that position and signed it "Lonely Orphan Girl" out of fear I would lose my job.

That letter got me a job as a reporter, but after a few searing articles about how the common worker was being mistreated, a group of businessmen paid a visit to my editor and I found myself covering weddings and funerals. . . .

Even after I made a daring trip to untamed Mexico at my own expense to show I could handle a foreign correspondent's job, I was still assigned a "proper job for a female reporter"—the society page.*

"I abruptly left my job in Pittsburgh and went to New York, certain my success would open doors for me. Instead, I found that there was no room for a woman reporter even in America's largest city. After banging on doors for months, and down to trolley fare, which I had borrowed after my last cent was stolen, I physically barged into the office of Joseph Pulitzer and informed the startled publisher that I could do a story that would turn the city on its head."

I describe for Sarah how I had to fool a boardinghouse landlady, police, psychiatrists, and a judge that I was insane.

Sarah laughs. "You should be on the stage."

"I find I can only act in real life. I have been on a stage just long enough to find out that I cannot fake it."

"Tell me why you have come knocking—pounding—at my door."

"Are you aware that a man was murdered in the marketplace in Port Said?"

She shrugs. "My steward said there was some native dispute."

"I don't think so . . ."

I relate the events from seeing the murdered man fall off his bike, to him whispering Amelia's name in the marketplace—omitting my search of Mr. Cleveland's cabin—up to my fall into the Tanis tomb and to the attack on me, characterized as "female hysterics."

The last bit got her on her feet, ready to storm the captain's cabin.

"No, please, if I antagonize the captain again, he'll drop me off at the next port. Besides, you'd have to reveal your identity."

After I finish my tale, she says, "Frankly, my dear, I don't think your little marketplace matter has a connection to the matter I am dealing with."

Little marketplace matter?

"Sarah, I need to know more about the situation you are in. If you'd share with me—"

She brushes away my need to know with a wave of her cigarette

* Nellie went to Mexico during a violent era of revolution and banditry and left after receiving a message that her life was in danger if she wrote any more exposés about conditions in the country. After she became famous, she wrote about her experiences in a book entitled *Six Months in Mexico*. —The Editors

holder. "I have been sworn to secrecy." She gives me a dark look. "Speaking to a newspaperwoman would hardly satisfy that oath. No word of it will escape from my lips even if I am being stretched on an inquisitioner's rack. However, I am frankly bored to death locked in this sardine can. Helping you with your little mystery would add some relief. Tell me what you know about this man Cleveland."

Admitting to my burglary, I tell her how I managed to get rid of the steward so I could make a search of Cleveland's room.

"You entered a strange man's room and searched it? That was naughty of you." She says it with a big smile.

Sarah's estimation of me has gone up.

She asks what I observed in the luggage and makes an exclamation when I come to the books and writings.

"That list of numbers you saw is a secret code. That's what one of the books was for, probably that law book that struck you as odd for a cutlery salesman to lug about. I once had a lover who was a spy. An Italian count. He used ordinary books for constructing his codes."

"How is it done?"

"It's so simple, a child could do it, but impossible to decipher unless you have the right book. The spymaster gives his spy a book that is not in general use in the foreign country where the spy is being sent—"

"That Yorkshire law volume would be perfect," I add.

"Exactly. To compose a message, they find the correct words in the book—"

"The numbers are the page, line, and position of the word."

"Nellie, you are quick, aren't you? Since both the spy and his supervisor have the same book, it's easy for them to decode messages. My lover sent his messages in invisible ink, especially the ones to me."

"Why did he use invisible ink?"

"He was married."

"Oh." I am awed by the fact the woman had a lover—and openly admits it. A married one, at that. What a daring and shocking admission for a woman. And very French, of course.

"Don't sound so prudish, my dear. Certainly you have had a love affair with a married—ah, yes, I see from your blush that you have. To read the messages, I ran a hot iron over the paper or held it over a warm radiator." She sighs. "He was a wonderful lover, warm to a woman's needs, and generous. They caught him spying and hanged him. Your spy, that cutlery salesman, he may have used invisible ink, too."

"The paper I saw had writing on it."

"Of course—a sheet of paper without writing on it would raise suspicion. The invisible words are written between the lines."

I snap my fingers. "Lemon juice, my brothers used it to make invisible writing when were children. Milk, too. What did your lover use?"

"Nothing so ordinary."

She leans forward and whispers in my ear. I blush from head to toe and quickly change the subject.†

"I suspect you're right about the books," I say. "It made little sense for a cutlery salesman from Liverpool to have a book on the laws of York, though I could understand why he might have one about Egypt. And you might be right about the invisible ink. The numbers I saw may have been a draft he prepared, to be turned into an invisible message between the lines of an otherwise innocent appearing correspondence."

"It's too bad you don't have the paper with the numbers on it and the book. Is the luggage still in Cleveland's suite?"

"No." I tell her about seeing an empty trunk hitting the water.

"Did all the luggage appear empty?"

"Now that you ask me, yes, I believe so." I shake my head to stir up the memory. "The way the boatman handled them so easily, taking them out of the lowered netting and tossing them back to his mates. They may well have been empty."

"So, the contents may still be aboard with your British lord sitting on them. Who may not even know the importance."

"I'm sure Lord Warton and the others must realize Mr. Cleveland was a spy. Or at least suspect it."

"That doesn't mean they know how the spy game is played. Or be aware that invisible ink could be part of what the chief of the Paris police calls modus operandi."

I have to wonder if the Parisian chief is her lover, too.

† Nellie is too inhibited to reveal the substance used for invisible ink by Sarah's lover, but a clue can be found in the story of Sir George Smith-Cumming, who entered British Intelligence in Victorian times and was the model for intelligence chief "M" in the James Bond stories. Smith-Cumming had his men use semen for invisible ink. —The Editors

Sarah lets out a great sigh. "Well, my dear, it is very late, and after listening to your tale, there is only one thing for you to do."

"Which is?"

"Go on with your own affairs, your race to beat the record around the world, and leave matters of spies and revolutions in the hands of the politicians. No matter what you do, you'll receive no thanks for your efforts and may in fact jeopardize your goal because politicians are devils."

It is good advice and much more palatable coming from this woman of the world who wants me to succeed than Mr. Selous, whose advice is based upon my gender.

I look her in the eye. "Sarah, do you want to share with me your—"

"No!" She gets up and dramatically sweeps to the porthole and opens it, staring into the dark night. "It is a secret I cannot share. If the secret is revealed, armies will march, empires will tremble."

I am awestruck. "Are you a spy? Entrusted with a national secret?"

"Me? A spy? Of course not."

"Then . . . then who's trying to murder you?"

"My lover's family, of course."

27

My head is pulsating when I leave the great actress to return to my own cabin. So many things have happened so quickly in this land of mystery and magic. Now I find Sarah Bernhardt, the most famous actress in the world, is on the ship—and she has become my friend and confidante. I wish I could wire Mr. Pulitzer and tell him about it. But she has sworn me to secrecy about her presence.

The ship is underway, moving down the canal toward Suez Bay, and I step out on deck to get air, joining other passengers seeking even the stingy breeze that the forward movement of the ship brings over the deck before I am banished below so the men can have the deck to themselves.

Crewmen are hanging lights at the front of the ship and a group of us watch them as they put the lights over the side.

I lean against the rail and eavesdrop as a man tells his companion that the lights are electric, powered by the ship's steam engine, and that before the introduction of electric headlights, ships were compelled to tie up in the canal overnight because of the great danger of running into the sandbanks.

Being near the bow reminds of me of my close call with the grim reaper. I didn't make an issue of it, but I'm not convinced that Sarah was the intended victim any more than I had leaned too heavily against the frail railing at Tanis or mistook "Amelia" for an Arabic word. I had been searched at Tanis for the key and I'm sure a Mahdi dagger man had come aboard to kill for the key, just as one had killed for it in the marketplace.

The death of Mr. Cleveland and the key are directly related to the political unrest in Egypt, I'm sure of it. What I can't comprehend, and without help from the great actress, is how those matters are related to her problems with her lover's family.

Having worked out nothing that sounds like a solution, I return to my cabin, certain that I will not get good sleep again.

As I step into the tiny cubbyhole that serves as my bathroom, I smell face cream.

My cream is in an airtight jar and I had not opened it since applying cream this morning. Opening it, I can see that the contents have been stirred around.

Bending down, I take a sniff of the drain opening in the sink bowl and smell a hint of cream.

Someone had opened my cream jar and stirred around the contents. In the process, a glob of cream had fallen into the sink and had been washed down to cover the intruder's tracks. They were obviously looking for the key.

I look around my cabin, seeking other clues that someone had invaded my personal space.

I find none, but have no other explanation for the condition of my cream jar other than someone had made a thorough search of my cabin and that the jar of cream was part of the search. Certainly my male steward had not been playing with my facial cream.

My room had been searched to find the key given to me by the man murdered in the marketplace.

"That settles that," I tell the room's walls.

There is no longer any doubt that the attacker on the bow had been an assassin and who the target had been. I feel like running back and telling the Divine Sarah she is wrong. I am not the understudy, but the star of this murder mystery.

My sense of having been violated once again chills me with anger, but a more practical thought sneaks in: Sarah's speculation that the contents of Mr. Cleveland's luggage might still be aboard.

From Sarah's description of the process, I'm certain that Mr. Cleveland had written a coded message, though I didn't know if what I had seen was the finished message or one in progress. Or if he had another message hidden on the papers in invisible ink.

Knowing what Mr. Cleveland wrote in the coded message might flush out my enemy.

How could I go about finding it without jeopardizing the race . . . or my life?

More urgent at the moment than secret messages is the matter of not being murdered in my bed by an intruder who returns to search my person.

I wedge the chair back under the door handle and crawl into bed, clutching my pair of scissors.

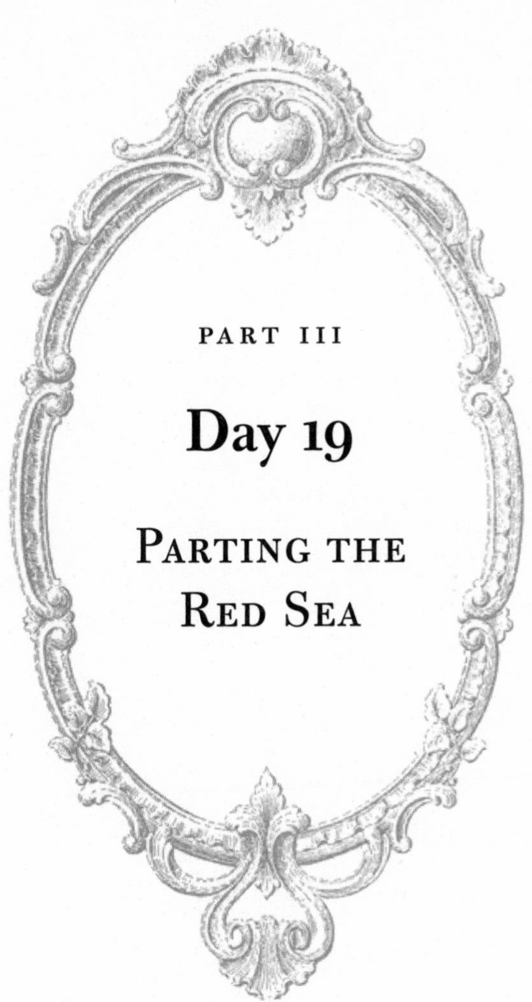

PART III

Day 19

Parting the Red Sea

28

Leaving the Suez Canal behind, the ship takes us the length of the Red Sea and to the Gulf of Aden at the western part of the Arabian Sea. Hopefully, I have left behind in Egypt the curse of the pharaohs that has brought so much hell into my life.

Just before we come to the British port known as the Aden Settlement, we pass high brown mountains.

"They are known as the Twelve Apostles," Von Reich informs me when we meet during an early morning deck stroll. "In Aden there is a tradition that the town dates back to Genesis and that Cain and Abel are both buried there."

Even though I had read the same thing in the ship's bulletin, I permit him to expound in his pedantic manner.

Watching his expression, I wonder if I can find a clue to any change in his attitude toward me since I have become a pariah to his British friends and the ship's captain. He signals nothing, not even the concern he had expressed earlier, but I suspect his lack of interest in me recently has been fed by the overtures I see him making to other women on board.

We come in sight of the British colony at Aden and it looks like a large, bare mountain of wonderful height, but even by the aid of a spyglass I'm unable to tell that it is inhabited.

I continue my morning constitution as Von Reich stops to watch a soccer ball booted back and forth on deck by a group of young men.

After the ship stops to drop anchor in the bay, the breeze dies and I escape inside. I am on a mission.

I give the assistant purser a big smile and a cheery "Good morning," and hope the devil has well oiled my lies.

It's obvious that Lord Warton has taken custody of Mr. Cleveland's possessions, but where are they now? While Warton could have some small items in his own cabin, the books for instance, he would have arranged for storage of the luggage as a whole because the only storage area in a cabin is for steamer trunks slipped under the bunks. I'm hoping that the pompous peer is as unfamiliar with the codes of spies as I suspect he is of growing wheat in Morocco.

"I'm planning to purchase a large item in Aden and will need somewhere to store it. Is there a place on board to store something too large for my cabin?"

"What type of item?"

"A Persian rug."

"I suspect Aden isn't the best place to find Persian rugs—Egyptian ports have a better selection—but if you do make a selection, you can store it in the Passenger Luggage Compartment."

"Where is that?"

"On the utility deck below the last passenger deck."

"I'd like to take a look at the facility, to make sure it's secure."

"Oh, it's secure all right." He nods back at a key on a large ring hanging on the wall behind the counter. "That's the key."

"May I borrow it to look over the area?"

"No, ma'am, we can't let passengers go down there; they might get hurt in the working area of the ship. Also, you know, some passengers have been known to rummage through the stored luggage of others. Not that you would do that, of course."

"Of course not."

"When you bring your purchase back, just give it to your steward. He will get the key and stow it for you."

In a pig's eye he will.

Trust the steward, poppycock! He has already been bought and paid for by Lord Warton. Offering him money would only whet his appetite to get more from others.

So how will I get my hands on the key if I can't enlist the steward's help?

Speaking of the devil, on my way back to my cabin I find the steward at my door with a written message.

"A chit from Mr. Selous. The gentleman requests a response."

The note is an invitation to join him in an hour to see the British colony.

It is signed, "Your Devoted Admirer."

The steward holds out a pencil. "Does Madam wish to reply?"

"Yes." And "Yes" is what I write on the chit.

Interesting. An invitation from a man who I left on sudden—and no uncertain—terms after he tried to keep me from the Ismailia cable office. My suspicious nature doesn't fail to register that the ship's bulletin says there is a cable office in Aden.

Frederick Selous isn't a stupid man or a crude one. He would hardly try the same trick twice, at least not one I had flung in his face.

The excursion will offer me the opportunity to see what I can discover from him, and to find out if he is trying to get information for Lord Warton. Besides, while I find my attitude morally weak, I admit that I find Frederick Selous very attractive.

When I am not angry at him.

As I come onto the deck, I find the heat very strong and am glad I have selected my silk bodice rather than my heavy wool waist. With my hat and umbrella, I feel ready to risk the sun. It feels even hotter than in the canal area, perhaps because we have travelled fifteen hundred miles closer to the equator since we left Port Said.

I hesitate as I see the Wartons approaching Frederick Selous at the accommodation ladder. I'm behind them and they haven't noticed me yet.

"Going ashore, too?" Lord Warton asks Frederick.

Frederick looks past them at me and says, "Yes, I have offered to show Nellie a bit of Aden. I've been here several times."

Both Wartons turn at my approach. Lady Warton gives me a crocodile smile from behind her mesh veil. "Would you two mind if we shared a carriage? That way we can all benefit from Frederick's wealth of knowledge."

"Of course not," both of us mumble, and I flash her a smile that I hope doesn't reveal too plainly that I'd rather take a pair of Egyptian cobras as companions than her sour personality and her arrogant arse of a husband.

Frederick gives me an I-didn't-plan-this look and I smile forgiveness because I don't think he did. The luck of the draw, the boys in the newsroom would say, and we had drawn the black queen and the knave for this hand.

As we await our turn down the temporary gangplank strapped to the side of the ship, her ladyship gives me a sweet-and-sour smile—a poor attempt at showing a friendly disposition toward me. His lordship is gravely neutral, almost as if he expects some gesture from me.

Perhaps he thinks a peasant like me should kneel and kiss his signet ring.

NEAR THE PIER where we land are shops, a hotel, a post office, and a cable office. The actual town of Aden is five miles distant.

Lord Warton tells us that Aden was first occupied by his country to halt piracy, some of it from Somalia, in Africa across the Gulf. "It is now an important station to take on coal and water for the steam engines of ships."

Not able to prevent a display of childish behavior, I give a good stare at the cable office as we pass across the street from it.

Frederick pulls me away toward a row of street vendors selling everything from ivory trinkets to salted fish. I already know why he has drawn me away from the others—to chasten me for my cable-office antic.

"You are an impertinent young woman." He says it with a smile, in a tone that hints if not of approval, at least of respect.

"And you, sir, are a scoundrel. Your last invitation was a bald-faced scheme to keep me from a cable office."

"Guilty as charged. But the fact that you had the opportunity to send a cable, and did not, clearly shows that you have no motive to stir up trouble for my country. I apologize for my rudeness."

"I accept your apology. And since this is a free country, you won't attempt to stop me from going over to that cable office and sending one off, will you?"

"Of course not. It's a free country, as you say, and I would exercise my freedom to inform the local authorities that you are an agent provocateur stirring up a revolt against the crown. And you can spend the balance of your eighty days pacing around a prison cell."

"Mr. Selous—"

"Frederick."

"Mr. Selous, the more I am around you, the more I discover what it is about you that I like."

"Which is?"

"Nothing. Absolutely nothing. You have no redeeming social graces that appeal to me."

He takes my arm and steers me toward a table of books.

"Actually, knowing your feelings toward me, I was hesitant to offer an invitation. I worried that you would return my invitation with a well-deserved slap to my face."

"I'm taking a rain check on the slap."

"Of course, there is that one comment you made that cut me to the bone." He gives me a narrow look.

"Ah . . ." I know exactly what he is referring to—the accusation of being Lord Warton's lackey. "Well, was it the truth?"

He purses his lips for a moment. "Yes, I was urged on by his lordship, but I also felt it was the right thing to do at the time."

"Then I owe you no apology."

He takes my arm in a gentlemanly fashion. "Do you know what I like about you, Nellie?"

"I'm afraid to ask."

"Everything. Your smile, your wit, your courage, the way you start throwing punches to protect yourself. But if you will forgive a man who has spent his adult life battling the worst that Mother Nature and the animal world can throw at one, you have a fault."

"A fault? No!"

"Nellie, you only know how to throw punches. You have to learn how to duck once in a while, even run when the odds are too great."

"Mr. Selous—"

"Please call me Frederick." He shakes his index finger in my face. "If you argue with me, I will be forced to tell Lady Warton that you are in deep need of her maternal ministration and wish to spend the rest of the voyage at her side."

"Ouch! I would rather swim with the sharks in the bay." I immediately regret my unladylike comment but he merely nods and mutters, "Amen to that."

I buy a back-scratcher, a stick with a carved hand on the end, not for a keepsake from Aden but because it occurs to me that I would have a use for it later, something that whoever carved it never dreamed of.

He suddenly reaches for a book. "What's this?"

The title is *Handbook on Aden*.

"Interesting," he says. He gives the vendor a coin and we walk away, ignoring the man's jabber in Arabic, no doubt an insistence that the book was a family heirloom worth many times more. He tucks the book into an inside pocket.

"A guidebook?" I ask.

"In a way."

"A spy manual?"

It was a shot in the dark, based on the book I saw in Mr. Cleveland's effects.

He stops and gives me a grave look. "As I said, you don't know when to duck. You're right, it is a book prepared by the Intelligence Branch at the War Office. There is a handbook for every country and colony detailing the political, economic, and military state of the country."

"Does it contain secret information? For spies?" I ask.

"Not the stuff of troop movements and war plans, if that's what you mean, but the information in the books is considered confidential, to be read only by high-ranking Colonial and Foreign Office officials. And spies, I suppose, to gain familiarity with a country." He locks eyes with me. "I am not a spy, if that's what you're wondering, but I do have friends in the Colonial and Foreign Offices and they have made references to the books."

Leafing through the book, he says, "I doubt that there is anything in here that would blow the lid off of Aden, but nonetheless it belongs in the hands of our administrators, not the locals."

"How do you think it got into a pile of odds and ends?"

He raises his eyebrows and shrugs. "Theft by a servant? A wife disposing of household items when packing for a return to Britain not realizing it's confidential? Quite the thing that would ruin a man's career if discovered." He smiles. "Or even cause the loss of the kingdom. Do you remember what Richard III said after his horse fell in battle? My kingdom for a horse?" He chimes:

Because of the nail, the shoe was lost.
Because of the shoe, the horse was lost
Because of the horse, the rider was lost
Because of the rider, the battle was lost
Because of the battle, the kingdom was lost
All because of a horseshoe nail!

"All because a housewife discarded an old book," I add.

"Quite. So you saw a *Handbook of Egypt* when you searched Cleveland's room, making you believe he was a British agent."

The casual remark by Frederick catches me off guard and I take a moment to respond.

"Actually, the fact that he sneaked off the ship in the wee hours, ran around Port Said with a brown stain on his face, and tangled with Mahdi killers in the marketplace made it rather obvious that he was on a secret assignment."

"What else did you discover in his room that you haven't told me about?"

I raise my eyebrows. "I'm sure you know better than I do the contents of his cabin. I had only the briefest moment to look through his things and saw nothing of consequence." A lie, but necessary.

"I never saw his personal effects."

"Ahh . . ."

"There's that revelation from the gods again."

"So Lord Warton has not shared his booty with you?"

Frederick gives me a twisted grin. "No, he hasn't. The *Handbook of Egypt* was a guess on my part. His lordship acts as if the survival of the British Empire itself has been placed upon his shoulders. Frankly, he strikes me as a rather small man who has stumbled into a rather big mess and who sees himself as the general leading a charge to rout the enemy."

Lady Warton approaches, raising a curious eye as she sees me and Frederick strolling arm in arm, no doubt her way of showing she's aware of a romantic interest between the two of us, but she reminds me more of a grinning shark than a matchmaker.

Lady Warton and I wander away from the two men, walking next to the edge of a cliff that provides a view of our ship in the bay below. When we are out of hearing range of the men, she pauses and eyes native women coming down the road.

"He married one, you know," she says.

"Who?"

"Selous. He married an African native woman and had a child by her."

"Really?" It's all I can think to say. I'm not sure why she is sharing this personal information with me.

"He's not really British, you know."

"He isn't? He sounds like it."

"He was born in England, but his great-grandfather was a French Protestant, a Huguenot who fled persecution in Catholic France."

By my calculation that made Frederick at the minimum third- or fourth-generation British, depending on how one counted. He might be British going back centuries on the side of one parent.

Lady Warton gives me a sympathetic look but my impression is that of a vulture eyeing a piece of meat.

"You poor dear, you must still be suffering from that terrible incident at the marketplace."

"Oh, no, I've forgotten the whole thing. All behind me, I'm feeling just fine. Should we join the gentlemen?"

I don't give her a chance to answer because I need to get away from the cliff's edge. I am too tempted to give her a shove over it.

A great ball of anxiety rises in my stomach, threatening to shoot up into my throat.

Frederick lied to me about being married.

What else is he lying about?

En Route from Aden to Colombo

Tonight we have a lantern slide* exhibition that is very enjoyable. The loyalty of the British to their Queen on all occasions, and at all times, has won my admiration, and it is once again apparent during the show.

Though born and bred a staunch American, with the belief that a man is what he makes of himself, not what he is born, still I cannot help admire the undying respect the British have for their royal family.

During the lantern slide exhibition, the Queen's picture is thrown on the white sheet which evokes a warmer applause than anything else that evening.

We never have had an evening's amusement that does not end with everybody rising to their feet and singing "God Save the Queen."

I cannot help but think how devoted that woman, for she is only a woman after all, should be to the interests of such faithful subjects.

With that thought came to me a shameful feeling that here I am, a free-born American girl, the native of the grandest country on earth, forced to be silent because I cannot in all honesty speak proudly of the rulers of my land, unless I went back to those two kings of manhood, George Washington and Abraham Lincoln.

Nellie Bly, *Around the World in 72 Days*

* A lantern slide show was an early form of slide projection. The slides were glass plates upon which pictures were painted. The slide could tell a story or show exhibits of art, history, etc. Over time, a technique was developed to use transparent photos and the modern slide projector came into being. —The Editors

Magic is on the schedule tonight.

Magicians will take to the stage to perform their acts, and I will attempt some magic myself, in a more private location. I just hope the wizardry I have planned doesn't come back to bite me.

I deliberately planned my scheme for tonight because the next port is Colombo, Ceylon, where I will change ships for the Far East leg of my journey. Since I will be getting off the ship anyway, the captain won't be able to go through with his threat to strand me at a port. However, my plan is so audacious, I have to wonder if he might take punitive action while I'm still aboard. The captain's wrath only comes into play if I am caught, of course.

The risk is worth it because I'm running out of time to search Cleveland's possessions and unsure what Lord Warton will do with the materials once he has to change ships. The British mission at Colombo is much larger than the one at Aden; he has to take the items off the ship, so it seems Colombo would be an obvious place to dispose of them to officialdom unless he decides to hold on to them for some reason.

After the lights are turned down in the entertainment room and up on the stage, a magic team comes out and introduces themselves: Carolina Magnet, a woman billed as the "Strongest Woman on Earth," and her assistant, who we already know is her husband.

Her husband is the master of ceremonies for her act, informing us that she is the strongest woman in the world and will prove it to us with "tests of strength in which she pits herself against the strongest men aboard the ship."

Quite a claim since the woman doesn't appear to be a particularly large or muscular specimen of womanhood.

"Any volunteers, gentlemen?" the man asks. "We need three men true and strong from the audience for Carolina Magnet to test her strength against."

Three large men, two fellow passengers and the ship's second officer, are coaxed onto the stage.

Carolina Magnet grasps a cue stick, holding it up about neck level as the ship's officer is instructed to also take hold of the stick by the master of ceremonies. "Carolina Magnet," he bellows, "has the ability to use the mysterious power called 'magnetism' to create a force that makes it impossible to move her."

The man steps to the side so the audience can get a full view of the woman and the ship's officer facing off, each grasping the cue stick.

It is obvious to me that without a "trick" up the woman's sleeve, the man will easily push her back. But, of course, watching her succeed is the fun of it.

"If this manly officer is able to push the strongest woman on Earth back a step, he will have accomplished a feat that no man has succeeded at."

"The man will best her," a well-boozed male shouts from the audience.

The tug-of-war begins and the officer can't push her, no matter how hard he tries. It's as if the woman's feet are nailed to the floor. I lean forward, trying to get a look at her shoes, wondering if they bear some sticky material that keeps her from sliding back, but even if her shoes were nailed to the floor, the man would be able to push back her upper body, and he can't do it.

There's a hand of applause and the other two men attempt to push her back and fail also.

I'm really intrigued and my curiosity as usual is chomping at the bit for an answer. To ensure that I get one, I've placed myself at the same table as Von Reich and swore literally on a stack of Bibles beforehand that I would never reveal the secret of any conjuring he explained. I know his loyalty toward the world of magic evaporates whenever his ego is excited by a woman's plea.

"How does she do it?" I whisper. "Please, I'll die if I don't know."

He grins smugly as he leans close to whisper. "If she pushed toward the men and they pushed back at her, she would be easily defeated. Instead, she holds the stick high and as a man pushes forward toward her, she pushes *up* on the stick. It takes very little effort on her part to hold back the much greater strength of the men because she has deflected their force up, instead of against her."

"It's that easy?"

"We can do it with a broomstick later and you'll see. If you push up, I won't be able to push you backward."

"Now the incredible Carolina Magnet will demonstrate her ability to use the mysterious power of magnetism again, this time by lifting more than twice her weight," her husband informs us.

A large dumbbell atop a wheeled cart is rolled out on a platform. The dumbbell, an iron bar with a large ball of iron on each end, indeed looks hefty—each ball is the size of a large round melon. It's obvious from the squeaking of the wooden stage that a heavy weight is being rolled.

Once again three men are invited up on the stage. None of the men is able to lift the big dumbbell off the cart.

With a roll of drums from the ship's band, the woman who claims to be able to manipulate the powers of magnetism, a secret which confounds the greatest scientists in the world, steps up to the dumbbell and lifts it, to the amazement and applause of all except Von Reich.

"Child's play," he snorts. "The dumbbell is very light, but the cart holding it is very heavy. There's a hidden latch that keeps the dumbbell stuck to the cart. When the men pulled up on the dumbbell, they were actually attempting to also lift the cart, which weighs several hundred pounds. When it's her turn, she releases the latch and easily lifts the fake dumbbell off the cart."

In some ways, it's better not to know the secret of how it's done. But from my point of view, the most interesting conjuring was about to be performed—my own.

I slip out of the entertainment lounge when the next magician billed as a master of Chinese rings comes on stage. I'll find out later from Von Reich how the magician manages to loop what appears to be solid rings in and out of each other.

The ship is rocking a bit from a tropical blow and people are leaving with me, some already queasy, making my own exit natural.

The interior corridor of the main deck is deserted as I hurry down it.

Passengers are either watching the entertainment, or in their cabin, while the service crew has retired to get some shut-eye before their early morning chores.

The assistant purser is on duty behind the counter, looking bored and sleepy.

"How is the show going?" he asks.

"Amazing. A small woman bested three large men at shows of strength."

"How does she do it?"

I lean across the counter and whisper, "Mirrors, it's all done with mirrors."

"Amazing what they can do, making it look so real."

"Incredible, isn't it? I want to make sure the rug I purchased in Aden made it into the passenger storage compartment."

He removes a clipboard that hangs next to the key to the storage area on the wall behind him. He sets it on the counter and I put my hand on it.

"One more thing. You keep a record of cablegrams passed to passengers, do you not?"

"Yes, ma'am. We have a board in back on which we post all cablegrams sent over to the ship from cable offices along with the time and date delivered to passengers."

"I believe a cable has fallen through the cracks some time since I boarded at Brindisi. Would you please check?"

"That will take a moment, ma'am."

That's the idea. "Thank you. I'll wait. I'll check on my rug while you look at the cablegrams."

The moment he disappears into the back room, I unhook the clawed back-scratcher that I have hidden beneath my dress and belly up on the counter in a very unladylike pose.

Extending it as I lean across the counter, I hook the Passenger Luggage Compartment key ring and bring it back, sticking it in my pocket and then quickly flip through the luggage manifest, turning immediately to Port Said.

Lord Warton checked in three boxes the evening Mr. Cleveland was killed. I had been with him and his wife for almost the entire time they were in the city and had never seen them make a purchase.

The log shows the boxes are stored at B5-3.

The assistant purser returns, shaking his head. "Everything has been delivered to you, Miss Bly."

"Thank you, that's a relief."

"Did you find your rug?"

"No, but I just remembered it might still in my room. I'll give it to my steward in the morning."

A passenger is coming up to the desk and I quickly move away, leaving the ship's officer a bit perplexed and still sleepy-eyed. I've already decided how I will get the key back to him after I search the luggage compartment. I'll come up to the desk, suddenly stoop down, and rise up, holding the key ring in hand, exclaiming I found it on the floor.

A bit of sleight of hand.

I'd be in awe of my own cleverness except that my stomach is tied in knots because I'm scared half to death by the realization of what I had done—I stole a ship's key to enter a restricted area and am about to search boxes belonging to a peer of the British realm.

Completely batty, that's what I am, no doubt about it. My ten days in a madhouse must have turned me into a real lunatic. Why in God's name would I put myself in harm's way again?

The real question is why I have these moments of remorse only after I have done something completely insane.

30

My nerves are still on fire as I quickly go down flights of stairs to the utility deck.

Opening the door to the luggage hold, I fumble with my hand until I find a switch on the wall. I turn it and a single naked lightbulb hanging in the middle of the storage area goes on.

Thank God they have installed a newfangled electric light, a single dim bulb, but one that at least takes the edge off of the darkness. Too bad it doesn't take the edge off of my jangled nerves.

Slipping inside, I leave the door open just a hair and place the key on the inside of the lock, rather than take the risk of losing it.

"This is not going to be easy," I mutter, staring at the walls of luggage and boxes.

Storage areas are on both sides of the aisle, three tiers, with luggage and boxes stuffed four or five high in compartments of each tier. Each compartment is screened in by a floor-to-ceiling netting that keeps the items on the shelves in heavy seas. When I find the correct section, I will have to release its netting in order to get access to the items piled on the shelves.

Getting close enough and squinting, I quickly learn the numbering system. The two lines of storage areas split by the center aisle are A and B, respectively, with B being the one on my right. It begins with storage compartment labeled B1-1.

Going down the narrow, claustrophobic passageway, with luggage and boxes on each side straining back and forth against the netting like a great beast's innards as it breathes, makes me feel like Jonah inside the whale.

Finally reaching the section I'm looking for, I groan. B5-3 means the items are located on the third tier, access to which is obtained by a narrow ladder that a monkey would find challenging, less more a woman in a full dress with heeled shoes.

Similar to a tall stack ladder in a library, the ladder is rolled sideways along the floor to where you want to ascend, but book ladders don't move all by themselves and this one does, sliding back and forth as the ship plows into seas whipped up by the blow.

I'll probably break my neck. They'll find my crumpled body when they empty the hold at the next port. But there's no turning back; it's too late. I have no place to go but up, literally. I've crossed the Rubicon and don't even have Caesar's army to back me.

Somehow I manage to reach the third level, unhooking the netting as I go up, but I'm only halfway home. Luggage and boxes are piled two deep and three or four high in the space. The only saving grace is that the items are not piled completely to the top, permitting me to move some of them as I hang on to a sliding ladder, worrying that the whole shebang will come flying off the shelves with the violent roll of the ship.

If I hadn't boasted to myself about my cleverness in plotting this ransacking of the ship's luggage hold, I would abandon the project. Only stubborn pride and a lack of good sense keep me going.

With very dim lighting it's hard to see the numbers on the individual items, but there are only five boxes and three of them should be the ones that Lord Warton has stored.

Now I am in a dilemma. I can't get them down to the floor to search and bring them back up because they are too awkward and heavy. They will have to be searched on the tier and that is only going to happen if I have two hands free instead of one clutching a ladder rung while grabbing out with the other to keep the ladder from sliding.

As I shove and restack everything, I manage to separate the luggage enough to create a hole big enough for me to squeeze in and I find myself standing upright on the third tier, hot and sweaty and a little nauseated from the ship's motion as I hang on to the top box of a stack I want to go through.

Never never never again will I be so stupid.

Each box has twine tied tightly around it and I don't have a knife. I am angry enough to rip it off with my teeth.

Lacking both a blade and strong enough teeth, I use an object from my hair that women all over the world for centuries have found as handy as the tools of men: a hairpin.

With sheer stubborn determination I manage to untie the string, open the box, and find the books.

Removing the piece of paper with numbers written on it and the Yorkshire book of laws, I take turns holding each of them in the direction of the light to see the printing.

The first set of numbers lead me to the word "extreme" in the law book; the second sends a quiver down my spine: "danger."

Hanging on tight as the ship rolls, I quickly check the written number scheme for page, line, and word place, and find the word "for."

My knees tremble with so much excitement, I'm ready to collapse.

As I'm reading the fourth set of numbers, I hear voices and the door opens. Petrified, I freeze in place.

"Here it is! In the door. You must have left the key here the last time you brought down luggage."

It's the purser, chewing out his assistant.

"But, sir, I would swear—"

The ship rolls again and I let out a startled yelp.

"Who's there?" the purser snaps.

The two men are sent staggering against the compartment to their left as the ship rolls again. The stack of boxes I'm using for support go and I throw myself deeper into the compartment to keep from being flung off the tier by the motion of the ship.

The ship pauses for a moment at the end of its roll and then starts to roll again in the opposite direction.

Frantically I grab at luggage as everything around me begins sliding off the shelves—*no longer restrained because I had removed the netting.*

Unable to keep my balance and with nothing left to hold on to, I follow the avalanche down, screaming bloody murder.

With thirty years experience at sea, from stoking the boiler to raising the sails and commanding the entire ship, I can tell you that despite any old sailors' tales, a woman is not bad luck at sea."

The captain is leaning back in his swivel chair, staring up at the ceiling as if he is expecting a missive from heaven.

Sitting perfectly still, I stare straight ahead, my hands in my lap . . . waiting for lightning to strike.

He leans forward and shifts a little to meet my eye but I turn away.

"Madam, my officers suggest that perhaps now there is something to the connection between women and bad luck aboard, but I reject that contention because you are not bad luck, you are a regular Medusa, worse than the plagues God threw at the Egyptians."

The purser and first officer are standing behind me, shaking with smothered laughter.

I just cringe. I know my face is flaming red and I am so angry that I have to struggle to keep my composure—not angry at the captain or the ship's officers, but at myself. I have made a complete fool out of myself. *Again.*

"Well, what do you think, gentlemen? What shall we do with the young woman who has disobeyed the laws of the sea?"

"Keelhaul her, Captain," the first officer says.

The captain leans forward in a pretense of gravity. "Do you know what keelhauling is, young woman? We run a line from one side of the ship to the other and tie an end of it around the miscreant. We then throw him into the sea and pull him back aboard . . . only we pull from the opposite side we threw him over so he is dragged under the keel, his flesh rubbed off by the rough barnacles that attach to the keel."

If this charade is not gotten over with soon, I will scream. There will be no punitive action against me except the one I dread the most—humiliation.

A pretty picture I must have made, flying off the tier and onto a mountain of luggage and boxes.

I'm mortified and so embarrassed at making a fool of myself. I will never go back out on deck where people can see me, never into the dining room, I will have to take meals in my room. Or drown myself.

What bothers me most of all is the dishonor I have brought to the death of Mr. Cleveland.

"Keelhauling is too harsh for a woman's delicate skin, Captain," the purser says. "I say we put her in irons and throw her—"

I leap out of my chair and push by the two officers and flee, their laughter flying at me faster than I can move.

Frederick is in the corridor outside the office and I rush by him, breaking into a run.

"Nellie! Wait!"

I shake my head without turning back and hurry to the stairway to my deck. Thank God it is late and there is no one in the corridor. I will throw myself overboard if anyone sees me running like a dog with my tail between my legs.

Not bothering to knock, I fly into Sarah's dark stateroom, pouring light in from the corridor behind me.

Her coffin lid is open and she sits upright, startled. Her face is covered with cold cream, her creamed hands are in gloves, her hair soaked in some other cream and bundled under a shower cap.

"What are you doing?"

"They've beaten me!" I wail.

"Who?"

"Warton, Frederick, the British Empire!"

"Well . . . that certainly narrows it down."

I cry for the damage I did to John Cleveland. And Nellie Bly.

"Nellie—"

"No, not Nellie, my real name is Elizabeth Cochran. Nellie Bly is the name of a reporter. I'm nothing, just a factory girl who thought she knew everything."

32

Lord Warton stalks back and forth, glaring at the pile of luggage and boxes that fill the end of the Passenger Luggage Compartment aisle.

He whips around and demands from the captain, "Well, where are they?"

The captain and the first officer look to the assistant purser, who squirms under their stares.

"The books were here," he says, "fell out of a box Miss Bly had opened before she took her tumble. When everything came off the shelves, the box dumped its contents. I saw them right there." He points to an empty spot on the floor. "Three books, scattered about along with some papers."

"If they were here," Lord Warton yells, "where are they now? I demand you search the room of that troublemaking reporter."

"She was with us when the books went missing," the captain answers. "Someone took them when my officer went to find crewmen to clean up the mess."

"Who? Who took them?"

The captain gives Lord Warton a tight grin that says he has had about enough with the man's demands. "Sir, obviously I don't know, but I suggest that in order to find out who, we start with *why*. What's the importance of these books?"

"You told me the woman said there were writings in a secret code," Lord Warton says, directing the statement at the assistant purser.

"That's what Miss Bly claimed when we got her untangled from the mess she created," the man responds.

"What secret was she talking about?" the captain asks Lord Warton.

"It is a matter of national security to which you do not have privity."

The captain looks to his officers. "Well, gentlemen, then I suggest none of us lose any more sleep about a matter to which *we* don't have privity."

"You!"

I let go of the handle to my cabin door as if it is a hot poker and whip around in surprise.

Lord Warton is the source of the exclamation.

"You are in deep trouble, young woman; more than you can imagine."

"I beg your pardon."

"Name your coconspirator, the one who took Cleveland's books, or I shall have you arrested."

"I don't know what you're talking about."

"You know exactly what I am talking about. You told the assistant purser that those books contained a code. I demand you turn them over to me so they can be given to the proper authorities at Colombo."

I'm speechless, not because of his demand but because it means he was unaware of the secret writing. I'm also not going to be bullied.

"I don't have the books and didn't even know they are missing. But now that you've explained the matter, I can see your problem."

"*Your* problem, you mean."

"No, sir, I'm not the one who appointed myself custodian of Mr. Cleveland's possessions. I'll leave it to you to explain to the authorities how you stored them in a *public* place and now cannot find them."

I slip into my room, throw the latch, and lean back against the door, breathless.

I can't believe Warton didn't know the numbers were a code. So why did he have the contents of Cleveland's luggage repacked into boxes and go through the charade of having the cases sent ashore?

In a strange way, I am greatly relieved, even elated to hear that someone has nicked the books. It validates my contention that they contain a secret.

I don't think the captain and his chumps will be laughing so hard now that they know I was on a serious quest. But I also find it strange that the captain had been amused rather than angry.

Completely exhausted and worn to the bone, my knees are wobbly as I shuffle to my bunk. I had talked with Sarah for over an hour and she had set me right about myself by telling me what she had gone through early in her own quest to establish a career.

When she was still a teenager and had ambitions to be an actress, her mother had pushed her into being a courtesan, literally providing "favors" to wealthy men in order to get acting roles.

She acquired roles, but they came with contempt from other stage players who were less fortunate. "And less talented," Sarah said. Ultimately, her God-given talent had won the day and the path she took for her first steps has been overshadowed by the universal proclaim of her talent.

"But along with success comes challenge," she told me. "You will never stop having to prove yourself."

Her story is a good reminder to me. I have always believed that the only course to be taken when I'm knocked to the ground is to get back up and fight. Perhaps Frederick is right, I don't know how to duck, I only know how to throw punches, but some of those punches land as one did tonight.

I had assumed that my adversary aboard is the British lord, who I now discover is in fact as inept at being a spymaster as he no doubt was instructing Moroccan farmers on how to grow wheat. Frederick basically told me that was his take on Warton, too.

The same person who searched my room for the key had taken the books, and it is someone who knows enough about my movements to allow them to slip in and steal the books in the wake of the chaos I have left behind.

A person hidden in shadows, one diabolical step ahead of me, all the way.

Someone I know and trust?

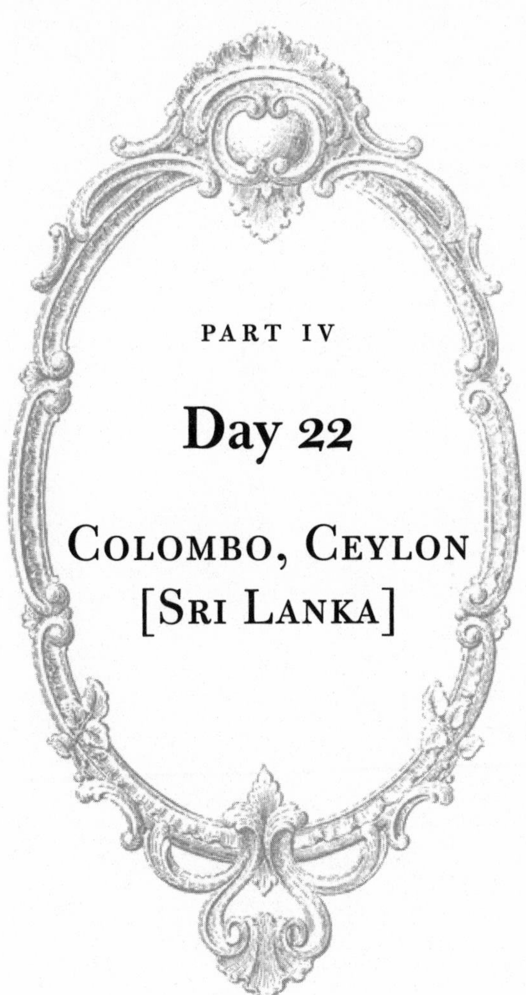

PART IV

Day 22

Colombo, Ceylon [Sri Lanka]

We steam into the bay at Colombo, Ceylon, on a bright day.

The large island of Ceylon is close to the southern tip of India, with the Indian Ocean stretching landless for thousands of miles to Australia and the Antarctic in the south.

I have to stay in the city for several days before I board the ship that will take me to the Far East. After checking into a hotel, my plan is to find the cable office and send a story back to my editor in New York. That cablegram won't contain anything about the incident in Port Said or my trials and tribulations since that will be written when I have the full story, but a second cable I send will concern the matter—a query to the paper's London correspondents for information about a cutlery salesman named John Cleveland.

Standing by with other passengers, I wait patiently for the ship to drop anchor. Once again, the bay is too shallow for our ship to reach the dock and we must be ferried ashore. A number of steam launches are already coming out to meet us.

With its abundance of green trees, the island appears restful and pleasing to my eyes after the spell of sweltering heat we had passed through on the Arabian Sea coming from Aden. The shoreline is dotted with low, arcaded buildings, which look, in the glare of the sun, like marble palaces.

Forming the background to the town is a high mountain called Adam's Peak. A man standing beside me explains there is a tradition in Ceylon that Adam and Eve were banished to the island paradise after they were cast out of Eden, and are buried here.

"The beautiful blue sapphires found on the island are the tears of

Adam and Eve that crystallized as they wept after being banished from the garden."

A charming anecdote and I make a note, as I did the link of Cain and Abel to Aden.

The beach, with a forest of tropical trees, looks as if it starts in a point out in the sea, curving around until it forms into a blunt point near the harbor, the line of which is carried out to sea by a magnificent breakwater surmounted by a lighthouse.

The land curves back again to a point where a signal station stands, and beyond that a wide road runs along the water's edge until it is lost at the base of a high green eminence that stands well out over the sea, crowned with a castlelike building glistening in the sunlight.

When I looked in on Sarah earlier to see if she wanted to accompany me to shore, her door was half open and she was pacing furiously, cold cream on her face, a cablegram in hand while her steward was packing a steamer trunk.

The pilot boat had delivered cables to the ship before the ship entered the bay.

She angrily waved the cablegram at me. "They will not force me to run for cover with their stupid threat!"

"What threat?"

She immediately drew back, tucking the message into a pocket of her dressing gown. "It's nothing, a small problem with a role I am to play." She whipped around and glared at the steward. "Much more important is what I shall do with this cretin. He has damaged my best hat with his sloppy packing."

"I dropped by to see if you wanted to go to the hotel together."

"I'll meet you at the hotel. If I am able to get off this ship with my possessions and mind intact."

I wondered about the cablegram as I went back out onto the deck and got in line to go ashore. A threat from her lover's family? What sort of threat would one send by cablegram?

Besides the cable and damage to her hat, it seems Sarah has another good reason for having a black day. Because we have to stay ashore, she must leave the sanctuary of her stateroom for a hotel—not a significant problem for most travelers, but no doubt fraught with complications for a woman who travels with a coffin.

I consider myself a well-seasoned traveler, but I would be hard-pressed to check into a hotel with a coffin, in Colombo or anywhere else in the world, yet Sarah appears more daunted by the condition of her favorite hat than the reaction that can be anticipated from hotel staff. Then again, there is a great deal of sheer drama in the mere notion of checking into a hotel with a coffin, and as the greatest actress in the world, she is a master of melodrama.

I will leave the *Victoria* with the only regret that the steamship *Oriental*, which will take me to China, is not prepared to sail yet because it awaits the arrival of a ship from Australia with passengers. Getting away from the bad service, poor food, and the looks I get from officers and crew will be a relief.

Colombo is a jumping-off point for ports in India, Australia, and New Zealand, besides the Far East. Thank God, most *Victoria* passengers will not be joining me to China.

However, I will not leave behind my reputation as an agent provocateur when I transfer ships: From prior conversations, I already know that the Wartons, Herr Von Reich, Frederick Selous, and many others will also be on the *Oriental*, and on the same ship as I am crossing the Pacific to San Francisco.

Each day of delay in Colombo will weigh heavily on me, but at least it will be spent in what I am told is one of the most beautiful places on Earth.

I am mulling over Sarah's reaction to the cablegram and wishing the slow-moving steam launches would move faster because the line to get ashore is a long one, when Frederick is suddenly beside me.

"If you're game for a little adventure, I can get you to the hotel while most of the passengers are still waiting to get ashore."

He catches me by surprise. He no doubt believes that I have deliberately avoided him since the fiasco over my search of the luggage hold, but it had come before that, in Aden when Lady Warton told me that he was married.

I am still contemplating my reply when he takes my arm and pulls me along.

"You'll have plenty of time to tell me what a cad I am on our way to shore. Your other option is to let everyone get ahead of you and book the best rooms at the hotel before you get there."

"You treated me callously by not rising to my defense," I tell him, as he leads me by the arm to a gangplank the crew is utilizing to unload luggage.

"I kept you out of the brig."

"I'm certain there is no brig on board this ship."

"True, but the captain had planned to lock you in your cabin."

"What!" I try to stop but he pulls my arm to keep me moving. "He wouldn't have dared."

"Perfectly within his right after the books went missing."

He gives me another pull along as I try to pause and defend myself. "The captain thought the whole matter was a joke."

"Only after I spoke to him and pointed out it would be wiser to laugh about it than have it appear a serious matter in his report to his home office."

"So you told him I was a clown?"

"Would you rather I told him you were a felon?"

"I'd rather you go to hell."

He gives me a sharp look. "Is that any way for a lady to talk?"

"If I wasn't a lady, I'd tell you what I really think of you, *Mr. Selous*."

"Frankly, *Miss Bly*, you should be thanking me. My biggest fear was not what the captain would do, but what would be told to the authorities after we docked. I'm sure you realize you could be arrested."

"Nonsense." But I suspect he's right.

"Don't worry," he says, "I've spoken to both the captain and Warton. Neither wants to have a chat with the authorities that will expose them as having been bested by a woman reporter, and having lost valuable materials."

I find myself once again vacillating between having warm feelings for this man—and deep distrust. I don't know what to expect from him. He lies to me, then protects me. Slams me down and lifts me up. Makes me grit my teeth one moment, then makes me want to snuggle up to him the next.

We pause at the top of the gangplank and I stare down at the cluster of odd-looking boats below.

"We are going ashore . . . *in one of those*?"

"We will if we don't drown."

The boats are awkwardly shaped, rudely constructed things, with a sitting area probably five feet in length and two feet in width across the widest part, narrowing down to the keel, until it is not wide enough to allow one's feet to rest side by side in the bottom. There are two seats in the middle, facing one another. The seats are shaded by a bit of coffee sack that must be removed to give room for passengers to get in.

A native sits with a paddle at each end of the peculiar boat. The paddle is a straight pole, with a board the shape and size of a cheese-box head tied to the end of it.

Too narrow to sit upright in the water without support, the little vessels are balanced by a log the length of the boat that is fastened by two curved poles that extend out three feet from the boat.

At the bottom of the gangplank, I step into one of these boats as gracefully as an elephant climbing into a bathtub, certain that I will end up swimming to shore.

When we are settled in, the oarsmen paddle rapidly. Unlike rowing a canoe, both paddles are used on the same side. We cut through the water at an amazing pace, passing steam launches that chug along.

"What do they call these things?" I ask Frederick.

"The locals call them catamarans, though tourists call them outriggers. Native fishermen consider them so seaworthy, they take them out to sea. I'm told that they are so secure against capsizing, no sinking has ever been reported."

On the dock, he guides me past the line of carriages awaiting passengers still to be deposited from the slow-moving steam launches.

"Carriages are slow on the crowded streets," he says.

He takes me to a line of two-wheeled carts with tops that can be raised to protect against rain. The carts resemble sulkies, the light, one-horse carriages designed to carry a single person, only the horsepower for these carts are human—short, small-built men.

With a little rough English and sign language, the first driver in line insists he can carry both of us. I'm not disagreeable about the notion of being pressed up against a handsome man with startling blue eyes, but I don't want the poor laborer injured.

"Are you sure he can pull us both?"

"The wiry build of Sinhalese men is deceiving. They're all muscle. They call these carts *jinrikisha*, shortened to 'rickshaw' by the rest of us."

As in all these hot countries, the men wear very little clothing and the *jinrikisha* men are no different—they wear little else than a groin sash, though their hats are broad affairs that remind me of big mushrooms.

The lovely castlelike structure I had seen from the ship was the Grand Oriental Hotel. Seeing it close up did not lessen its elegance.

After we step out of the rickshaw, Frederick asks, "Will you join me for a cool drink after we check in?"

I hesitate but give him a "Yes."

"Followed by lunch?"

"If I am still speaking to you. I don't think I like you very much."

"I don't blame you. I don't like myself much, either."

I wave away his attempt at humor with my hand. "Why didn't you tell me you were married?"

"Ah, yes, I see, a little gossip from her ladyship?"

"The source is not important. The fact that you are a barefaced liar is."

"You asked if I was married, I told you truthfully that I am not. Had you asked whether I had ever been married, I would have told you the truth, that yes, I had been. My wife passed away. She was African and was taken by one of those fevers that seem to come suddenly out of nowhere and leave a path of death behind it. I have a son in school from that union."

"I'm sorry. For your loss and for my rudeness."

Two things weigh heavily on my mind as I make my way to the front desk. Will Frederick change his mind and put the police on me if he finds out about the Cleveland cablegram I plan to send? That thought is coupled with an insight about the disappearance of Cleveland's books and code.

Frederick proved to me that he knew the importance of the handbook when he showed concern and ransomed one in Aden. But Cleveland had gone far beyond just a handbook. Yet Frederick showed little concern when he talked about the missing books.

He must have stolen the books.

Now he has gone out of his way to keep me from of the hands of the police.

Why? Is he trying to help me? Or does he have something worse up his sleeve?

34

I check in first before Frederick and wander a bit, looking over the hotel as I wait for him.

The Grand Oriental is a fine, large hotel, with tiled arcades and airy and comfortable corridors, furnished with easy chairs and small marble-topped tables which stand close enough to the broad armrests for one to sip the cooling lime squashes or the exquisite native tea or to enjoy the delicious fruit while resting in an attitude of ease and laziness.

I have found no place away from America where smoking is prohibited, and in this lovely promenade the men smoke, consume gallons of whiskey and soda, and peruse the newspapers, while the women read their novels or bargain with the pretty little copper-colored women who come to sell dainty handmade lace, or with the clever, high-turbaned merchants who snap open little velvet boxes and expose, to the admiring gaze of the charmed tourists, the most bewildering gems.

My wide eyes see deeply dark emeralds, fire-lit diamonds, exquisite pearls, rubies like pure drops of blood, the lucky cat's-eye with its moving line, and all set in such beautiful shapes that even the men, who would begin by telling the vendors, "I have been sold before by some of your kind," would end by laying down their cigars and papers and examining the glittering ornaments that tempt all alike.

"I could take up permanent residence here," I tell Frederick when he joins me in the lobby.

I immediately plop down on a large lounge chair, feeling wonderfully lazy, sipping a lime squash, while Frederick enjoys a cold beer and a fine cigar.

He is both intriguing and attractive, when I'm not annoyed at him. I have met men like him before, men of the West who live by the gun—shooting buffalo and bears of course, not lions and elephants. Generally, they are hardened, solitary souls, rough-hewed in all aspects, who prefer the companion of prairie dogs over humans.

Frederick, though, is a cultured gentleman. Educated at prestigious Rugby, he told me that he had prepared to become a lawyer before abandoning law for stomping through the jungle, facing dangers, and treading where no European or American has ever been.

When I am with him my suspicions melt and I feel warm and comfortable, even a sense of freedom, feelings I don't often get with men. Too often a man tries to pigeonhole me into a role as helpmate, a sex mate, or a kitchen maid—anything but an independent woman with a career.

Frederick nods toward a high-turbaned merchant who has snapped open little velvet boxes and exposed all types of jewelry to guests seated nearby. "You'll find that most of the jewelry bought and sold in Colombo is sold in the corridor right here, in the Grand Oriental Hotel. It's much pleasanter than visiting the shops."

"I heard on the ship that the gems in Colombo are a good value."

"Quite so. No woman who lands at Colombo ever leaves until she adds several rings to her jewelry box, and these rings are so well known that the moment a traveler sees one, no difference in what part of the globe, he says to the wearer, inquiringly, 'Been to Colombo, eh?' Let's get him over to show his wares."

"Sounds like fun, but I can't afford it, nor can I add anything to my valise—there's no space."

"Then, you can add it to your finger or around your neck so your case remains unburdened." He holds up his hand to quell my objection. "I know I have been a bore and cad toward you. I want to make it up to you."

I catch my breath. This gorgeous man is going to buy me a gem. I would love a blue sapphire to match his dazzling eyes.

He turns to call over the gem merchant when a woman so beautiful that she puts to shame the sparkling rubies and sapphires of Ceylon glides toward us.

Frederick pauses in mid-motion, freezing in place, and gawks as if the Queen of Sheba has entered.

"Oh there you are, Nellie dear." Sarah flutters her handkerchief at me. She is not wearing her netted veil, but has it in her hand. "I was worried that we'd end up at different hotels."

"Good heavens!"

The exclamation comes from Frederick. It was a shout, but one that was barely audible, a shouted whisper, hoarse and full of awe, surprise, and amazement.

I hear his quiet exclamation loud and clear, and I know exactly what the next words will be.

"Sarah Bernhardt!"

A man of the world, cultured and educated, would no doubt have seen her on the stage in London and Paris. His tone is that of a love slave worshipping a goddess.

The gem merchant gives me a look and I shake my head, sending him away.

Like all men who have gazed upon the Divine Sarah, Frederick's mind was gone, destroyed, no longer capable of rational thought or action. At the moment Frederick wouldn't remember to buy me a lump of coal if I was freezing.

Scrunching back, I shrivel up, tucking in my chin, clutching my arms to my body, curling my fists, feeling small and gawky, an ugly duckling in the presence of a graceful swan.

35

We part for our rooms to unpack and freshen up with an invitation for Sarah and me to join Frederick in two hours for *tiffin*, which he tells us is the name for lunch on the Indian subcontinent.

The invite places me in the awkward position of grinning and bearing the fact that I must share his attention with one of the most desirable women in the world . . . or sulk in my room.

I graciously accept rather than succumb to my lower instincts and appear petty and jealous.

After a cool, refreshing bath, I dress hastily and leave my room. I have an errand to run and need to get it done before I meet them for lunch.

I decide a rickshaw will get me to my destination faster than pedaling my feet.

There is a definite scent as we move along the street, and it is not the city making it. Besides dressing in nothing but a sash around their private parts, these rickshaw drivers cover themselves in an oil or grease. When the day is hot and they run and sweat, one wishes they were wearing more clothing and less oil! The grease has an original odor that is entirely its own.

I have a shamed feeling about going around the town in a cart drawn by a man, but after I have gone a short way, it occurs to me that this work is the way the man earns an income to feed his family.

The roads I've seen are perfect. I can't decide, to my own satisfaction, whether the smoothness of the road is due to the entire and blessed absence of beer wagons, or to the absence of the New York street commissioners.

My destination is the local newspaper office at which I find two clever young Scots who run both of the city's newspapers. They are quite excited by the story of my trip and ask many questions.

Inquiring about news coming out of Egypt, I'm told that there have been reports of murderous attacks by Mahdi terrorists but no mention of one in a Port Said marketplace, and I do not pursue the subject further.

When it is time for me to leave, I put into action my plan of deceit.

Knowing that the newspapermen are in constant touch with the local cable office, I pass them the draft of my cables and money to cover the transmissions to my editor in New York and to the London correspondent of the *World*. "Could I get you to send these off for me?" I ask sweetly. "I am tied up this afternoon . . ."

They kindly take charge of the dispatches, promising to cable them as soon as possible.

The New York message contains a brief summary of events since I left Port Said, omitting any reference to the attempts on my life or the incident in the marketplace; the London cable asks the correspondent for information about cutlery salesman John Cleveland and a background check.

I request a reply to Hong Kong since that would provide time for a thorough check.

Now I don't have to worry about being followed to the cable office or being treated like an agent provocateur.

As I make my way back for *tiffin*, I leave the rickshaw a few blocks from the hotel so I might enjoy the exotic sights on the streets, especially the snake charmers. They are almost naked fellows, sometimes with ragged jackets on and sometimes turbans on their heads, but more often the head is bare. They execute a number of tricks in a very skillful manner.

The most wonderful of these tricks, to me, is that of growing a tree. They show a seed, then place the seed on the ground and cover it with a handful of earth. They cover this little mound with a handkerchief, which they first pass around to be examined, that we might be positive there is nothing hidden in it.

Over this they chant, and after a time the handkerchief is taken off and having appeared up through the ground is a green sprout.

Those of us gathered around look at it incredulously, while the performer says, "Tree no good; tree too small," and covering it up again he renews his chanting. Once more he lifts the handkerchief and we see the sprout is larger, but still it does not please the trickster, for he repeats, "Tree no good; tree too small," and covers it up again.

This is repeated until he has a tree several feet high. Then he pulls it up, and shows us the seed and roots.

Then the trickster asks if we want to "see the snake dance?"

I say that I would, but that I will pay to see the snake dance and for nothing else.

All of us take steps back as the man lifts the lid of a basket, and a cobra crawls slowly out, curling itself up on the ground.

Like its Egyptian cousin, this is one of the deadliest creatures on Earth, yet the snake charmer moves casually about it, as if he's dealing with a harmless garden snake.

The "charmer" begins to play on a little fife. The serpent rises up steadily, its neck fanning as it darts angrily at the flute, rising higher at every motion until it seems to stand on the tip end of its tail.

The snake suddenly darts for the man, but in a flash he cunningly catches it by the head and with such a grip that I see the blood gush from the snake's month.

He works for some time, still firmly holding the snake by the head before he can get it into the basket, the reptile meanwhile lashing the ground furiously with its tail.

When at last the snake is covered from sight, I draw a long breath, and the charmer says to me sadly: "Cobra no dance, cobra too young, cobra too fresh!"

Quite right; the cobra is too fresh!

I generously tip the charmer for the sake of his family. I suspect snake charming is not an occupation with a bright future.

"Aren't you going to ask me how the trick is done?"

Von Reich gives me a grin. I hadn't seen him approaching.

"This one is obvious, isn't it? The snake sways to the music—"

He is already shaking his head. "It cares nothing for the music. It's the motion of the flute that the snake is following. Cobras are used because they seem to get transfixed by the motion and are relatively slow moving when they strike, at least compared to other snakes. That one was too young; it needs to be housebroken, so to speak."

"Are you staying at the Grand Oriental?" I ask as we walk in the direction of the hotel.

"No, unfortunately, a lesser establishment. By the time I arrived, all the rooms were taken. I did not have the benefit of a seasoned traveler in these parts racing me to shore."

I let the remark fly by without retort, but praise the Lord that the Wartons are probably not at my hotel, either.

The Viennese gentleman strokes his long golden mustache and gives me a look out of the corner of his eye as we walk.

"I am hurt, Fräulein, that you find the company of that English hunter much more pleasant than mine."

"Not at all. I have accepted Mr. Selous's overtures a few times because you have been busy romancing every available woman on board. Not to mention some who are supposed to be *unavailable.*"

He gives me a small chuckle. "I am merely trying to give a little companionship to lonely women."

"Some of these lonely women I see you flirting with have husbands."

"I'm doing their husbands a favor, too. They can enjoy their cigars and brandy, and I can enjoy their wives."

He gets a big laugh out of his own wit and I join him.

"Well, at least you are honest about your evil intentions." I decide to go on a fishing trip. "Did, uh, Lord Warton tell you that he made some rather nasty allegations against my character?"

"Little mention is made of you around his lordship because he tends to go into a fit of apoplexy whenever your name is spoken."

Another roar of laughter from him.

"You understand, of course," I say, "I am entirely innocent of wrongdoing."

"Of course you're *not* innocent, at least to him. He believes you are a nosy newspaper reporter who is determined to stick her nose into a controversy over who will keep control of that ditch that connects the Mediterranean to the Red Sea."

"And what do you believe?"

"I believe you have a very pretty nose. And that it is going to get cut off if you keep sticking it in places where you shouldn't."

Arriving back at the hotel, I find Sarah and Frederick waiting at the dining room door. They are engrossed in conversation like old friends.

Putting on my bravest smile, I let him guide us to the dining room, determined not to reveal my feelings of jealousy and inadequacy, emotions

I hate and would not reveal in public even if I was suffering the infamous Chinese torture of a thousand cuts.

"I've stayed here before," Frederick says. "The food is very good."

"Then you should order for us," Sarah says. "We will be helpless, otherwise."

Oh my God—she really knows how to warm the cockles of a man's heart. Her veil is back on. Too bad she hadn't worn it earlier. Even worse luck, it would have been nicer if she had missed out like Von Reich at getting a room at the hotel.

Petty, petty, petty . . .

The dining hall is pleasant in its coolness, interesting in its peculiarities, and matches the other parts of the hotel with its picturesque stateliness. The small tables are daintily set and are beautifully decorated daily with the native flowers of Colombo, rich in color, exquisite in form, but void of perfume, which I personally like. I don't know why, but many perfumes give me a headache. I believe it's a quirk I acquired from my mother, who never wore perfume, complaining it gave her a headache.

Frederick explains the cooling system. "Those strips of cloth are called *punkahs.* They are an invention of the people in this hot climate of the subcontinent."

The embroidered *punkahs* are long strips of cloth, fastened to bamboo poles that are suspended within a short distance of the tables. They are kept in motion by rope pulleys, worked by men and boys. They send a lazy, cooling air through the building, contributing much to the ease and comfort of the guests.

As Sarah asks Frederick a question about the beautiful breakwater we had seen from the ship, I look around, soaking in the atmosphere and the scent of exotic foods.

The people of this tropical island are pleasant and polite, being small of stature and fine of feature, with very attractive, clean-cut faces, light bronze in color.

The hotel waiters wear white linen apronlike skirts and white jackets. Noiselessly they move over the smooth tile floor, in their bare, brown feet. Their straight black hair is worn long, twisted in a Psyche knot at the back of the head, though that coil of hair is a woman's hairdo fashion in America and Europe.

My reverie about the beautiful people and food on the picturesque island is interrupted by an exclamation and a clap of Sarah's hands.

"I'd be delighted," she says.

"After dinner about nine would be the right time to head out," Frederick says to me.

"Sorry . . . I was thinking about something."

"There's a magic show tonight I'm sure you both would enjoy. And Sarah wants to see the famous breakwater. We can stop there on the way to the show."

"Why don't you two—" I begin, my feeling like a sore thumb taking over.

"You must come," Frederick says. "It's a once-in-a-lifetime opportunity to see a performance of the world's greatest magic trick."

"Please, Nellie, it'll be such fun."

"All right."

The only thing stronger than my jealousy is my curiosity—and dread of being left out of anything. My mother says she never deprived me of anything as a child, but perhaps my fear of being left out came from being a young child in a family of thirteen children.

While climbing the steps to return to my room, a thought pops into my head, filling in a blank that I wasn't even aware was there.

Sarah wore her veil to lunch.

She always wears her veil in public.

But not when she met Frederick and me in the lounge area. She had it in her hand.

Why would someone who is so easily recognizable have taken off her veil?

Finally, a question to which I have a ready answer.

She wanted to be recognized by Frederick.

But why would she want him to recognize her?

36

Sarah's cablegram.

The answer to Sarah not wearing a veil when we first met at the hotel came to me when I tried to nap before dinner.

She had revealed herself to Frederick because of the cablegram.

Stupid threat, she had said. A physical one? One that would make her seek out the friendship of a well-known hunter for protection?

Threats of bodily harm are not sent by cable—the message had to be more subtle than that—but from her anger, there is no doubt that the contents were meant to intimidate her. Certainly it infuriated her and drove her to make contact with Frederick.

I mentally draw a line connecting the cast of characters, as Sarah would call them: Frederick has a connection to Cleveland . . . now Sarah has a connection to Frederick. Did that mean Sarah has a connection to Cleveland?

Sarah's friendship isn't a safe harbor for me. She's part of the intrigue that began in the marketplace and that still touches me, reaching out from Port Said like the tentacles of Jules Verne's giant squid.

I never have been comfortable with the notion of there being two separate intrigues aboard, but making a connection between a love affair of the famous French actress, a fanatical religious uprising in Egypt, and the intrigues of great nations over control of the vital Suez Canal, threaten my small brain with a big headache.

Since any kind of rest is futile, I pull myself off the bed. Maybe a leisurely bath will relax me for the evening that I will spend with a beautiful actress who obviously has an interest in the same man I do.

After viewing myself in the mirror, I decide that the only way I could get Frederick to notice me when Sarah is present would be to throw myself in front of an oncoming train. And then it would only be the sound of the train's horn that directs his attention to my mangled body. . . .

Frederick and Sarah are waiting for me at the carriage stand in front of the hotel when I come out.

I keep a blank face but I find the way they stand and talk interesting for its sheer subtlety. Rather than standing face-to-face as one would when conversing with an acquaintance, they each face slightly away from one another, almost as if they don't want anyone to know they are talking. A casual observer might not even realize they knew each other. Or had been talking.

Why the charade? What are they up to?

We board a carriage and set out. From the number of people on the streets, it seems that everybody at the hotel and the city at large has come out for a drive, the women and many of the men going bare-headed as a cool evening breeze sweeps in.

When we are out of sight of other Europeans, Sarah takes off her netted hat to get the full benefit of the light breeze. She looks rather young for a woman who became an actress probably about the time I was born. It makes me wonder how old she is. I am twenty-two years old and I suspect she must be a decade past that.*

The carriage takes us at a leisurely pace through the town, down the wide streets, past beautiful homes set well back in tropical gardens. We go along Galle Face Drive that runs along the beach just out of reach of the waves that break on the sandy banks with a deeper mellow roar than I have ever heard water produce.

"We're going to the breakwater," he says, "Sarah wants to see the dedication plaque."

The breakwater, which is a good half mile in length, is a favorite promenade for the citizens of Colombo, he tells us. "Morning and evening, gaily dressed people can be seen walking back and forth between the lighthouse and the shore. When the stormy season comes the sea dashes a full forty

* Sarah is forty-five years old, but looks younger and lies about her age. As stated earlier, Nellie also lies about her age, claiming to be twenty-two but has taken three years off her age to create a "girl reporter" image. She was twenty-five when she made her trip around the world. —The Editors

feet above the promenade, which must be cleansed of a green slime after the storms are over before it can be traveled safely."

Well, maybe there will be too many people around to dispose of me, but I am still irked that they are up to some sort of shenanigans and I am excluded.

Sarah buys a rose from a street vendor and places it on a plaque that says Britain's heir to the throne, Edward, Prince of Wales, had placed the first stone for the breakwater fifteen years ago.

"It is considered one of the finest breakwaters in the world," Frederick says.

I take his remark as filling in conversation because he must find her dedication to an old brass plaque a bit unusual. She acts perfectly natural about putting a rose on an old brass plaque—and I mean *act*—that it arouses my own curiosity.

A tidbit about Sarah from the gossip columns back home stirs in my head. "Wasn't there a rumor a while back that Sarah and the prince—"

"Quite," Frederick snaps. "We must hurry to make it to the magic show."

I have inadvertently hit a sore spot and scratched open that British sense of total loyalty and defense to their royals. Her name, of course, has long been linked with love affairs with European royalty, but Prince Edward is not just known for his flirtation with Sarah. He is a playboy of international esteem, known for his taste for beautiful women, fine food, aged brandy, and champion racehorses.

As we walk back to the carriage, I can't help but think about Sarah's remark the night I first met her when she told me her lover's family was out to kill her. I can't see Queen Victoria setting out to kill her son's lover. Of course, if Sarah were pregnant or had already produced a claimant to the throne, who knows what a loyal Brit might do without the Queen's permission . . .

I let out a long sigh and tell myself that I have enough mysteries to contend with without creating another.

"Did you say something, Nellie?" Frederick asks.

"No. Probably just thoughts leaking from the holes in my head."

"I beg your pardon?"

"Sorry. An old American expression."

That I made up, but it's how I feel.

37

The Indian Rope Trick is not just considered the most amazing feat of illusion ever performed," Frederick tells us, "it's almost as old as the Himalayas. Claims are found in ancient Greek and Egyptian texts that the magic trick was observed centuries before the birth of Christ. Marco Polo saw it performed during his travels six hundred years ago."

We listen to Frederick's explanation of the trick as we sit on logs set out in rows from a mostly open air stage formed by cloth over large pieces of bamboo. Gaily colored sheets of cotton covered the sides and back of the slightly elevated stage. The top was partly open with lengths of bamboo coming across to connect the walls.

The back side of the stage enclosed the trunk of a tall, bushy pear tree.

A drum beats and the *fakir*, the Indian term for a worker of wonders, comes on stage. The *fakir* has the robes of a monk, wisdom's white beard, and the dark eyes of a traveling snake-oil salesman. A native boy about ten years old wearing a turban and loincloth joins him.

After much hand-waving and spoken incantations in what I imagine is the language of Ceylon, the old man's demand to the boy is obvious—he wants the boy to go up the tree and bring back something.

"A fruit so tasty only a god is permitted to eat it," Frederick whispers. "The fruit is guarded by the god's *jinnis* in the tree."

The *fakir* stands over a wide woven basket and plays a horn.

I expect an angry cobra with its neck fanning to glide up but instead it is a piece of rope. The rope continues up and disappears in the foliage of the tree.

"It's being pulled up by a thin line, fishing wire maybe," I whisper to Frederick and get a noncommittal shrug in return.

After the rope disappears into the spread of the tree, and after a bit of coaching, the boy grabs onto the rope. He begins to climb.

The audience cheers in amazement as he climbs hand over hand until he disappears into the foliage of the tree.

The *fakir* stares up at the tree, then moves about the stage yelling up at the boy, obviously demanding the boy come back with the fruit.

Instead of the boy descending, shouting is heard above, then cries of pain as the tree's foliage shakes as if a struggle is taking place among the leaves and branches.

Something drops and the entire audience—including me—lets out a gasp.

It's not a piece of fruit but an arm belonging to a small boy.

The *jinnis* guarding the fruit are obviously bloodthirsty little demons.

Then another piece drops. A leg.

A woman screams.

I begin to laugh hysterically and Frederick grabs my arm and whispers, "Don't."

He's right, it's purely rude, and I smother my laugh.

More pieces drop with the head coming last. By now the audience is on the edge of their seats. And staring at the basket.

The old man goes over to it, stares down into it, and shakes his head sorrowfully. Leaning over the basket, he begins to play his horn.

Soon the hair of a head appears . . . and then the head.

It's the boy. A raw red gash around his neck with stitches shows that his head has been sewn back onto his shoulders. As he slowly unwinds from the basket we see that his arms and legs have been sewn onto his torso.

Finally he steps out of the basket and runs off stage with the *fakir* yelling at him for having failed at his task.

The audience responds with loud clapping and coins rain onto the stage, the three of us throwing not a few.

"Amusing," I tell the other two as we wait for the crowd to disperse.

"You're not impressed?" Frederick asks.

"Of course not. The boy disappears into the front of the tree, climbs down the back, puts on the bloody makeup, and goes through a short tunnel that ends up in the basket. There's a hole in the basket and a tunnel beneath."

Frederick stares at the stage. "I wouldn't be certain of that. The stage is off the ground enough so that you can see beneath it. We would have seen the boy come up."

"Mirrors," I say, "it's all done with mirrors."

After the *fakir* and the boy clean the coins from the stage and leave, I make a dash for the stage to prove my point.

On stage I grab the basket and lift it. There's no hole in the bottom of the basket, no hole in the stage beneath it, no mirrors anywhere.

"A twin then," I decide. "There was a twin to the boy hidden in the basket. A child could easily wrap themselves around the inside of—"

Frederick grabs my arm and firmly pulls me off the stage.

"You are the most impetuous young woman I have ever met."

"I need to examine the tree."

"I'm getting you out of here before that *fakir* casts a magic spell and turns you into a mouse."

"A mouse? I deserve to at least be a tiger."

Report of an English Traveler Who Observed the Rope Trick in 1681

I want to relate a matter which defies all belief and which I would hardly have dared to insert here had there not been a thousand eyewitnesses of this as well as myself. One of this same company took a coil of rope of which he held one end in his hand and threw the rest into the air with such force that we could barely keep the other end in our sight. Then he clambered so high up the rope that we could no longer see him. I stood, amazed not knowing what would transpire when a leg tumbled down from the sky. A wizard picked it up and threw it in a basket. A moment later a hand fell down and then the other leg, and soon all the rest of the body flew down and were thrown in the basket. The very last piece was the head and as soon as it was thrown in, the basket was upended and we saw before our very eyes all the parts join together again as a perfect human being again who could move without showing any injuries.

Never have I been so astonished as when I saw this miraculous work and now I did not doubt any longer that these benighted people were assisted in this by the Devil . . .

—Edward Melton

38

On the way back to the hotel, Frederick instructs the carriage driver to stop at a marketplace. "You'll enjoy this place," he tells us.

The three of us split up wandering about, looking at the exotic merchandise—gems and tapestries, silk so light it seems to float, and perfumes that come with a guarantee that the scent alone will seduce your lover.

Sarah goes for the aphrodisiacal scents, Frederick wanders to the huts of the gem merchants, and I step over to a vendor selling cool lime and mint drinks.

I know better than to get interested in beautiful things—my valise is designed to meet my needs, not my desires.

Wandering about with my drink, for the first time since leaving America I see American money. A silk vendor is wearing it—as jewelry.

He speaks a good bit of English and he tells me that American gold coins are very popular in Colombo as jewelry and command a high price!

"It goes for little as money," he says.

I already knew that. When I offered it in payment for my bills I was told it would be taken at 60 percent discount. Gold is gold, but American gold is discounted when offered to pay a bill! But not if it's to be worn.

"The Colombo gem merchants are very glad to get American twenty-dollar gold pieces and pay a high premium on them," the silk merchant says.

The only use they make of the money is to put a ring through it and hang it on their watch chains for ornaments. The wealth of the merchant can be estimated by his watch chain, they tell me; the richer the merchant the more American gold dangles from his chain.

As I wander about, I see men with as many as twenty pieces on one chain. Women preferred daintier jewelry.

Dodging an oncoming group of children running after each other, I step off the main walkway and take a shortcut around a hut to a silk shop when a man says to me, *"Beau jour, Mademoiselle, nous devons parler."*

It's a disreputable-appearing sailor, a European, who has stepped out from behind the shop. His pants are stained with black smudges, his boots scuffed, his shirt has only been washed by sweat and rum, no doubt, for some time. He has a cockeyed sailor's cap holding down a mop of unruly dark hair. Add his unkempt beard and the man looks pretty much like the seafarers who hang around the saloons at ports all around the world . . . sailors who can't find a berth because their reputation for dereliction of duty and greater sins has spread.

The man was saying in French that "we need to talk."

"I don't speak French," I lie, and turn to walk away from him.

"Hey, sorry, lady, thought you were a Frog."

He had reverted to a working-class cockney accent, using "Frog" vulgarly for a person of French descent.

Turning my back and walking away only emboldened him.

"Have a drink with me and I'll show you my tattoos. I've got one that dances."

Frederick is suddenly between me and the man.

"Get out of here. You've made a mistake. Now move on."

The man leers at Frederick. "And who are you to give me orders?"

"I'm the man who will beat you enough so you can't crawl far before the police drag you out of the gutter."

The rude sailor's hand goes to the hilt of a knife he has strapped on his hip. He gives Frederick an appraising look.

Frederick stares back, giving the man a small smile as he taps his heavy walking stick on the ground. Walking sticks are carried for protection for good reason—they often conceal a weapon, not to mention that the head of the stick can deliver a powerful blow.

A man who has stood his ground with charging bull elephants, Frederick, tall and broad chested, has the posture of a soldier at the ready.

"Blimey!" The sailor takes his hand off his knife and raises his eyebrows giving both of us a look of mock surprise. "Unfriendly blokes, aren't you?" He removes his hat and waves as he bows. "Your lordship, ladyship."

He moves off and Frederick offers me his arm.

"Thank you," I tell him.

"I only intervened to keep you from thrashing the man."

I warm to the great hunter. There is nothing like a man defending a woman's honor to raise her esteem of him.

"Unpleasant chap," he says. "Probably lost his berth for tapping into the rum cask too often and lives off the beach. You find them often enough in the warmer regions, beachcombers too lazy or dishonest to work, living off fish, fruit, and what they can steal."

As Sarah joins us, Frederick says, "Here is something to remember Colombo by."

He gives each of us a gold charm. "This is the Monkey King who brought peace to the island by ridding it of demons. He brings good luck to those who desire to spread peace in the world."

We both express our appreciation, but petty woman that I am, I have still not forgotten that he was about to get me a gift before he saw the Divine Sarah.

Oh, well, the golden monkey is quite cute.

Back at the hotel, Frederick escorts us to our rooms. We first say good night to Sarah and are at my door when he surprises me with something.

"You are a very special person, Nellie Bly. When I saw this, I knew it should belong to you."

Hanging from a gold chain is a blue sapphire—the color of his eyes.

I am speechless. Thrilled. Instantly guilt-stricken because of my jealous thoughts.

"I . . . I don't know what to say."

I grab his lapels and stand on tiptoes to give him a kiss on his cheek. "Thank you."

As I turn to leave he takes a hold of my shoulders and turns me back to face him. Before I know it, he bends down and gives me a kiss. A long kiss. "You're welcome." He leaves me speechless.

I float into my room and hold the necklace against my chest.

My heart is beating. I am breathless, and feel warm all over.

I recognize the symptoms.

I am infatuated with Frederick Selous.

THE BLACKBOARD IN THE HOTEL corridor bore the information that the *Oriental* would sail for China the following morning at eight o'clock.

This is my last night in Colombo—I hope. Tomorrow I board a ship for the leg to China—I hope. I fall asleep easily, tired from the day, but wake up sweating because I hadn't left my balcony doors open.

Getting out of bed, I take a blanket and pillow with me to set up camp on the wicker chair on the balcony and to enjoy the mild night breeze and the bright moon.

My balcony looks down on the large courtyard in the center of the hotel. The courtyard is dark, but the hotel lounge where men gather for their drinks and tobacco is still open. Men are on the patio of the lounge, enjoying their brandy, tobacco, and conversation.

A familiar figure off to the left of the lounge patio catches my eye. I recognize the big, broad-rimmed, rugged hat that Frederick wears.

It is too dark to make him out or identify who he is talking to, but I keep watching, the thought of his special gift again warming the cockles of my heart.

The discussion breaks up and he approaches the patio doors and goes back inside. Passing under the gas lamp, I can see that it is definitely Frederick under the hat.

The person he had been talking to is crossing the courtyard for the exit to the street. When he walks under a gaslight, I gape.

It's the rude sailor from the marketplace.

39

My wake-up knock has been arranged for five o'clock, and some time afterward I leave for the ship.

Since Sarah had already informed me it would be much too early to even contemplate opening her eyes, I set out alone.

She did ask if I would go with her later that morning to buy some jewelry, but I told her I was so nervous and anxious to be on my way that I couldn't wait a moment longer than was necessary to reach the boat that was to carry me to China.

In truth, I needed to be alone to deal with all the thoughts rattling in my head.

Frederick and the sailor carried off a deception at the marketplace. They knew each other. So why did they pretend otherwise?

What did Frederick say to the man? *You've made a mistake.* It was a message telling the man he'd approached the wrong woman.

He was supposed to approach Sarah.

Frederick hadn't protected me from the man; he protected the secret that was behind whatever they're concocting. And Sarah is part of it. A starring role, of course.

My role? A bit player cast as the romantic interest of the leading man, but who in reality is there to draw attention away from whatever schemes the two stars are involved in. That is when I'm not being battered as the understudy of the female lead.

That special sentimental gift he gave me, the sapphire that warmed the cockles of my heart?

"A bone thrown to a dog."

I speak loud enough for others on the street to turn and look.

When I think about Frederick in the light of day, my mind unaffected by my feelings, it always boiled down to one thing: If it wasn't for Frederick's statement that he had personally spoken to Mr. Cleveland, my insistence that the man had been killed in the marketplace would carry some credibility.

An interesting angle to my ricocheting relationship is his statement that he worked on Warton and the captain to keep me from being arrested.

Why would he go out of his way to keep me around?

Is my next role the sacrificial lamb to slaughter?

AFTER AN HOUR of walking the streets of Colombo for the last time, I head for the dock to find that passengers are being ferried out to the *Oriental.*

Frederick is there, talking with the Wartons and Von Reich, and Sarah arrives on my heels. I get in line to rub shoulders with my enemies as we wait for a boat to take us out. As the boys back at the newsroom would say, It's the only game in town.

Frederick turns to me and says, "Too windy for an outrigger."

A fresh breeze is up, creating whitecaps on the bay.

I agree. "I already had a bath."

Everyone either has one hand on his or her hat or is making a mad dash for one headed for the bay. Watching women, Sarah and Lady Warton among them, hanging on desperately to their elaborate hats, many with veils to protect against sun and biting insects, I am again thankful for my simple, unfashionable cap that stays put.

A man and two women disembarking from a carriage catch my attention because of his unusual outfit. He has a wide-brimmed hat not unlike Frederick's distinctive jungle-tromping headgear, along with shirt, vest, pants, and boots with an unmistakable Australian Outback rancher look that I've seen in drawings and pictures.

While the outfit would be considered ordinary work clothes on an Aussie ranch, at a Ceylon dock it appears more like an eccentric taste in male attire . . . or a costume.

A gust of wind comes up that nearly blows off my own hat and rips the hats off of many a head. Lord Warton makes a dash for her ladyship's hat and Frederick chases his hat and uses his foot to stop it from taking a swim in the bay.

The Aussie outbacker looks toward us and yells, "Well, hello there!"

I don't know which of us he's hailed, but there's no response and he hesitates for a moment, as if he is puzzled or unsure, and then turns to the two women who even at this distance appear obviously to be yapping at each other in a heated manner.

"That outfit the Aussie is wearing looks almost like a costume," I say to Frederick as he joins Sarah and me on a steam launch.

"It is. I've been told he's an entertainer. His name is Hugh Murdock, an Aussie who bills himself as the best marksman in the world."

"Aren't you the best marksman in the world?"

"Perhaps the best hunter, if you will pardon the boast, but I have always been a terrible marksman. Quite wretched, really. I have to let beasts get so close that I can smell their hot breath before I pull the trigger."

He nods back at the Aussie group gathering their trunks on the pier. "I hear he also catches bullets in his teeth from a gun his wife fires. Magicians who perform on board get a discount on their fare, so perhaps he'll give us a demonstration."

"He better hope the seas are calm when she shoots," Sarah says.

I no longer had to wonder whether my reputation as a hysterical female and general troublemaker had preceded me. The purser checking off names on the passenger manifest does a double take when I give mine. I can only attribute it to the fact that someone who had previously boarded befouled my reputation. My prime candidate for that someone was Lord Warton, though my list of enemies has more names on it.

Too antsy to remain in my cabin, I stand at the rail and watch the steam launches deposit waves of passengers on the gangplank. As the Aussie sharpshooter comes aboard, it's not hard to see that the hostility between the two women has flared again.

"His wife and his assistant," Von Reich tells me as he appears at my elbow. "The one who looks young enough to be their daughter is the assistant. His wife is also a marksman, though not as good as he is."

"Looks like the assistant has annoyed the wife."

He grins and strokes his handlebar mustache. "I hear the annoyance may be that the wife resents sharing the marriage bed."

"Ah . . ."

That the Aussies' personal lives are already making the rounds of the ship's passengers doesn't surprise me. A ship churns out rumors faster than a society ball.

"I've heard that the man claims to be the best shot in the world," I tell Von Reich. "And that he catches bullets in his teeth."

"His claim of being the best shot is not valid. I know for a fact he has been beaten by a much better shot."

"Annie Oakley is the best I've ever seen. How can he make the claim of being the number one if he's been bested?"*

"My dear, it's show business; he can claim the moon. Besides, the other sharpshooter suffered an identity crisis after rising from the dead and isn't performing. As for catching bullets in his teeth . . ." He grins smugly.

"You know how he does it, don't you?"

"Of course."

"Really? Tell me, please."

He shakes a finger at me. "No, no, no, that would take all the enjoyment out of it. I am an amateur magician myself. It would be a violation of the code."

A violation he's made to me and every other woman on board who teased his ego. But he's right—I'd much rather see the bullet-catch trick and take a guess myself as to how it's done . . . before I'm told the secret.

As the Aussies go by, I think for a moment that the wife is going to slap the young assistant as the wife hisses, *"Bitch."*

I give Von Reich a sage nod. "I suspect that statement sums up the relationship between the parties."

At one o'clock, we sail and I stand at the bow, torn with conflicting emotions. I am on my way again! The race is still on! But knowing that the mystery sparked by Cleveland's words in the marketplace may have also come aboard, I am sick to death of the dark cloud hovering over me. With Egypt thousands of miles away, I have resolved not to play whatever game is afoot with Frederick, Sarah, and whoever else is involved in the intrigue.

When I am back in the States, I will put the matter before the British Ambassador in Washington and demand that Mr. Cleveland's Amelia be

* Nellie was taught to shoot by Annie Oakley when Nellie participated in Buffalo Bill's Wild West show. Both women were five feet tall and lied about their ages to keep a "girl" image. Annie performed for Queen Victoria and other royalty; at the Prince of Prussia's request, she shot the ashes off a cigarette held by him. An interesting slant on her aim that day is that had she missed and hit the prince, World War I might have been avoided because he became Kaiser Wilhelm II of Germany. —The Editors

contacted and the odd key that is still in the heel of my shoe be given to her.

The whole sad affair has not just taken some of the joy of the journey away, but threatens to rain on my quest to complete the trip in less than eighty days. Besides, there is one thing I know about game playing—when someone else names the game and has all the advantages, you are bound to lose.

So, I will just concentrate on the stories I'm doing about my travels and finishing the race on time. I'll step on no one's toes and set out on no adventures.

How can I get into any trouble just minding my own business?

40

Hugh Murdock comes out of his cabin bathroom and into a hornet's nest. "Will you two please shut up? You have been clawing at each other like two cats for hours."

"Get rid of this bitch and I'll have some peace," his wife Irene says.

"Go to your cabin," Hugh tells Cenza, the assistant.

Cenza points an accusatory finger at his wife. "She put me in a room so deep in the hole, I'll have fish for companions."

"I hope they're sharks!" the wife hisses.

Irene and Cenza exchange one more poisonous look before the younger woman leaves.

"I'm divorcing you as soon as we get back home," Irene tells him. "You brought that little slut along to humiliate me. She approaches you just before we're ready to sail from Australia and you use some of our last money to buy her a ticket. She can't shoot, she can't—"

He waves away her ire. "Be quiet, something's happened."

"Something? *Lots* of things have happened besides your infidelities. You're not just a bad husband, you're a bad gambler and a bad businessman. What you haven't lost at cards, you threw into that crazy scheme to raise camels in the Outback. We're stranded, we don't have the money to get back home. We don't even have the money for a hotel when this damn ship docks."

He ignores her and stands at the porthole chewing on his lower lip.

"What's the matter with you?"

"Someone's on board that I know."

"Someone you've slept with? I'm not surprised considering how many bitches you've crawled into bed with."

He turns and meets her eye. "You don't understand. The person I saw can solve all of our problems."

"Our problem is that we're broke—"

"That's what I'm talking about. I smell money."

Irene calms down. "Tell me more."

He grins. "Something's afoot and I can smell money. And I'm going to cut myself into a piece of it."

"You mean *we* are going to get a piece of it."

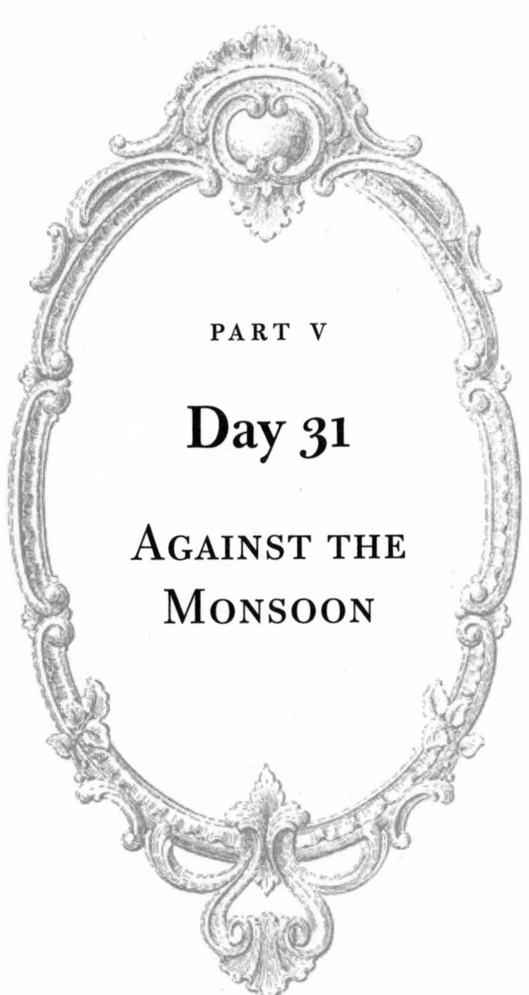

PART V

Day 31

Against the Monsoon

41

At first it is so wet-warm in the Straits of Malacca, so sultry and foggy, and so damp that everything rusts, even the keys in one's pockets, and the mirrors are so sweaty that they cease to reflect. Then the winds they call monsoon pick up and the seas punish us as we sail for the Far Eastern ports of Penang, Singapore, and Hong Kong, with the headwinds making the run slower than I had hoped for.

I work on the story about Colombo, both the one I will cable back and the one that will be placed in a secret journal I have begun. I am logging everything that happened since I saw Mr. Cleveland leave the ship in the wee hours that first day at Port Said. If I am lost overboard for whatever reason, I don't want his last wish to die with me. And I am petty enough to want to see my killer hanged by the neck if my trip to Davy Jones's locker comes from any hand but that of my Maker.

The bane of ocean traveling soon strikes and almost all of the passengers disappear into their cabins to hide their misery as seasickness becomes epidemic.

During dinner, the chief officer relates the woes of people he had seen suffering from seasickness that threatens now to even overpower the captain. I listen for quite a while, merely because I cannot help hearing, but finally his stories of miserable passengers makes me get up and run outside for the rail. After I do my duty and avoid having it slapped back at me by the wind, I straighten my shoulders and make a determined march back to my dinner plate rather than let the malady control me.

It is amazing that Sarah is able to stay in her stuffy cabin and only occasionally seek a breath of fresh air. I am still clueless about the purpose of her goal to keep her presence a secret, but have no doubt that her journey is intertwined in some way with the events at Port Said. My nose is dying to snoop further despite my vow of abstinence from foreign intrigue, but at the moment the most I can hope for is that I keep my sea legs under me and don't have to use them to swim if the ship goes down.

While I occasionally see Frederick and other passengers I know, it appears almost everyone has fallen victim to the violent motion of the ship in the monsoon sea and are too miserable to leave their cabins. I am secretly pleased that I have fared better than the great hunter.

The terrible swell of the sea during the monsoon, the rise and fall of mountains of water, is beautiful. I sit breathless on deck watching the bow of the ship standing upright on a wave then dashing headlong down as if it intends to carry us to the bottom.

In a moment of insanity, I fell in love with a cute monkey in Penang and bought it on impulse. The seller assured me it did not bite, but I soon discover that the little beast has a worse temper than Medusa, sending me fleeing for safety after I made the mistake of opening his cage after it got banged around by the ship being tossed in the angry seas.

During the night the monsoon sea washes over the ship in a frightful manner and my cabin fills with water, which, however, does not touch my berth. Escape to the lower deck is impossible, as I can't tell the deck from the angry, pitching sea.

As I crawl back into my bunk, a feeling of awe creeps over me and with it a conscious feeling of satisfaction. I think it is very possible that I have spoken my last word to any mortal, that the ship will doubtless sink, and if the ship does go down, no one will be able to tell whether I could have gone around the world in seventy-five days or not. The thought is comforting, for I feel I might not get around in even a hundred days.

I don't worry myself over my impending fate because I am a great believer in letting unchangeable affairs go their way. "If the ship does go down," I think, "there is time enough to worry when it's going. All the worry in the world can't change it one way or the other, and if the ship doesn't go down, I will have wasted time worrying."

So I go to sleep, lullabied by the sloshing water on my cabin floor, and slumber soundly until the breakfast hour. The ship is making its way laboriously through a very frisky sea when I look out in the morning, but the deck is drained, even if it is not dry.

With the seas slowly returning to normal, I make my evening constitutional with less concern that I will be washed overboard, but worry whether I will get to Hong Kong in time to board the ship that will take me across the Pacific.

I'm absorbed in my own thoughts when I hear the voice of the Aussie sharpshooter.

"That's my demand."

He is standing under a stairwell. I can't see him in the darkness well enough to recognize him, but it's his voice and I can make out that distinctive Outback rancher hat he sports. I can't see who he is talking to, but his tone had been a hard one, as if in response to an argument.

My poor nose twitches at the prospect of not finding a reason to tarry and loiter around to find out, but feeling that the eyes of his companion might be on me, I keep moving, hoping he will say something that gives a clue as to what his demand is—and to whom it's directed.

When mentioning the incident later to Von Reich, who finds little intrigue in what I observed, he suggests a way I can ask the sharpshooter myself about the conversation:

"Volunteer to have him shoot a cigarette from your lips."

I am omitting my unladylike reaction to his comment. However, as with all the other passengers and crew that can squeeze into the dining room, I show up to watch the Aussie sharpshooter's performance.

Von Reich kindly signals me to join a table that includes Lord Warton, the captain, an Italian count, and his wife from Lombardy. I spot Frederick standing along the back wall with others unable to find a seat in the packed room.

I don't bother asking Lord Warton about his wife's absence. Her ill disposition to seafaring is well known.

The lights are turned down in the room and up on the stage as Hugh Murdock's wife comes out and introduces her husband as the "world's most amazing and accurate marksman!"

He appears, stage right, to a burst of applause.

The Aussie puts on a demonstration of marksmanship, shooting playing cards on a spinning wheel and shooting the flames off of candles. A thick wood barrier stage left is used to catch the bullets.

The assistant appears stage left and after she is introduced, takes up a position before the barrier and holds up a wood kitchen match.

The Aussie counts twelve paces back from her, placing him nearly in the curtained area stage right, and fires from that position, the bullet nicking the match head and igniting it.

"It's not over yet!" Von Reich whispers to me, "I've seen these sort of acts performed in Budapest and London."

The assistant lights a cigarette with the burning match. Taking aim, the sharpshooter fires and knocks the tip off the cigarette.

The assistant doesn't move and the Aussie fires again, exploding the cigarette in its entirety.

A well-deserved round of standing applause erupts.

The Aussie holds up his hand to silence the applause.

"Now, ladies and gentlemen, we will present the most death-defying physical feat ever performed on a stage. My wife will fire a bullet at me . . . and I will catch it in my teeth."

The Aussie holds his hand over his eyes, trying to see out into the dark audience. He is not wearing his Outback hat. "Yes, there he is, Mr. Frederick Selous, the noted hunter and explorer. Please come forward."

Frederick joins the sharpshooter on stage.

"I'm sure you all know that Mr. Selous is the world's greatest hunter, a man who has trekked the wilds of the Dark Continent and bagged the most fierce creatures found anywhere. No one has greater expertise than this renowned hunter on how to load and fire a weapon. His life has depended on such skill a hundred times over when he faced charging beasts."

The assistant brings out a small table covered with a black velvet cloth and sets it in front of the two men. The wife places a rifle on the table and two cartridges next to it.

"Mr. Selous, would you please load the rifle with one of the cartridges and fire it into the barrier. A light-caliber weapon is being used to keep down the noise," Murdock tells the audience.

Frederick fires into the barrier.

"Are you satisfied that the weapon is fully functional and capable of bringing down a charging lion?" he asks Frederick.

"I wouldn't want to face a lion with this caliber, but a well-placed shot from it would certainly bring down smaller game."

"Would it kill a man, sir?"

Frederick smiles. "Certainly. Men are small game."

Murdock hands Frederick a small knife with its blade open. "Please carve your initials on the lead part of the bullet."

Frederick marks the bullet and offers it back to the sharpshooter, who holds up his hands to block the handoff.

"No, please, I don't want to touch the bullet or the gun. If I did so, the audience would justly believe I had substituted another bullet by sleight of hand and have the marked one already in my possession. Please load the rifle with the bullet and place it back on the table."

Frederick slips the cartridge into the chamber and places the rifle on the table.

Murdock has Frederick leave the stage amidst a hand of applause and then has his wife join him and asks her if she is ready to shoot a bullet at him.

"If I must," she says.

"Make sure you are satisfied with the weapon and it is ready to fire," he tells her.

She examines the weapon briefly, cocks it, and lays it back on the table.

"I am ready, but—"

"No buts, my love, these people have paid good money . . . well, would have paid good money had they not been a captive audience on a ship. Either way, they deserve to see the most dangerous and incredible feat ever performed onstage!"

She starts to hand him his distinctive hat and give him a peck on the cheek, saying, "I'll try not to miss, dear," but he steps back and holds up his hands, telling her, "We must not touch, there must be no trick of a hand faster than the eye of the audience."

Finally, the Aussie takes up his position in front of the barrier with the wife, rifle in hand, on the other side of the stage. The assistant has gone offstage, behind the wife.

The Aussie appears a bit nervous and pats sweat on his forehead, but it's easy for me to see it's an act.

A drum starts with a low tempo and slowly builds up as the wife gets into a shooting stance, cocks the rifle, and slowly raises it to aim.

She starts a countdown as the drum beats louder : "One . . . two . . ."

"Three" is lost in the bang of the drum and the sound of the shot.

The man's head snaps back, blood sprays, and his whole body slams back against the barrier. His mouth gapes open and a bullet falls out.

A moment frozen in time occurs as no one moves or breathes in the room.

A cry of surprise and agony breaks the silence.

The sound is from the wife.

The rifle slips out of her hand and onto the stage.

The Magician Who Stopped a War

In 1856, magician Jean Robert-Houdin was sent to French Algeria by Emperor Louis-Napoléon to use his conjuring skills to break the influence of the Marabouts, Islamic religious fanatics who claimed to have magic powers to drive the French from the country.

After putting on shows in cities, Robert-Houdin went into the desert and performed the most dangerous trick of all for rebel tribal leaders: the bullet catch.

He had a rebel put a distinctive mark on a lead bullet, then he placed the cartridge in the rebel's own rifle, and had the man fire it at him—stunning the rebels when he caught the bullet in his teeth.

Robert-Houdin, through sleight of hand, had switched the real cartridge for one in which the bullet appeared to be lead but was actually wax mixed with lampblack.

When the cartridge was fired, the wax "bullet" completely dissipated—and the magician, who had slipped the real bullet in his mouth, spit out the bullet as if he had caught it with his teeth.

On another occasion before rebel leaders, to demonstrate that his magic was even more powerful than the *jinnis*, the demonic spirits of the desert, he suddenly shouted that a *jinni* was in front of a building. He fired his pistol at the "spirit" and then raced to where the bullet had left a mark on the building. As he ran his hand over the bullethole, he smeared a red substance—and told the amazed tribesmen the spirit had bled from the gunshot wound.

By the time Robert-Houdin left Algeria, there was no doubt that French magic was more powerful than that of the fanatics.

Jean Robert-Houdin, who died in 1871, is considered the Father of Modern Magic.

His name was immortalized by a disciple named Ehrich Weiss—who took the stage name of "Harry Houdini" as a tribute to the great conjurer.

42

Before most of the ship is awake, I am at Frederick Selous's door. He surprises me by being fully dressed and ready to leave his cabin.

"I was expecting you," he explains. "Let's walk."

"Why were you expecting me?"

He gives me a sour frown as he steps out and shuts his door behind him. "I've learned to expect you at the scene of a sensational news story."

I stop him short in the corridor. "I beg your pardon, *Mr. Selous*, you make it sound like I find my way to crime scenes chasing police wagons. That's hardly been the case. If anything, I've been the one chased."

"You're right, I apologize. I was up half the night with the captain and others going over the accident."

"Accident?" I deliberately say it with a tone of sarcasm.

That gets a lift of his eyebrows and shake of his head. "Let's take a brisk walk before it gets too warm. I need to clear my head from the captain's cheap cigars and immature brandy."

We walk briskly, indeed, with me almost running to keep pace with his long legs.

After a complete lap around the ship in stony silence, I wait until we are out of ear reach of others and then stop to get my curiosity satisfied.

"What happened last night? What went wrong?"

"Two things. The first is that Murdock chose to add what is considered magic's most dangerous conjuring trick to his simple sharpshooting act. And he got careless."

"Is it the first time he tried to catch a bullet?"

"No, he's done it a number of times over the past few months. But it only takes one error to end a life. Do you know how the trick is done?"

"No, but I think Von Reich does."

"Yes, he volunteered to assist the captain in the investigation because he is an amateur magician. However, Mrs. Murdock explained the trick and we examined the weapon to confirm her statements."

"Which were?"

"There was a malfunction. There are different ways to perform the trick, but with some common features. A member of the audience is asked to mark the bullet so it can be identified later."

"As you did."

"Yes. In most cases the magician uses sleight of hand to substitute the marked bullet for a fake one that will not fire because it has an insufficient load of powder, or is made of wax, or is otherwise rendered impotent. The fake bullet is fired and the magician, who has palmed the real bullet, pretends to catch it and spit it out into his hand."

"But I watched closely. Murdock never touched the weapon. And you fired it to make sure it was real."

"I put a cartridge with a lead bullet head into the gun and fired it. The cartridge I placed next into the weapon, the one Murdock is supposed to catch in his mouth, is also real, but the lead head has been altered so the wife is able to slip it off."

"How could she slip the head off the cartridge? It was in the gun."

"There's a trick to cocking the gun that permits the cartridge to drop out, into her hand. The cocking action brings a blank into the chamber to be fired."

"How does the bullet get to his mouth?"

"He had a bullet hidden in his mouth when the act started. When the blank is fired, he spits out the bullet as if it's the one I marked."

"How does he get the one you marked to show to the audience?"

"As he steps forward with the wet bullet in his hand, his wife gives him a handkerchief to wipe it. The handkerchief—"

"Has the real bullet in it. And he switches bullets. Clever. It's sleight of hand, after all. Handing him the handkerchief would be a natural thing for her to do. What went wrong?"

"It appears that Murdock had been negligent in preparing the weapon. He placed a live bullet rather than a blank in the secret chamber. It's quite easy to do, they look alike. It's not the first time a mistake like this has happened. A moment's lack of concentration will do it, and from what his wife said, he had been indulging lately in not only liquor, but what the French call 'white angel.' "

"Cocaine."

He gives me a surprised look.

I shrug. "You'd be surprised at what a crime reporter has to deal with. What did the wife say was driving him to drink and worse?"

"She intimated at financial problems, but naturally we didn't probe any further."

"Naturally."

He doesn't miss the sarcasm in my tone and he becomes noticeably stiffer.

"All right, Nellie, why don't you tell me why we should have stretched the poor woman on a rack to get a confession out of her for killing her husband."

"I don't know that she killed her husband. Maybe she didn't, but someone did and she may have information that leads to the killer."

"Come now, blank cartridges are made to look like real ones. It's not that difficult for a mix-up to occur."

"A deadly mistake."

"With a trick that has a history of going astray. Von Reich said that of the nine magicians who've regularly performed the act over the past half century, five have died. Because it's so complicated, it is inevitable that something will go wrong if the trick is performed enough times. And when it does, the result is deadly."

"Hmmm," I say, a response that makes his eyebrows arch. To keep the conversation going, I add, "I would think that since she pulled the trigger, and everyone on board knew she was angry at her husband over whatever he had going on with the pretty young assistant, at least the notion of the wife shooting her cheating husband might have been discussed."

"That thought was bandied about last night and, in fact, the captain bluntly asked her."

"What was her reply?"

"If she had been in a killing mood, she would have shot the bullet into the assistant's mouth and not into her husband." He grins. "The captain found the logic rather convincing."

So do I, but I'm not ready to admit it.

He clears his throat. "Nellie, my advice to you is to not go any farther with your suspicions than you have with me."

"Or you will once again police my actions?"

He stops and confronts me. "I believe I have apologized profusely for my clumsy attempt to do what I thought was the right thing for my country in Ismailia. For some reason, since we left Colombo, you seem to have had . . . shall we say, a change of heart from the warm relationship we were developing."

He is getting tight jaws but I don't know how to defuse the situation without lashing out with an accusation about intrigues involving Sarah and the rude sailor in Colombo.

"Nellie, it is inevitable that you will attempt to make something out of this event that already antagonizes the captain. There is nothing here but an accident of the sort that has happened before. Do you understand that?"

His authoritative tone makes me fume because I know it is his way of chastising me and he has no right to do so.

"Maybe if you can see beyond your nose, Mr. Selous, you might learn something. I observed several unusual incidents in regard to Mr. Murdock, the most obvious being the marital difficulties. But he also recognized someone at the dock who didn't acknowledge him in return."

Frederick throws up his hands in exasperation. "Perhaps the person didn't hear him, maybe he was mistaken about who he was hailing, and just maybe you are making the proverbial mountain out of a molehill."

"I overheard him making a demand on the person."

"A demand for what? From who?"

"I . . . I don't know."

"And your interpretation of this demand you know nothing about?"

"He wanted money."

"That's a giant leap."

"Hardly. It fits nicely with his wife's admission that they needed money."

"And from this you have constructed a murder plot?"

"There are questions that need to be asked and answered. If that leads to a murder plot, then so be it."

"You are amazing." He shakes his head. "Completely amazing. You really do have a lively imagination. I can understand why Lord Warton considers you a rabble-rouser. The pieces you have put together, the tiny fragments that could fit in so many different ways, simply don't make the picture you have constructed."

Once again he throws up his hands in frustration. "Next you will be telling me that you believe Murdock's death is connected to the marketplace murder you witnessed."

So that he can't see my face and read my thoughts, I turn away.

He grabs my arm and turns me back to face him. "Don't you dare attempt to tread that path again. If you start rumors flying about that incident at Port Said, I will personally suggest that the captain lock you in your cabin for the duration of the voyage."

Jerking my arm free, I take a step back. "To protect whom?"

He flinches. "Why . . . you, of course."

"I'm not so sure about that. I do recall that you are the sole witness to Mr. Cleveland being alive. Now you handled the weapon that the sharpshooter was killed by. Is it possible you *accidentally* substituted a live bullet for a blank?"

His face flushes with anger and I fear I've crossed the line. I turn and leave, pedaling my feet as fast as they will go. And groan aloud at my stupidity.

Why does the devil make me do these things?

43

It is the evening of December 23, and I am sitting on deck in a dark corner by myself listening to men singing and telling stories. We are approaching Hong Kong and I will be leaving this ship for another after a several-day stopover.

Plagued by guilt for literally accusing Frederick of murdering the Aussie sharpshooter, I hid out in my cabin until I could not tolerate the screeches of the monkey who appears even angrier at me than I am at myself.

In remorse over my stupidity and rudeness, I had my steward take a sealed chit to Frederick that contained the beautiful sapphire necklace he'd given me in Colombo. My message was simple and to the point: "I do not deserve this."

In a funk since, I had come out on deck and hid in the darkness rather than stay in my cabin and stare at the walls while the monkey howled accusations.

I'm beating myself mentally when Frederick sits down beside me. I cringe back at the recriminations I deserve and am sure I will get.

He hands me the sapphire necklace. "This was given to me by mistake. It belongs to you."

"I told you, I don't deserve it."

"You didn't earn it, it was a gift given out of respect and admiration."

"You couldn't have respect after my accusation."

"Your accusation? You mean that little matter of accusing me of murdering a fellow passenger? Don't worry about it, I simply tucked it away with the ones charging that I'm Lord Warton's lackey and I talk to dead men on beaches."

I start to get up to flee and he takes my arm. "Please, I'm only joking. I'm guilty of throwing a few your way, too. I have to keep in mind that you really do know how to punch. The moment I pushed, you lashed out."

"I had big brothers. I had to learn how to defend myself."

"May I escort you around the sights of Hong Kong?"

I ponder the question for a moment. I am shamelessly pleased that he wants to be with me and also worried that it is to keep an eye on me.

"Thank you, but I have already made other plans. From the dock, I have to go immediately to arrange passage to San Francisco before exploring the sights. Then I'm going to pay a visit to nearby Canton to see a notorious prison."

"Excellent. Then it's settled."

"Settled?"

"As to you contacting me when you get your passage resolved so I can escort you to the prison, and that you're no longer angry at me."

"I suspect we shall both be old and gray before that happens."

"That's good. It means we'll still know each other." Then he leans over and puts the necklace around my neck and gives me a long kiss. "Good night, Nellie," he says, and he leaves me once again speechless.

I go down to tell the monkey he will soon be in Hong Kong. "Do you have any idea what Frederick's motives are for wanting my companionship?"

He gives out a screech as loud as the ship's emergency siren.

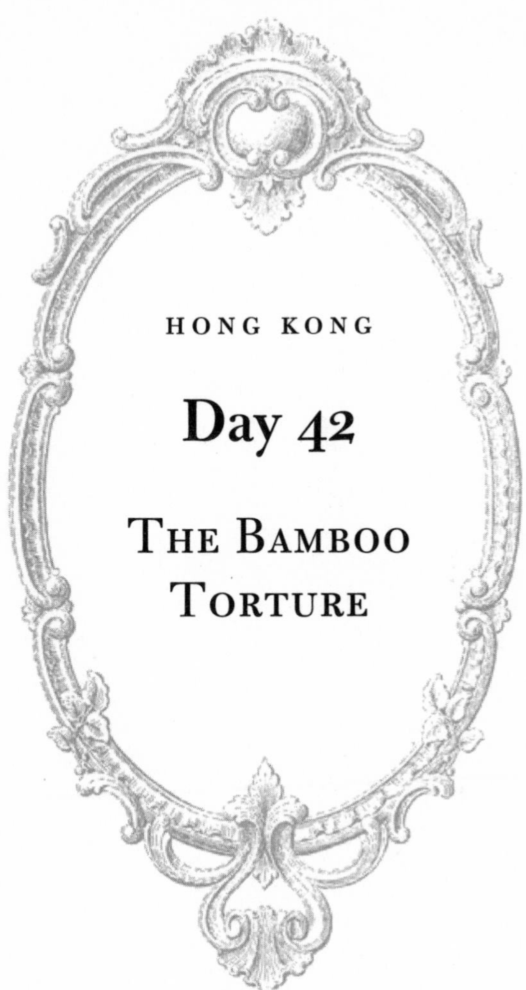

HONG KONG

Day 42

The Bamboo Torture

44

Our first glimpse of Hong Kong is in the early morning: gleaming white, castlelike homes terraced on a tall mountainside. The ship fires a cannon as we enter the bay, as this is the custom of mail ships, according to the captain.

The bay is a magnificent basin, walled by high mountains. Mirrorlike in the bright sun, it is dotted with strange crafts from many countries: heavy ironclads, torpedo boats, mall steamers, Portuguese lorchas, Chinese junks, and sampans.

A Chinese ship wends its way slowly out to sea, its strange, broad stern hoisted high out of the water, an enormous eye gracing its bow.

An exotic, graceful thing, I think, but I hear an officer call it awkward in rough seas.

I leave the boat with Frederick and walk to the pier's end where we select sedan chairs to carry us to the town. I expected to travel in a rickshaw, but until we reach town, the steep roads are not suitable for wheels.

The sedan carriers are as aggressive as the hackmen around railway stations in America, competing for our attention and patronage.

This is my first experience with these strange passenger conveyances that were common in Europe and America during previous centuries. They are literally a rectangular box standing long side up with two poles attached front and rear. Inside the box is a chair one sits in.

We follow the road along the shore, passing warehouses of many kinds and tall balconied buildings filled with Chinese families, on the flat-house plan. Garments are stretched on poles, after the manner of hanging coats so they will not wrinkle, and those poles are fastened to the balconies until it looked as if every family in the street had placed their clothes on exhibition.

Turning off the shore road our carriers go up a road that winds about from tier to tier up the mountain, and then back down it. When we reach the business district, I wave good-bye to Frederick. I have to get to the office of the Occidental and Oriental Steamship Company and learn the earliest possible time I can leave for Japan to continue my race around the world.

Only forty-two days have passed since I left New York and I am in China—halfway around the world. The *Oriental* not only made up the five days I had lost in Colombo, but reached Hong Kong two days sooner than I expected, and that with the northeast monsoon against her.

I go to the O and O office feeling very much elated over my good fortune, with never a doubt but that it will continue.

"Will you tell me the date of the first sailing for Japan?" I ask a man in the office.

"In one moment," he says, and going into an inner office he brings out a man who looks at me inquiringly.

When I repeat my question, he asks, "What is your name?"

"Nellie Bly," I reply in some surprise.

"Come in, come in," he says nervously.

I follow him into an office. After I am seated, he says, "You are going to be beaten."

"What? I think not. I have made up my delay."

Despite my optimism, I am surprised by his statement, wondering if the Pacific has dried up since my departure from New York, or if all the ships on that line have been destroyed.

"You are going to lose it," he says with an air of conviction.

"Lose it? I don't understand. What do you mean?" I demand, beginning to think he is mad.

"Aren't you having a race around the world?" he asks, as if he believes I am not Nellie Bly.

"Yes, quite right. I am running a race with Time."

"Time? I don't think that's her name."

"Her! Her!" I repeat, thinking, *Poor fellow, he is quite unbalanced.*

"Yes, the other woman; she is going to win. She left here three days ago."

I stare at him stupidly. "The other woman?"

"Did you not know? The day you left New York another woman started out to beat your time, and she's going to do it. She left here three days ago. You probably met somewhere near the Straits of Malacca. She says she has the authority to pay any amount to get ships to leave in advance of their time. Her editor offered a thousand dollars to the O and O if they would have the *Oceanic* leave San Francisco two days ahead of time.

"They wouldn't do it, but they did do their best to get her here in time to catch the English mail for Ceylon. If they had not arrived here early, she would have missed that boat and been delayed ten days. But she caught the boat and left three days ago, while you'll be delayed here five days."

"That is rather hard, isn't it?" I say quietly, forcing a smile that is on the lips, but it comes from nowhere near the heart.

"I'm astonished you did not know anything about it. She led us to suppose that it was an arranged race."

"I don't believe my editor would arrange a race without advising me," I say stoutly. "Have you no cables or messages for me from New York?"

"Nothing," he replies.

"Probably they don't know about her."

"Yes, they do. She had worked for the same newspaper you do until the day she started."*

"I don't understand it," I say quietly, too proud to show my ignorance on a subject of vital importance to my well-doing. "You say I can't leave here for five days?"

"That's correct, and I don't think you can get to New York in eighty days. She intends to do it in seventy. She has letters to steamship officials at every point requesting them to do all they can to get her on. Have you any letters?"

"Only one, from the agent of the P and O requesting that the captains of their boats be good to me because I am travelling alone. That is all," I say with a little smile.

"Well, it's too bad because I think you have lost it. There is no chance for you. You will lose five days here and five in Yokohama, and you are sure to have a slow trip across the Pacific in this season."

* The woman is Elizabeth Bisland, who had worked at the *World* and became an editor at *Cosmopolitan*. When *Cosmopolitan*'s publisher heard about Nellie's trip, he sent Bisland with only hours' notice around the world travelling in the opposite direction, certain that the west-to-east route would beat Nellie's time. Nellie relates how she learned of the "race" in Hong Kong but never mentions Bisland's name in *Around the World in 72 Days*. —The Editors

"I promised my editor that I would go around the world in seventy-five days, and if I accomplish that I shall be satisfied," I stiffly explain. "I am not racing with anyone. If someone else wants to do the trip in less time, that's their concern. I promised to do the trip in seventy-five days, and I will do it."

I LEAVE THE STEAMSHIP COMPANY OFFICE with thoughts chasing their tails in my head. My statement that I am not in a race is, of course, an attempt to hide my horror that I might actually be beaten by someone who has stolen my idea and is able to make better connections than me because of the weather.

Put the fear away in a dark cabinet, I tell myself. I will surely lose if I go about dreading failure rather than anticipating success.

I'm in a rickshaw en route to my hotel when I see a familiar figure in another one, turning into a street ahead. *Lady Warton.*

I find it odd that the woman is alone. I'm also without a companion, but that is my way and lot in life. Her ladyship, however, is of a social milieu that would frown upon her presence on the chaotic streets of Hong Kong without an escort. She's also more reclusive and conservative in her social affairs than I imagine most women of her position.

More out of curiosity than anything else, I signal my driver to turn at the same corner. The first thing that comes to my reporter's mind is that the woman is on a romantic rendezvous . . . with someone besides her husband, of course.

As we come around the corner I spot her stepping from the cart in front of a restaurant.

Two men are standing by to greet her.

I'm so startled I forget to tell the rickshaw driver to turn back around and end up going by them. I turn my head in the opposite direction as I'm carried past the group as they head into the restaurant.

My heart is pounding and my mind is swirling.

Frederick Selous is one of the men who greets Lady Warton.

The other is the drunken sailor who was so offensive in the Colombo marketplace.

I continue on to my hotel, where a room has been secured for me by the purser of the *Oriental*. The purser also had the monkey sent over to the steamship *Oceanic*, with my instructions that it be cared for by my cabin steward until we sail.

When I'm crossing the lobby to go to my room a woman approaches me.

"Miss Nellie Bly?"

"Yes."

"I'm John Cleveland's wife"

"Amelia?"

"Yes, Amelia Cleveland."

I suffer a rare infliction of speechlessness and simply stare at her. She's a bit older than me, about thirty perhaps. An attractive, conservatively groomed woman with heavily rimmed eyeglasses, and very blond hair pulled back in a bun and mostly hidden under her hat, she's wearing widow's black and speaks with a British accent.

"I understand you observed the terrible incident." She dabs the corner of her eye with a lace handkerchief.

"Yes, yes, I did. It was . . . a tragedy."

Getting my wits together, I direct her to a couch so we may sit sidesaddle facing each other.

"What a surprise," I tell her. "I didn't realize you were in Hong Kong. I was prepared to track you down to the ends of the Earth once I returned home." I shake my head, still bewildered by her sudden appearance.

"John planned to meet me here. His cutlery company was posting him here after he finished visiting accounts in Egypt. It must have been nightmarish for you to see him cut down before your eyes."

I can only nod. How do I tell her about the lifeblood gushing from his wound, the anguish on his face?

"He spoke your name to me. His last thought was of you."

"Oh . . . oh my." She stares down at her lap and appears ready to collapse in grief.

"I'll get you a glass of water."

She grabs my arm as I rise.

"Did he give you anything for me?"

"Oh Lord, I forgot! Of course he did. I'll get it."

I hurry away toward the stairway up to my room, leaving her on the couch. I can handle most things in life but I am not good with grief. I flee rather than confront it. My mother says it's because I grieved so when my father was taken from us when I was six. Disappearing to my room to get the key out of my shoe will give me an opportunity to regain my composure.

I'm stopped short of the stairway by a clerk who hands me an envelope that bears the insignia of the cable office. I open it and read the response from the London correspondent as I go up the stairs.

JC 34 YR OLD BACH—WORKED CUTLERY CO 8 YRS—
DIED CONSUMP 2 YR LONDON—WENT GRAVESITE

I freeze in place halfway up the stairway and stare at the message. John Cleveland had indeed been a cutlery salesman, for eight years. But he died of natural causes two years ago at the age of thirty-four. The correspondent had visited the gravesite to make sure he really was dead and buried.

Most important, the man had been a *bachelor.*

Spinning around, I stare at the woman who had gotten up and is now standing by the couch. Whatever she sees in my face causes her to panic. She turns and runs for the entry.

I start after her and become entangled with a man and woman coming up the stairs. Brushing by them, their "How rude!" remark follows me as I race for the entrance.

Once I am outside, I look right and left, starting this way and that way, but she is gone, swallowed by the crowds of people on the sidewalks and an army of sedan chairs and rickshaws flowing in both directions on the street.

Reluctant to give up the chase, but knowing it's hopeless, I slowly go back inside.

As I head for my room, a thought strikes me, and I am able to confirm it as soon as I get there and check the exact positions of my personal effects: My room had been searched.

Having so few possessions on the trip, it's easy for me to check and see that nothing is missing, not even my jewelry, which makes it a certainty that the intruder was not a sneak thief.

At the window I stare down at what appears to be organized chaos on the street below. Hong Kong is a city that never sleeps, and I shall get little of it myself this night as my mind wrestles with the singular events of the day.

No matter what I do, the marketplace incident thousands of miles behind me seems to dog my heels like a witch's curse.

Lady Warton has apparently joined whatever scheme Frederick, Sarah, the sailor, and Lord knows who else has cooked up.

My room has been searched, and now a woman has pretended to be the widow Cleveland.

However I toss the pieces, they don't fall into a revealing pattern like Chinese tea leaves, though I do get one revelation: I'm glad I took Frederick up on his invitation to spend time together. While he is keeping an eye on me, I can keep an eye on him.

46

A chit slipped under my door the next morning from Frederick informs me that he will be delighted to see me—in an hour.

I groan aloud and stumble back to bed and under the covers to deal with the situation. I have many questions to ask the great hunter, but from my experience with him I know that a frontal attack will not work. I shall have to be more subtle than in the past.

Mr. Selous has declared war on me.

I shall respond in kind, but rather than engage in verbal fisticuffs, I must be clever and subtle, neither of which are my strong points. I must show restraint and learn something from him rather than showing what a weak hand I have been dealt.

I have to learn how to duck.

I'm still completely perplexed about the incident with the woman last night who claimed to be Amelia Cleveland and her desire to obtain what John Cleveland had given me.

Had she known it is a key, I'm sure she would have asked for it.

What the key is for, who the woman is, and which of my shipmates are in league with her, are all a puzzlement to me.

Neither moping nor hiding my head under the blankets will prove fruitful, so I get up to prepare my body and mind for my meeting with Frederick.

When I come down from my room and into the lobby, I give Frederick a pleasant smile. As a proper young lady, all books on etiquette decree that I am to shine in conversation—though not so brightly as to eclipse my male companion—and listen intently with eyes open a little wider than normal as he relates his triumphs of manhood.

In other words, I will know my place in the presence of a man this morning.

He gives me a gentlemanly bow. "And how are you today, Nellie?"

"In a hurry. There are many things to see in Hong Kong and I intend to see them all. Let's get going."

I fly by him, biting my tongue to keep from lashing out at him about his rendezvous with Lady Bitch.

Outside the entrance I let out a big sigh and pause to let him catch up. So much for Miss Manners. This will not do.

I have to change my attitude or I shall not be able to flush out my game.

"Please forgive me, Frederick. I received some bizarre news at the steamship line company yesterday and it has me quite befuddled."

After quickly telling him that I have found myself in a competition not of my making, I ask what we will see first.

"We are going to scale the highest mountain on Hong Kong Island."

VICTORIA PEAK, ABOUT EIGHTEEN HUNDRED FEET HIGH, and named in honor of the Queen, is fortunately "scaled" first by taking an elevated tramway that takes one to Victoria Gap, two-thirds of the way up.

Opened two years ago, the fare is thirty cents going up and fifteen cents coming down. Before the tram was completed, people were carried up in sedan chairs.

Frederick explains in the tram that during the summer months Hong Kong is so hot that those who are in a position to do so seek the mountaintop, where a breeze lives all the year round.

At the Gap we secure sedan chairs, and it requires three men to a chair ascending the peak, just as it did over the rough terrain from the pier. At the Umbrella Seat, which is merely a bench with a peaked roof, everybody stops long enough to allow the carriers to rest, before we continue on our way, passing sightseers and nurses with children.

After a while the carriers stop again, and we travel on foot to the signal station.

My mood is greatly refreshed looking out because the view is superb.

The bay, in a breastwork of mountains, lies calm and serene, dotted with hundreds of ships that seem like tiny toys. The palatial white houses come halfway up the mountain side, beginning at the edge of the glassy bay. Every house we see has a tennis court blasted out of the mountainside.

They say that the view from the peak at night is unsurpassed, that one seems to be suspended between two heavens because thousands of boats and sampans carry a light after dark, which along with the lights on the roads and in the houses, creates the impression of a sky more filled with stars than the one above.

"This is heaven," I tell Frederick. I mean it and am pleased that I have kept my tongue on a leash.

"Quite. Now if you are game for an overnight boat ride, we will descend to Dante's Inferno—that prison in Canton you want to see."

"Unlike the colony, Canton is a real Simon-pure Chinese city," Captain Grogan tells us after we board the coastal ship *Powan*.

The captain, who has lived for years in China, is a very bashful man, and a most kindly, pleasant one.

Soon after the *Powan* casts off from Hong Kong, night descends and I slip away alone and go on deck where everything is buried in darkness.

Softly and steadily the boat glides along, the only sound—and the most refreshing and restful sound in the world—is the lapping of the water. To sit on a quiet deck, to have a star-lit sky the only light above or about, to hear the water kissing the prow of the ship, is, to me, paradise.

They can talk of the companionship of men, the splendor of the sun, the softness of moonlight, the beauty of music, but give me a willow chair on a quiet deck, where the world with its worries and noise and prejudices are lost in the distance, and the glare of the sun and the cold light of the moon are blotted out by the dense blackness of night and I am in heaven.

My reverie is interrupted by my own good sense of reality. It seems there is always a snake to spoil paradise and news that I am in a race not of my making has tainted some of my pleasant feelings about the race. No matter haw dark things had gotten since the marketplace at Port Said, the race has always been nothing but pure pleasure. Now I have to worry not only about beating a fictitious character but a fellow reporter, all the while wrestling with the intrigues and machinations about the key that seem to be all around me.

Frederick has not given me the slightest clue as to what schemes he may be involved in. Had I not recognized the cur of a sailor with Frederick, I would have imagined the meeting with him and Lady Warton as a romantic one.

Not wishing to work my brain or keep my tongue quiet any longer, I send a message to Frederick that I have retired, and go to my cabin.

Before daybreak we anchor at Canton.

47

While we are having breakfast, the guide whom the captain has secured for us comes aboard and quietly supervises the luncheon we are to take with us.

The first thing he says to us is "A Merry Christmas!" and as it has even slipped our minds, we appreciate the polite thoughtfulness of the Chinese guide, Ah Cum.*

Ah Cum tells us that he has been educated in an American mission located in Canton, but he assures me, with great earnestness, that English is all he learned. He would have none of the Christian religion.

The captain says that besides being paid as a guide, Ah Cum collects a percentage from merchants for all the goods bought by tourists. Of course, the tourists pay higher prices than they would otherwise, and Ah Cum sees they visit no shops where he is not paid his fee.

"A very clever fellow," Frederick grumbles.

Ah Cum is dressed rather colorfully, with beaded black shoes with white soles on his feet, and navy-blue trousers, or tights—more properly speaking—tied around his ankles and fitted very tightly over most of his legs.

Over this he wears a blue, stiffly starched shirt-shaped garment, which reaches his heels, and atop that he has a short padded and quilted silk jacket, somewhat similar to a smoking jacket.

His long, coal-black queue, finished with a tassel of black silk, comes all the way down his backside to touch his heels. On the spot where the hair braid begins rests a round black turban.

* Ah Cum was the name of Nellie's guide in her book *Around the World in 72 Days.* —The Editors

Ah Cum has sedan chairs ready for us as we step off the gangplank. His own chair is a neat arrangement in black: black silk hangings, tassels, and fringe, and black wood-poles finished with brass knobs. Once in it, he closes it, and is hidden from the gaze of the public.

Our plain willow chairs have ordinary covers, which, to my mind, rather interfere with sightseeing, and we have them tied back.

We have three carriers to each chair, which is not very equalitarian since Frederick's carriers are burdened twice as much as mine are. The carriers are barefoot, with tousled pigtails and navy-blue shirts and trousers, much the worse for wear both in cleanliness and quality than Ah Cum's dandyish garb.

Ah Cum's own carriers wear spotless white linen garments, gaily trimmed with broad bands of red cloth, looking very much like a circus clown's costume.

Ah Cum's chair leads the way, our chairs following, as we push down the crowded streets and are carried along dark and narrow ways, in and about fish stands, whence odors drift, until we cross a bridge that spans a dark and sluggish stream.

What a picture Canton makes. They say there are millions of people in Canton, yet the streets, many of which are roughly paved with stone, seem little over a yard in width.

The shops, with their gaily colored and handsomely carved signs, are all open, as if the whole side facing the street had been blown out. In the rear of every shop is an altar, gay in color and often expensive in adornment.

I am warned not to be surprised if the Chinese should stone me while I am in Canton. The anger and bitterness over the Opium Wars that forced them to sell the foul substance to their own people, and other injustices from the Western nations, runs deep.

Captain Grogan says that Chinese women have spat in the faces of female tourists when the opportunity offered. However, I have no trouble. Instead, as we are carried along men in the stores rush out to look at me, not taking interest in Frederick, but gazing at me as if I am something new. They show no sign of animosity. The few women I meet stare curiously at me, and less kindly.

The people do not appear happy; they look as if life has given them nothing but hard work and little gain, and wear expressions not unlike those of coal miners in my own home state of Pennsylvania.

Surprisingly, the thing that seems to interest the people most about me are my gloves. They always gaze upon them with looks of wonder and sometimes are bold enough to touch them.

When Ah Cum tells me that we are in the streets of the city of Canton, my astonishment knows no limit. The streets are so narrow that I think I am being carried through the aisles of some great marketplace. It is impossible to see the sky, owing to the signs and other decorations, and the compactness of the buildings; the open shops are like stands in a market except that they are not even cut off from the passing crowd by a counter.

Sometimes, our little train of sedan chairs would meet another train of chairs, and then we stop for a moment, and there is great yelling and fussing until we have safely passed, the way being too narrow for both trains to move at once in safety.

As we are approaching the prison I want to see, Ah Cum tells us that it is the place where political executions are conducted. There is much dissent against the tyrannical rule of the Dowager Empress, and a great deal of that dissent ends up in spilled blood on the execution grounds.

"Why do you want to see a prison?" Ah Cum asks me during a rest stop.

"The high drama of life and death is meat and potatoes for a crime reporter," Frederick answers.

I hope it is my reporter's instincts and not a perverse desire to see the macabre.

48

We go in through a gate where a stand erected for gambling is surrounded by a crowd. A few idle people leave it to saunter lazily after us. The place is very unlike what one would naturally suppose it to be. At first sight, it looks like a crooked back alley in a country town.

As we pass a shed with half-dried pottery, a woman stops her work at the potter's wheel to gossip about us with another female who had been arranging the wares in rows.

"The execution grounds," Ah Cum says, indicating with a sweep of his hand an area about seventy-five feet long by twenty-five feet wide at the front, narrowing at the other end.

The ground in one spot is very red, and when I ask Ah Cum about it, he says indifferently, as he kicks the red-colored earth with his white-soled shoe, "Eleven men were beheaded here yesterday."

Frederick wanders off, back to the pottery, telling me, "I've seen enough blood of men and animals for several lifetimes."

Ah Cum adds that it is an ordinary thing for ten to twenty criminals to be executed at one time. The average number per annum is something like four hundred. Ah Cum also tells me that in one year, 1855, over fifty thousand rebels were beheaded in this narrow alley.

I shudder at the thought of that many souls being violently sent off to heaven or hell because of political differences.

While he is talking I notice some roughly fashioned wooden crosses leaned up against the high stone wall. Supposing that they are used in some manner for religious purposes before and during the executions, I ask Ah Cum about them.

A shiver waggles down my spinal cord when he answers, "When

women are condemned to death in China, they are bound to wooden crosses and cut to pieces."

"Good Lord!"

"Men are beheaded with one stroke unless they are the worst kind of criminals," the guide adds. "The worse are given the death of a woman to make it the more discreditable. They tie them to the crosses and strangle or cut them to pieces. When they are cut to bits, it is done so deftly that they are entirely dismembered and disemboweled before they are dead. Would you like to see some heads?"

The Chinese guide could no doubt tell stories as large as those of any other guide—who can equal a guide for highly colored and exaggerated tales?—so I say coldly, "Certainly; bring on your heads!"

As Ah Cum instructs me, I tip a man with a silver coin. With the clay of the pottery still on his hands he goes to a barrel, which stands near the wooden crosses, puts in his hand, and pulls out a head!

"The barrels are filled with lime," Ah Cum says, "and as the criminals are beheaded their heads are thrown into them. When the barrels become full they are emptied out and reused. Prisoners dying in jail are always beheaded before burial."

He tells me that if a man of wealth is condemned to death in China he can, with little effort, buy a substitute. Chinese are very indifferent about death; it seems to have no terror for them.

I follow Ah Cum to the jail and am surprised to see all the doors open. The doors are rather narrow; when I go inside, I see that all the prisoners have thick, heavy boards fastened about their necks, so it is no longer a surprise that the doors are unbarred. There is no need of locking them.

We go next to the law court, a large, square, stone-paved building. In a small room off one side we are presented to some judges who are lounging about smoking opium. In still another room we meet others playing fan-tan. At the entrance there is a large gambling establishment!

"Now you must see the tools of persuasion." Ah Cum chortles.

Two judges lead us into a room to see the instruments of punishment: Split bamboo to whip with, thumb screws, pulleys on which people are hanged by their thumbs, and other such pleasant things.

Two men are brought in who have been caught stealing. The thieves are chained with their knees meeting their chins, and in that distressing position are carried in baskets suspended on a pole between two carriers.

The judges explain to me through Ah Cum that because these offenders had been caught in the very act of taking what belonged not to them, their hands will be spread upon flat stones and, with smaller stones, every bone will be broken.

Afterward, they will be sent to the hospital to be "cured."

I elect not to see the punishment.

I thought I had heard of the most bizarre and painful punishment man could conceive after an American who had lived many years near Canton told me there is a small bridge spanning a stream in the city where it is customary to hang criminals in a fine wire hammock, first removing all their clothing.

A number of sharp knives are laid at the end of the bridge, and every one crossing while the man is there is compelled to take a knife and give a slash to the wire-imprisoned wretch.

However, Ah Cum tells me that the bamboo punishment is the worst—and not as uncommon in China as one would naturally suppose from its extreme brutality.

This most gruesome and horrifying torture is exceedingly cunning in its ability to deliver not just slow, excruciating, literally unimaginable pain, but an unbearable anticipation of the suffering to come.

Offenders subjected to it are pinioned naked in a standing position with their legs astride, fastened to stakes in the earth. *This is done directly above a bamboo sprout.*

To realize this punishment in all its dreadfulness it is necessary to give a little explanation of the bamboo. A bamboo sprout looks not unlike the delicious asparagus, but is of a hardness and strength not equaled by iron. When it starts to come up, nothing can stop its progress. It is so hard that it will go through anything on its way up; let that be asphalt or any other substance, the bamboo goes through it as readily as though the obstruction didn't exist.

The bamboo grows with marvelous rapidity straight up into the air for thirty days, and then it stops. When its growth is finished it throws off a shell-like bark, its branches slowly unfolding and falling into place. The branches are covered with a soft airy foliage finer than the leafage of a willow.

As I have said, nothing can stop a bamboo sprout when it intends to come up. Nothing ever equaled the rapidity of its growth, it being affirmed that it can really be seen growing! In the thirty days that it grows, it may reach a height of seventy-five feet.

Picture then a convict pinioned above a bamboo sprout and in such a position that he cannot get away from it. It starts on its upward course never caring for what is in its way; on it goes through the man who stands there dying, dying, worsening by inches, conscious for a while; then fever mercifully kills knowledge, and at last, after days of suffering, his head drops forward, and he is dead.

"But that is not any worse than tying a man to a stake in the boiling sun, covering him with quick-lime, and giving him nothing but water to quench hunger and thirst," the guide assures me. "The man holds out and out, for it means life, but at last he takes the water that is always within his reach. He drinks, and when he perspires it wets the lime and the lime begins to eat."

I am dizzy and my mind is shutting down as we leave the torture area with Ah Cum droning on about another delight of a professional torturer: suspending a criminal by his arms, twisting them in back of him.

As long as a man keeps his muscles tense he can live, but the moment he relaxes and falls, it ruptures blood vessels and his life floats out in a crimson stream.

The unfortunate is always suspended in a public place, where magistrates watch so that no one may release him.

Friends of the condemned flock around the man of authority, bargaining for the man's life: if they can pay the price extorted by him the man is taken down and set free; if not, he merely hangs until the muscles give out and he drops to death.

They also have a way of burying the whole of criminals except their heads. The eyelids are fastened back so that they cannot close them, and so facing the sun they are left to die.

Sticking bamboo splints under the fingernails and then setting fire to them is another happy way of punishing wrongdoers.

"Stop!" I yell at the startled guide. "No more descriptions. You are torturing me."

"Are you superstitious?" Ah Cum asks me.

"Superstitious? I suppose so, at least as much as everyone else."

"Do you wish to try your luck?"

I think about the race to the finishing line imposed upon me and I answer in the affirmative.

"Come. We will go to the Temple of Five Hundred Gods, and you can see your fortune laid out before you."

With Frederick also in tow, at the temple Ah Cum places joss sticks in a copper jar before the luck-god. Then he takes from the table two pieces of wood, worn smooth and dirty from frequent use, which, when placed together, are not unlike a pear in shape.

With this wood—he calls it the "luck pigeon"—held with the flat sides together, he makes circling motions over the smoldering joss sticks, once, twice, thrice, and then drops the luck pigeon to the floor.

"If one side of the luck pigeon turns up and the other turns down, it means good luck. If they both fall in the same position, it means bad luck. Since they both turned the one way, I will have bad luck."

He did not appear pleased with the result.

I take the luck pigeon. I am so superstitious that my arm trembles and my heart beats in little palpitating jumps as I make the motions over the burning joss sticks.

Dropping the wood to the floor, one piece turns one way and one the other, and I grin with relief.

I'm going to have good luck.

It is Frederick's turn and he refuses a try.

"I make my own luck," he says.

49

Ah Cum takes us to a building he says will be a pleasant place to enjoy our luncheon. Once within a high wall we come upon a pretty garden with a mournful sheet of water undisturbed by a breath of wind. In the background the branches of low, overhanging trees kiss the stillwater where long-legged storks stand, graceful birds made so familiar to us by pictures on Chinese fans.

He leads us to a room which is shut off from the courtyard by a large carved gate. Inside are hardwood chairs and tables.

While eating we hear chanting to the weird, plaintive sound of a tom-tom and a shrill pipe.

"We are in the Temple of the Dead," the guide tells us.

I realize it is Christmas Day. "We are eating Christmas luncheon in the Temple of the Dead," I tell Frederick.

"Let's hope the dead don't interfere with this fine food."

Ah Cum explains the death ritual.

"It is customary at the death of a person to build a bonfire after night, and cast into the fire household articles, such as money boxes, ladies' dressing cases, and the like, while the priests are playing shrill pipes.

"The demon which inhabits all bodies leaves the body to save the property of the dead, and once they trick him out, he can never reenter, so souls are saved."

I climb high stone steps to the water-clock, which, they say, is over five hundred years old, and has never run down or been repaired.

In little niches in the stone walls are small gods, before them the smoldering joss sticks. The water clock consists of four copper jars, about the size of wooden pails, placed on steps, one above the other. Each one has a spout from which comes a steady *drip-drip*. In the last and bottom jar is an indicator, very much like a foot rule, which rises with the water, showing the hour.

On a blackboard hanging outside, they mark the time for the benefit of the town people. The upper jar is filled once every twenty-four hours, and that is all the attention the clock requires.

I am near the gate at the bottom of the steps when a man dressed all in black suddenly grabs my purse and gives me a shove at the same time, sending me down while he runs through the gate.

I am on my feet and rushing for the gate when a group of people on the outside suddenly converge upon the gate, keeping me from opening it.

Frederick is outside the gate. He yells "Stop!" to the fleeing man and gives chase while I push at the gate with ever-growing anger until I blow my stack and throw myself screaming at the obstacle.

The people pressing against the gate scatter as I come through and head off in the direction I had seen Frederick and the thief disappear. I have not gone a dozen paces when Frederick comes around a corner of a building holding up my purse in triumph.

"Got it. He dropped it as I gave chase. Is there anything missing?"

"Thieves always have time once it is in their hands, it only takes a second." I rummage through the purse. "Nothing is missing."

"Excellent. So the pigeon luck machine was right—you have good luck."

"Luck has nothing to do with the thief grabbing my purse. And it didn't have anything to do with people suddenly keeping me from pursuing him. Like you, some people make their own luck."

I am steaming and instruct Ah Cum to get me back to the *Powan* immediately.

It's obvious that the purpose in grabbing my purse was not to steal my money, but to search for the key.

Just as evident is how convenient it was that Frederick Selous lures me to a place where it could be easily arranged, which means that our tour guide is an accessory.

I am cold and distant to Frederick afterward.

"Ask your friend the thief for a tip," I tell Ah Cum when I refuse him a gratuity after he delivers us back to the ship's gangplank.

He says nothing but glows with guilt and resentment.

I draw the line at paying to get mugged.

On our return to the *Powan* I am conscious of an inward feeling of emptiness. It's Christmas Day and I think with regret of dinner at home, although I know it is past midnight in New York.

Suffering from a sick-headache, I go to my cabin, and shortly we are on our way to Hong Kong.

The thief got nothing from me except my last hope that Frederick had spent the time with me because of his feelings for me.

That and my sense of security. I am in China, thousands of miles from the Mahdi and the blood spilled in the marketplace, and I'm still not safe.

I feel as if I have lost another battle.

50

On my last night in Hong Kong I am badgered by the purser of the *Oceanic* and a fellow passenger who will join me on the ship when we cross the Atlantic to see *Ali Baba and the Forty Thieves* as performed by the Amateur Dramatic Club of Hong Kong.

They tell me that the theater in Hong Kong knows only a few professional troupes, but the amateur actors in the English colony leave little to be desired in the way of splendid entertainments. The purser says that the very best people in the town take part, and they furnish their own stage costumes. The regiments stationed here also turn out very creditable actors in the persons of the young officers.

We come to the theater in sedan chairs instead of carriages, the narrow streets not being inviting for horse-drawn conveyances. The sight of handsomely dressed women stepping out of their chairs and the daintily colored Chinese lanterns—hanging fore and aft, marking the course the carriers take in the darkness—is very impressive. It is a luxury to have a carriage, of course, but there is something even more luxurious about owning a chair and having full-time carriers in one's employ.

A fine chair with silver-mounted poles and silk hangings can be bought, I should judge, for a little more than twenty dollars. Some women keep four and eight carriers; they are so cheap that one can afford to retain a number. Every member of a well-established household in Hong Kong has his or her own private chair with carriers waiting to pick up the poles.

Many men prefer a coverless willow chair with swinging step, while many women have chairs that close entirely, so they can be carried along the streets secure against the gaze of the public. Convenient pockets, umbrella stands, and places for parcels are found in all well-appointed chairs.

The *Arabian Nights* tale is a new version of the old story filled with local hits arranged for the club by a military captain; the music is by the bandmaster of the Argyll and Sutherland Highlanders. The beautiful and artistic scenery is designed and executed by two army men, as are the limelight effects.

Inside, the scene is bewitching. A rustling of soft gowns, the odor of flowers, the fluttering of fans, the sounds of soft, happy whispering, a maze of lovely women in evening gowns mingling with handsome men in the regulation evening dress—what could be prettier?

If American women would only ape the English in going bonnetless to the theater, we would forgive their little aping in other respects, and call it even. Upon the arrival of the governor the band plays "God Save the Queen," during which the audience stands. Happily, they make it short.

The play is pleasantly presented, the actors filling their roles most creditably, especially the one taking the part of Alley Sloper.*

After Ali Baba discovers the cave of the Forty Thieves and brings part of their treasure back to his brother's house, he meets Morgana, a clever slave girl.

I cannot take my eyes off of Morgana because I recognize her. "What do you know about her?" I whisper to the purser, who has made himself an authority on Hong Kong plays.

"Professional actress. Aussie, I think. Traveling drama group went broke and stranded her here. Name's Virginia Lynn."

I resist the impulse to tell him that not long ago she identified herself as Amelia Cleveland and fled my hotel with me on her heels.

Begging the pardon of my companions, as soon as the play is over, I part company with them and station myself at the stage door.

She comes out with two men but goes in a different direction from them. I catch up with her.

"Good evening, Amelia."

She throws me a glare. "Go away."

"You can talk to me," I tell her back, "or to the police."

That stops her. She swings around and confronts me. "I've done nothing for the coppers to take an interest in me."

* "Alley Sloper" was Victorian slang for a person who snuck out when the landlord came to collect the rent and sloped down an alley to sneak away. —The Editors

I get almost nose to nose with her and lock eyes. "Nothing except attempt to steal a valuable object through impersonation."

She takes a step back. "No. I was just a messenger."

"A messenger? We'll see if the Hong Kong police think that is as funny as I find it."

"What do you want? Go, get away from here, go on that silly race you're doing. Leave me alone, I've troubles enough."

"You're going to have more troubles if you don't tell me why you told me you were John Cleveland's wife."

"It was a part I was hired to do, that's all."

"Who hired you? Selous?"

"Who?"

"Tell me who hired you."

"A woman offered me two quid to go to the hotel and tell you I was John Cleveland's wife and came to get his property."

"What did she look like?"

Virginia Lynn gave that one some thought. "I can't really say. Met me out here in the dark, just like you. I never really got a look at her. She wore one of those high-fashion hats with a thick veil."

"What was the color of her hair?"

The actress shrugged. "Not really sure. Maybe brown." She shakes her head. "Not really sure."

"What did her voice sound like?"

"I don't know. You have an American accent. Hers was British."

"What else did she tell you?"

"She said she was John Cleveland's wife and that Cleveland had given you something that belonged to her family."

"Did she tell you what it was?"

"No. She said just to say I was his wife and you'd know what to give me."

"Did she tell you why she didn't ask herself?"

"I asked her that. She said she was too emotional about it. That's all I know. I got two quid and now a headache. Leave me alone."

"Anything about the way she dressed that stood out? Broach, necklace—"

"Her shoes. Tall heels, really exotic leather, light brown, had bumps on it, bumps with holes or nicks, maybe some kind of snake or something."

We part, her at almost a run, and I secure a chair to take me back to my hotel.

Two women obviously fit the description the actress gave: Lady Warton and Sarah. The accent wasn't important. I've heard Sarah imitate a British accent.

It's also obvious that half the European women in Hong Kong probably fit the vague description.

Nor did it let Frederick Selous off the hook. He has intrigue going with both women and probably arranged the charade. Having a woman hire the actress was clever because it is easy for a woman to disguise herself behind big hats and scarves and veils. A woman's size, shape, and age are much easier concealed than a man's.

Murder in Egypt and international intrigue that has already extended thousands of miles to Hong Kong and threatens to follow me around the other half of the world is too much for a young woman from Cochran's Mills, Pennsylvania, population exactly 534.

Especially when I had another woman to worry about—the one giving me grief by turning my adventurous race against time into a competition.

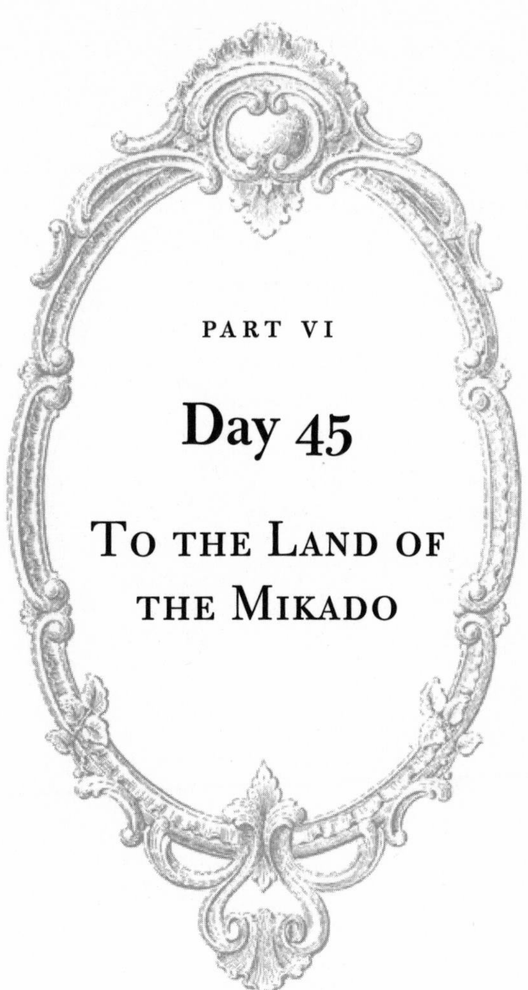

PART VI

Day 45

To the Land of the Mikado

51

My first order of business upon boarding the *Oceanic* is to get quickly to my cabin and make sure both my possessions and my little simian friend transferred from the *Oriental* are in good order.

I meet the stewardess in the corridor and ask about my monkey.

"We have met," she says dryly.

She pulls up her sleeve to reveal that her arm is bandaged from wrist to shoulder.

"What did you do?" I ask in consternation.

"I did nothing but scream; the monkey did the rest!"

I hasten away from her complaints and go into my cabin to confront the little devil. He sees me and screeches as he throws nuts at me through the bars of the cage.

"Keep it up and you will have to swim back to land."

He replies in monkey talk that I gratefully cannot decipher.

Shortly before we are to push away from the pier for the voyage to Japan, I step outside my cabin door and find the ship's most mysterious recluse in the corridor reading a cablegram.

Sarah gives a grimace. "Well, at least I am as important as a race-horse."

I raise my eyebrows and she shakes her head. "Nothing, my dear, just mumbling. I came to insist that you come with me to see Madame Xi Shi."

She pronounces the name Zee She.

The monkey screeches at her.

"What is that?" she asks.

"A mistake."

On our way to the outer deck, Sarah explains that she'd heard the famous Chinese spiritualist is waiting at the gangplank for the purser to clear her boarding papers.

"I saw her perform in Paris three years ago. She has a true gift of calling forth spirits of the dead."

"Maybe I should ask her to give John Cleveland a call."

We take a place at the railing along with the others who had gathered to watch the entrance of the spiritualist. An elegant sedan chair with tightly closed curtains is at the foot of the gangplank with carriers standing by. A Chinese man and two women, all dressed in black, servants to the spiritualist I assume, are standing by the chair.

The assistant purser comes onto the deck and shouts down permission to board, and the sedan chair starts up the gangplank.

"Well, she is certainly privileged," I say. "I'm sure even a queen would walk up."

"She would never make it up the gangplank. You'll see why."

At the top of the ramp, the curtains are opened to reveal a tiny woman much shorter than my own barely five feet of height. She reminds me of a ceramic doll, very beautiful, delicate, and even fragile. A wrong movement and she'll break into a million pieces. Her skin is pale white, emphasizing her red lips and cheeks. Her eyes are done in turquoise eyeshadow and lined in a deeper green. Raven black hair is twisted in coils, making a fat bun on the top of her head. Sticking out of the bun are little Oriental sticks with very small yellow feathers at each end. I can't see her hands; they are hidden in the silk, flowered robe that hides any figure.

Her red silk dress is exquisite, with dainty patterns embroidered with gold and silver thread, set off with a red silk umbrella.

As she is assisted out of the sedan chair by the female servants, I realize why the gangplank would have been a mountain to her. Her feet, encased in red slippers, are abnormally short and stubby.

"Lotus feet," Sarah whispers.

The male servant leads the way and the two female servants assist Madame Xi Shi as she walks across the deck and through a door to the interior. Even with the assistance, she sways more than a person ordinarily would . . . yet her movements are graceful. The way the woman sways could even be considered sexually suggestive.

"I've heard of this," I tell Sarah. "Feet that have been deformed by binding."

"Yes. Her feet would have been bound as a child so they grew bunched up rather than straight out. Her feet are only about three inches long. She's a Golden Lotus because that is considered the most desirable length."

I look down at my feet. They are not excessively long for a woman, but compared to Madame Xi Shi's, they look like planks.

"The comparison is to a lotus," Sarah says, "because of reverence for the flower in the Far East. That swaying walk is called the 'Lotus Gait.' It's caused by the deformity of her feet. Chinese men consider it quite erotic. I've read about the process and consider it a brutal deformation of a woman's body performed to satisfy the prurient desires of men."

"Amen to that! If men like deformed feet so much, they should have their own bound."

I can see enough of Sarah's expression under the veil to know that she is about to land a good one.

"Better yet, men who encourage this type of torture should have their penis bound so it is distorted like a lotus foot."

We shamelessly giggle like little girls. Eager for knowledge, even of oddities, I ask Sarah to tell me how lotus feet are created.

"It begins by bandaging the foot at about six years of age. It's done before the little girl's arch is fully formed. Toenails are cut way back so they can't become ingrown and all the toes and the arch are broken."

I shiver. "Good Lord. Why do they break the toes and arch?"

"So the toes can be folded under the foot, up against the sole. That way the front half of the foot grows backward and bunched up. Rather like an odd-shaped stump."

"This happens all at once when the girl is six?"

"The process takes some years. Until the foot is fully deformed and stops growing, the binding is tightened each day to give it a little less room to grow."

The sheer horror of it is mind-boggling to me.

"Chinese sex manuals list dozens of ways for a man to play with a woman's feet that have been deformed," she says. She shakes her index finger at me. "But it's not just the men of China who enslave women sexually. Arabic men insist upon hiding their women beneath veils—it's a form of sexual slavery, keeping the woman all to themselves and chained to the hearth. European and American men do it by keeping control of a woman's life, from money to education, frowning at a woman reading a newspaper or discussing politics. Women can't vote, control their own property—"

I change the subject. "Did you get to know Madame Xi Shi when she was in Paris?"

"No, I was busy with a play but a friend was quite taken by her when she opened a channel between him and his dead mother. Her name, of course, has historical significance in China. It's the name of one of the Four Beauties of ancient China. Do you know the story?"

"Vaguely." I am lying of course, trying to appear intelligent to this amazing woman.

"Four women in the history of China were of such incredible beauty, legends about them arose. Their physical features were so dazzling that if they walked by a pond of fish, the fish would drown because they forgot to swim; birds would fall out of the sky because they would stop flapping their wings—"

"Flowers would faint and fall over," I interject as a guess.

"The legend is that flowers would close their petals in shame, but I suppose that's close enough."

Sarah retreats to her cabin and I stay at the railing and watch two other passengers board. The two women are familiar to me—the widow of the Aussie sharpshooter and the young assistant—but I find their mannerisms toward one another strange: Instead of two cats snarling at each other, they are cheerfully yakking as the widow shows the younger woman a jade bracelet on her wrist, while behind them comes a line of porters carrying not just their luggage, but boxes of new purchases. Many boxes.

The widow appears to have made a nice recovery from having killed her husband in front of an audience. The gods have smiled upon her financially, too, since she complained about her money problems.

It is simply too much for my paranoid brain to believe that the death of the sharpshooter isn't connected to the intrigues that have been sailing with me since Port Said. I'm still convinced that the Aussie sharpshooter saw someone on the Colombo dock who he could blackmail.

I have a feeling the wife knows who it is. And if I don't ask, I won't find out.

Mind your own business, my good sense tells me, but I'm not listening.

52

Two hours later, when I'm certain the woman has unpacked and settled into her stateroom, I am at the "grieving" widow's door, knocking.

The door whips open. "Put it—" She is wearing a robe, her wet hair is in a towel, and she is barefoot. She stares at me, her expression turning sour. "I thought you were the steward. What do you want?"

"My name is Nellie—"

"I know who you are, you're that nosy newspaper person."

I smile sweetly. This isn't going well. Her face is flushed; whiskey and cheap perfume radiate from her. Rather early in the day for libations.

"I was a great admirer of your husband—"

She lets out a coarse burst of laughter. "Well you'd be the only one. Was he diddling you, too? He never could keep it in his pants."

"I'd like to do a story about the situation."

"I know what you're up to, but you came knocking on the wrong door. I'm not telling you anything."

"Your husband was murdered." It is a shot in the dark to stun her and to see how she reacts—which is hostile. I take a step back as she moves forward, ready to lunge at me.

"You little bitch, you better mind your own business or you'll be answering to me."

She steps back into the room and I move closer. "I'll pay you to tell me who your husband recognized at the dock."

The door to the stateroom bathroom opens and the assistant steps out, naked, wiping her wet hair. She sees me and stops. "What—" She recovers quickly and grins, not bothering to hide her nakedness.

The widow leers at me. "What's good for the goose is good for the gander."

I stumble back, avoiding a broken nose as the door slams in my face.

Whew.

Making my way down the corridor, I try to read the tea leaves again. It had not been a wasted visit. Before I knocked on the door it had been obvious to me that someone had given her a financial reward, but now I have added pieces to the puzzle: She had been warned not to talk to me. And her relationship with the assistant was a far cry from what they had earlier demonstrated in public.

Her liaison with the assistant is not something that would erupt overnight while her husband's body still lay warm. That raises an interesting question: What was the purpose of the public clawing at each other if they were having an intimate relationship?

Had Mr. Murdock been aware of his wife's affair with his assistant? More important, did the affair play any role in his death?

My session with the woman had not added to the biggest question of all: Was there any relationship between his death and the Port Said matter?

Well, this leg of my journey is turning out to be very interesting. Upside down on the bottom of the world, everything looks a bit cockeyed.

STEAMSHIP RMS *OCEANIC*
HONG KONG–TO–SAN FRANCISCO RUN

53

We are sailing between Hong Kong and Yokohama, Japan, as the New Year approaches. Standing at the bow, the forbidden zone, I let the wind and ocean spray blow at me as I stare at the horizon and wonder why I have been so fortunate as to find myself on this great adventure—and worry that I will not succeed, that the copycat reporter will not just steal my thunder but humiliate me into leaving reporting.

Black and white—that is how I've been told I see things. Win or lose. No compromises.

It is a fault, I know, but it is how I feel. That fault of mine is probably why I also so furiously hold on to Mr. Cleveland's memory—like a dog that's hopped onto the back of a meat wagon, I have clamped my jaws on the matter and all the kicking in the world won't make me let go.

Casting aside dark thoughts about my many imperfections, I ruminate about the race. My fate lies with the ship because this last leg of my journey by water is by far the longest on any conveyance I've used—over sixteen hundred miles to Yokohama, Japan, and then nearly five thousand miles across the wide Pacific to San Francisco. After that, by Iron Horse across the continent to the East Coast.

The quiet of the sea and my avoidance of company on this leg has left me alone with my thoughts, a dangerous situation that too often gets me into trouble. Pondering over the fact that a magician on board whose specialty is reading sealed messages will put on a New Year's Eve performance is exactly the sort of thing to stir up that overactive imagination Frederick Selous and Lord Warton accuse me of possessing.

Naturally, I have hatched a plot to shed some light on the mystery with a little sleight of hand myself, and before the ship's bell rings in the New Year it will be time to put my plan into effect.

In just hours the year 1889 will be found only between the pages of history books, and 1890 will take birth.

The day has been so warm that we wear no wraps. In the forepart of the evening the passengers sit together in the social hall talking, telling stories and laughing. I don't feel like socializing, but I force myself to participate because the audaciousness of my plan has me nervous.

The captain owns an organette, which he brings into the hall, and he and the ship's doctor take turns at grinding out the music.

Later in the evening we go to the dining hall where the purser has punch and champagne and oysters for us, a rare treat which he had prepared in America just for this occasion.

Afterward, a jolly man from Yokohama, whose wife is equally jolly and live spirited, teaches the assembled a song consisting of one line to a melody quite simple and catching: "Sweetly sings the donkey when he goes to grass, Sweetly sings the donkey when he goes to grass, Ec-ho! Ec-ho! Ec-ho!"

I sip punch as I listen to the passengers singing and laughing. I don't dare imbibe in the champagne because I will need steady legs and my wits about me.

The magic show is announced and we assemble in the dining room once again where a small stage has been erected.

It's time for my own magic to come into play. The plan I've concocted is to make whoever hired "Amelia Cleveland" in Hong Kong expose themselves.

To carry out my scheme, I needed Sarah, Lord and Lady Warton, and Frederick at the same table.

To accomplish this, I sweet-talked the captain into inviting me and the people on my list to his table, and threw in Von Reich for good measure because he seems to be joined at the hip with the Wartons.

Getting Lady Warton and Sarah to the table was a challenge because they are both recluses. Lady Warton attends few events, but the captain convinced her to attend, though she still wears a veil.

I have coaxed Sarah from her cloister by challenging her to attend in disguise. It was a challenge she couldn't ignore and she assumed the character of an elderly Russian dowager, a role she once played.

No matter what my suspicions are of Sarah's role in the matter, I not only admire her as a person, but like the rest of the world, I am awestruck by her talent. Frederick confided in me that he once saw her on the stage in Paris in a role in which she never left her chair—yet mesmerized the audience and overshadowed the other performers.

I got them to the captain's table, which is the closest to the stage, because I will be there myself—and I want to see their faces when I spring my trick.

The magician who claims to be able to "read" messages placed in envelopes calls himself the Great Nelson. There seem to be quite a number of magicians with a first name of "Great."

At the beginning of the show, paper, pencils, and envelopes are provided to members of the audience, who are invited to jot down a short message, no more than ten words, and place the paper in the envelope and seal it.

The envelopes are made of paper too thick for the magician to see through even if he held them up to a light.

When it is time to collect the envelopes from the passengers, the magician says, "Now I will need a volunteer to collect the sealed messages."

I jump up from my seat at the captain's table and immediately begin gathering envelopes.

"Madam, please make sure the messages are sealed and that there is no envelope among them that the human eye can see through."

Gathering the envelopes, I slip in my own, making sure it is close to the top so it will be selected early in the performance. I hand him the stack on stage and turn around to return to my seat.

"You are not done, young lady." He turns to the audience. "To prove that I am using my miraculous ability to see through the envelopes, I will have this charming lady hand them to me one at a time."

"Oh, I can't—"

"Let's have a hand for this young woman who has so generously volunteered her services."

I smother a groan as the audience claps. I needed to be back at the table, watching my companions.

"Please hand me the first envelope," he tells me.

I grimly hand it to him. He hardly looks at it and announces, "The message inside reads: THIS SHIP IS THE BEST SHIP."

He rips open the envelope and reads the message aloud again, exactly as he had stated it before he looked. Peering out to the audience, he holds up his hand to shield his eyes from the stage lights which make it much brighter onstage. "Is that correct?" the magician asks someone, then holds up the message in triumph to the audience. "As you witnessed, I read it correctly *before* opening the envelope."

Another round of applause and I hand him the second envelope. He repeats the message inside without looking, then tears open the envelope and reads the writing aloud, confirming its contents about the size of a hat with a woman in the audience whom I recognize as having been a fellow passenger with me since Colombo.

My envelope is the third one read.

"Now this is a bit unusual," he tells the audience before opening it. "It reads, VIRGINIA LYNN SENDS HER REGARDS." He opens the envelope and extracts the paper I wrote on. He reads the message aloud and then shields his eyes and asks the audience, "And would the author of this missive confirm that I am correct?"

No answer, and he repeats the question. Finally, not wanting to see the man embarrassed or threaten his reputation because of my machination, I timidly raise my own hand. "I wrote it."

"And is it correct?"

"It's correct."

Standing sadly on the stage, handing the magician another envelope, I suppress a desire to leap off the stage and run out of the room screaming. What a fiasco! The words of Robert Burns come to mind about the best-laid plans of mice and men going astray.

Defeated by stage lights! I had planned to be at the table and see the faces of my suspects when Virginia Lynn's name was spoken. Instead, I am onstage and unable to see the audience because of the bright lights.

All I have managed to achieve is to look ridiculous to at least one person in the audience: whoever hired Virginia Lynn.

Rather than return to my companions when my envelope duties for the Great Nelson are finished, I pause by the table and whisper to Sarah, "I have a headache," and leave for my cabin to mope.

I get only a few paces out of the dining room before Sarah is on my tail.

"You must tell me how the envelope trick is done. You're the only one Von Reich will reveal magic secrets to."

"He made me promise not to reveal the secrets to anyone."

"Tell me or I will start a rumor that you have the Big Pox."

"That is disgusting." The Big Pox is syphilis, the dread of every good woman whose husband drops his pants outside the home in too many places. "All right, he actually never made me promise specifically for the envelope trick, though he did for each of the others." A technicality, but one I would take advantage of.

"So tell me."

"He opens the first envelope and reads the message, but tells the audience something entirely different from what the person in the audience had written on the paper."

"Something different?" she repeats. "I don't understand."

"Remember before he opened the first envelope, he told us that the message was about the ship being the best. Then he opened the envelope, read the note inside, and announced that he was right."

"Yes."

"The message he read to himself was actually the one a woman had written about the size of a hat, but he lied and told us it was about a ship so he didn't have to reveal that he had read the hat message."

"Someone confirmed the ship message."

"No. If you think about it, you'll realize you never actually heard anyone confirm aloud that it was the correct message. The Great Nelson simply looked out at the audience and pretended someone had written it. It was very dark in the room, so no one would be suspicious if they didn't see anyone wave or nod to confirm he was right."

"So he makes up a message and has an imaginary person confirm it."

"Exactly."

"What did that accomplish?"

"It permits him to read the *first real message*. So now he knows that the message in the first envelope speaks of a hat because he has already opened and read it when he pretended to confirm his ship version. Then he opens the second envelope—"

"I get it. He reads the second message to himself so he knows what it says, but actually tells the audience *what the first one had said*. He's always one step ahead, pretending he's reading messages through the envelope when he has actually already opened up the previous envelope and memorized the contents."

"Always such simple solutions to complicated tricks," I tell her. "So unlike life."

She gives me a frown and I wonder if she is going say something about my failed attempt to expose the person who hired the woman in Hong Kong. If she does, I will know she is the one who hired the imposter.

"You should get off to your cabin and crawl into bed," she says. "You do look worse for wear. Take your headache powders. If that doesn't work, I have a bottle of coca wine."

I turn down the coca wine, a strong wine mixed with cocaine, and retreat to my room, my tail between my legs.

The monkey starts to screech and jump up and down in his cage when I walk in but immediately shuts up when he sees the look on my face.

I sit on my bed, unsure if I should scream with rage at myself or cry out of pity. What a blunder. Those damn stage lights.

"I will not give up," I tell the monkey.

I shall simply bide my time and make my move when I am ready, while I keep taking one step forward at a time. Even if they are tiny steps I will be that much closer to accomplishing my goal.

The stewardess pounds on my door shortly before midnight. "Your friends insist you come back and usher in the New Year with them."

Knowing that I must face others in the morning anyway, I reluctantly return to the dining room where champagne is being passed around. Frederick hands me a glass.

"I have made a fool of myself," I confess.

He looks puzzled and shakes his head as if he doesn't know what I'm talking about. Or does he? Is he that good of an actor? Or am I wrong in naming him as a culprit in the Amelia Cleveland charade?

When eight bells ring, we stand and sing "Auld Lang Syne" with glasses in hand, and on the last echo of the good old song toasting the death of the old year and the birth of the new, we shake hands all around, each wishing the other a happy New Year: 1889 has ended, and 1890, with its pleasures and pains, has begun.

Frederick escorts me back to my cabin and we stand in the hallway and face each other knowing that we harbor secrets from one another. There is an awkward silence for a moment before he speaks.

"Nellie, hunting big game is a dangerous business. It also requires great stamina and the ability to live under the most trying conditions. I have never taken a woman on an expedition with the unknown before and have sworn I never will, but after meeting you, I realize that I'm wrong. You would be more capable than most men, yet only half the size."

I glow with immodest pride.

"Not only are you capable," he goes on, "but you're also beautiful and charming."

"And you are a great liar," I say, still glowing. "Go on."

He smiles. "I'm glad I met you Nellie, and I hope that one day you will accompany me on one of my trips. I think we would make a good team."

My heart melts when I look in his soft blue eyes.

"I should like that very much." But there is a small part of me that wonders if it is just an empty promise since I am not totally confident of his intentions. I still don't trust him.

"Very well then, it's settled."

Before he leaves, he leans slowly forward and kisses me on the lips. "Happy New Year, Nellie."

Shortly after, I go to sleep lulled by the sounds of familiar minstrel melodies sung by the men in the smoking room beneath my cabin, the taste of Frederick's warm lips on my mouth, and the feel of his body against mine.

54

Sarah and I leave the ship at Yokohama, Japan, because we will be in the country for five days and wish to stay in a hotel.

Full of surprises, she meets me on deck disguised as a man—clothes, hair, even a nice thin mustache, which, unless she can perform miracles, is false.

"What-ya-up-to, girl," she says, with a Brooklyn accent.

"Why?" I ask. Not as to why she is disguised, that I know, but why she is dressed as a man.

"I get bored being just a woman; I like variety in my roles. I've played Prince Hamlet, my dear. Believe me, playing an American will not be as challenging."

Her voice is not too masculine, but it will suffice.

We are taken from the ship, which anchors some distance out in the bay, to the pier in a small steam launch. The first-class hotels in the different ports have their individual launches, but like American hotel horse-drawn omnibuses, while being run by the hotel to assist in procuring patrons, the traveler pays for them just the same.

Frederick joins us on the shore launch. He is in a pleasant mood and gives me a nice grin, but when I see him look at Sarah with a smile in his eyes I am ready to plunge a knife in his heart.

The port on Tokyo Bay has a pleasant, cleaned-up Sunday appearance. The Japanese rickshaw men are clad in neat navy-blue garments, their legs encased in unwrinkled tights, the upper half of their bodies in short jackets with wide-flowing sleeves. With their clean, good-natured faces, peeping from beneath comical mushroom-shaped hats and their blue-black, wiry locks cropped just above the nape of the neck, they offer a strikingly "clean-cut" contrast to the rickshaw men of other countries. Their crests are embroidered upon the back and sleeves of their top garment as are the crests of every man, woman, and child I see.

Rain the night previous has left the streets muddy and the air cool and crisp, but the sun, creeping through the mistiness of early morning, falls upon us with most gratifying warmth.

We are both staying at the Grand Hotel, a large structure, with long verandas, wide halls, and airy rooms, commanding an exquisite view of the lake in front.

It takes a little persuasion, but finally I convince Sarah to join me in seeing the sights of Yokohama. "Oh my . . ." is all I can say when Sarah meets me later in the hotel lobby. She has transformed from a saucy young man from Brooklyn to an elderly woman—white hair in a bun, a cane, a little slouch to her walk, even a big broach in the center of her chest just like my grandmother always had. The lady is indeed an actress.

"Why?" I ask again, always at a loss for words around the great actress.

"I have been informed that the Japanese are extremely respectful of their elders, so I thought, What could be more perfect then a daughter out seeing their city with her grandmother?"

"All right. I thought we'd see Yokohama and then take a trip to nearby Tokyo. Think you can handle it, Gram?"

A rickshaw is taking us down a neighborhood street filled with men, women, and children playing shuttlecock and flying kites when Sarah gives me a coy smile. "I saw you looking at that handsome devil Frederick like a lovesick adolescent, so why didn't you have him join you instead of me?"

"Nonsense, you saw nothing of the kind. Besides, I enjoy your company better than his."

"Rubbish. I've seen the way you two look at each other with bedroom eyes."

"With *what*? You're not intimating that—"

"That you two are destined to be lovers? Of course I am. If you're going to keep your passions hidden under a blanket, my dear, do have a man there to share them with."

"Sarah, you are scandalous. Please . . . there is nothing between me and Mr. Selous."

"My dear Nellie, you can't fool me. You're dying for him to water your garden." She leans closer with a lewd whisper. "How long's it been since a man put his—"

"Stop it! Or I'll jump from this contraption." My cheeks are burning but I can't make up my mind whether to laugh at or run from her impudence.

"Nellie, you're a grown woman; you've obviously dreamed of him whispering sweet nothings in your ear as you lie with him and he caresses your—"

"Stop! I won't listen to you." I put my hands over my ears.

She leans close enough so I can feel her lips on my hand covering my ear. "Tell me you don't lie awake at night and massage your love button while you dream about him fondling it?"

I let out a scream that causes the poor rickshaw man to stumble and almost fall as he brings it to an abrupt halt.

"Sorry," I tell him. "Keep going, please."

I put my hands back over my ears and she pulls one off. "Stop being a child. I expect better of you. I'm giving you the best advice you will ever get. Go enjoy the magical, sensual passion he'll give you. You won't regret it."

"And will I enjoy returning home as an unwed mother?"

"Come now, every woman knows there are ways to avoid conception. If you don't know, I'll show you, but I don't think you're a virgin. Wait!" She leans closer and whispers, "Do you prefer women?"

"I prefer you stop harassing me and deliberately embarrassing me. But since you raised the subject of lovers, why don't you tell me what is going on between you and your mystery man that has put a cloud over us since Port Said?"

"Look." She points to Japanese women happily playing shuttlecock in the streets. "Wouldn't you say they are some of the prettiest women in the world? One would think an artist painted their faces . . . those perfectly shaped cherry lips and rosy cheeks. Not to mention their silky black hair. What amazes me is the graceful way they move while walking in those god-awful wooden sandals."

In other words, she has changed the subject.

"My maid at the hotel says that rather than carry a purse, the women put money, combs, hairpins, anything they will need when they leave the house up their sleeves." She gives me a sympathetic look. "Like most women, I'm sure they carry their hearts on their sleeves, too."

The rickshaw drops us off at a covered market where everything from fish and rice, to cloth and chopsticks, are sold from booths. Sarah wanders off by herself to find a blind person to give her a bath and massage. "It's a profession the Japanese reserve for the blind and they charge almost nothing." She grabs my arm. "Come with me, it will loosen you up for Frederick."

I jerk my arm out of her grasp and she leaves me laughing. Despite her teasing, I admire her. I believe I'm a modern woman with a proper rein on my passions, while she is completely free and uninhibited toward men and sex. A quality I secretly envy.

Wandering through stalls of goods, I find myself daydreaming about what it would be like between me and Frederick if I had Sarah's sense of freedom until I spot a pair of shoes on a woman's feet that cause me to stop and stare.

I can't see the woman because she is on the other side of a wall. The stalls are partitioned by bamboo walls that leave a wide space at the bottom for air to circulate beneath and it's that space that reveals the shoes—and the leather that catches my attention. It matches the description that the fake Mrs. Cleveland used in Hong Kong to describe the shoes of the woman who hired her: light brown, with bumps that have little holes or nicks on them.

My heart is already racing as I make my way through the ceramic shop I'm in and go into the shop next door to see who is wearing the shoes.

I hurry around the corner and almost fly into a woman, quickly taking a step back and exclaiming, "Sorry."

"Perfectly all right."

The young assistant to the Aussie sharpshooter smiles at me. I look down; she's the shoe wearer.

"What's the matter? Have I picked up a little something on my shoes?"

"No, not at all," I stammer. "I'm sorry, I don't mean to be rude, but I saw your shoes and wondered if they are sold here."

A complete lie. Her shoes are a high-top laced shoe similar to my own, an Occidental style completely unlike the five-inch-high Japanese sandals that make people look as if they are walking on stilts.

"Hardly the local style, don't you think?" she says.

I had assumed she was an Aussie like the Murdocks, but while her accent is British, it carries a hint of some other European country. She has dark hair, green eyes, and a tanned complexion.

"It's the leather I find interesting, the bumps and all, I've never seen it before. What kind is it?"

"Ostrich, those big birds that don't fly."

"Ostrich? Really. My name is Nellie Bly."

"Cenza."

She offers no last name.

"We almost met—once."

"Oh yes, with me baring it all. I'm glad you didn't appear offended. Most women have been so indoctrinated by their husbands to the point that they would faint at the suggestion of love between women."

"I have learned that there is nothing wrong with people of like desiring flocking together." I give the shoes another look. "I've heard of ostriches. Their feathers are popular. Are they an Australian creature?"

"There are ostrich ranches in the Outback, though I believe the big birds are native to Africa." She glances down at my feet. "If we wore the same size, I would give mine to you since you are so enamored with them."

"Actually, it was Virginia Lynn who told me about them. You were wearing them the night you hired her."

She raises her eyebrows. "I'm sorry, I'm afraid I don't know your friend. Wasn't that the name you mentioned during the magic act?"

So much for my frontal assault. I should have guessed she had been in the audience.

She brushes against me as she leaves. "If you want a little fun, drop by our cabin. Otherwise, piss off, bitch."

Amazing. She's hard and nasty not far beneath her skin. I have a strong desire to go after her and demand she tell me what she knows, but not only would I get nowhere, I'd probably go to jail for punching her the next time she used foul language on me.

"Nellie!" Sarah comes toward me, walking much too spryly for a granny. "What a wonderful experience. He had the hands of an angel." Seeing the look on my face, she adds, "And you look like the devil just spit in your eye."

55

Frederick calls on me soon after I return to the hotel and I meet him in the lobby.

"What do you know about ostriches?" I demand, before he can get a word out of his mouth.

"Ostriches? Big, fast, nasty beasts. Full-grown males weigh in at over three hundred pounds and are dangerous if cornered. A man I knew climbed drunk into a corral of them one night. They kicked him to death. He probably forgot they kick forward, not back like a horse. Why do you ask?"

"When I was in Hong Kong, a woman approached me in the hotel and said she was Amelia, John Cleveland's wife."

"*What?* Why didn't you tell me?"

"I didn't tell you because I assumed you hired her to get something from me."

"What are you talking about? I didn't hire anyone. Nellie—"

"Stop." I hold up my hands. "You say you didn't hire her. So it could have been your friend, Lord Warton."

"I don't monitor Lord Warton's actions—nor does he mine. We're not working together, we just have a common interest of queen and country, but that is all we have in common. Did the person in Hong Kong get . . . what did you say it was?"

"Look me in the eye and tell me from the depths of your heart that you have not worked with Lord Warton to lead me astray on this investigation."

He locks eyes with me and says with sincerity, "You have my word as a gentleman."

I sigh. He's lying, of course, but there is no use pursuing it. We would simply end up again with a standoff, each bluffing while pretending to be completely innocent, neither wanting to show their hand. "Did you want to see me about something?"

"Quite so. A Japanese diplomat I met in South Africa has invited me to dinner tonight and there will be a special performance afterward—dancing girls called geishas. Would you like to go?"

"I would love to," I tell him. He had used the magic words, of course—it is not in me to miss something special.

"I'll call for you at six. Now what's this about ostriches and something you have? You must tell me—"

I step by him. "You'll have to excuse me, I have to freshen up for dinner tonight."

THE DINNER IS HELD IN A TRADITIONAL Japanese home that forms a great contrast to what I am accustomed to back home. The house is small and dainty, like a playhouse indeed, built of a thin shingle-like board that is fine in texture, despite the fact that our host is a man of some position.

Nothing was said on the way over about the Hong Kong ostrich mystery. Frederick has an uncanny ability to pretend complete disinterest in the intrigue that seems to be whirling around and under every rock I turn over, while I am determined not to give him an ounce of what I know until I get a pound of his secrets.

"Chimneys and fireplaces are unknown in the country," Frederick tells me.

I find the design of the house both unusual and clever. The first wall of the house is set back, allowing the upper floor and side walls to extend over the lower flooring, making it a portico built in instead of on the house. Light window frames, with their minute openings covered with fine rice paper instead of glass, are both doors and windows in one. The frames don't swing open and shut as do our doors, nor do they move up and down like our windows, but slide like rolling doors. They form the partitions of the houses inside and can be removed at any time, throwing the floor of two rooms together.

Both the host and hostess speak English and when I tell them that I am interested in learning more about their culture and customs, they satisfy my yearnings.

In a private moment, the hostess tells me that women of her country have tested European dress, but finding it barbarously uncomfortable and inartistic, they went back to their exquisite kimonos, though they retained the use of European underwear, which they found more healthful and comfortable than the utter absence of it, to which they had been accustomed.

"Gracefulness is taught in our schools," she says. "As girls, we are taught graceful movements, how to receive, entertain, and part with visitors, how to serve tea and sweets gracefully, and the proper and graceful way to use chopsticks."

It is a pretty sight to see this lovely woman use chopsticks—and an ugly one to see me make use of them! At dinner the instruments are laid out for us on rice paper. The chopsticks are probably twelve inches in length, but no thicker than the thinner size of lead pencils. The sticks are whittled in one piece and split only half apart to prove that they have never been used. One breaks the sticks apart before eating, and after the meal they are destroyed.

My regret as I dine with these charming people, and the only regret of my trip, and one I can never cease to deplore, was that in my hasty departure I forgot to take a Kodak. On every ship and at every port I met others—and envied them—with Kodaks. They could photograph everything that pleased them; the light in those lands is excellent, and many were the pleasant mementos of their acquaintances and themselves they carried home on their plates.*

After dinner, in the cool of the evening we go to a house that has been specially engaged to see the geisha girls. Several others, members of foreign diplomatic missions, are also attending.

At the door are the wooden shoes of the household, and we are asked to take off our shoes before entering, a proceeding rather disliked by some of the diplomatic party, who refuse absolutely to do as requested. A compromise is effected, however, by putting cloth slippers over our shoes.

The second floor has been converted into one room, with nothing in it except the matting covering the floor and a Japanese screen here and there. We sit upon the floor, for there are no chairs in Japan, but the exquisite matting is padded until it is as soft as velvet. It is laughable to see

* Cameras used "glass plates" coated with a chemical to take pictures. —The Editors

us trying to sit down, and yet more so to see us endeavor to find a posture of ease for our limbs. We are about as graceful as elephants dancing.

A smiling woman in a black kimono sits several round and square boxes containing burning charcoal before us. These are the only Japanese stoves. Afterward, she brings a tray containing a number of long-stemmed pipes—Japanese women smoke constantly—and a pot of tea and several small cups.

Impatiently, I await the geisha girls. The tiny maidens glide in at last, clad in exquisite, trailing, angel-sleeved kimonos. The girls bow gracefully, bending down until their heads touch their knees, then kneeling before us murmuring gently a greeting that sounds like "*Konbanwa!*" and drawing in their breaths with a long, hissing suction, which is a token of great honor.

The musicians sit down on the floor and begin an alarming din upon samisens, drums, and gongs, singing meanwhile through their pretty noses. If the noses were not so pretty I am sure the music would be unbearable to one who has ever heard a chest note.

The geisha girls stand posed with open fan in hand above their heads, ready to begin the dance. They are very short with the slenderest of slender waists. Their soft and tender eyes are made blacker by painted lashes and brows; their midnight hair, stiffened with a gummy wash, is most wonderfully dressed in large coils and ornamented with gold and silver flowers and gilt paper pom-poms. The younger the girl the more gay is her hair.

Their kimonos, made of the most exquisite material, trail all around them, and are loosely held together at the waist with an obi-sash; their long-flowing sleeves fall back, showing their dimpled arms and baby hands. Upon their tiny feet they wear cunning white linen socks cut with a place for the great toe. When they go out they wear wooden sandals.

The Japanese are the only women I have ever seen who can wear rouge and powder and not be repulsive, but the more charming because of it. They powder their faces and have a way of reddening their under lip just at the tip that gives them a most tempting look. The lips look like two luxurious cherries.

The musicians begin a long chanting strain, and these bits of beauty dance. With a grace, simply enchanting, they twirl their little fans, sway their dainty bodies in a hundred different poses, each one more intoxicating than the other, all the while looking so childish and shy, with an innocent smile lurking about their lips, dimpling their soft cheeks, and their black eyes twinkling with the pleasure of the dance.

After the dance the geisha girls make friends with me, examining, with surprised delight, my dress, my bracelets, my rings, my boots—to them the most wonderful and extraordinary things—my hair, my gloves. Indeed they miss very little, and they approve of all.

They say I am very sweet, and urge me to come again, and in honor of the custom of my land—the Japanese never kiss—they press their soft, pouting lips to mine in parting.

"You were a big hit with the Japanese women," Frederick says as he escorts me into the hotel lobby. "The fact that you are on a great adventure is amazing to them."

"It's amazing to me, too," I say, giving him a coy look. "So many interesting things have occurred on my journey."

"Is there something you'd like to tell me?" he asks.

He delivers the question with a stern tone, the kind used by fathers to children and overbearing husbands to wives.

"Yes, there is. I had a wonderful time tonight. Thank you. And I do have a question. How was John Cleveland dressed the day he told you on the beach that he was staying at Port Said?"

"What kind of nonsense is this? He was wearing clothes, not native garb, the clothes any British wears in a city."

"Ahh . . ."

He stares at me, his lips working but not knowing what revelation I'd gotten from the gods this time. But my triumphant grin tells him he gave the wrong answer.

He stamps off, his face a map of frustration.

Why did I do that? His tone had irked me, of course, not to mention his one-sided demand that I confide in him while he keeps his cards face-down.

Oh well, it's not in me to let sleeping dogs lie, anyway. From the time I'd met him, I've been bugged by his claim that he spoke to Mr. Cleveland on the beach and the business about the clothes just popped into my head. I don't know if he had actually spoken to a man on the beach, but even if he had, it certainly wasn't Mr. Cleveland who left the ship wearing sailor's work clothes and would have had room in his small sea bag only for his Egyptian disguise.

56

Frederick doesn't send over any invitations for the rest of my stay in Japan, but I have a pleasant time and even get Sarah to visit Tokyo with me.

The incident with Cenza and the ostrich shoes spiked my paranoia, and I keep an eye out for trouble when I should be totally relaxing in the exotic atmosphere. I have no clue as to the woman's place in the intrigue; she didn't board until long after Port Said—but she spooks me. She strikes me as someone who could smile to my face while she slips a knife between my ribs.

One of the pleasant events of my stay is a luncheon given for me on the USS *Omaha*, an American war vessel lying in the bay. Afterward, I return to the hotel and gather my possessions. A number of new friends in launches escort me to the *Oceanic*, and when we hoist anchor the steam launches blow loud blasts upon their whistles in farewell to me, and the band upon the *Omaha* plays "Home, Sweet Home," "Hail Columbia," and "The Girl I Left Behind Me," in my honor.

I wave my handkerchief so long after they are out of sight that my arms are sore for days.

Sarah simply shakes her head at the sight of the battleship hailing me. "All my success on the stage and I have never had an entire warship crew adore me. All of those men . . . wasted on a woman with a virgin mentality."

Everything promises well for a pleasant and rapid voyage. Anticipating this, Chief-Engineer Allen caused to be written over the engines and throughout the engine room, this date and couplet:

For Nellie Bly,
We'll win or die.
January 20, 1890.

The runs are marvelous until the third day out and then a storm comes upon us. They try to cheer me, saying it will only last that day, but the next day finds it worse, and it continues, never abating a moment; head winds, head sea, wild rolling, frightful pitching, until I fretfully wait for noon when I can slip off to the dining room to see the run, hoping that it will have gained a few miles on the day before, and always being disappointed.

When the storm doesn't pass, a rumor becomes current that there is a Jonah on board the ship. It is thought over and talked over and, much to my dismay, I am told that the sailors say monkeys are Jonahs.

"Monkeys bring bad weather to ships, and as long as the monkey is on board we will have storms," my steward assures me.

The chief engineer asks if I will consent to my monkey being thrown overboard. A little struggle between superstition and a feeling of justice for the monkey follows as I ponder the matter. Just then someone explains that ministers are Jonahs; they always bring bad weather to ships. And we have two ministers on board!

I tell the chief engineer quietly, "If the ministers are thrown overboard, I'll say nothing about the monkey going with them."

As soon as the weather becomes manageable, I decide it is time to put into action my plan to ferret out the person involved in the death of John Cleveland. People will go in many different directions when we land in San Francisco and this is the last leg of the journey in which I can learn the truth behind Mr. Cleveland's death. And who has tried to kill me.

Lying awake at night, I imagine the clock ticking, each moment bringing me closer to San Francisco, closer to my personal goal but also meaning that little time is left to expose an injustice. And I still know so little. If John Cleveland had spoken just another word or—

I sit straight up in bed, then get out and pace in my bare feet, a little silver moonlight taking the edge off the darkness.

My monkey opens his sleepy eyes and just watches me pace the floor back and forth. "Why not have him tell us who arranged his murder?" I ask him. Stepping up to his cage, I lock eyes with him. "It's no more crazy than committing myself to an insane asylum to get a job."

He bares his lips and snaps his white teeth together in a clatter, and I take it as a sign of approval that John Cleveland be brought back so he can confront the person who caused his murder. And I know exactly how it can be done.

"I'm going to raise the dead," I tell the monkey.

He bounces up and down in the cage and screeches loud enough to wake the dead. "Shh," I plead but it's too late; the man in the next compartment pounds the wall and shouts an ungentlemanly remark.

The idea stays with me back in bed. "Too risky," Mr. Pulitzer would say if I told him my idea. But he's said that about many of my ventures, from acting crazy to get into a madhouse, to walking the streets as a prostitute and tracking a killer to Paris. That's why Mr. Pulitzer hired me—I take chances to make things happen. Including a rise in his circulation figures. The attempt certain for failure is the one we don't try.

John Cleveland didn't live long enough to tell me everything that he wanted to say. But there is a person on board who can help him speak his piece.

57

A note to Madame Xi Shi requesting a private audience and hinting at financial reward is all I needed to arrange for an interview with the famous spiritualist who acts as a medium between this world and the beyond.

"Audience" is the precise word I used in my missive, hoping it conveyed the proper sense of servitude and admiration to the regal woman. Polishing an apple, the boys in the newsroom would call it.

On my way to her stateroom, I ponder over a more mundane problem: How would I account to Mr. Pulitzer for a fee paid to raise the dead? Not a man in tune with the unworldly, he'll be raisin' Cain with me if I don't find a clever way to bury the expense.

My feeling about spiritualists is similar to the professor William James who debunked many claims of spiritualists until he met Leonora Piper, a woman who had her first connection with the dead at eight years old when her aunt whispered to her—the very moment the aunt was dying elsewhere.

After studying the Piper woman, Dr. James was not willing to dismiss her out of hand just because all the other "psychics" he'd studied proved to be frauds. He characterized his feelings by saying that it takes only one "white crow" to prove that not all crows are black. In other words, it would take only one incidence of spiritual contact to prove the existence of a world of the dead despite all the fraudulent attempts.

Is Madame Xi Shi a white crow?

Only the dead know for sure because a séance, is, of course, necromancy—communication with the dead. In earlier days such an attempt would be considered a black art that got the practitioner into hot water—hot enough to peel one's skin off—but it is now considered a parlor game that some take very seriously.

As for my own feelings about paths between the living and the dead, I am a practical, commonsense person, and try not to close the door on things just because I can't see them. I share the belief of many that life continues beyond the grave.

When I heard about a spiritualist in New York last year who was impressing high society with his ability to call forth the bodiless essence of dead loved ones, I decided to attempt to contact my sweet father, who passed from this life when I was six.

A friend laughed when I told her what I was going to do but it was not a joking matter to me. I hoped that love would penetrate even the grave.

After listening to a shadowy figure mumbling unintelligibly while rapping was heard and the table suddenly levitated, I leaped from my chair and threw on the light to expose the fraud, showing how the medium's feet maneuvered hidden wires to create the rapping and table movement and the garbling came from a person in the adjoining room speaking in a tube that led to the chandelier overhead.

I had practiced a bit of fortunetelling myself for the event that night. Anticipating my action might stimulate a violent reaction, I had taken along a police detective who howled with laughter as he got me safely from the angry "spirits."

A FEMALE SERVANT LETS ME INSIDE Madame Xi Shi's stateroom and I resist the impulse to curtsy as I enter. The spiritualist is sitting in a high-back wicker chair that is low enough to the floor for her tiny lotus feet to reach, yet conveys the impression of a queen on a throne.

Chee Ling, her chief assistant, henchman, whatever his function, is standing beside her with his arms crossed and his hands slipped up his sleeves. Dressed entirely in black, his features narrow, he reminds me of the predator bird of prey that the desert prince had back in Egypt.

Accepting an offer of tea, I take a seat and address the predator bird who I'm told is her interpreter.

"Madame Xi Shi is world renowned for her ability to contact the spirits of the dearly departed," I say.

He nods. "Renowned in this world and *others*."

"I have come to request that she use her great powers at a séance in which she makes contact with a man who died rather . . . violently."

"Your loved one?" he asks.

"Actually, a stranger to me, at least until the last few seconds of his life."

"Madame Xi Shi does conduct private sessions." He looked pained. "Naturally, it would be necessary to make a small gift to aid her work with the spirit world."

"Her great work deserves to be richly rewarded so she can help others. There will be nine guests at the séance."

Chee Ling shakes his head. "Madame Xi Shi requires seven guests in order to achieve the proper balance of energy between this world and the spirit world. Seven is considered auspicious because during the seventh month, the Ghost Month, the gates of hell open and the dead may visit the living."

"Uh, well, frankly, I hope the spirit I wish contacted comes from a slightly cooler climate than hell. I must have nine people. I will compensate Madame Xi Shi for the additional psychic energy."

The spiritualist gets a translation from Chee Ling and nods her approval.

"We will need a room about the size of this one," Chee Ling says, "but completely empty except for a round wood table and chairs. We will need time to prepare it in a manner that will permit entry of spirits."

"I can arrange that; I understand that there are a couple of empty staterooms."

"There will be no lights and no interference of any sort."

"I need to have a candle lit."

He shakes his head. "Impossible."

"I need at least a small one, in the center of the table." I wouldn't be able to see the effect on the guests if it was completely dark. "I will, of course, add an extra donation for Madame's work with the spirit if a small candle is permitted."

More discussion and then I am told the medium will make an exception and permit a small candle.

I take a sip of tea as my heart starts beating faster. "Let me explain exactly what I need to have done."

Lord help me if this goes wrong.

Leaving Madame Xi Shi's stateroom, I am approached by the steward assigned to the corridor.

"Mademoiselle Aisse requests that you drop by to see her."

Sarah has booked herself under a different name at each leg of the journey. My guess is that the names are roles she has played on stage, and for reasons that I can't fathom, she may believe that her actions will confuse her enemies.

Whoever, wherever, or whatever they are.

That I had been seen going into the spiritualist's stateroom did not surprise me. The steward probably saw me and told Sarah who now wants to know if there is any juicy gossip to share. There is little privacy on a ship at sea.

Sarah lets me in. She is wearing a sailor's watch cap, a navy shirt, and bell-bottom trousers.

"Planning to hoist the sails, matey?" I ask.

"After this long, dreary journey on the seas, I feel as if I have saltwater in my veins. Perhaps I shall play Odysseus when I return to Paris, tied to the mast with stagehands throwing water on me as I resist the song of the Sirens."

She resists the crashing waves as she goes across to her closed coffin and sits with her feet extended down on the lid and her back to the wall. She takes a puff from a cigarette extended on a long holder and waves me to a chair, but I am too antsy to sit.

The smoke doesn't smell like any cigarette I'm familiar with, which makes me wonder sometimes about Sarah and her bohemian lifestyle.

She points the cigarette holder at me. "So tell me, girl reporter, what did you talk to the Dowager Empress of the Spirit World about? If she's any good, I have some questions about an ex-lover to ask her. The scoundrel passed onto the next world without telling me where he hid a diamond necklace that he promised to me."

"You are scandalous, Sarah. I just interviewed her for my readers. Interviewed that aide-de-camp or whatever that skinny man in black is."

"He's a eunuch."

"*No.* You mean like a harem guard?"

"Yes, an old Chinese tradition. There are thousands of them employed by the imperial family, but not as harem guard. They are considered the most trustworthy servants and political counselors in the land—almost all of whom got their status voluntarily."

"You mean by cutting off their man things?"

She grimaces and waves smoke away from her. "I am always amazed at how perfectly ridiculous grown women make themselves sound by using children's words to describe human anatomy."

"They cut off their testicles?" I ask to show I am indeed modern.

"They whack off their balls," she says in a throaty sailor's tone. "Not personally, but they are sliced off by a man who travels around and does ball-whacking with a sharp knife."

"I can't imagine a man having this done just to get a job."

She shrugs. "People do worse things to themselves."

"Why are eunuchs considered more trustworthy?"

"With no wives or children to share their loyalty, they are able to devote their entire lives to the imperial family. Like priests, except once they take up the cloth, so to speak, there is no going back. The rewards can be incredible. Some eunuchs have literally ran China in the name of emperors."

"I shudder at the thought of what they must feel when the knife blade begins to cut."

"Women have been turned into eunuchs, too. A British surgeon named Brown has made a name for himself and a good income by slicing off the clitorises of women."

"*No*. Why?"

"He guarantees it will get rid of undesirable passions in women. Husbands love the operation; it ensures their wives do not stray and doesn't bother the husbands because they satisfy their own passions outside of the home. It also thwarts masturbation, that great evil of sexual pleasures that so many learned medical men claim can lead to madness, nymphomania, and even the brothel." She gives me a narrow look. "Do you do it?"

I turn crimson from head to foot. "D-do what?

"That self-abuse called onanism, masturbation, the unnatural act, you know what I mean. Admit it . . . you play with the little mushroom button between your legs to relieve your unnatural pass—"

I am out the door in a flash, but not soon enough to hear her howl of laughter as I flee her room.

I am a modern woman. But not *that* modern.

My next stop is the captain to wangle him into hosting the séance. How else will I get the suspects there?

I approach him with the idea that it will be entertaining and memorable for the passengers. "A pity if we didn't enjoy the services of the most famous medium in the world when she is on board."

"Why would anyone want to contact the dead?" is his response.

"Queen Victoria had a séance so she might contact her beloved Albert." I don't know if that is true, but the whole world knows that the grieving for her lost love is transcendental so it is at least a credible lie.

"Really . . ." This gets him thinking. "Well, if the Queen can contact the dead, then I see no reason why we can't give it a go. Besides it's all for fun. Right?"

"Quite!"

58

Madame Xi Shi must have commanded all the spirits of the sea to haunt our ship tonight as the séance I arranged will unfold. A fog, heavy with gloom and swirling wisps, shrouds the ship, making it impossible to see everything but easy to imagine anything.

Nights like this remind me of a time as a young girl when I stayed too late playing with other children and had to walk home alone through dark woods. I broke into a run, flying breathless into the house, sure *something* in the darkness was chasing me. My mother shook her head and said, "What the eyes can't see, the mind will."

"Oh well," I tell the sea, pushing back from where I have been standing at the rail, gathering my courage for the drama I have schemed—a *denouement*, a fancy French word for revealing the killer in a play or a book. I just hope Madame Xi Shi's Chinese spirits are up to a bit of mystery-solving.

Shivering as I carry a little of the chill night back inside with me, I conclude that no one could have asked for a better setting to summon a spirit.

Midnight, and the living I have summoned are arriving to meet the dead.

The rendezvous is an empty stateroom the captain has donated for the evening and that Madame Xi Shi's assistants have turned into a—

"Crypt!" Sarah declares, stepping into the room that is completely draped in black—walls, floor, ceiling. "Even the air looks black."

"Like the inside of a coffin," I suggest. "With the lid down."

She shudders. "That happened once."

Amazing. Sarah is frumpy tonight, a middle-aged woman with some parts needing support. And she does it with little makeup, mostly it's just an attitude, though drab clothes add to the dowdiness. She has a central European accent tonight.

The only furniture sits in the center of the room: the round wooden table and bare wooden chairs have deep groves in them from years of use. As I requested, one thin, church like, white candle is in the center of the table, held by a plain silver candlestick.

Sarah pats the table. "Reminds me of a set piece in one of my plays. A table in a medieval castle. When the candle went out, the spirits of people tortured in the dungeon came to life."

"Perfect." Except for the candle going out.

The Wartons enter; a lip-pressing look of annoyance from his lordship, an ominous frown from her ladyship that reminds me of the Queen of Hearts's command of "Off with her head!" in Alice's adventure.

Oh well. I can always throw myself overboard if everything goes to hell tonight.

They come in, most dressed in black, men and women alike, as has Sarah. Why, I don't know; I had considered it myself, but didn't have a black dress. Perhaps it is a show of respect since black is the color of death. Cenza doesn't bother with respect; her choice of color is red. The little tart has chosen *harlot red*, and she has clutched onto Von Reich, much to the annoyance of the widow Murdock.

"Isn't she the prima donna?" Sarah whispers.

No matchmaker would team Von Reich and Cenza, and unless the attraction is to the Viennese's money, I have to wonder why the public display of affection.

Chee Ling seats the nine of us: Sarah, the Wartons, Von Reich, the harlot in red, the widow wearing a whiskey flush, Frederick who doesn't recognize Sarah, the captain looking handsome in a dark navy blue uniform, and one scared rabbit.

"There must be no talking during the performance," Chee Ling instructs us with the tone of a disciplinarian schoolmaster. "Complete silence is required for Madame Xi Shi in order to contact the spirits."

The candle is lit, the door is shut, and the lights go out. It's quickly evident why the spiritualist had little objection to the candle—with nothing to reflect the light, it hardly takes the edge off of the complete darkness in the room. All the faces are in dark shadows and I can barely make them out.

Von Reich tells us, "The purpose of the candle is to create a light for the spirits to find us. Isn't that so . . . uh, where are you?"

Chee Ling has vanished in the darkness.

I didn't volunteer that the real purpose of the candle is to let me spot the living guilty.

Everyone, everything is in position, except the outcome. I start a little prayer and stop, seriously doubting that I should bring to the attention of the Almighty that I am orchestrating black magic.

Regrets that I have devised this scheme are welling up in my throat as Madame Xi Shi appears, floating in the air, coming to the table. A tiny light from the front of her clothes gives light and shadow to her frail features.

There are murmurs, a gasp I think from the widow Murdock, and a whisper to me from Sarah: "Nicely done." She's talking about the showmanship.

The small candle I insisted upon gives away the trick, at least to me, closest to the spiritualist. I can make out that she is sitting on a pillow placed on a small platform painted black, the tubular shape conveying an impression of bamboo. The assistants carrying her are covered completely in black, appearing as just the slightest hint of movement in the darkness.

Very clever. Without the candle, I would not have seen anything except the glow of her features from her own light. That tiny light takes another shade off the darkness, enough for me to make out that people at the table are all focused on the spiritualist.

When I had first seen her, she reminded me of a ceramic doll, one of those beautiful China dolls craftspeople in Hong Kong make so cleverly. Tonight she strikes me as a goddess of the exotic and mysterious East, a deity of the shadow world.

Madame Xi Shi lowers her head and puts her hands in a prayer form, and we hear the whisper of wind, a cold stirring that causes the candle to flicker and which gives me a shiver.

Wind? The portholes are covered; the entire room is cloaked in heavy black drapes. I don't know and don't want to think about it.

A sound comes from Madame Xi Shi. Not words, at least not any that I can understand or even distinguish as words of another language, but more of a hum, a chant, and Chee Ling's voice finds us in the darkness.

"Madame Xi Shi's spirit contact is a Tibetan monk whose physical body passed beyond sorrow three hundred years ago but whose spirit is strong. He is her guide into the world beyond."

A childhood memory flashes in my mind: After my father died, my mother stood in front of my father's casket, looking down at him. The minister stood beside her. She asked him, "How long does it take for a soul to leave its body?"

His answer never left me. "It depends if the person died peacefully."

Mr. Cleveland died violently. Does this mean his spirit is still here waiting for justice? Maybe she really will summon John Cleveland's spirit.

The hum slowly rises, until it fills the room with its powerful tone.

A ghostly image flashes across the room and everyone gives a start.

Cenza giggles and that releases the tension in the room.

"Probably a light trick—" Von Reich says, but is silenced by a loud hiss from somewhere in the room. Chee Ling, no doubt.

Another voice is heard, a deep rumble, and I sense someone is behind me. I want to look, but in truth, I'm afraid to. This is all getting too real for me.

A dark mass materializes behind Madame Xi Shi, more a shadowy darkness that doesn't seem to have any definite shape to it.

It *floats* closer to her and an animated conversation erupts between the dark mass and Madame Xi Shi, words that sound like the gibberish I once heard in a holy roller church; "speaking in tongues" some call it.

A gong sounds and then complete silence as the dark form vanishes into the night air.

A strange guttural noise emits from Madame Xi Shi and she sits upright, and *stares right at me*.

She opens her mouth and an eerie male voice comes out. "Amelia—"

"You poor man!" Lady Warton shouts. *"You were murdered! God help you! You were murdered!"*

She stands up and grabs her chest and starts gasping for air. Her breathing becomes labored and she falls back into the chair. *"My heart! My heart!"*

Frederick quickly throws open the door to the corridor to let in light and jerks the covering off the electric light next to the door.

"Someone get the doctor!" the captain shouts.

I'M IN A FOG. Imprisoned by stunned arms and legs to my chair, unable to move, unable to talk, as the drama around Lady Warton unfolds. A prisoner to my own sense of shame and doom, I don't even turn my head as she is taken out of the room in a wheelchair.

The ship's doctor hovers over her as Von Reich wheels her out. Lord Warton comes at me and Frederick is suddenly there, restraining him.

"You're a devil!" Lord Warton spits at me. "If this ridiculous trick of yours kills my wife, it will be on your head and I'll make sure you are prosecuted!"

"Leave her alone!" Sarah yells at him as she puts her arms around my shoulders.

I can't say anything; all I can do is shake my head as Frederick guides the irate husband out of the room.

The captain is suddenly in my face. "What is Lord Warton talking about?"

Frederick comes up to the captain and answers his question for me as I sit paralyzed.

"Nellie, the Wartons, and Herr Von Reich witnessed the murder of a man, John Cleveland, at a Port Said marketplace. She also feels I had some part to play in it."

I cringe when he says the words.

"The moment the name Amelia was uttered, it became obvious that she had concocted this farce to smoke out the killer. She only had the best of intentions."

"Nonsense!" The captain glows with anger. "That makes no difference. What in heaven's name were you thinking?"

I have no answer. I am lost.

"The poor woman has had a heart attack!" Now he's yelling. "You may have killed the wife of a British peer with a cruel and tasteless joke. Everything I have heard about you is true. You are a troublemaker!"

The first officer has arrived and the captain turns to him.

"Officer, escort this woman to her cabin. You are not to leave without my permission," he snaps at me. "You will not cause any more trouble on my ship. If you do, I will have you put in chains."

The first officer reaches for my arm and Frederick is suddenly there again. "I'll escort her for you."

Frederick offers me his arm and I slowly rise and take it, my knees so weak I must walk stiffly to keep from collapsing.

Ahead of us in the hallway, Cenza, walking with the Murdock woman, turns and laughs. "Everyone has a price," she shouts.

I have no idea what she is talking about. Suppressing the urge to vomit, I keep up with Frederick, walking stiffly, like a zombie.

When we get to the cabin, the first officer pardons himself. "Sorry, Miss Bly. You know the whole crew is rooting for you."

I just shake my head. I have let them down, too.

Frederick puts his arms around me and gives me a hug. I let him pull me into him, but I don't squeeze back. I am completely drained of emotion.

He holds my head in his hands. "I know your motives were pure."

I bend my head down, unable to meet his gaze. "I'm an idiot. I should be shot."

"The captain won't go that far. I hope." He smiles. "Just joking."

"Thank you for protecting me. You are truly a gentleman. And more than I deserve."

Escaping into my cabin, I shut the door behind me and stagger to my bed.

I'm still sitting on the edge of the bed, my life passing before my eyes, when Sarah opens the door. "Bread and water for the prisoner," she says.

She has a bottle of champagne and a small cake.

"You'll be happy to know that Lady Warton has not slipped off to the spirit world. In fact, she never went to the ship's infirmary, but had them take her to their stateroom."

"To her room? After shouting 'heart attack'? Now I know what she meant when she said everyone has a price."

Sarah sets down the "prison food" and gives me a look. "Lady Warton said that?"

"No, Cenza, the one in red. She laughed at me and said everyone has a price."

"Meaning?"

"Chee Ling the Eunuch, the spiritualist's mouthpiece, henchman, whatever. He sold my scheme to other people."

"Ah, well, that explains that."

"Explains what?"

"Why Lady Warton's heart attack sounded so contrived. I've died from a broken heart on stage much more realistically than her pathetic moans and groans."

I bang myself on the forehead. "They set me up. The whole bunch of them. I *should* be shot for my stupidity."

"Don't say that too loud, darling. The captain might hear."

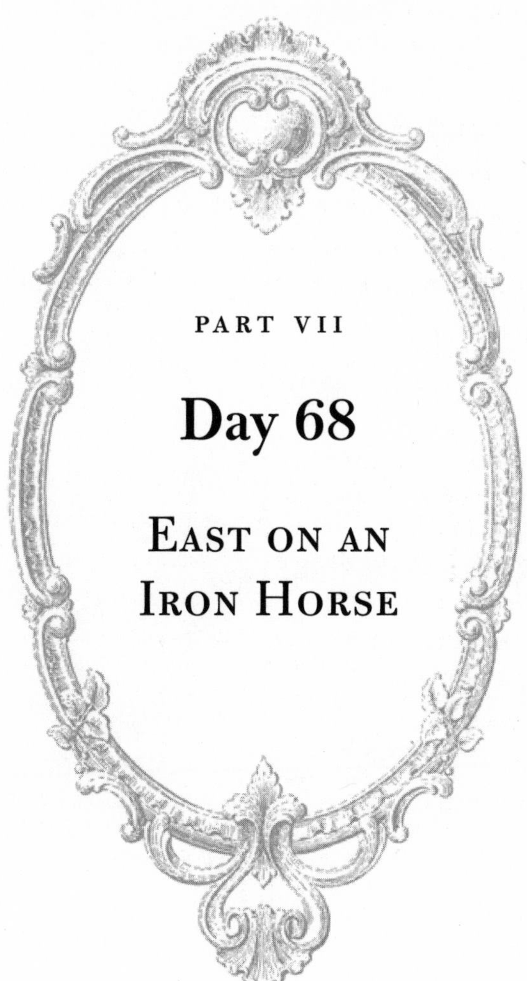

PART VII

Day 68

East on an Iron Horse

ON TIME!

Nellie Bly Arrived Yesterday at San Francisco and Is Speeding Home.

M. JULES VERNE OUTDONE.

A Rousing Welcome for "The World's" Globe-Girdler.

KIND GREETINGS EVERYWHERE.

The Long Trip from Yokohama Comes to an End and Miss Bly Starts in on the Homestretch—The Escort Corps Had a Perilous Time of It but Caught Her at Last—The Circumnavigator Sends a Despatch—Welcomes en Route.

NELLIE ARRIVING IN SAN FRANCISCO

I arrive at the gateway to San Francisco Bay on January 21, 1890. A gray morning with wet chill air and choppy seas adds to a sense of gloom and doom that grips me as I stand on the deck of the tugboat and look back at the *Oceanic* as it slowly fades into a dark shadow in a bank of fog.

Frederick, Sarah, and Von Reich are among the passengers lining the deck to see me off or there just to get a look at the first sight of land in nearly five thousand miles. I'm sure the Wartons and the Aussie widow and assistant are on the crowded deck, too, if for no other reason than to make sure I have left.

Getting off the ship and onto the tug leaves me breathless with anxiety and anticipation and now that the umbilical cord has been cut, I feel a bit disconcerted, a sense of unease and I know the cause: unfinished business.

So many unanswered questions are still on the ship. Sarah and Frederick—two people I am fond of, yet unable to fully trust because I know they harbor secrets. I feel a warmth toward Frederick that surpasses friendship despite the lies and charades we both practice, though I am not fool enough to believe that he would ever trade the green jungles of Africa for the hard concrete ones of New York.

Now as the little tug is taking me away from the people I have gone more than halfway around the world with, people who might have the answers to my question, I cannot help but feel loss and despair.

Worse than my feeling of loss, is my feeling of inadequacy. I failed to expose an injustice. I never learned why Mr. Cleveland died in an Egyptian marketplace. He secreted to me a scarab with a key inside as he whispered a name—Amelia. Who is she? His lover? *Who?* Certainly she was not that actress in Hong Kong.

My sense of confidence has been trampled because a man dies in my arms and passes to me the hidden reason for his death, and I have been unable to unravel it.

"Nellie, stop this!" I tell the ocean air. Sulking and moping won't heal the wound and definitely won't make me feel any better.

I wave good-bye one more time to the *Oceanic*, Frederick, Sarah, and all the rest, even though I know they won't see my gesture. I have to accept the fact that I am forever separated from the mystery and must move on.

Now I have only one thing to do: finish the race in first place.

It's no exaggeration of my feelings when I say I would rather die than suffer the humiliation of defeat at the hands of the woman from *Cosmopolitan* magazine, who shows she is without honor and common decency when she started a race against me without even telling me.

My estimation is that she has already set sail from a French port. It takes about the same time to cross the North American continent by rail as it does the Atlantic from Calais to New York by ship—if the railroad line over the Sierra Mountains is not buried in snow.

The news that it is shouldn't have surprised me—it is January, the heart of winter.

The mountains becoming impassable because of winter storms is the reason her editor must have chosen the east-to-west route—she would have crossed the Sierras over two months ago.

Soon I will be at the train station, and from the telegraphic communications that the railroads use to relate status of their routes, I'll know whether I have already lost. If by some miracle the rails are cleared, we will be neck and neck to the end and I shall have no peace until—unless—I cross the finish line *first*.

It is my fondest hope that my competitor is washed overboard in an Atlantic gale and finishes the race in Davy Jones's locker.

Moving from the stern of the tug, I turn my back on the *Oceanic* and go to the bow, having this silly notion that by doing this I will pass through the channel called the Golden Gate a second or two quicker than if I had I been at the rear, fantasizing that these seconds will help me win the race.

Even though there are still thousands of miles to go, I have a wonderful sense of relief knowing I'm back in my own country where I don't have to fear arrest or harm for having become entangled in the intrigues of men and nations. Best of all, I don't have to constantly keep a watch over my shoulder for someone who wants to give me a shove overboard or put a knife between my shoulder blades.

With the key still hidden in my shoe, I still don't know what it unlocks, why it was important to Mr. Cleveland, or why others so desperately want it. One conclusion I reached is what to do with it: I'll turn it over to the British Embassy in Washington, after extracting a promise that they will assist me in contacting Mr. Cleveland's Amelia. She can't have the key because it would put her in danger.

This key has already left two men dead in the marketplace in Egypt and another on a magician's stage in the middle of the ocean, and very nearly caused the loss of my own life, not once but twice.

If only I could rub the key like a jinnie's lamp and have its secret revealed.

A man comes out of the pilot house and joins me at the bow.

"Welcome to San Francisco, Miss Bly. I'm Henry Stewart from the office of the Port of San Francisco. It's my job this morning to get you to the Oakland train terminal as soon as possible."

"That's kind of you. Is there any news about the mountain passes? Are they still snowed in?"

"We won't know until we reach the terminal, but that was the case two hours ago. You know, there is another route, down the central valley and across the southern desert."

"Isn't that much farther than over the mountains?"

"Yes, it would add quite a bit of time to your record."

A ferry on its way from San Francisco toots its horn at us as we pass through the Golden Gate.

"The railroad ferry on its way to Sausalito," Mr. Stewart says. "They say someday there will be a bridge across the Golden Gate channel, but that Frenchman who writes fantastic novels also says someday we'll fly to the moon. I wouldn't put my money on either ever happening. At two miles, the gap is too wide and the water too deep to support a bridge. It's just physically impossible."

That "Frenchman" is, of course, Jules Verne, and I am not one to doubt any of Monsieur Verne's predictions.

As the tug steams close to a pier in San Francisco, I'm surprised to see a group of people waving and cheering my name.

"Welcome Nellie Bly! Welcome Nellie Bly!"

Smiling, I return their greeting. "How did they know I arrived?"

Mr. Stewart chuckles. "You're the talk of the town, the talk of the whole country. When news came that you had left Yokohama, everybody got excited."

Unlike the Atlantic and Indian oceans, no cable spanned the Pacific, so the news that the *Oceanic* had left Japan would have traveled opposite my route around the world, transmitted on undersea cables back from the Far East to India, Africa, Europe, and across the Atlantic to New York, then by telegraph wires strung across the continent to San Francisco.

The fact that a message can be sent as Morse code dots and dashes nearly around the globe over a piece of copper wire is a scientific miracle that makes me believe that almost anything Jules Verne can dream up, people will someday be able to accomplish.

"If it's okay with you, we'll get closer to the Frisco piers as we wrap around the peninsula to Oakland on the other side of the bay," Mr. Stewart explains. "The people of San Francisco want to get a glimpse of you and it'll only add a few minutes to your trip."

"That's fine," I say, dreading the loss of the minutes. "I regret that I don't have time to see your beautiful city and thank everyone for their support."

"Actually, since some of the most famous parts of the city are built on hills facing the bay, you'll see a great deal right from this tug." He points at a streetcar crawling up a hill. "That's a cable car. Do you know how they came about?"

I shake my head no.

"A man named Hallidie saw horses being whipped while they struggled on the wet cobblestones to pull a horse-car up a steep hill. The horses slipped and were dragged to their death as the horse-car rolled back down the hill. He decided enough of that and invented a way to pull the cars with an underground cable."

"Thank God for Mr. Hallidie."

As Mr. Stewart chats about the city's colorful history, I continue to wave at the people who stand on the piers and cheer me on. The sun has come out and some of the gloom and doom I felt leaving the ship has evaporated, but the anxiety is still with me.

People are hailing me as the conquering hero, as if my journey around the globe is for all Americans, helping to bond us with so much of the world that knows so little about us—but the race is not won yet and the cheers of success could easily turn into the stings of defeat.

No bridge has been built to link San Francisco with the east side of the bay, either, so the transcontinental railroad ends at Oakland and passengers and goods are transferred by boat to San Francisco.

Mr. Stewart confers with men waiting at the pier as soon as we dock and returns with a smile. "The train has also been waiting for your arrival in readiness to start the moment you board it. Everyone wants to make sure you win your race."

"The pass over the mountains?"

"Still blocked, but I understand other arrangements have been made."

"Still blocked" sticks in my head as I'm escorted to a train that has only one passenger car. I'm staggered when I'm told that it's a special train just for me.

The *Miss Nellie Bly Special* consists of the *San Lorenzo*, a handsome Pullman car, the engine called the *Queen*, one of the fastest on the Southern Pacific line, the tender car that carries coal and wood to keep the steam engine going, and a caboose.

"What time do you want to reach New York, Miss Bly?" Mr. Bissell, general passenger agent of the Atlantic and Pacific system, asks me.

"No later than Saturday evening."

"Very well, we will put you there on time," he says quietly. "At least the first leg, the *Queen* will carry you to Chicago."

"How will you get me there on time if the pass is still closed?"

"We are taking a route that Mr. Pulitzer chose," he says, "which I must say is quite clever. Instead of going directly east to Chicago, we're sending you hundreds of miles south and then across the southwest deserts through Arizona and New Mexico before turning north to the Windy City. It's five hundred miles longer, but it has less snow and rail traffic."

As I board, the conductor, porter, engineer, and fireman introduce themselves.

"I'll keep the throttle wide open," the engineer proudly states.

"And I will keep the boiler red hot," the fireman says.

I'm so tickled by their enthusiasm, I feel like I should also contribute.

"If you tire of shoveling coal," I tell the fireman, "I'll help you shovel until the *Queen* is flying."

Changing my mode of conveyance from steamship to steam locomotive makes me reflect upon how dependent I've been for the past couple of months on the strong arms of men shoveling coal into boilers and how fortunate I've been so far that the engines themselves did not fail me.

Crossing my fingers, I pray my luck will continue

While we are doing some fine running the first day, the horn blasts and there's a bump as if we strike something. Brakes screech, we come to a stop and go out to see what has occurred. My first thought is there'll be a delay.

It is overcast, with rain in the air, and it's hailing when we step out and see two men coming up the track. The conductor meets them and returns to tell us, "We hit a handcar." He points down the track to a piece of twisted iron and a bit of splintered board—all that remains of the four-wheeled platform with a hand pump that rail crews used for transportation.

When the men come up, one remarks, with a mingled expression of wonder and disgust upon his face: "Well, you *are* running like h—!"

"Thank you, I am glad to hear it," I say, and we all laugh.

"Is anyone hurt?" I inquire.

"No." They assure me they are not.

With good humor being restored all around we say good-bye, and the engineer pulls the lever, and we are off again.

At Merced, our second stop, a great crowd of people dressed in their best Sunday clothes have gathered about the station.

"Are they having a picnic? I ask the conductor.

"Oh, no . . . they've come to see you."

"*Me* . . . oh my."

A loud cheer, which almost frightens me to death, greets my appearance and the band begins playing, "By Nellie's Blue Eyes."

A large tray of fruit, candy, and nuts, the tribute of a dear little newsboy, are passed to me, for which I am more grateful than had it been the gift of a king.

After waves to the crowd and yells of *"Thank you!"* we are off again.

The three of us in the train car have nothing to do but admire the beautiful country, through which we are passing as swiftly as clouds along the sky, or to read, or count telegraph poles, or pamper and pet the monkey.

Having little inclination to do anything but to sit quietly, I rest, bodily and mentally. There is nothing left for me to do now. I can't hurry anything or change anything, and this makes me realize the same goes for Mr. Cleveland's murder. It is completely out of my control—it's done, it's over with. I can only sit and wait until the train lands me at the end of my journey and then I shall go to the British Embassy and give them the key and Amelia Cleveland's name.

With this resolution, I close my eyes and enjoy the rapid motion of the train so much that I dread to think it could stop.

AT THE NEXT STATION, the town turns out to do me honor and I am the happy recipient of exquisite fruits, wines, and flowers—all the products of Fresno County, California.

The men are interested in my sunburned nose, the delays I have experienced, the number of miles I have travelled, the women want to examine my one dress in which I have travelled around the world as well as the cloak and cap I've worn, and are anxious to know what is in the little valise, and all about the monkey.

A man on the outskirts of the crowd shouts, "Nellie Bly, I must get up close to you!"

The crowd evidently feels as much curiosity as I do about the man's objective, for they make way and he comes up to the platform. "Nellie Bly, you must touch my hand," he says, excitedly.

Anything to please the man. Reaching over, I touch his hand and then he shouts: "Now you will be successful. I have in my hand the left hind foot of a rabbit!"

Well, I don't know anything about the left hind foot of a rabbit, but later my train runs safely across a bridge that was held in place only by screw jacks and fell the moment we crossed it; following that near disaster, the engine which had just switched off from us, loses a wheel. At such moments I think of the left hind foot of a rabbit and wonder if there is anything in it. I also wonder if it will counteract any of the bad luck that seems to be associated with the key in my shoe heel.

Another place, where a large crowd greets me, a man on the limits of it yells, "Did you ride on an elephant, Nellie?"

When I reply, "No, I didn't," he drops his head and walks away, leaving me to feel that I'd let him down.

Then we stop at another place where the policemen have to fight to keep the crowd back; everybody wants to shake hands with me, but at last one officer is shoved aside and the other, seeing the fate of his comrade, turns to me, saying: "I guess I'll give up and take a shake," and while reaching for my hand he is swept on with the crowd.

My entire trip down California's central valley and across the deserts of the southwest went on like that—leaning over platforms and shaking with both hands at every station, and when the train pulls out crowds run after us, grabbing for my hands as long as they can.

My arms ache, but I don't mind the pain, my trip being a haze of happy wishes, congratulating telegrams, fruit, flowers, loud cheers, rapid hand-shaking, and a beautiful car filled with fragrant flowers attached to a swift engine that is tearing like mad through flower-dotted valleys and over snow-tipped mountains, on—on—on!

During this time I find myself living in the moment and forgetting all my cares and worries. Mr. Cleveland no longer exists to me. I am home, safe, and very happy.

"Come out here and we'll elect you governor," a Kansas man says, and I believe they would have, if the splendid welcomes they give me are any criterion.

It's impossible to mention one place that was kinder than another. Over ten thousand people greet me at Topeka. To say I feel honored is an understatement. Everyone has been so kind and as anxious that I should finish the trip in time, it's as if their personal reputations are at stake.

It's only when I'm alone at night, in my bunk, listening to the rails sing as we roll along that little doubts and fears sneak back into my head. Sometimes I feel as if there's a spider in my ear, whispering a question that became a mantra to me when things went from bad to worse.

When will the other shoe fall?

60

I'm sleeping late when George the porter knocks and tells me we will be arriving on the outskirts of Chicago shortly.

I dress myself leisurely and drink the last drop of coffee there is left on our train, for we have been entertaining anybody who cared to travel any distance with us, before joining my two train mates in the stateroom.

There is little for us—Henry the conductor, George the porter, and myself—to do in the Pullman car except watch the fields and hills slip by as we roar down the tracks with the throttle wide open.

I listen with interest as they talk about the history of the Pullman car, how not too long ago it revolutionized train travel, literally creating a hotel on wheels for the ordinary traveller and palatial luxury for the rich.

The inventor of the sleeping car, George Pullman, designed his car after spending miserable overnight trips sitting up in a train seat. The other option was to sleep on the dirty floor, using one's bag as a pillow.

Mr. Pullman's concept of berths that fold up by day, a washroom for men and one for women, clean sheets, towels, and pillows, became so popular he built cars just for sleeping while travelling.

The car on my "special train" had thick carpeting, draperies, carved mahogany paneling, French upholstered chairs, a stocked bookcase, a card table, a chandelier and oil lamps rather than candles, plenty of head room, and water provided from an overhead system of tanks. And, of course, "George" the porter. All Pullman porters are called "George"—the name being taken from George Pullman.

George tells me my special car pales in comparison to the private cars for wealthy people that are built specifically to their specifications, with as much attention to detail as the construction of their yachts. But, Abraham

Lincoln so disliked the ornate railroad car supplied for his service as president, he only rode in it once—when it carried his coffin.

"The Lincoln funeral train is still running on the tracks, filled with ghosts," George says. "Every April it comes through at midnight, following the route it took when it carried his body home. It passes by with long black streamers waving, a band playing, and skeletons sitting around."

I stare out the window watching telegraph poles flying by as I listen idly to their conversation about railroading when I hear a name that gives me a start.

"What did you say, George?"

"Ma'am?"

"What was that name you just said?"

"You mean Amelia?"

"Yes, what about Amelia?"

"Why, *Amelia*'s the finest private rail car in the country. I spent a month serving on it last year when a porter friend took ill."

"Who does it belong to?"

"To Stirling Westcot, the wealthy railroad magnate."

Westcot. His name is recognizable not just to me, but to people in all forty-two states as one of the richest men in the nation. He owns railroads and coal mines. His name is also synonymous with ruthless business practices.

"Is Amelia his wife's name?"

"No, ma'am, it's the name of his horse that won the Kentucky Derby last year."

What had Sarah said to me just before we sailed from Hong Kong? Something about her being as important as a *racehorse*.

Pieces fall into place. Amelia. Sarah's remark about a racehorse. A Pullman car named *Amelia* owned by a rich horse-racing enthusiast.

A coincidence?

The hair quivering on the back of my head says it's not. So do the knots in my stomach. Getting up, I pace back and forth, thoughts flying through my head, none of them forming a coherent pattern.

How do I make a connection with a murder in an Egyptian marketplace, a holy war to drive the British from Egypt and the Suez Canal, a train car named *Amelia*, the world's greatest actress, and an American racehorse enthusiast as rich as Midas?

No matter how the pieces are twisted, they don't fit together. Connecting them requires a romantic link between Sarah and Stirling Westcot. While he is immensely wealthy, he also is very short with an oversized head, and is famous for being as mean as a snake and as cheap as a Memphis minister.

A man with enough money can attract beautiful lovers, even if he looks like a toad and acts like a cad. But when Sarah spoke of her mysterious lover, there was real passion in her voice. A fire lit up in her eyes and she got that "glow" only real love can produce.

Stirling Westcot doesn't fit with her passion. And neither do fanatical terrorists halfway around the world and the struggle to control the Suez Canal. Westcot makes money, not nations.

"There's no connection between them despite the name," I tell the conductor and George.

They both agree without knowing to what they have assented.

Sitting down, satisfied that I have reached the correct conclusion, it occurs to me there is one more item concerning Mr. Cleveland that I have not resolved.

As the men go back to talking, I slip off my shoe and twist the heel to let the key drop into my hand. "What do you turn, little fellow?"

George the porter stares at my key and then checks the ring he carries on his belt.

"What is it, George?"

"Sorry, ma'am, for a moment I thought you had my key."

"You have a key like this?"

"Of course I do. All porters have them. It opens the storage area beneath the car."

Oh my God.

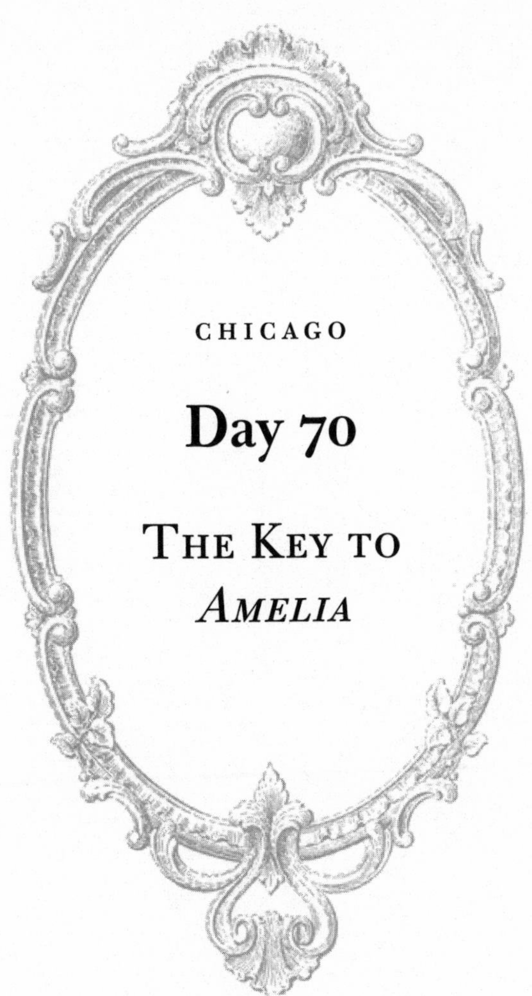

CHICAGO

Day 70

The Key to *Amelia*

61

Just before the train is to pull into a station outside Chicago, I slip back into my compartment with the excuse of needing to freshen up, but I want the time alone to get my wits about me.

There is a connection between the killings in Port Said, Sarah, the struggle for Egypt and the Suez Canal, and one of the richest men in America: The sleight of hand that weaves them all together is the key.

No longer is there any doubt as to what the key opens—for over twelve thousand miles, I have carried a key that unlocks the storage bin in the underbelly of a private Pullman car.

Now I am completely stumped by the importance of the key.

Why it was hidden in a scarab seems obvious—it allowed the key to be passed secretly on to someone without drawing attention. Whoever passed it or received it must have believed that they would be watched and didn't want the key to be seen exchanging hands.

Mr. Cleveland intercepted it, literally grabbing it and running, so it wasn't meant for him. And it got him killed.

A scarab is a good choice to hide the key in. Of all the things a European tourist might purchase in an Egyptian marketplace, a souvenir scarab ranks very high on the list, probably at the top, beating out cartouches and hieroglyphic art painted on papyrus. Definitely avoids attracting attention.

The scheme starts to take some shape in my mind, at least the passing of the key. The person who was supposed to receive the key was a European, probably someone from our ship. While many passengers on board may have visited the marketplace, only a few of them stand out in my mind, Lord and Lady Warton and Von Reich, and only because I accompanied them. It was Lord Warton who insisted we go to that area of the marketplace because he wanted to pick up something for his sister.

That doesn't meant that there weren't a dozen other passengers in the area or that the pass off wasn't to take place later. That snake magic had me engrossed and I wasn't paying attention to what was happening around me.

Whoever picked up the scarab-key intended to carry it to America and open the storage area underneath Westcot's private train car. But why?

What is in that locker that is so important it triggered murder and intrigue halfway around the world, has some connection to a holy war in Egypt against foreigners, and can rattle the sabers of the British Empire because their hold on the Suez Canal is threatened?

From the news stories I read about Stirling Westcot, he was an unlikely candidate to be involved in international intrigue or anything across the seas. He prided himself on making money, period, and the only business he had with politicians were the stuffed envelopes he slipped them when he wanted something. Other than gouging as much money as he can from coal mines and railroads, his only passion is horse-racing. If it wasn't for Sarah's cryptic remark about a racehorse, I would not be able to make a connection between Egypt, the canal, and a Pullman car called *Amelia*.

The secret I still have no clue about is the contents of the storage box, but no matter how I stirred the pot, it all boils down to one thing: When the key is used on the *Amelia*, it will open Pandora's box. And it will trigger something with international consequences. There is no other explanation for a Mahdi connection.

Somehow Sarah is mixed up in the intrigue, but I'm certain it's an innocent involvement. I found her too blunt and open about her thoughts and feelings to picture her as a schemer. Nor does she strike me as politically zealous. I'm sure Sarah could care less whether the Suez Canal belonged to Egyptians, the British, or the man in the moon, and she is definitely too melodramatic for spying.

Whatever earthshaking events are unfolding, they don't seem to relate to Sarah but to the important man she is clandestinely rendezvousing with. And try as I might, I can't see her romantically connected to Stirling Westcot. A man had to have more than money to capture her heart. Perhaps Westcot has a son Sarah has become involved with? One in the diplomatic corps?

No matter how I try, I can't get the pieces to stack into nice, neat piles.

Maybe I'm building a mountain out of a molehill; perhaps I'm wrong, a train car named *Amelia* might just be a bizarre coincidence—but it sounds right to me.

Now I'm worried for Sarah. I need to contact her, find out where she is going and where this train car *Amelia* is. But how?

I must finish my race. Too many people are counting on me. I've gone this far, there's no turning back. *Damn!* What I desperately need is time, which I don't have.

George knocks on my door. "Miss Bly, there's a reception committee here for you."

I find the social area of the car quite filled with good-looking men.

"Hello, Miss Bly, I'm Mr. Cornelius Gardener, the vice president of the Chicago Press Club." He steps forward, with his hat in his hand. "We've come to Joliet to escort you to Chicago."

"Thank you."

Before the train departs the station, I give the conductor a telegram to run in to the station office, a query to Mr. Bissel, the kind railroad executive I met in Oakland. I request a most urgent reply; I'm hoping that I will find a response at Chicago, our next stop.

Before we are into the station I have answered all the questions of the newsmen, and even joked about my sunburned nose and discussed the merits of traveling around the world with only one dress and a devilishly clever—and bad-tempered—monkey.

Since I'm changing trains in Chicago, I bid a teary-eyed farewell to the wonderful men of the rails who have brought me safely and speedily two-thirds of the way across the continent in record time. It was done only because the crew on my train and many dozens of trainmen on the Santa Fe route made my winning the race a part of their own lives and I shall be forever grateful to them.

The *Miss Nellie Bly Special* was given the right of way along the entire route and all speed limits were ignored. As news of the train's impending arrival flashed over the telegraph lines to the next station, switchmen, engine changers, and coal and water tenders were standing by and went into action like a race crew, breaking many records, including switching an engine in forty-five seconds.

Because of their efforts, we set a new record for a run from the San Francisco Bay to Chicago—nearly 2,600 miles at an average speed of 37 miles per hour and occasional bursts of 60 miles per hour.

The rails between Chicago and the Eastern Seaboard are too crowded with rail traffic to permit my special train to dominate the tracks, so now I must leave the *Miss Nellie Bly Special* to board a regular passenger train for the rest of the race.

My train in Chicago is not ready to depart when we arrive and carriages are waiting to take me and the group of newsmen to the meeting room of the Press Club.

As I step aboard a coupe I shall share with Vice President Gardener, George the porter comes huffing and puffing from a good run to catch up with me and thrusts the reply to my telegram in my hands.

"Here you are, Miss Bly. God's speed to the finish line!"

The query to the Oakland manager had requested the progress of certain passengers from the *Oceanic* who had left behind me. It is easy for a railroad man in a very short time to determine the progress of trains because most of the telegraph lines across the country follow the tracks.

My specific question is about Sarah, Frederick, the Wartons, and Von Reich. The answer: They left together on the train that crossed the mountains and are due to arrive in Chicago several hours *after* I am scheduled to leave.

Mr. Gardener interrupts my thoughts.

"Sorry, I was lost in thought," I apologize. "What did you say?"

"My dear, Miss Bly, I am strongly tempted to steal you. You are quite a lady."

"Well, Mr. Gardener," I say, giving him my innocent young-woman smile that worked many times with Mr. Pulitzer, "that is an opportune suggestion because I do indeed need to have you and the Press Club members steal me for a few hours. I'm changing my departure time so I can join up with friends coming in from the west."

"Isn't that risky?"

"I hope not." But I know it is.

Those words that have become a mantra with me, "If I lose the race, I will not, cannot return to New York," create a lump in my throat and a knot in my stomach.

I can see the headlines: NELLIE BLY FAILS! SHE FAILED AMERICA AND WOMEN! Instead of HURRAHS, I'll be receiving BOOS.

But there is no other choice. Delaying my departure to join my former shipmates is the only honorable thing for me to do. I'm certain Sarah is in danger, more than she realizes.

War, death, illicit love—deadly sins are all in some way wrapped up in Sarah's journey, events not far from her description of armies marching on darkling plains.

"You appear sad, Miss Bly." Mr. Gardiner gives me a kind smile. "I hope it's because you know that you will only spend hours in our beautiful city."

"I was just thinking about how peaceful it was when I was very small and had not one care in the world."

62

In the beautiful rooms of the Press Club I meet the president, Stanley Waterloo, and a number of clever newspapermen. They weren't expecting me in Chicago until noon. The club had arranged an informal reception for me, but when they were notified of my speedy trip and consequently earlier arrival, it was too late to notify the members.

After a most delightful reception they escort me to Kinsley's, where the club has a breakfast prepared. Owing to some misunderstanding, none of the men has had anything to eat since the night before. After breakfast, the members of the Press Club, acting as my escort, take me to visit the Chicago Board of Trade, the commodities exchange, where I encounter two surprises.

First: Their billboard lists my name as a guest for this day to address the commodities traders.

Second: Mr. Stirling Westcot, the millionaire and owner of the *Amelia*, is listed below my name. He is going to address the commodity traders tomorrow night.

I must have been staring at his name because my escort notices.

"Acquainted with Mr. Westcot?"

"Only by reputation, but I would like to meet him."

"Unfortunately, you'll miss him on this trip. He addresses us tomorrow and leaves for the West Coast the following morning."

Going west in his private train car, of course. And I'm going east. So are my shipmates. Sarah wouldn't come all the way to Chicago just to turn around and head west. Maybe there is more than one Amelia in this world and I have been focusing on the wrong one.

When we enter the commodities trading room, the pandemonium that seems to reign all during business hours is at its height.

My escorts take me to the gallery and just as we get there a man raises his arm to yell something to the roaring crowd, but he spots me and yells instead: *"There's Nellie Bly!"*

In one instant, the crowd that has been yelling like mad becomes so silent a pin could have been heard falling to the floor. Every face, bright and eager, turns up toward me; instantly every hat comes off, and then a burst of applause resounds through the immense hall.

I am in shock. People can say what they please about Chicago, but I do not believe that anywhere else in the United States can a woman get a greeting which will equal that given by the Chicago Board of Trade.

The applause is followed by cheer after cheer and cries of *"Speech!"*

I take off my little cap and shake my head at them for I can't speak. I just pray I can hold back my tears; I can't have these men seeing me cry . . . it's just so incredible.

My gesture only serves to increase their cheers.

It is late afternoon when Press Club members escort me to the Pennsylvania Station, where I reluctantly bid them good-bye, unable to thank them heartily enough for the royal manner in which they have treated a little sunburned stranger.

From Mr. Bissel's telegram, I already know the Wartons and Von Reich have compartments in one car. Frederick Selous and Sarah are in other cars. My compartment is in the same car as Sarah's. Sarah and I will be next-door neighbors and the rest closer together than when we were on ships. It will be interesting to see what happens with all of us sandwiched together like sardines.

Right now I'm very curious as to how they will react when they see me. And what Sarah tells me when I demand answers from her.

A group of people boarding pause and look in my direction as a man takes off his hat and yells, *"You're on the last lap, Nellie! Get going and get across that finish line!"*

Smiling, I wave and mouth a "thank you" to him. God, I hope I will.

Well, the cat's now out of the bag.

Lord Warton, who is entering a Pullman, two cars down from the one

I will be riding in, turns and gives me the sort of frown and grimace I would expect a hanging judge to cast down on a prisoner in the dock. As for her ladyship, she merely glances in my direction, lifts her chin, and gives me her back. An ice-cold wind would have been a warmer welcome.

Inside, I drop my bag and ulster in my own compartment and knock on Sarah's door.

"This is the police," I whisper at the door. "We are investigating a mystery woman."

A scream of joy comes from the other side of the door and it flies open. *"Nellie!"* She gives me a genuine, warm, enthusiastic hug. "Come in!"

Pretending to peek around the tiny compartment, I ask, "What, no coffin to sleep in?"

She dramatically puts the back of her hand against her forehead. "Alas, it ended up in the baggage car. I'm so delighted you are here! I thought for sure we had seen the last of each other."

"Me, too." I close the door behind us. "Sarah, I have to talk to you."

She takes a seat, while I remain standing.

"What is it, dear? You look positively alarmed."

"We need to talk about your rendezvous. You have to tell me—"

She almost shakes her head off her shoulders. "No no no, you must not ask, you must stay completely out of the matter."

"I have to know. Especially about Amelia—"

"Out!" She jumps up and slides open the door.

"Sarah—"

"Out." She gives me a little push. As I start to step out she gives me a kiss on the cheek. "Some day I will make it up to you, but right now you are persona non grata to me."

"Sarah, I think you're in danger."

"That's so sweet; you are such an innocent little thing. Sometimes I feel like the whole world is in danger."

"Armies marching on darkling plains . . ."

"Exactly." She gives me another peck on the check. "Now run along, dear, and"—she leans close and whispers—"don't come back unless I call for you."

She slips back into her compartment and closes the door.

For a moment I stare at the door, tempted to slide it back open; then I hear the lock engage. Well, for now that takes care of that, and I start to enter my compartment but change my mind.

"George, what car is Mr. Selous in?"

"The next car up. But I saw Mr. Selous in the smoking car a moment ago. That's three cars up."

"Thank you."

Smoking cars are my least favorite part of a train. I'd rather ride in the train's coal tender with the fireman and the smoke from the furnace blowing back at us than be forced to breathe thick clouds of evil-smelling cigar smoke, a fact that I have shared more than once with men on a train. To no avail.

Lord and Lady Warton are there when I enter, with her ladyship's charming personality fortunately hidden behind her veil, along with whatever she thinks about the fact we have been reunited as travelling companions. They're in a group that includes Frederick, who is engrossed in conversation with another man and doesn't realize I entered.

The Bluenoses both completely ignore me despite the fact I hear my name buzzed around the room and several people give a friendly smile of recognition. I feel like asking her if she's faked any more heart attacks, but leave well enough alone.

"What do you gentlemen think of the Westley 303?" a man asks Frederick.

"A what?" Lord Warton asks.

"It's a tiger gun, isn't that so, Frederick?" Lady Warton says.

She demonstrates her knowledge of the weapon to put herself ahead of a simple little peasant girl like myself. That word my mother always dislikes me using, "bitch," comes to mind whenever I am around Lady Bluenose.

"Yes, it can bring down a tiger," Frederick says, giving me a big smile as he spots me, "but you better hit at a kill point or you'll end up with six hundred pounds of charging beast in your face with the force of a locomotive."

I move along, waiting for Frederick to disengage himself from men who want to ask questions of the renowned hunter, when I spot more familiar faces.

The widow Murdock and Cenza—her assistant, lover, whatever—and the gregarious Von Reich, are sitting together at the back of the car. The Viennese explosives expert is leaning back in a chair with glass in hand and appears to have enjoyed quite a few drops of the nectar of the grape. The widow is smoking a cigarillo, a small, thin cigar. She has a glass of brandy and judging from the flush on her cheeks it isn't her first.

Cenza gives me a smirk that implies she knows something I don't, and it's about to drop on my head.

Smirking, perhaps, is a permanent deformity of her lips, if not of her mind.

It's difficult for me to imagine Cenza with the Murdock woman. They are just not a match, whatever their personal sexual preferences. There has to be something else that glues them together and the only thing I can imagine is the pot of gold the widow acquired after her husband's bizarre demise.

I reverse direction to stay away from them and find Frederick breaking away, calling out, "Nellie! I'm so delighted you're here."

Lord Warton gives me his back again, takes his charming wife by the arm, and exits. I catch something about "the bad penny is back" as they leave.

"I apologize for Warton," Frederick says, taking me out of hearing range of others. "He's a rude bastard. Under different circumstances, I would take him to task for his boorish behavior toward you."

"What exactly are the circumstances that make the mere sight of me so offensive to him and prevent a gentleman from coming to my rescue?"

He chuckles. "Nellie, you have a wonderful sense of inquisitiveness. But you must learn to control it."

"Does Amelia control it?" A shot in the dark.

His eyebrows go up. "Amelia? Isn't that the name you thought you heard—"

"Yes, *thought* I heard, but I realize now that I was wrong. The truth is I never heard anything. I was never in Port Said. I don't even know who you are. Or who I am."

"Nellie, I think—"

"Please do. In the meantime, I'll take some headache powders or something stronger for my weak feminine disposition or maybe I'll just have some of Sarah's damn coca wine."

If I wasn't a lady, I'd . . . instead, I spin on my heel and am out of there without looking back, retracing my steps to my compartment. I enter and slam the door shut behind me. And lock it.

Why did I do that? I went to talk to him in a civilized manner. I was happy to see him and could tell he wanted to see me. And what do I do? Blow up at him.

My only excuse is that I'm angry, frustrated, befuddled, and bewildered because what I'm certain is a murderous conspiracy seems to be unimportant to others.

"What is going on?" I demand from the wall separating me and Sarah.

Maybe I am just a fool. I must be. I have risked winning my race to save Sarah and she doesn't want to be saved. Doesn't even want me around.

I'm beginning to wonder if they are right, that *I'm* the one with the problem.

Why else would I jeopardize the race my life depends upon to come back and travel with people who appear surprised—and some definitely annoyed—that I am still on the planet?

Sarah adores me, but slams her door in my face and tells me to stay out of anything involving her. Frederick is laughing at me or, at the very least, has developed a patronizing amused tolerance of my antics. Lord and Lady Bluenose treat me like a leper. Von Reich ignores me. And Cenza, who radiates malice with her smug grins, gives me the willies.

I know I am supposed to hide my head in the sand and pretend nothing is wrong, but despite the doubts that roll in my mind, my gut keeps telling me another shoe is about to drop.

What do these people know that I don't?

63

Instead of having an entire deluxe Pullman car at my disposal, I have but a stateroom, and my space is so limited that all my floral and fruit offerings had to be left behind, which I so do miss. I also miss the speed of travel my first train had. This train creeps along like a snail, and I fear I will not make this last leg of my journey on time.

Before I reach my compartment, George hands me a telegram that was meant to be delivered in San Francisco, but has just caught up with me.

The message gives me great pleasure and changes my mood:

> MR. VERNE WISHES THE FOLLOWING MESSAGE TO BE HANDED TO NELLIE BLY THE MOMENT SHE TOUCHES AMERICAN SOIL: M. JULES VERNE ADDRESSES HIS SINCERE FELICITATIONS TO THE INTREPID MISS NELLIE BLY.

Oh, how I could use Jules' help right now.

THE TRAIN IS RATHER POORLY APPOINTED and it's necessary for everyone to get off for meals. Our first stop is Logansport for dinner.

When I reach the platform, a young man whom I've never seen before or since, springs up on another platform and waves his hat shouting, *"Hurrah for Nellie Bly! Hurrah for Nellie Bly!"*

A delegation of railroad men wait upon me and present me with beautiful flowers and candy, as does a number of private people. The crowd claps and cheers, and after making way for me to pass to the dining room, they press forward and their cheers go up again. They even crowd the windows to watch me eat.

After I sit down, several dishes are put before me bearing the inscription, SUCCESS, NELLIE BLY.

Despite all the attention I've gotten since I left the *Oceanic*, I'm not comfortable with the public displays of admiration. It makes me sad and angry—here are people who do admire me and are counting on me to finish and in a way I may have betrayed them because I could be hours ahead. How stupid I've been.

I spoon my soup very carefully so at least these wonderful people won't have the memory of soup running down my chin or dropping on my blouse.

An ancient old dowager at another table has a note delivered to me. I open it, reading between sips of soup:

> I don't even get this type of treatment when I'm in a hit play. Next time I need attention I shall travel around the world at great speed.

Glancing over at the old woman, I get a subtle nod in return and give back a wry grin.

What an actress she is.

On my way back to the train I'm informed there will be a delay because a switching locomotive is adding another car behind the one my compartment is in. It provides a golden opportunity for me to walk along the tracks in the cool night air and to enjoy a moment alone to myself. Not much privacy has been available to me during the more than two months I've spent on ships, trains, and in hotels.

Even though there are other people about, every now and then I can't help taking a look behind me. It's dark and I still have the key someone has killed for.

A short distance down the tracks they are connecting a Pullman car behind mine. It's a beautiful car, polished forest green with a substantial gold trim that obviously shows it belongs to someone with an abundance of wealth.

I stop and stare at the nameplate on the side of the car, the name engraved in gold on a silver plaque.

Amelia.

My heart beats a little faster and I get a flash of a man speaking her name as his lifeblood poured out onto the ground.

A porter steps down from the *Amelia* and lights a cigarette, and I saunter over to him.

"Good evening."

"Evenin', ma'am."

"Isn't this Mr. Westcot's car?"

"Yes, ma'am, it is."

"I met him once. Would you mind taking my card to him?"

"Can't do that, he's not aboard."

"Really? Who's using the car?"

A grunt comes from above us. A man is standing on the top of the Pullman's steps looking down at us.

The porter mutters, "'Scuse me," and goes up the steps, the man moving aside for him without ever turning his eyes from me.

Another man, a chip off the old block of the one that's staring down, appears from behind me.

Feeling boxed in, I quickly move away.

Obviously they are plainclothes policemen; they have the thick necks, beefy frames, and Irish whiskey noses of New York City's Finest, with the roomy cheap suits that all seem to be cut from the same cloth.

They also could be Pinks, a nickname crooks have given Pinkerton's private detectives. Many Pinks are former policemen and to find them protecting a millionaire's rail car would not be unusual. The men employed by the agency founded by Allan Pinkerton, an immigrant from Scotland who was Chicago's first police detective, are much favored by businessmen as investigators, guards, and strike breakers ever since the Pinks foiled a plot to assassinate President-Elect Lincoln when he traveled by train to the inauguration in Washington.

Why are two coppers guarding the *Amelia*? Or, more likely, whoever is in it. It certainly isn't its owner, Westcot; he's on his way to count his money out west.

Turning around, I smile politely and give them a "Good evening."

Not particularly friendly greetings are returned, along with tips of their hats.

Very interesting . . . coppers, for sure. But I did get a surprise—their accents are British.

So why are two British dicks protecting the train car of Sarah's lover?

Who is important enough that one of the richest men in America gives up his luxurious Pullman so his guest can have a romantic tryst with an actress?

It's a very short list, for sure . . . but who?

An answer comes to mind as to the possible identity of the lover, but it's so incredible, so far-fetched that not even my vivid imagination will accept it as gospel. It's simply not within the realm of reason that one of the most important men on the planet is in that train car. Not even what Frederick thinks is my overworked imagination can make me believe that he is in that car. If that were the case, it would be on the front page of every newspaper in the country.

It just can't be . . . which only leaves me aching to find out who is in that Pullman.

I can't sleep.

Lying awake, I listen for the telltale sounds of Sarah leaving her compartment for a romantic rendezvous with the mysterious occupant of the *Amelia*, but I don't hear it. She might have sneaked out too quietly for me to hear over the noise of rolling wheels on the rails and the creak of the train cars.

I finally doze off but in the middle of the night I'm jolted awake as the brakes screech, bringing us to a stop to take on coal and water.

The moment I wake up I know what my next step must be. I quickly dress, and remove the key from my shoe heel and slip it into my pocket. As I put my hand on the compartment's doorknob, I pause for a moment and ask myself: *Should I really go through with this?*

The train has stopped, it's the dead of the night, and the rest of the world is asleep. I have the key to *Amelia*. This is an opportunity that might not be repeated.

If there are easier ways to find out what's in the storage locker rather than sneaking around in the dark, they all avoid me at the moment.

Fighting the jitters, I lean my forehead on the door and close my eyes. Do I really want to do this? *Now or never,* that's the answer. If I am ever going to do it, it has to be now.

I squeeze the key in my hand. I made a promise to a dead man to get the key to "Amelia." Well, this is the only way that promise can be kept.

It's time to open Pandora's box and see what is inside.

64

Slipping by the snoring porter's curtained bunk, I quickly open and close the exit door behind me to keep a breeze from sneaking in and awakening him.

The night is cold and dark as my feet touch the rocky rail bed and I immediately regret that I didn't wear my ulster.

Down toward the front of the train, I can make out the chute that is feeding coal to the tender car and a line from a water tank to the boiler. It's a fuel stop in the middle of nowhere, with no houses, no station. I am at the far end of my train car from the *Amelia* and I have to walk slowly and cautiously to keep my footing on the rocky bed. After everything I have been through, it would be a fitting conclusion to my race around the entire world if I were to fall and hit my head and be left on the side of the tracks while the train continues on to a triumphant arrival at New Jersey—minus me.

No light shows in any of the *Amelia*'s windows. The undercarriage storage locker is about halfway down the length of the car.

Despite the *crunch-crunch-crunch* noise I'm making, I pick up my step because I don't want to run into someone who decides to stretch their legs and get a breath of fresh air.

Crouching down in front of the locker, I wish I had had the foresight to stick a kitchen match in my pocket because it's too dark to see the lock hole. Fortunately, exploring with my fingers, I find it.

A serious case of the jitters has set my nerves on fire, as if my body knows something I don't—but should.

Fumbling, I drop the key onto the rocky train bed that is black from soot and coal dust. Patting the ground I find it, and using two hands to guide it, I slip the key in the lock and turn it. The brackets make an awful metal grating noise that makes me cringe as I lift the lid. *Damn.* I'm so jittery, I'm sure the scraping is loud enough to wake the dead. And I can't see anything in the locker; it's just a black void. Either it's completely empty or whatever is inside is farther back, hidden in the darkness.

I reach back as far as I can, but feel nothing. Pandora's box is empty? I edge back and stare at the box, refusing to believe the obvious—the key to *Amelia* has opened an empty box.

Footsteps crunch to my right and I turn to a gun in my face.

"You called that one right, Mr. Selous. The woman's a troublemaker—that's a certainty for sure."

The speaker is one of the British coppers, a redheaded one. The train has finished fueling and we are in the common area of the car containing Frederick's compartment. While the redheaded copper had pointed his gun at my nose outside, his mate ran up behind me, putting aside his own pistol only long enough to handcuff me.

Treating me as if I'm a dangerous criminal when I'm investigating a case does so remind me of my interactions with New York's Finest.

Lord Warton has joined the others trampling me underfoot, poetically at least, but the night is young. They may still kick me like a dog.

His lordship has a whiskey glow and he's unsteady on his feet. Obviously he has been sucking on a bottle in the middle of the night. Whatever demons drive him to find relief with John Barleycorn seem to have intensified since I last saw him aboard the ship.

Frederick had come to my rescue and had them put away their guns and remove the cuffs, telling them, "She's not dangerous . . . just nosy."

Listening with a cold sense of fury to the men boasting and backpatting themselves and each other, I keep my peace because I have no defense.

Frederick refuses to meet my eye, which is fine with me because I'm more angry at myself than at him. He had guessed my intent and told the coppers, and they set a trap. Walking into it was inexcusable.

Other passengers, who had poked their heads out of their compartments to see what all the commotion was about when I went ballistic at being manhandled, were ordered back to bed. Sarah never showed her face.

Vigilance committee. That is how I have come to think of the Brits who have seized me as if I am a criminal. Like the groups of men who cleaned up San Francisco and many another Western towns by stringing up the bad guys to the nearest trees, the British coppers act with authority when they have none. That the two coppers have guns, muscles, and look very much like police detectives, make them the natural administrators of justice at the moment.

When I reach my fill of the abuse as they debate how to "restrain" my "wild impulses," I start throwing verbal punches. "At the next stop, I'll have the sheriff remove all of you from the train," I tell the redhead, "and place you, your cohort, and the rest of this posse of vigilantes under arrest for manhandling a woman."

"I'll have you know *we* are police officers," the redheaded copper snaps back.

"Then you're thousands of miles outside your jurisdiction. You're a bunch of foreigners who have attacked an American citizen."

Frederick reaches to pat my hand and I jerk it away. "Nellie—"

"What is *your* authority, Mr. Selous? And the rest of you, tell me, who granted you a license to kidnap a woman and hold her prisoner?" I look from one to the other, giving a good stare to each. "It's pretty obvious that you have plotted with my competitor to keep me from winning. In case you haven't noticed, the local police have been at every stop to cheer me on."

That is not completely true, but I threw it in for good measure.

"When I step out at the next stop and inform the crowd that you have physically assaulted me, do you have any idea what the men in that crowd are going to do?"

The redheaded copper looks at Selous. "I thought you said she wasn't dangerous."

"She needs to be locked up," Warton manages to say.

His drunken slur reminds me of my drunken stepfather who abused our entire family with his bad words and beatings. I hated that man. I step up to Warton to make sure I am right in his face.

"I am filing charges of slander and abuse against you at the next stop. You can look for your next bottle of whiskey in a jail cell, if you aren't strung up to the nearest tree by the crowd first."

Lord Warton takes a step backward, almost falling as he stumbles. The man is so horrified, he appears ready to totally collapse.

"I'll have you horsewhipped." He points a shaky finger at me.

"Another threat for the police!" I snap.

Frederick steps in between us. "Show his lordship back to his compartment," he orders the redheaded officer. "Return to your duties," he tells the other officer.

Frederick grabs my arm and I jerk it loose. "You're also going to jail."

He starts laughing and that spikes my rage.

"Stop, please," he begs, "I'm not laughing at you, I'm laughing at the way the others got out of here so fast."

There seems to be an eternal silence as we stand staring at each other.

Naturally, I break it. "I meant it when I said I'd have the whole gang of you arrested."

"I'm sure you could do it; you're America's sweetheart. But after what I've been through since I met you, a long prison term sounds like paradise."

"*What you've been through?* I have blood on me from murder and nearly was killed myself not once but twice. I hope a big, strong man like you wasn't too terrified as I fought killers."

Satisfied that I have gotten the last word in, I start for my room. He follows, whispering magic words: "I have answers to your questions."

Weak person that I am when it comes to a story, my feet stop.

He touches my arm again, gingerly, as if he's afraid I'll bite. "Please join me for a moment in my compartment where we can talk in private."

We sit across from each other. Pushing the wrinkles out of my dress, I sit back and clasp my hands together.

"First," he says, "let me tell you what I meant when I said I'd had nothing but trouble since I met you. You aren't the cause of the trouble, it just happens that it began about the time we met."

"Tell me everything," I command. "Everything. Start at the beginning. And try not to lie too much."

"Before I begin, I must have your word of honor that what I'm about to tell you will never find its way to the public during the lifetimes of any involved."

"I can't promise that, I'm a reporter. Besides, I already know a great deal."

"Your promise is required for me to go on."

"How can I make a promise when I don't know all the facts? What if you tell me something that in good conscience should be revealed to the public or the proper authorities?" I hold up my hand to stop his objection. "I will commit to this. If you give me a good reason why I shouldn't do the story, I won't do it. *But* . . . only if I find the reason compelling. I've already put together much more than you realize and I don't care what country ends up controlling the Suez Canal. And I'm positive that I know the identity of the mysterious personage whom Sarah is visiting."

Much of what I "know" qualifies as wild guesses, but I doubt he's going to be completely honest with me anyway. I don't know how many chords I hit—he appears a bit amused—so I lock eyes with him in order for him to get the full impact of my knockout punch.

"How is good old Bertie?" I ask, attempting a cockney accent.

That wipes the humor from his face. His eyes narrow and his forehead folds into wrinkles. "You are dangerous."

"Start talking," I command again. It feels good to have the upper hand after scraping bottom. "Start with the murder in the marketplace."

"Fine. The events that led up to that deadly confrontation began some weeks earlier, at least for me. I was visiting an old hunting chum in Cairo, a Turkish collector of exotic animals who has dealings with a wide variety of individuals in Egypt, including those who are ardent followers of the Mahdi movement. Let's call him Bey. He heard a story that I didn't find credible, but when I passed it on to the head of our mission in Cairo, I was shocked to discover that there was credence to it.

"Bey told me that a plot had been hatched by the Mahdi to galvanize the entire Egyptian population behind them by striking a blow against Britain that would shock the entire world. The plot is to assassinate a very important personage—"

"Bertie," I interject.

"The plot is to kill the individual while he is on a, uh—"

"Romantic tryst?"

He clears his throat. "While he's on an unreported horse-racing venture in America. As you must know from reading newspapers, the gentleman is an ardent racehorse owner who regularly enters his horses at important British meets and on the Continent. He has had for a number of years a friendly competition with Mr. Westcot about who has the fastest three-year-old filly in the world. The track time of the two horses are the same and the only way they can settle the matter is to race them together. So, the . . . uh, the personage decided to bring his horse to America and hold a private, and of course, secret meet at the track where the Kentucky Derby is run."

I raise my eyebrows. "Obviously, such a race could have been arranged much more easily by simply shipping only horses rather than people, so my guess of a romantic rendezvous is most likely the correct one."

Selous gives me a diplomatic smile of conciliation. "Let's just say that there is more than one motive for the trip. The person we are speaking of is noted for occasionally travelling incognito."

"Fine. So how did word of this trip get all the way to Egypt and to the ear of terrorists?"

"In a manner that is not as unusual as you might think. The individual who is second in command of Britain's mission to Egypt is part of the personage's inner circle back home. The friend learned of the trip while in London. When he returned to his duties in Cairo, one night over dinner he told his wife about it—"

"With servants present," I interpose.

"Yes."

"You're right, it's not unusual. There's more than one servant in New York who got rich leaving his ears open while serving an employer who talks business over cigars and brandy. It's pure arrogance by men who don't consider servants as people."*

"Quite so. The servant was a Mahdi loyalist who passed the information on to higher ups, who hatched the plot. They knew that their target would be travelling by Pullman car. It so happens that they had once killed an important member of my government, along with several high ranking Egyptian officials, with a bomb on the Alexandra-to-Cairo run."

"You're going to tell me they placed the bomb in the locker under the train. And used a Pullman key to do it."

"Exactly. The keys are easy enough to steal; there are Pullman cars in Egypt."

"And Mr. Cleveland intercepted the key. I take it he was a British agent?"

"A naval officer—"

"Mr. Cleveland's been dead for two years."

Frederick clears his throat. "We used Cleveland's identity not only because he no longer needed it, but his profession as a cutlery salesman serving Egypt fit the need for a cover. The naval officer was given the assignment because he spoke Arabic. My government doesn't have many full-time spies and none fluent in Arabic. My own initial involvement was simply to fulfill a request that I meet Cleveland in Port Said and fill him

* Nellie once went undercover as a servant girl to expose the abuse of employers. —The Editors

in on what I had learned from Bey, who had told me that the key was to be passed by a scarab merchant in the marketplace to the hired assassin."

"The Mahdi hired an assassin rather than use one of their own. Because their own people would have stood out."

"Yes. Cleveland was to go to the marketplace to observe the handoff, as you know, and ended up with the scarab in his own hand. We don't know why he suddenly grabbed the scarab, perhaps from inexperience in dealing with such a situation, or maybe the man mistook him for the assassin and at first offered him—"

"The scarab, and then called for his death when he realized the mistake."

He nods. "Poor devil. He appears to have acted on impulse, as a soldier would have, obviously knowing about the subtleties of spying."

"Your Cleveland disguised himself as an Egyptian when he could have blended in with other Europeans in the marketplace. Isn't that true?"

"Yes, I agree, Nellie. What does that tell you?"

"He planned from the first to get the key. And he had had a conversation with the man selling the scarabs, at least enough to be told that the target car was *Amelia*."

"You're quite right, I see what you mean. He didn't go there just to observe as he'd been ordered, but to pull off a coup."

"How close were you when he was killed?" I ask.

"Not as close as you. Back quite a ways, as a matter of fact. I didn't see the killing. I made contact with Lord Warton after you and her ladyship left."

"Uh-huh. And began trying to make me the fool."

He shrugs and spreads his hands on his lap. "Not out of malice, let me assure you."

"And you took Cleveland's place?"

"Right. His superior drafted me to continue the mission because there was no one else available. As it so happens I had already obtained a ticket for India to attend a safari, so my appearance on the boat wouldn't arouse suspicion."

"And you concocted the story that Cleveland was alive."

"It seemed the appropriate way to proceed at the time."

"Why didn't you just ask me for the key?"

"Nellie, you never told me you had it."

"True . . . actually, I didn't know I had it until I began to see conspiracies swirling around me."

"That wasn't intentional. There was also a question about your potential involvement. Bey was told that the assassination team was composed of two people. It could have been a man and woman."

"You thought I was an assassin? And planned a race around the world to carry it off?"

"I didn't know who you were at the time. I soon decided you were a genuine reporter—"

"Well, that was kind of you. And clever."

He clears his throat. "But then another problem arose. The scarab wasn't on Cleveland when I searched his body. And I found fragments of a scarab when I searched your room."

"So you knew I had the key. And we began a game of cat and mouse."

He smiles. "And you were the cat. With sharp claws."

"So after you knew I had it, why didn't you just ask me for it?"

"There were complicated reasons."

"Complicated reasons . . . ah, I think I understand. The hired assassins would also want the key. And if you watched me, you would see who they were . . ."

"Quite."

"As they murdered me."

He clears his throat again and grins. "I was hoping to prevent that possibility."

"And you are just an innocent bystander, roped in to serve queen and country."

He tries unsuccessfully to smother a smirk. "I thought I adapted well to the role of spy."

"Not bad," I say with a shrug, "though you must watch your back more. I was able to follow you to your meeting with Lady Warton and that rather offensive sailor friend of yours in Hong Kong." I didn't volunteer I had stumbled onto them by accident.

"So, the spy was spied upon! Very good. Gary plays the role of offensive seaman, quite well, don't you think? He's actually with Navy Intelligence."

"He didn't play it that well. He spoke French to the wrong woman, so I knew you had hatched something with Sarah. I take it there was an effort to get Sarah to go home and forget the rendezvous?"

"Yes, but like you, Sarah follows her own drummer."

"What were you hatching with Lady Bluenose in Hong Kong?"

"Lady Warton wanted to relate her feelings about Von Reich. Her husband is quite taken with the man, but her ladyship doesn't like him and was offended by some anti-British statements he had made."

"Her husband's tolerance, I take it, is a result of him being paid to introduce the man to government officials."

"Quite."

"So . . ." I think for a moment. "The plan was to put a bomb into the Pullman locker. As they did in Egypt."

"Yes."

"But you prevented that?"

"The attempt was blocked, yes, hours earlier than your use of the key. We knew it was going to be attempted and were ready. When the culprit was spotted, he dropped the bomb on the ground and fled. But we know who it is and your police will catch him. If nothing else, his heavy accent will trip him up."

"An accent? Von Reich? Von Reich's the assassin?" My astonishment is evident.

"Yes, he fills the bill rather nicely. An explosives expert, a foreigner, was at the marketplace—"

"He's not the type."

Frederick raises his eyebrows. "Nellie, dear, assassins aren't produced from a cookie cutter."

"But—"

"No buts. You simply must accept it."

"You and those coppers actually saw Von Reich?"

"It was too dark to see the man's features, but his hat fell off as he ran away."

"What's his motive?"

"Money, of course. The Mahdi can pay vast sums in gold. They may have done business before. No doubt he prepared the explosives for the Egyptian train car assassinations."

"You have no confession? Don't know where—"

He held up his hand to cut me off. "The man is on the run. But, I'm sure you're aware from your reporting that fleeing from the scene of a crime is tantamount to a signed confession."

He gets up, leans down, and kisses me on the cheek. "Get some rest, sweet lady. We'll talk about this some more in the morning. You must conserve your energy to finish your race."

Back in my compartment, I undress and climb back into bed again, worn to the bone and down to the marrow. Frederick's right, of course; the mystery of the key to *Amelia* is finished and I still have mountains to climb, rivers to cross, castle walls to storm . . . and a race to win.

I didn't fail to note that Frederick forgot to obtain my promise not to use the story. The revelations will be sensational. Mr. Pulitzer will be thrilled, not to mention extra benefits for me—a pay raise, choices of stories to cover. Not only will I finish my trip on time, I will come back with another sensational story.

This settled, I close my eyes and will myself to sleep when a thought electrifies my tired brain: *Poor Von Reich.*

Now why did I have such a thought? The man's an assassin, a murderer—

I sit straight up in my bed. But he's not a runner. The portly gentleman would hardly have given the coppers a run for their money. And dropping his hat. "How convenient is that?" I ask the ceiling. He leaves his hat behind so there would be no mistake in identification?

The shoe doesn't fit Von Reich no matter how I try to slip it on.

Stop it, Nellie!

I restrain myself from shouting the command. It's over with, done, finished, time to move on.

Von Reich is the obvious villain. He's a professional bomb maker; the crime fits him like a glove, so why can't I accept it? I pull the blanket over my head. I hate it when my mind won't shut off and let me sleep.

There's a light tap on my door and the porter asks, "Miss Bly? Are you still awake? I have a note for you."

Giving me the note, he apologizes. "Sorry, ma'am, I was given this hours ago and forgot to give it to you."

"Who's it from?" I ask as I unfold the note.

"Don't know, ma'am. Another porter handed it to me. Good night."

George leaves and I step back into my compartment to read the message.

I MUST SEE YOU 7201C—VR

The author's initials blaze with fire in my mind's eye.

What does he want with me?

65

Not a creature was stirring, not even a mouse, plays in my head as I step lightly down the corridor to the porter's bunk. The only evidence of life in the train car is the rasps of snoring. Once again, everyone is asleep except lucky me.

Tapping next to the bunk curtain, I whisper George's name and he sticks his head out.

"Sorry, George, but what car is 7201?"

"Two cars up, ma'am."

"Who occupies compartment C in that car?"

"I can't say, ma'am. The porter in 7201 has that information. Did you want me to—"

"No." I slip him a silver dollar. "Thank you. Go back to sleep."

Two cars up is the one that I had seen the Wartons entering.

Frederick's car is next. The corridor is as deserted as my own, as is that of 7201 when I reach it. Hushing the porter with *"shh"* and a silver dollar, I ask who occupies compartment C.

He unhooks a clipboard from a hook and consults it. "A Mr. Lazarus, ma'am."

"What does he look like?"

"I don't know. He's sick, never comes out of his compartment."

"How do you know he's sick?"

"The young lady told me, the one with the other Australian woman. She said not to disturb him 'cause he's under the weather."

Questions rattle in my head as I go to compartment C. Who's Mr. Lazarus and why is he harboring Von Reich? Why is the caustic Cenza making excuses for Lazarus? And what does Von Reich want with me?

Gathering my courage, I stare at the compartment door, knowing that I might be throwing myself into the hands of a dangerous killer, and that I should get Frederick. But then I'd never get to the truth of what's happening. He'll bust in, arrest Von Reich, and I'll still have no final answer.

Looking up and down the corridor to ensure that I am not being watched, I tap lightly with just the tip of my fingernail. No response and I tap again, a little louder. Silence. Taking a deep breath, I slowly slide open the door an inch, just enough to see that it is dark inside.

I pull the door open wider and give a startled cry.

Von Reich is on the bench seat, hunched over, his right shoulder against the window frame. A streak of blood has run down the side of his head. On the seat beside him is a derringer.

A woman pokes her head out of the next compartment.

"What's going on?"

"*Murder,* there's been a murder!"

She screams. I stare at her dumbfounded.

She screams again.

Compartment doors start opening, heads poke out.

I feel like screaming myself so I take a deep breath and let out a wail of pure frustration.

66

I am back in the hands of the coppers and the other vigilantes. Under ordinary circumstances I would welcome the professional attention being given the matter, but since I'm being treated as a suspicious person, if not an actual suspect, by the high-handed flatfoots, I find no fault on my part in challenging their conclusions or their authority.

Shocked, sick at seeing a man dead that I knew and rather liked, a companion on a long trip who had shown me courtesies, I permit myself to be ushered to the common area in Frederick's car. I don't know what to think. I'm out of answers, at the moment. I'm even out of questions. Everything is too unreal for it to really sink in. For a moment after I opened that door my first thought was that the death was staged, a joke by Von Reich, but that thought was erased by the funeral pallor of his skin.

Half the train awoke from the hysterical cries of *"Murder!"* that resounded down the aisles. Order was finally restored, people assured of their safety, and the vigilance committee met to receive the "official" pronouncement from the coppers who were examining Von Reich's body—which is now wrapped in blankets and being transferred to the baggage car by the two coppers.

Frederick is with me, as is Lord Warton, looking the worse for wear and carefully not looking in my direction.

No one is happy I found the body. No one considers me completely innocent. They look at me as if I was caught rustling their cattle and will soon be kicking at the end of a rope.

Frederick reads my mind and rubs his forehead as if it will remove a headache.

"I find you completely amazing. A friend of mine in the raj is quite taken by the belief in India that our lives are predestined, that the paths we take are determined at birth by our fate, our karma. Nellie, I have to wonder what it is about your karma that draws murder to you like bees to honey."

The two coppers return, saving me from trying to justify my existence.

They give a nod to Frederick and a glance at Warton, who appears to have slipped into a drunken slumber. His lordship's chin has dropped down to his chest with a dribble of saliva threatening to drop off at any moment.

"Suicide," the redheaded copper announces.

"Nonsense." That retort comes from me, of course.

The copper sucks in a sharp breath through bared teeth and Frederick throws his hands in the air. "Why does that proclamation not surprise me? Officer, let's hear the facts of your thorough investigation before Miss Bly entertains us with her guesswork."

My temper spikes but I clamp my mouth shut.

"It's laid out quite neatly, sir, the pieces falling together to form the answer to a puzzle. There are no powder burns on his head; however, the burns are on the small pillow provided for seat comfort. He used it to muffle the shot."

"Why would he use a pillow to muffle a shot?" I ask.

The copper chews on it for a moment before deciding to answer me, using a tone he probably reserves for children—and women. "Obviously one muffles a shot so it can't be heard."

"It doesn't make sense that someone on the run from the police, and so panicked and depressed that they are driven to take their own life, would bother muffling a shot."

"Crazy people don't have to make sense," the copper replies, miffed.

"Well, I spent weeks travelling on the same ships with Von Reich. Being crazy was not one of his faults."

"I warned everyone about her." Lord Warton has come to life.

His drunken, slurred statement, made without opening his eyes, grabs the attention of all of us for a moment, but he quickly falls back into his slumber.

The redheaded copper gives me a stern look that I'm sure has frightened a confession out of more than one criminal.

"This is a police matter and I would inform you in no uncertain terms that you will find yourself in serious trouble if you interfere in an official investigation. Do we understand each other . . . *madam*?"

"As I have pointed out, you have no *official* authority in this country. And if you interfere with my *official* investigation as a journalist, I shall have the sheriff of the next town take you into custody. Do you understand me . . . *sir*?"

His mouth flaps open in an attempt to deliver a reply but the words don't come. He looks to Frederick for help.

"Nellie, please, the officer is just trying to help out in a delicate situation. Let him finish his report. Officer?"

The copper clears his throat. "Yes, sir. The most important and telling piece of evidence is the weapon used by the deceased. It is a Rhine brand single shot derringer. And on the bottom of the butt," the officer gives me a look of triumph, "appears a plate bearing the name 'Von Reich'."

The other chimes in. "Naturally we considered the matter of motive. The deceased was on the run from the law, facing financial ruin and spending the rest of his life in a prison cell. Motivation for suicide, if I ever heard it."

Frederick nods. "Quite so; good work, officers. Isn't that so, your lordship?"

Lord Warton snaps awake with a sputter and looks about him as if he's unaware of his whereabouts.

The redheaded officer gives the peer a frown and says to Frederick, "We'll be moving on." He nods in the direction of the *Amelia*. "Have to make a full report of the matter."

I wait until they have stepped by me before I direct a comment to Frederick, who has started up from his seat. "There is that unanswered question . . ."

He flops back down on his seat and looks to the two officers who have paused in the corridor. Poor devils—they would very much like to ignore me but don't dare, out of fear that a mere woman will show them up.

"All right, Nellie." Frederick sighs. "We're all tired, as I'm sure you are. Please, do tell us what you're referring to."

That's it. I get up and head for my compartment.

"Nellie!" Frederick yells. "You'll not be able to sleep unless you get it off your chest."

He is right, of course, but I would like to make them sweat a little, so I pause at the compartment door before I turn and give them a wan smile.

"What about Mr. Lazarus?"

"Lazarus?" Frederick asks.

"This investigation is not over with until the matter of Mr. Lazarus has been resolved."

"Why should we care about this Lazarus person?" the mouthy red-headed copper demands.

"Well, I would be curious as to the man's whereabouts since Von Reich was found dead in his compartment. If you are actually right about Von Reich being a mad bomber, and if he knew Mr. Lazarus well enough to kill himself in his compartment, well . . . I guess I would be wondering about whether this invisible man makes bombs, too."

Passing halfway into my compartment, I toss another volley over my shoulder. "Kind of strange, don't you think? . . . No one has ever seen the man. I think I'd ask that Aussie sharpshooter's assistant, Cenza, why she made excuses for him."

"She left the train," Lord Warton says. "I saw her get off at the last stop."

I throw my hands in the air. "Well, there it is. You spent so much time harassing me that all the bad people were able to duck for cover. Good luck finding a man no one has ever seen after you let the only witness escape."

As soon as I close the door behind me, I lean back against it. My heart is ricocheting in my chest, my mouth is dry, my stomach feels ready to erupt volcanically. Despite my attempt at a firm tone, I am shaking. However, I'm glad I threw that last punch.

The devil oils my tongue and makes me do these things, but it feels good, at least for the moment.

Lazarus rose from the dead. That's what it says in the Bible, if my memory of a Sunday school lesson remains true.

That thought about the name wraps around me like the arms of an octopus as I lie awake and listen to the rumble of the train wheels in the early morning. I can't shake it. Lazarus rising from the dead is connected back to something Von Reich had said on the dock at Colombo when the Aussie sharpshooter had shouted to someone as if he recognized the person.

Von Reich also said someone else was a better shot than the Aussie, and something about an identity crisis and rising from the dead.

Another thought with the grip of octopus tentacles grips me. If no one saw Lazarus besides Cenza, a doubtful source, was he ever actually in the compartment?

I try to move on but my thoughts are fuzzy. Being in a room that is small and confining doesn't help, and I make another try at getting Sarah to work with me.

A knock on her door reveals that she has not returned from her previous engagement. Sliding it open to see if she has simply slept through the knock—my excuse for being nosy—I find her personal effects have been removed. The Divine Sarah has either moved into the baggage compartment to sleep in her coffin, or she is ensconced in her lover's bed. I'd guess the latter.

Knowing that she is enjoying the tender caresses of forbidden love while I wrestle with the world's problems doesn't endear her to me at this moment.

The parlor area at the head of the car is empty and I go there to pace. Most of the passengers on the train had boarded after attending a wedding and got off at the last stop, leaving me as the only occupant now that Sarah has taken up residence in more luxurious quarters.

George comes behind me carrying a long, narrow box. He gives me a smile as I eye the odd-shaped package.

"Golf clubs for that British lord. I stored them for his porter because there was no room in his car. I can't imagine why he'd want them while still on the train."

"Maybe he plans to hit balls down the aisle."

George finds the idea amusing and is still chuckling as he goes through the connecting doors to the next car.

I also find myself wondering at the odd request. Unless Lord Warton has had a miracle cure, he will be fortunate to get out of bed today, much less play golf aboard a train.

I kneel on the bench seat and lean my arms on the bottom of the windowsill and stare out, miserable. I hate it when I can't shake off one of those unsettled feelings I have when things just aren't right and there's no easy solution to putting them back on track.

The train is travelling through hilly terrain, going up grades, and snaking around turns that permit good views of the other cars on inside bends, giving me the opportunity to shamelessly stare at the *Amelia*, hoping to get a look at the "personage" with her. Like all passenger cars, the Westcot's Pullman has large windows, but my car is too closely attached for me to get a good broadside look when the opportunity arises. Cars farther up the train would have a clearer view.

What I do get is a glimpse of the storage locker beneath the train car and that gets my thoughts churning.

So busy defending myself as a woman, a reporter, and a human being to the vigilantes, I have not shared a thought with them about the storage locker and have not given enough reflection on it myself. Now a worrisome matter about it tugs at me: *It became useless as a hiding place for a bomb when the key was taken by Mr. Cleveland.*

The full impact of that thought blows the top off my mind. Resisting the impulse to run and tell Frederick, I keep my feet firmly planted because my thinking isn't completely organized.

While the blood was still wet in the Port Said marketplace, the conspirators had to know that Mr. Cleveland had passed on the key and the name of what it fit, and pretty much could guess I had been the recipient. He died in my arms and I made no secret in the marketplace that he spoke the name to me. Not long afterward, Frederick knew I had the key and told Lord Warton, who would have passed it on to Von Reich and Lord knows who else.

When that happened, the plot to place a bomb in *Amelia*'s storage locker became unusable not because they couldn't get another key, but because it was obvious that the locker would be carefully watched. But the storage locker could serve another purpose for the plot: a red herring to direct the authorities' attention elsewhere while the killing is carried out another way.

The thwarted attempt to place the bomb in the *Amelia* was at best inane—walking up to the train car with bomb in hand, knowing that the authorities had been forewarned and knowing that two armed guards were standing by, was hardly a workable scheme. Managing to leave behind a hat conveniently allowed the perpetrator to be identified.

It made sense only if it was done to disarm the suspicions of the guards. They were told there would be a bomb attempt, there was one, the would-be assassin was identified, and is now conveniently dead.

With a wave of a magician's wand and a shout of "*Abracadabra!*" everyone can relax and the lovers can enjoy their forbidden tryst.

So what is the real plan? Guns, knives, another bomb plot . . .

We go around another inside bend and I get a view of Sarah and her lover through the window, briefly but enough to see the broad build and the dark beard of the man. Too far away to see him well enough to put a name to the face, in my heart I believe I know who it is, but I dare not utter the name even to myself until I am positively certain. Still, it does strike me that he can be an easy target for a sharpshooter on the ground or even on the train. In fact, because a rifleman in another carriage is travelling at the same speed, it makes it a much easier shot.

Why, going around the curves as we are, if I had a rifle, I could—

The thought petrifies me.

A man named Lazarus is somewhere on the train, a person who Von Reich intimated is a world-class sharpshooter. Shooting from a train car farther up from mine to the *Amelia* would be a turkey shoot for a good marksman when we go around an inside bend.

But Frederick and the coppers must have searched the train and it would be extremely difficult for Lazarus to hide—unless someone is helping him, someone who is above suspicion and whose quarters would not be searched.

Lady Warton demonstrated her knowledge of a high-powered but little-known rifle last night. One her English huntsman husband wasn't even familiar with. She hadn't named the rifle out of necessity, more to show off. Hardly the sort of thing a proper woman, a well-bred lady, would have done, especially one who prides herself on her womanly social skills as she does.

If she and her husband are working with Lazarus, it is information that she could have gotten from the mysterious marksman. It sounds far-fetched only because Warton is a British peer. But he's also a drunkard, a gambler, and apparently so broke he has to sell his integrity to literally act as a doorman for businessmen who want access to government officials. Desperate enough to aid an assassin because he might lose his estates? Men have done worse for less.

Thinking about it, Warton had always been Johnny-on-the-spot. He took charge in the marketplace, set out to discredit my suspicions from the very beginning, kept possession of Mr. Cleveland's effects even though he could have sent them ashore to British officials in Port Said. Von Reich knew something about Lazarus and was involved in some way with the man. Lord Warton was Von Reich's sponsor and even volunteered the information that the woman Cenza had left the train, ensuring no one would look for her.

Now he orders his golf clubs. A golf bag would be a perfect place to hide a rifle.

My mind is swirling and I press my temples. All nonsense? A house of cards? But it fits so nicely.

"Head hurtin' from all the excitement?"

Cenza. With a gun, a small, wicked-looking one.

"There are people looking for you. And they have bigger guns." Brave talk but I'm petrified.

"This? It's only a backup. When the two guards come out of *Amelia* and run down this corridor, I'm going to step out of a compartment and shoot them—hopefully in the back. If I don't get them, my brother will."

"Lazarus?"

"That's his stage name, from an act when he was a kid and rose from a coffin that had been burned to cinders. Bela kept it when he became a sharpshooter."

"He's the one who Murdock recognized in Colombo and tried to blackmail. He shot Murdock backstage with you. He fired at the same time Murdock's wife did. She knew, of course. Bought off?"

"Bought off in more ways than one. Bela's very smart. He knew the Murdocks were booked on the ship and sent me down to join them. It wasn't hard. I just climbed into bed with both of them."

A strange calmness engulfs me as I talk to a woman who has come to murder me. Electrified shock, not courage, keeps my lips moving.

"Why didn't you just buy him off instead of killing him?"

"Tried. But Hugh had a big appetite."

"What about Von Reich? When you didn't need his explosives—"

She scoffs. "He knew nothing about explosives. He was a road manager for Bela's magic-and-sharpshooting act and made some money selling gunpowder to the Mahdi. He talked too much. You are clever, I give you that. You have the curiosity of a cat." Her malicious grin widens. "But with eight less lives. Have you figured it out?"

"I think so. It'll happen around one of these bends, when your brother can get a clear shot at the man in the *Amelia.* The rifle's in the golf bag. You paid off Lord Warton to help."

"Very good, you would make a good detective—if you weren't going to be dead very soon. But you're not all right."

Keep her talking, someone will come along.

"How much did you pay Warton?" I ask. "Even if he needed the money—"

"That souse's so busted, he'd sell his soul to keep off the foreclosure of his estates. But it's more than that. Bela can destroy his reputation, too. A sex scandal that no one can crawl out from under."

"Did you—"

"Turn around." She checks her watch. "Now. We're through talking."

"They'll hear you if you shoot me."

"Don't worry, I'm not going to shoot you."

There is wicked glee in her voice.

I turn, my knees suddenly weak. I can barely keep them from buckling. I hear a movement and out of the corner of my eye I can see she's taken off her belt and is folding it. My head explodes in a burst of sparks. The leather strap loops over my head and onto my neck, her knee presses into the small of my back, my wind is shut off as she jerks back. My neck feels crushed and I can't break her hold even with the strength of my panic.

The pressure suddenly snaps, and she falls against me and slides to the floor as I push myself away and get up, nearly falling back down.

"You okay?"

Holding my burning throat and gasping for breath, I stare into the wonderful face of my porter. He's holding a silver platter and there are breakfast rolls scattered on the floor.

He gestures at Cenza. "She was choking you. Is she crazy?"

"Mean crazy."

Cenza starts to push herself up and I grab the heavy platter from George. Lifting it high in the air, I bring it down on the back of her head, collapsing her back down on the floor. Just for good measure, I give her another whack.

"You could kill her!" George says.

"I doubt it, but hope so." She's still clutching her small pistol and I take it. "Watch her, she's dangerous."

"Who is she?"

"A killer."

Giving him the platter, I make a dash for the connecting door to the adjoining car where Frederick's compartment is, yelling back at George. "Tell those British coppers to make sure their man is away from the windows and then come to Mr. Selous's compartment."

Dashing into the next car, I slide open Frederick's door. Empty.

"Where is he?" I shout at his porter who stares at me like I'm a maniac.

He shakes his head as he backs away, holding up his hands. "I don't know."

I realize I'm pointing the gun at him and aim it at the floor. "Find Mr. Selous. Tell him it's the Wartons."

"What about the Wartons?"

"Tell him they're the ones."

I rush by him.

"Where are you going?"

"To stop a murder!"

68

A few feet from the Wartons' compartment, I stop and stare at the small caliber revolver in my hand.

What am I doing? I'm about to face a sharpshooter who's armed with a rifle and I've got a peashooter. Cenza's small revolver holds five bullets in the cylinder, less than the six-shooter I learned to fire but it feels like a cannon right now.

"Don't think," Annie Oakley had said when giving me a lesson, "just look where you want the bullet to go, then point and shoot."

Point and shoot. Pulling back the hammer to cock it, I fumble the gun in my hand and nearly drop it.

Forcing myself forward, one step at a time, I'm shaking so badly I have a hard time opening the connecting door out of the car and the one into the next.

The corridor is deserted and I move slowly down, holding the gun out in front of me with both hands. A shadow created by someone in the parlor area at the other end of the car moves and I freeze in place.

Lord Warton steps into my line of aim, swaying, and almost loses his balance.

"Go back to your hole," he slurs.

He's so drunk, I'm not sure he even recognizes me.

"Put your hands up!"

"Stupid woman." He goes back around the corner, out of my sight.

Half from panic, I run toward the parlor area holding the gun out in front of me. As I go by a half-open compartment door, Lady Warton flies out, swinging a rifle stock that knocks the revolver from my hand.

She jerks the rifle back and slams the butt into my stomach, crippling me with pain and shock. My knees fold and I grab at her for support as I start to fall, getting a hold of her hair. The whole head of hair comes off, leaving a bald head.

She—he?—grabs me by my own hair and jerks me up, sticking the gun under my chin as I rise to wobbly knees. My eyes are glazed, a wheezing breath feels like it's on fire.

"Give me any trouble and I'll blow your head off."

Her voice is no longer feminine, though softer than most men's. The identity problem Von Reich spoke of is obvious—Lady Warton is not a woman. I now understand Cenza's remark about Lord Warton facing a sexual scandal.

"Bela," I spit out.

He hits me across the side of the face with the back of his hand. *"Shut up."*

His features are so similar to his sister's, I might have made the connection if I saw them side by side—without a netted veil.

He forces me down the aisle, one hand on my hair, the other holding the rifle he has stuck against my side. Tears roll down my cheeks, not from sobbing, but from the excruciating pain.

In the parlor area he shoves me down on the couch next to Lord Warton who's clutching a bottle of Scotch as a life preserver.

Bela lifts my chin with the tip of the rifle barrel. "Where's my sister?"

Unable to speak, I shake my head as tears flow and I'm still trying to breathe.

He slaps me and my neck stretches as my head feels like it's ready to fly off.

"If they have her, I have you, and we'll trade when I'm ready. And if she's been harmed . . . I'll kill you."

He raises his hand to slap me again and I slide down on the couch, turning my head away and sobbing.

Bela looks beyond me, leaning down to squint as the train tracks form an inside bend that gives him a clear view of the *Amelia.*

"Can't do this," Lord Warton slurs, "not what we agreed. Can't do it."

"Shut up, you old sot. I'm saving your estate from creditors."

Warton shakes his head. "Can't do it, not this."

"Shut up and drink your milk."

The window suddenly explodes behind my head and I fall forward as glass shatters toward me. Bela drops to his knees and I grab onto the rifle with both hands. He jerks it, rising up from his knees, but I hang on for dear life and go with him until we are standing face-to-face with the rifle between us. He lurches forward to shove me back and I push up on the rifle, displacing his force as Carolina Magnet did. He pushes again and I push up, shrieking with glee as his face turns purple from rage.

Jerking me to him, he twists the rifle but I hang on as he pulls me around in a circle when he can't break my hold. He tries again, this time pushing me back toward the wall and I push up again and we stop in the middle of the parlor. His rage has now turned into a wild animals howl.

He lets one hand go of the rifle and hits me across the side of the head, sending me sprawling. Rifle now to his shoulder, he aims down at me but it is Lord Warton who comes to my rescue when he flies off the couch with his bottle of Scotch and swings, hitting Bela on the side of his head.

Bela falls back against the opposite wall and screams, "You stupid fool!" He fires, slamming Lord Warton back onto the couch.

Gunfire erupts and I lay flat on the floor as bullets smack the walls around me. Bela is knocked backward but keeps his feet and fires the rifle from the hip once before his body jerks as a rain of bullets hit him.

My ears are ringing; the air is full of gun smoke. Both Bela and Lord Warton are down and neither is moving. Or breathing.

The redheaded copper is coming down the corridor with a gun in hand.

"Don't shoot!" I yell at the top of my lungs as I lay my head back down. If he said anything, it is lost in the ringing of my ears.

A few minutes later, I am seated in Frederick's compartment. He is giving me an apology, which my numb brain doesn't process.

"Cenza—" I interrupt.

"Jumped from the train. Probably dead." He kneels before me. "Sweet Nellie, I almost got you with that shot through the window, but I had to try it."

"Had to try it? Had to risk killing me to get a shot at that man, woman, whatever he is?"

"You have to understand—"

"That you were willing to risk killing me for queen and country?"

"I fired from the *Amelia* at Lazarus, Lady Warton, whatever that monster is called."

"And almost got me? You—the world's greatest hunter?"

"I told you I was a poor shot. I have to—"

"See the white of their eyes, I remember." I get up slowly, resisting Frederick's offer to help me.

"Nellie, I need to talk to you about what you've seen and heard. A revelation about the personage in the *Amelia* having an affair with an actress could have a dire effect on an elderly woman whose health and welfare is of prime importance not just to my country, but to the world at large."

I brush by him and slide open the compartment door.

"Where are you going?" he asks.

"To freshen up and get the glass out of my hair. And keep myself from finding a gun and showing you what it's like to nearly get your head blown off."

"Please. Another Nellie nearly killed her with grief. Don't be the one who actually puts her in a grave."*

"I still have an issue to resolve with you."

His eyebrows go up. "Just one?"

"One at a time. Did you fight off that assassin the night I was attacked on the bow?"

"Nellie, sweet Nellie, I wish I had so you would remember me for something besides a near miss."

"Then it must have been Von Reich."

"Lord Warton saved you."

"What?"

"Sarah confided in me that she saw him running away when she found you lying on the deck. Warton was not a good man, not even a very pleasant one, but as you found out today, he will stop short of murder."

"I will have to thank him in my prayers. After I forgive him for getting me almost murdered in the first place."

"You are not a forgiving woman, Nellie Bly."

"Mr. Selous," tapping his chest with my forefinger, "I have been battered, slandered, beaten, and kicked . . . and I have endured and fought for truth, and justice, and the American way. Or something like that. And right now—"

He pulls me to him, embracing me, smothering me with his warmth

* Frederick Selous is obviously referring to Queen Victoria. The reference to a death blow from "another Nellie" is dealt with in an historical note later because Nellie never explained it in her journal. —The Editors

and masculinity. Our lips touch and a warm flush flows all the way down to my toes.

I finally push him back with weak knees. "Don't go away."

Before I slip out the compartment door, I tell him, "I'm taking you up on your offer to join you on a safari. You need someone to teach you how to shoot properly. Point and shoot, just point and shoot, don't aim; I'll show you how."

"Don't make promises you can't keep"—he looks back at me with those blazing blue eyes—"because I'm going to hold you to that one."

For a moment we just look at each other before I race down to my compartment and start picking the shards of glass from my hair.

He almost killed me. And yet I want nothing more than to rush back and have him take me into his arms and never let me go.

The race is still on. I will crawl to the finishing line if I have to, but for just a few precious moments I want to be held in his strong arms, feel his warm breath against my neck, and have him kiss me.

Maybe I'll cry, but that's a woman's prerogative, isn't it?

"Take a deep breath," I tell myself. I have people counting on me to finish the race and that is exactly what I am going to do.

NELLIE ARRIVING AT FINISHING LINE IN JERSEY CITY

L'ENVOI

Almost before I knew it I was at Philadelphia, and all too soon to please me, for my trip was so pleasant I dreaded the finish of it.

A number of newspapermen and a few friends joined me in Philadelphia to escort me to New York. Speechmaking was the order from Philadelphia on to Jersey City.

I was told when we were almost home to jump to the platform the moment the train stopped at Jersey City, for that made my time around the world. The station was packed with thousands of people, and the moment I landed on the platform, one yell went up from them, and the cannons at the Battery and Fort Greene boomed out the news of my arrival. I took off my cap and wanted to yell with the crowd, not because I had gone around the world in seventy-two days, but because I was home again.

To so many people this wide world over am I indebted for their kindnesses that I cannot, in a little book like this, thank them all individually. They form a chain around the Earth.

To each and all of you, men, women, and children, in my land and in the lands I visited, I am most truly grateful. Every kind act and thought, if but an unuttered wish, a cheer, a tiny flower, is imbedded in my memory as one of the pleasant things of my novel tour.

From you and from all those who read the chronicle of my trip I beg indulgence. These pages have been written in the spare moments snatched from the exactions of a busy life.

For the Record

I covered 21,740 miles in 72 days, 6 hours, and 11 minutes.

I spent 56 days, 2 hours and 4 minutes in actual travel, and lost by delay 15 days, 17 hours and 30 minutes.

My average rate of speed was 28.71 miles per hour.

First-class tickets around the world (ships and trains) cost $805 (not counting the special train).

Nellie Bly, *Around the World in 72 Days*

COVER OF NELLIE BLY'S BOOK
AROUND THE WORLD IN 72 DAYS

HISTORICAL NOTE

Who was the man in the Amelia?

For reasons that are not clear but perhaps arose from a sense of respect that Nellie had for Queen Victoria, the grande dame that an entire age of history is named after, Nellie never, even in her secret journal, revealed the name of Sarah's lover, "the personage" in the *Amelia.*

However, looking at the evidence, we find that the man had British "coppers" as bodyguards when he travelled, his very presence in the United States was a well-protected secret, and he was an aficionado of horse-racing.

These facts all fit Edward, Prince of Wales, Queen Victoria's oldest son, a playboy who angered her when her beloved consort, Prince Albert, died two weeks after travelling ill in the dead of winter to an army camp to chastise Edward for having an actress smuggled into his tent.

This was the probable source for Frederick Selous's comment that a "Nellie" had almost killed the Queen with grief: The actress was Nellie Clifton.

Queen Victoria never forgave her son. She wore mourning black the rest of her life and wrote her daughter about Edward, saying, "I never can, or shall, look at him without a shudder."

Prince Edward, who enjoyed the night life of Paris, was a rumored lover of Sarah's, but the "smoking gun" of the evidence was Nellie's facetious remark, "How is old Bertie?"

"Bertie" was the pet name given to Edward by his family.

Prince Edward assumed the throne after the death of his mother, and is remembered by history as Edward VII, an able monarch who also has a period of history carry his name: the Edwardian Era.

THE EDITORS

EDWARD, PRINCE OF WALES